TABLE OF CONTENTS

DEDICATION

THIS BOOK IS DEDICATED TO MY CHARMING, POSITIVE AND LOVING family. My wife, Elsie, and our daughters, Karen and Tracy, have nudged, encouraged, and supported the writing of Seaside Glitter through every stage of its creation, refinement, and endless edits. Special hugs of thanks and love are also given to two very special ladies in my life—my granddaughters Amy and Ella.

ACKNOWLEDGMENTS

I WOULD LIKE TO ACKNOWLEDGE THE ENORMOUS LOVE, SUPPORT and encouragement I received from my parents, Clifford and Anita-Nora Turner. They proudly exclaimed to family and friends, 'This is our son the writer,' before I saw myself in that role.

I would like to thank my siblings, Noreen, Penny *(Penelope)*, John and Steve for the many adventures we've shared, both willingly and otherwise. Looking back at our childhood years as an adult has inspired me and added both creativity and humour to my written words.

To my daughters, Karen and Tracy, thank you for the special moments and learning experiences that a loving daughter adds to a father's life. I love you both dearly. To my daughter, Karen the teacher, I thank you for the adventurous suggestions and the grammatical corrections marked with your red pen. Like many students, I questioned your assessment. However like every student, I discovered that sharing ideas and listening to feedback really does accelerate one's personal growth and quality of life. May all your students benefit from your red pen as the readers of *Seaside Glitter* and I have.

And finally to my soul mate and loving wife, Elsie...Love You More, Darling. Thank you for the hugs and belief that I am still a "keeper" after more than 48 years together.

PREFACE

A YOUNG FAMILY IS DEVASTATED AND LEFT REELING BY THE LOSS OF their grandparents and parents in a tragic accident. Exploration of Grandfather Ramsay's attic uncovers the 1796 diary of Grace Ramsay. The handwritten pages offer a fantastic tale of ghosts, lost treasure, and family connections that have long been lost. John is quick to discard the diary's contents as the over active imagination of a young girl in a new land. His young wife and brother search for something more in the diary.

Determined to learn more about the diary, they set off to explore the original family homestead in East River, Nova Scotia—a small community of hearty fishermen that is a stone's throw away from the town of Chester and fabled Oak Island. Soon enough, they find themselves retracing the footsteps of Grace's father and uncle, the brothers who once told the terrifying tale of staring directly into the eyes of Hell's Master. How could the written stories of a young girl from two hundred years ago be connected to the lives of John, Richard, and Lyndsey?

Join the adventure to find out.

CHAPTER 1

LYNDSEY HELD THE ANCIENT DIARY IN HER LEFT HAND AND dusted its cover gently with her right. She turned it sideways and marveled at the yellowed pages held securely within the leather bindings of her surprise find. The puzzled yet curious look on her face drew the attention of her husband John.

"A penny for your thoughts," he offered up.

A glance into John's eyes brought a hesitant frown to Lyndsey's face as she leaned forward and passed the diary to him. The urge to embrace her husband faded, fed by John's ongoing rejections of her affection. Silently she fretted over having hinted to John her desire to start a family. A desire fed by memories of a passionate mother-daughter relationship shared with her Mom, Letitia—Lettie, lost to cancer two years past. Over the past six months John's sex drive had faded, then abruptly vanished, replaced by late nights he spent toiling over major sales proposals at work. Lyndsey struggled to suppress the tears in her eyes.

John held the diary but remained silent. Lyndsey suspected the look on John's face meant the tragedy that had blindsided their family in early April once again clouded John's mind. The tragedy had destroyed John's family reducing it to Richard, his brother, and Lyndsey. The three had been sandbox companions throughout their childhoods. Her parents had been likewise to Lyndsey's in-laws. The

Ramsey homestead a second home and to Lyndsey her in-laws had been a treasured second family throughout life. They'd stood with her and her Mom at the passing of her Dad. Again on her Mom's lost battle with cancer, they had embraced and supported her. To her John's parents had transcended the realm of in-laws and simply become mom and dad. The tragic loss of Bill and Mary Ramsay—mom and dad, and grandparents, William and Maureen Ramsay, who had died in that fiery traffic accident drew the threesome closer together, yet cast them in a shadow of sadness that impeded their efforts to move forward in life. Both John and Lyndsey had personally witnessed the tragic accident. The horror of its reality was etched in their minds forever. Opting on the side of discretion, Lyndsey decided to allow John to work through his inner thoughts. Silently she prayed that together they could embrace life's positives and one day experience the love both their parents and grandparents had extolled, experienced and lived throughout their lives.

Quickly, John lost sight of his surroundings. He stared blankly into Lyndsey's eyes; slowly his troubled thoughts took control of his mind. He found himself drifting beyond his Grandparents' attic.

As a child he had not been permitted to enter this area of the family's homestead. That did not mean he was unfamiliar with its surroundings. *The term angelic had never been used to describe John and his younger brother Richard as children and very few adventurous opportunities slipped by the Ramsay boys unnoticed.* Many thoughts of those days past spent with Richard, in the loving care of their grandparents, flashed though his mind.

A teardrop quickly raced down his cheek. The idea of never enjoying another warm hug in Grandma's arms saddened him. He fought to hold back the sad emotions held within, then fought hard to accept the fact he'd lost not only his grandparents, but also his parents in that tragic accident. The family reunions of their childhood had been joyful events. Reunions of recent years often suffered the effects of a feisty edge centred on the elder Ramsay men not condoning John's life values. Grandmother had always stood up for John on those occasions. She'd held Grandfather and John's Father, in check, and prevented the not uncommon rows from erupting. *To hell with them*, John thought. *Now I'm the eldest Ramsay. It'll soon be my way or no way.*

The tragedy replayed itself in John's mind. First, he had the joy of watching his parents Mary and Bill Ramsay, grandparents Maureen and William walking towards him and Lyndsey in the airport. It had been a month since he'd last enjoyed the pleasure of his Mother's company. Business had been declared the focus of their Parents' and Grandparents' extended trip to B.C. John's detail driven mind had questioned the trip from its announcement. Failure of both his Dad and Grandfather to share the trip's details and progress over the past month rattled John's nerves to no end. However, hugs from Mom and Grandma quickly set John's mind at ease. A quick walk to the baggage area had retrieved their luggage then he led them to the terminal exit and passenger pick up area. Dad had accepted the Buick's keys from Grandfather then he had headed off to the daily parking lot, where Richard had parked Grandfather's Buick two days earlier. John accompanied him to retrieve his Honda Civic. It irked John to no end that little Richie got to drive their Grandfather's vehicle and he did not. He questioned Richard's excuse for not being available to meet their returning parents and grandparents. However he accepted Richie's lame work related excuse. Once they had returned John quickly loaded the sets of luggage into the Buick's trunk. Then family tradition had stepped forward and they'd parted company for the ride to the family homestead. Tradition, he silently cursed, held that the family's elders travel together, allowing discussion of matters that did not concern the young. To hell with their traditions John mused after tomorrow...I will be the kingpin, the eldest Ramsay and will definitely alter future family traditions!

In his mind John recalled driving down the Toronto airport exit ramp towards the express highway. Traffic that day had been heavy but moved smoothly. He had quickly settled comfortably in the centre express lane a safe distance behind his Grandfather's Buick. John held that thought, Lyndsey's presence pulled him back into the attic and life's reality. He wiped away the stream of tears that flowed freely down his cheeks. He sobbed, struggled briefly with his inner feelings and then returned to the scene being replayed in his mind. John sensed the salty tang of tears on his lips. He did not feel the tissue as it moved in loving strokes over his face. He did sense that the tissue's holder was his wife but he quickly replaced her with the image of his mistress. Tessa stirred John's sexual desires.

Lyndsey fed an inner hunger; she kissed John softly and with a gentle passion. The kiss lacked Tessa's aggressiveness and she faded from John's mind. Lyndsey pulled away from John her kiss having touched unresponsive lips.

Back behind the wheel of his Honda Civic, Lyndsey seated at his side the tragedy replayed itself in John's mind. Out of the corner of his eye, he spotted a transport truck as it raced past him in the express lane. The tractor-trailer's brake lights flashed on followed by a loud squealing as the truck's brakes took hold. Without warning, the transport truck jack-knifed. Witnesses had stated that its driver had been cut-off by an erratically-driven pickup truck that had blown a front tire, causing its driver to lose control of the vehicle.

John's right leg jerked in response to the scene unwinding in his mind. He hit the brake pedal hard. The Honda's nose dipped as its brakes took hold. John then released and quickly reapplied the brakes. The brakes and tires screamed; within split seconds the vehicle swerved sideways, and came to a screeching halt. He turned sideways and stared blankly out the window of the driver's door. The sounds of Lyndsey's terrified screams were not heard by John.

John watched in horror. He relived the last seconds of his Parents' and Grandparents' lives. The tractor-trailer swerved to its right, and the Buick disappeared from sight for a second—or was it two? Then it reappeared for another second its roof and windows were gone. A second more and the vehicle disappeared in a ball of blazing flames.

John's hand reached for the door handle and fought to open the door. Nothing happened; he remained frozen in the driver's seat. The blare of sirens in the distance and the memory of a graveside service brought John's remembrance to the end of its replay.

Through tear-filled eyes, he looked quickly at the diary held in his hands and then over to his wife, Lyndsey; finally, his eyes came to rest on the old diary.

Lyndsey placed her hands on John's shoulders. She stared deeply into his hazel eyes and pulled him closer. Slowly, she worked her way over his brow and down over his tear stained cheeks with warm touching kisses. She whispered, "Feel the pain darling embrace it," then she moved her lips to his. Slowly, she increased the passion of her kiss, while drawing him closer. Warmth spread from her lips into her cheeks, and she sensed John slowly responding to her actions. Two firm breasts pulsed as their nipples grew firm. A passion quickly worked its way through Lyndsey. She felt John's growing passion expand against her belly, a dusty, old diary pressed against both their chests. John's mind released some of the tensions that had burdened his heart. Passion raced to reach the levels that Lyndsey lovingly administered. He released both hands from the old diary and wrapped them tightly around Lyndsey while pulling her closer. Slowly, his hands worked their way down her back and onto Lyndsey's buttocks. Once there, they slowly and methodically massaged and toyed with the treasure held in their grasp. John's fingers needed no directions. They worked their magic and ever so slowly raised the hem of Lyndsey's cotton dress, exposing more and more of the backs of her long slender thighs. The hem quickly found itself pressed against the arch of Lyndsey's back exposing her white panties. John ran his fingers along the elastic band of Lyndsey's panties then slowly slid them under the elastic. In his mind, he pictured Tessa's black bikini panties and tanned buttocks. John's heart pounded rapidly as he raced to fulfill the sexual fantasies of his mind.

Lyndsey sighed and responded with joy to John's aroused sexual state. Anticipating pleasures she'd been denied over the past days, weeks and months, Lyndsey shuddered and cast aside doubts about her ability to satisfy John's needs. Her body melted in John's arms.

Footsteps on the old staircase stopped dead in their tracks. The owner grabbed the handrail and braced himself. Instinctively, he bit down hard on his lip, suppressed the words that sat fresh on his tongue, and grimaced at the wet ball of yellow fur that had almost sent him spiraling back down the old staircase. Silently, he cursed Bailey, the life-long companion of his departed Grandfather.

Inside his chest, a pounding heart slowed, and the tingling sensation disappeared from his scalp. The ache in his heart did not abate. Richard recalled the cause of his late arrival. He had driven to the cemetery and visited his parents and grandparents at their graveside. In an attempt to allay and ease his feelings of heartfelt loss and total abandonment, he paused and shook his head in disdain at Bailey. Richard's blue eyes watched the culprit disappear over the top of the staircase. His unheard footsteps resumed their climb up the old staircase to the attic.

Bailey's head twisted back towards his tail, and the old feline looked back down the staircase. A well-rehearsed snicker appeared then quickly vanished from the old cat's face. He whipped his head forward and set off in search of his master. Little doubt remained in his mind how the master would handle this intrusion into their space. Bailey believed that same young man would be sent back down the staircase and away from the domain he and his beloved master had shared for so many years. He did not anticipate the obstacle that stood in his path of flight. Thump! Bailey came to a crashing halt. His cold, wet, furry body in full flight hit the back of Lyndsey's exposed thighs.

M…eow! One shocked feline fell, hit the floor and quickly scampered off and disappeared in the old attic.

Lyndsey screamed, "A…aaah!" then fell backwards and came to a shocked rest when her back hit the attic floor. Her blue eyes stared at the rafters in stunned disbelief. She did not move—could not move. Her body had suddenly been pinned to the floor with John pressed hard against her.

"Hey!"

John's and Lyndsey's faces turned together towards the staircase and the late guest.

"Sorry for showing up so late. Or was I a tad early?" Richard teased. He covered his eyes in jest, allowing his brother and sister-in-law time to partially recover but treated himself to a short peek at Lyndsey's exposed thighs and panty line. As he turned slowly away from the couple, Richard noticed a dusty old book she held to her belly.

John extended his hands to the floor, pushed hard, and lifted his weight off Lyndsey. Their eyes locked briefly and silently promised to revisit their shared moment later that night. He pushed harder and their hips separated. Erect and steady on his knees, John looked down at Lyndsey; Tessa's black bikini panties replaced Lyndsey's. He spotted the old diary and retrieved it from Lyndsey's belly. He took one more wishful look at Lyndsey's flat belly and panties with hesitation he pulled Lyndsey's cotton dress down over the objects of his desire. He stood up, paused, and then stooped down and offered his hand to Lyndsey.

Lyndsey accepted John's extended hand, followed the flow of his strength, and soon stood, head tilted back, and again locked eye-to-eye with John. She extended herself up on the tips of her toes and then lovingly touched her lips to John's and shared a kiss that promised more. Their lips parted, Lyndsey released John and she turned and ran over to Richard.

Richard accepted Lyndsey's greeting. He wrapped his arms fully about her, and returned her hug. The hug was short, but not without emotion. There were no words spoken between the pair of in-laws. Deep within himself, Richard knowingly stored the moment among the many memories of treasured times once spent with Lyndsey the love of his childhood. Gazing at her lips he savored their sweetness. They separated, smiled warmly at each other, then stepped back and created a space for John, who had joined the pair.

John stepped up and grasped Richard's hand. The brothers exchanged a short but hearty handshake. Their hands parted and the greeting extended into a brotherly hug. An extra squeeze brought the greeting to its end, and the brothers stepped back from each other. Richard smiled and repeated his greeting—apology in jest, "Sorry for showing up so late."

"No you're not late," John said, "We just got started."

"So I noticed," Richard replied with a smile that concealed his heart's true passions and desires.

"Looking through Grandma's old trunk," John added. He then looked down at the old diary he held in his left hand and said,

"Lyndsey just found this old diary, and we were about to look through it when you showed up."

"Right!" a smiling Richard responded.

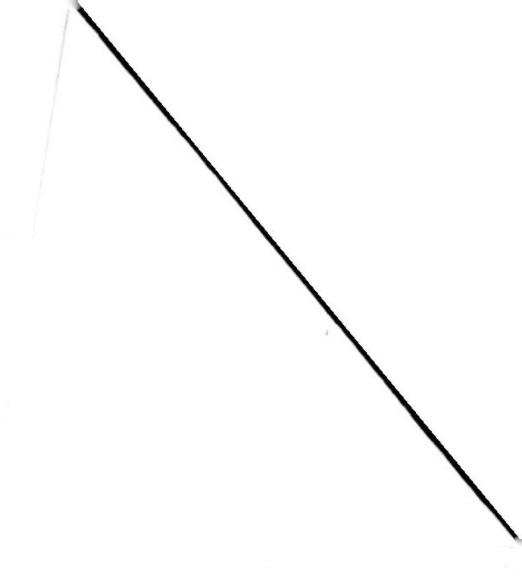

CHAPTER 2

JOHN TOSSED THE DIARY AT RICHARD, WHO GRABBED IT AS IT FLEW through the air towards him. He drew the diary towards himself, paused, and then untied the diary's leather binding laces. At first, the bindings resisted his efforts, then loosened under Richard's renewed efforts.

Lyndsey and John looked on as Richard finally pulled the binding laces fully apart. They watched Richard flip the front cover open. Their curiosity had grown; they stood and waited for him to comment. The comments did not come as quickly as anticipated. They watched his eyes and facial expressions grow in intensity.

"What's it say?" both Lyndsey and John asked in unison.

Richard did not respond. The diary had touched his curiosity. The first page had taken a quick hold. The top entry was all it really took. The dates and location had hooked him. He pondered, *Could this be from the pencil and hand of a long past relative? Did his family's tree stretch that far back into time's endless journey?* Richard read on, oblivious to his surroundings and companions. Forever the fabled family dreamer, had fate or a weary soul from the past placed this treasure in his hands? It read:

Diary of Grace Ramsay
East River Nova Scotia
1796

Mother and Father presented me with this diary today, November 22, 1796 ... my 11th birthday. I feel at a loss for words, tongue tied really. I do not know what to write into the pages of my treasured gift. My dear friend and companion Alice told me to keep my entries short and to the point. She said I must never enter a hurtful thought or word. For one day, they may come to be. My teacher Miss Cruthers said write of things that came my way ... feelings of what happened and why ... of how I felt ... and lastly good things I wish to come my way.

Surely somewhere in between the two, the answer I need will arise. Not too short, but also not too long ... for the pages within this treasured gift are less than I feel I'll need ... but more than I've ever dreamt of possessing. I do love Mother and Father so dearly ... They seem to know my every waking dream and desire. One day I truly wish that I may come to know the love they share.

Nothing too revealing about our family's past, if it is in fact our family, Richard thought. He flipped through to the diary's centre pages. The entry he found there caught and held his attention.

Sunday, August 18th, 1797 ... Today, Father and Uncle Richard returned home early from their day of fishing. Not all is right! Father looks scared ... a look I've never seen on his face before this day. Uncle Richard has seen a ghost, of that I'm most certain. Only yesterday his hair stood robust and full of flowing black curls. Today, not a curl to be found and his once black curls are now straight and white as the snow of winter.

"Hello!"

Richard's mind snapped him back into his Grandparents' attic. He looked up from the diary's pages and over to the asking faces of John and Lyndsey.

"You'll never believe what I've just read," he said then continued to speak, "This diary is very old, and not from the pencil of Grandfather or Grandmother. More likely it belonged to their Grandparents' Grandparents or beyond."

Both John and Lyndsey looked blankly at Richard, then moved quickly and took up positions at each of Richard's shoulders.

No words were spoken. Richard remained silent and allowed time for them to read the entry he'd just read. Then he turned the page, and together they read onward of the thoughts and feelings of a young Grace Ramsay.

> *They sent us to bed early tonight. Tom cried but has since fallen quickly asleep. Not I ... I must confess. The candlelight outside our room is flickering. It casts an eerie pallor over Father and Uncle Richard. Mother has taken out Father's jug of rum. She encourages Father and Uncle Richard to drink of its contents. This is something I've never seen her do before, such a fine lady and staunch follower of our Lord's ways. It seems more than Father and Uncle Richard's world has been turned upside down. My hand cannot keep pace with all I hear and see. So I'll but listen and watch. Later I'll return with pencil in hand to write of what I now hear and see.*

The three family members turned and looked directly into each other's eyes. What they'd just read surpassed their wildest dreams and expectations of what they'd find inside the pages of the dusty old diary.

Richard picked a sales receipt out of his shirt pocket, and inserted it into the old diary, to mark their current page. He closed the diary, dusted its cover anew, and then passed it to John.

In silence the three separated, then walked over and sat down in front of the old trunk. They sat in silence facing each other, while their minds raced over the words and pages their eyes had just read.

Lyndsey broke the long silence and said, "For better or worse… we avowed our love, John." She then smiled and continued to speak, "What kind of family secrets have I married into?"

"A loving one to start," replied Richard.

John frowned, he did not respond to Lyndsey.

Richard added, "Normal? I'm feeling the seeds of doubt take hold. Ghost, an ancestor of old whose hair turned snow-white, from the sights and beings he'd seen?"

Lyndsey smirked and said, "Alas, we know of your family's love of white rum and its storied connection to family deeds and tales of yore."

"Speaking of which, my taste buds are aroused," John injected, and licked his lips.

"Say no more!" replied Lyndsey.

She leaned forward, kissed her husband, and then jumped up and said mockingly, "Doth me Lordship require glasses? Or will a jug suffice?" She turned and walked off towards the attic staircase.

John called out, "Fine crystal…me wench…and make sure the jug be full."

John looked down at the old diary that sat on his lap. He'd never imagined a family past that traveled beyond the old family homestead. He'd never traveled far afield of the Toronto-Newmarket area. His view of Canada as a whole had been limited to schoolbooks, newsprint, and an old reliable, the trusted…TV screen. The idea that a whole new family past existed outside of his worldly realm both intrigued and worried John. The thought of unfamiliar family members stepping forward and laying claim to a share of his inheritance angered him. Richard he could handle, strangers with legal eagles in tow he reasoned could test his status as the newest Ramsay Patriarch. Numbers and money had successfully driven him throughout life. Silently he resolved to disenfranchise any imposters that stepped forward with claims.

"Boo!"

John smiled back at Richard.

Richard said, "Intriguing to say the least, big brother."

"Yes. A little more than I expected to find in Grandmother's old trunk," John answered.

Together, they moved closer to the old trunk. John followed Richard's lead and rose up onto his knees. They gazed into the trunk's contents. John set the diary down on the attic floor. Richard reached into the trunk. He tossed aside a couple of old dresses, probably from the wardrobe of his Great-grandmother. To him, they did not have the look or feel of his Grandmother. Digging deep into the trunk, he picked out an old photo album that looked to be a mate to the diary. He pondered the advent of photography and wondered if the two books could be related.

John grabbed the photo album from Richard and opened it. The unfamiliar faces eased his concerns. Satisfied no threat existed to his inheritance, he dropped the album onto the floor. He'd heard Lyndsey's footsteps on the attic staircase.

The two brothers watched Lyndsey as she re-entered the attic. John eyed the tray carried by his wife. It contained his every wish come true…almost. The first item tempered his taste buds a crystal flask of white rum missing half its original contents. Next, he eyed three short frost covered crystal tumblers. They had obviously been retrieved from the freezer. A family tradition and trademark of their Grandfather's that Grandma sustained by maintaining a healthy stash of crystal tumblers in the freezer. He suspected the stash had been overstocked in anticipation of the family reunion that was never meant to be and never would be. The crystal ice bowl that was filled to overflowing, along with a bottle of cola, topped off his wish list…almost. He pondered over the missing item…Tessa... then brushed her image aside.

John disguised his wishful lust and looked beyond the tray. His eyes rested a second on the two full and firm breasts that he'd somehow grown tired of. His eyes continued upward and locked onto Lyndsey's baby blues. His mouth formed a quick kiss. He sent it through the dusty attic air towards Lyndsey's waiting rosette coloured lips. In his mind…John watched his kiss land on a pair of deep red lips—Tessa's.

Richard looked up and smiled past the tray at the partially concealed face. A dreamer of renown, Richard's wish list contained one item: a time machine. *Oh!* Richard thought, *If I could only relive that fateful moment over again.* He didn't regret the mistake of three years past. Any regrets dwelt repeatedly upon the consequences of his actions. *If only Lyndsey had been a twin,* he thought. *Then,* he reasoned, *perchance a second chance would have been within his grasp.*

Lyndsey walked across the attic floor in short but sure steps. She quickly found herself standing before John and Richard. In a maidenly manner she stooped down and placed the tray before the pair then curtly said, "I trust my lord finds this offering worthy and to his palate's delight." After a pause for effect, Lyndsey smiled, then stepped back and sat down.

John reached forward and lifted the flask of white rum from the tray. He removed its cap and administered the appropriate doses to each of the three frosted tumblers. After a brief pause, he poured a topper to his tumbler, replaced the flask's cap, and returned it to the tray. He frowned on seeing the flask stood next to empty. The trio then took turns adding ice and cola to their own taste.

Three tumblers were raised in harmony in a toast as Richard spoke, "Together today we are a family of three. I make a toast to the love of our ancestors that brought us to be. Drink slowly, brother and sister of these spirits, then follow by my side, and we'll travel the roads once traveled by those whose love we'll forever cherish in our hearts and minds."

"Here!"

"Here!"

"Yes, and so it must be," a smiling Richard proclaimed.

John ignored the recently uncovered photo album. He picked up the old diary and passed it to Richard. After a quick nod of his head he said, "Let the honours be yours, brother. Read to us, the words and thoughts once written by our newly discovered and dearly loved ancestor."

"Quick, open it up," Lyndsey begged, "reveal a piece of our family's past."

Richard raised his icy tumbler to his lips and took another taste of the ice-cooled spirits. He set his tumbler down by his side and opened the family's old diary to the pages marked by his sales receipt. He removed the receipt and returned it to his shirt pocket. With his left hand, he reached out and turned the yellowed page he'd last read. He glanced quickly over the contents of the newly uncovered page. Its contents caused his lips to form and then release a quick frown which both Lyndsey and John missed. Richard licked and moistened his lips and then proceeded to read aloud from the pages of the old diary.

> *August 25th 1797 ... So much has been spoken, that I must recall and write into my diary today. A week has passed since last I guided my pencil upon these pages. Uncle Richard's once black and curly hair remains whiter than snow to this day. I have looked out upon the sea more than once this week past. Most days the fog has possessed the bay. There was an occasion or two when I was blessed with sunshine and believe I did lay my eyes upon what must be the island of which Father and Uncle Richard have spoken. I did on those occasions feel an eerie tingle run up and down my spine. They have not returned to the sea to fish since that day. Father hints to Mother that she has no need to fret or worry. The Lord has finally provided he tells Mother. She replies that it is more like to be the Devil from what has befallen poor Uncle Richard. Father said it all happened as he and Uncle Richard jigged for their daily catch of cod and mackerel off the northwestern tip of Sinner's Island. He hinted at having spotted the far off elusive Floating Islands on the horizon. So named he says because on a hot sunny hazy day, to fishermen they appear to float above the surface of the sea. He swears that on such days he's almost certain they move about and change their location upon the sea. Mother says she'll have no such talk in her home.*

Richard paused, caught his breath, looked about and reconfirmed the reality of his surroundings. He reached down and picked up his tumbler of rum and raised it to his lips. He glanced at Lyndsey. Richard took in the minute delights presented to him. The rum had altered his senses. He unknowingly allowed the glance to linger on Lyndsey longer than he'd intended. A quick snap of his head found him looking directly at John. There, he realized that the expression of curiosity on Lyndsey's face—had been twinned on his brother's. Encouraged, he accepted what he thought to be the truth. The two of them had become mesmerized by the events being revealed to them in the old diary. The old, yellowed pages called out…summoned him to read deeper into the story its author had once written. His gaze returned to the diary's pages. The words on its yellowed pages had faded and blurred as dusk's shadows embraced the attic and its occupants.

John, the consummate doubter, missed Richard's extended gaze into Lyndsey's eyes. Richard reacted to the attic's fading light he shouted, "Lights please!"

John uttered a silent curse. Frustrated with the diary's tall tale, John's mind had captured him in a wide sexual fantasy with his mistress Tessa. He jumped up then briefly wavered on two severely cramped legs. He turned towards the attic entrance and took a first step towards the light switch. After what seemed a lifetime, his first footstep landed shakily on the attic floor. A tad dizzy from the alcohol, John forced the second step and then a third. Each step he took came easier to him. On reaching the light switch, he flicked it on. The bright light temporarily blinded him. The sensation passed quickly. John turned about and walked back towards Lyndsey. He did a quick side step as he passed between Lyndsey and the old trunk then sat down by her side.

The trio sat in silence and allowed time to digest the images the diary's contents had painted in their minds. Not one of them could recall having ever traveled to Nova Scotia; they definitely had never stood on the pristine, rocky shores of its southern coastline before today. Yet at this moment Lyndsey, John, and Richard each found themselves lost in their personal thoughts and standing alone on the shores of East River Bay, looking out onto the blue-green sea-waters that stood before their eyes. In each case, the object of their attention was unique. Using their hands to shield the sun, through squinted eyelids they each sought out the islands revealed to them by Grace Ramsay in the pages of her diary. Sea breezes caressed their faces then embraced their minds cascading their hair freely in the grasp of each passing breeze. The alluring taste of the sea captured their imaginations; John gazed upon the sensual image of Tessa and her lips that silently called out to him, Richard sighed on hearing a youthful Lyndsey's lips whisper, "Kiss me Richie, and ignite a passion in my heart."

Lyndsey gazed upon an image of John with Richard at his side. Confusion and hesitation stood between her and the men she loved and had loved. Her eyes closed and doubts entered her mind. In each of their minds an imagined hazy mist floated far out from shore and denied them of their quest, an image of the islands they'd discovered in the pages of Grace Ramsay's diary. While in the heart of their minds images fed the desires and doubts their hearts struggled to embrace and accept.

Thump! Crash! Meow! The threesome were shocked back into the reality of the attic. Richard broke into hearty laughter. He'd caught a glimpse of Bailey in mid-flight as the old cat tumbled from atop his Grandfather's old bookcase. He also viewed Grandfather Ramsay's prized picture of an unknown seashore crash towards the floor, and sure destruction. Bailey landed with a loud thud on the attic floor. A short distance from Bailey the picture lay with its protective glass shattered.

CHAPTER 3

BOTH LYNDSEY AND JOHN JOINED RICHARD IN LAUGHTER ON SEEING the bewildered look on Bailey's face. Lyndsey felt a pang of pity for the old feline then recalled their earlier encounter. All traces of pity quickly vanished as a tingle ran up her thighs. The recollection of Bailey's cold wet fur and what had been interrupted brought a smile to her face.

Richard picked up his tumbler and raised it to his lips. He stopped just before the tumbler reached his lips. Holding the glass out for closer inspection, Richard was repulsed by a heavy deposit of yellow cat hairs inside his tumbler. A frown appeared briefly on his face. It vanished quickly, replaced instead by a childish smile. He realized the truth behind Bailey's dilemma. The old cat was drunker than a skunk. A picture of Grandfather Ramsay sitting at his writing desk stood out clearly in Richard's mind. Off to the side of the desk, a much younger Bailey appeared. Richard chuckled as he spotted the cat dish from which the younger Bailey indulged himself. The dish's contents had grown to be a family legend over the years. Richard's smile grew as the image of Grandfather Ramsay and the young Bailey faded from view. His attention returned to a much older and dazed Bailey, sprawled out at the base of the bookcase.

Bailey rolled over into an upright position. He thrust out both front paws and pulled himself up into a sitting position. After a short pause, he rose up into a full four-legged poised cat stance. He casually tossed an indignant glare at the threesome, then lifted his front paw and took a bold first step forward.

Thump! All three laughed together as Bailey tumbled sideways and fell back onto the floor. Their laughter died out, and all three watched in earnest as the object of their attention struggled to escape his current situation with dignity.

Slowly, the old feline recovered into a sitting position once more. Using a rear paw, he applied a vigorous scratching session to his ample belly. After a quick shake of the head, Bailey stood up on all fours and proceeded to walk across the attic floor. Though not a smooth catlike strut, it did carry an intoxicated Bailey to his destination. He stopped at the top of the attic staircase, cast a glance back at our threesome, and then disappeared.

Lyndsey stood up and briskly rubbed her thighs; the rubbing relieved the cramps in her legs. She turned, looking across the attic and out the attic's dormer window. A dark night stared back at her. Time had truly taken flight, a glance down to her watch cast a look of surprise on her face. The digital display proclaimed the hour to be 9 pm. She walked towards the broken picture, thought better of it, and then turned about and returned to the old trunk. Stooping down, she picked up the three tumblers and placed them on the tray, accepted a kiss from her husband, stood up with the tray, and walked off towards the attic staircase. On reaching the staircase, she paused and called out, "I'm starved. Am I the only one with a grumbling belly?" Lyndsey disappeared down the staircase.

Richard called out to her, "Nothing too heavy, Lyndsey! Our current state of mind would never stand up to it." He then marked their place in the diary with his sales receipt and set it down on the floor.

"Then soup and sandwiches shall be the order of the day," Lyndsey offered up.

With no protest registered, the menu was set in place. The two brothers sat across from each other in silence. Each appeared deep in thought over the facts and possibilities that had been revealed by the old diary. Richard, forever the dreamer of the two, found himself lost in a sea of possible explanations, while John sat stern faced and sought out logical explanations. He did not subscribe to Richard's view of life. Take or be taken had always been John's life motto.

John reached to his side and picked up the old photo album. He opened the front cover and began to search for answers. The first pictures were extremely old, as evidenced by their yellowed edges and backgrounds. He did not recognize any of the people in the photographs. All the men bore long, whitened beards and moustaches—a trait he'd never seen in any remotely recent family pictures. Quickly, he flipped through the remaining pages, but failed to recognize any of the people or places captured in the pictures. In the last few pages, he admitted a few of the facial features could be family traits of the modern day Clan Ramsay.

"Mind if I take a look at the album, John?" Richard asked.

"Not at all Rich, be my guest! Sorry to say I don't recognize any of the people or places. Just a tad before my time...our time, I'd hazard to guess."

Richard chuckled and accepted the photo album from John. He pulled the front cover open and proceeded to lose himself between the covers of the old album. A consummate history buff, Richard dove into the minute details of each of the pictures set before him in the album. He quickly recognized common features in many of the photos. They had been taken in the vicinity of the sea which created a link between the photo album and the old diary. The album held Richard's thoughts so firmly that he failed to notice John's departure. Each page received Richard's undivided attention. Photos on the last few pages were coloured not black and white and yellowed like the album's earlier photos. Richard guessed them to be photos dating through the late 1960s and early to mid 1970s. He studied them closely.

"Come and get it!"

Richard looked up from the album's landscapes. Lyndsey's meal call awakened a hunger that until then had been suppressed. He closed and set the album aside on the attic floor, then stood up, and set off to join John and Lyndsey in the kitchen downstairs. The aroma of tomato soup and grilled cheese sandwiches quickened his pace as he drew near to the kitchen. A short visit to the sink removed traces of the attic's dusty residue from his hands and face. Richard turned away from the sink and joined the meal in progress.

The pile of grilled cheese sandwiches and pot of tomato soup soon disappeared under the assault of a hungry threesome. Richard stood up and started to clear away the dishes from the table. He paused and offered up compliments to the chef, "Thanks Lyndsey. That really hit the spot and filled a couple of hungry men." Before Lyndsey could respond, Richard had the table cleared and dishes deposited in the kitchen sink. Next, he engaged the drain plug, turned on the hot water, added a dash of dish detergent, and chased the chef and John out of the kitchen with an offer quickly accepted. "Leave the rest to yours truly. I'll join you in the den in ten or fifteen…and thanks again Lyndsey, those sandwiches were great."

John and Lyndsey walked out of the kitchen then turned down the hallway towards the den. Once out of Richard's sight, Lyndsey picked up her pace, turned back towards John and whispered, "I'll join you in the den soon as I take care of a nagging thought."

John stopped dead in his tracks. Taken aback by Lyndsey's unexpected departure, he smiled at her and passed her his approval with his trademark facial twitch. He knew better than to question or attempt to change his wife's decision. He watched her departure and longingly eyed her hips as Lyndsey quickly moved towards the staircase to the second floor. Good God he thought! *If she would only learn to use those hips like Tessa,* then John reasoned, *he would possess every real man's obsession the best of two worlds, sex and more sex!* Experience told him Lyndsey's wanderlust had been peaked by the old diary. He heard a faint squeak as Lyndsey's footsteps hit the only loose step on the attic staircase. John turned and entered the family den. He made his way across the den floor, stopped in front of the loveseat, turned once more and plunked himself down on the seat's beckoning cushions. A tired head leaned backwards and found instant comfort on the soft, cushioned backrest. He spoke his thoughts aloud, "Best hurry back my dear." Two tired eyes blinked and then closed firmly; John's mind drifted towards dreamland. The Sandman carried John's thoughts away to his mistress's apartment.

Lyndsey's footsteps carried her up the attic staircase. She reached the top rung of steps and proceeded across the attic floor. The object of her attention lay on the floor in front of Grandma's old trunk. On reaching her goal, Lyndsey stooped down and retrieved the old diary. Satisfied, she stood up turned and walked back towards the attic staircase. Lyndsey stepped smartly down the attic staircase. At its base, she flicked off the attic lights, and proceeded to walk with a light-foot back to the den on the main floor. She stepped through the arched entrance and smiled across the room at her husband.

Lyndsey proceeded across the den floor, stopped in front of the loveseat, stooped over and kissed John gently on his cheek. John grunted and pulled away from Lyndsey's kiss. She rose up, twisted about, and then sat down next to him. After snuggling up against John's side, Lyndsey frowned and pondered the recent lack of spontaneity and passion in their relationship. Their earlier interrupted connection in the attic had eased her recent concerns. Bailey entered the den and leaped up onto Lyndsey's lap. Frustrated, she quickly shoved the old feline off her lap. Bailey landed on the floor then quickly set off in search of companionship. Once Bailey had parted company with a frustrated Lyndsey, she flipped open the old diary to the page marked by Richard's sales slip and scanned the yellowed pages of the diary. She picked out the spot where Richard had ended his narration. Each word she read heightened Lyndsey's intrigue of the life and times once lived by Grace Ramsay. Her imagination raced ahead of each word read. It sought reasonable explanations for the facts exposed by the diary. Page after page added fuel that drove her imagination further along its journey. Her eyelids fluttered and fought to remain open. It proved to be a battle she'd never win. The diary dropped out of her hands and landed on Lyndsey's midriff; she did not feel its weight. She shifted slightly then snuggled closer to John. The Sandman had successfully claimed his second victim.

Richard quickly worked his way through the dishwashing and stacked the cleaned dishes in the drying rack. He grabbed a dish-towel and proceeded to dry the dishes and returned them to their proper place in Grandma Ramsay's kitchen cupboards. Over the years, he'd assisted Maureen Ramsay with the current task at hand more than once. With the last dish safely stored away, Richard used the spray attachment on the sink to wash away the remaining soapsuds in the drained sink. This completed, he picked up the dishcloth and walked about the kitchen, wiping off the counters, stove top, and kitchen table. Satisfied that the job was now complete, he placed the dish cloth on its drying rack, then dried his hands on the dish towel and hung it over the oven door handle. He turned about and walked off towards the family den to find Lyndsey and John.

On entering the den, Richard stopped dead in his tracks and looked across the room to the love seat. A smile broke out on his face. Seated on the love seat were John, head tilted sideways towards Lyndsey, who had managed to snuggle up tightly against John before the pair had dropped off into dreamland. Richard swung about and walked out of the den. In the hallway, he turned off the light switches for the den and living room, walked to the front door, which he locked, then headed upstairs. There, he flicked off the light switch to the downstairs hallway and headed to the guest bedroom. The bed called out to his tired soul. He removed his shoes and socks, undressed then pulled the bed covers back and sat on the bed's edge. After a pause he crawled under the covers. A short period of tossing and turning ensued, until finally he snuggled up into the bed's soft spot and quickly drifted off into a deep and sound sleep.

CHAPTER 4

LYNDSEY UNCONSCIOUSLY PULLED HER LEGS UP ONTO THE LOVE-seat and tucked her cold feet between the cushion and loveseat's side arm. Her left hand slipped under John's golf-shirt, and sought out the warmth of his chest. She settled back into a deeper sleep. Drifting deeper into dreamland, the events of her day tugged at an active sub-conscious mind.

The diary's author Grace Ramsay and her words owned Lyndsey's imagination and dreamland adventure. Those words cast Lyndsey into the essence and persona of their author. She squinted and peered through an opening in the door of Grace's bedroom. In Lyndsey's mind Grace's words and recorded experiences became a reality. A strange and unfamiliar scene revealed itself to her through the opening. Uncle Richard's appearance sent a chill straight through to her bones and caused her skin to tingle. He was not what one would call an old man. However to be thirty years old she reasoned would amount to ancient status in the eyes of a niece eleven years old going on twelve. Toss in the visual effects of hair whitened to match the snow of a winter squall, an ashen face, and a low, incoherent voice—what was a young lass to think? Yes! She felt and sensed with Grace's reassurance in 1797 to be *thirty years old was definitely over the hill and halfway down the far side.* She longed to see the other Uncle Richard: the one Grace had grown to love—the one whose presence set her young heart to pitter-pattering, and never failed to cause a smile to burst forth on her freckled face. She looked away from the door and picked up the treasured diary, flipped it open to the next blank page, and with pencil in hand guided by Grace started to record the scene revealed to her through the opening in the door. A quick flick of her fingers snapped the diary shut. The words spoken by Grace's mother had startled and frightened the young girl of Lyndsey's dream.

"John! Bring out your jug of rum this minute. I'll have none of your denials…we both know where you keep it hidden."

John tried a mild denial, "What? Pray…tell me of this secret place you speak of my Love."

"I'll have no more of your denials John!" Sadie answered, "Take but one honest look at your poor brother. He needs all the comforting effects that your hidden sinful treasure can offer. The poor man—I'm sure has seen a ghost or worse. Where you two have been, and what you've done, I'll not hear of until poor Richard has received the care he rightly needs this hour."

Before Sadie stopped speaking, John had slipped quietly over to the corner nook, retrieved the jug of rum, and reappeared at her side. Sadie took the jug from him, poured a healthy portion into a mug that sat on the kitchen table and then set the jug down on the table. She picked up the mug and offered its contents to a visibly shaken Richard. John stood motionless beside the table and watched Sadie crouch down in front of his brother.

"Richard, drink this. It will help calm your nerves," Sadie said, then held the mug up to Richard's trembling lips. She tipped the mug upward, and the clear fluid trickled over Richard's trembling lips into his mouth.

Through Grace's eyes, Lyndsey continued to stare out through the door's opening at the action as it unfolded. A hurt settled on her heart, and tears trickled down her cheek. Subconsciously Lyndsey tasted the tears. The sight of Uncle Richard deeply unsettled her mind. She thought, "*What dreadful deed has brought Grace's uncle to this terrible state?*" Through the opening, she felt Grace pining to reach out and comfort her much-loved uncle. Her extended heartstrings hesitated briefly on contacting those of Uncle Richard's troubled heart, then slowly wrapped themselves about their target and stood ready to protect Uncle Richard from further harm. Uncle Richard's emotions touched her through Grace. The faded and blurred image of a fearsome, bearded adversary reached out and touched her. She shuddered as Grace drew back, the evil sensed at first frightened her then she relaxed on sensing Grace's resolve to protect her beloved uncle. She felt his deep hurt and terrified emotions. Grace's willpower broke through and connected fully with the being of her Uncle Richard. His essence flowed eagerly and sought refuge within its Garden of Eden—Grace.

Uncle Richard sat trembling on an old wooden kitchen chair. He stared straight ahead into the eyes of Sadie. The words that formed inside his mind stood motionless. They refused to move forward towards his trembling lips, and thus, remained unspoken. Visions of hell and beyond flashed intermittently in Uncle Richard's troubled mind. Uncle Richard's taste buds raced forward and sucked hard on the fluid that trickled over his lips and into a waiting and eager mouth. It passed over a dry parched tongue. Its powers set to work on the tensions that stood in its path. Slowly, warmth started to build inside Uncle Richard's chilled body. The tremble of his lips lessened. A dash of the old Uncle Richard's charisma worked its way towards the surface and exterior of his body. He allowed his lips to open further. This allowed the flow of rum over his lips to increase. A tint of colour worked its way into Uncle Richard's cheeks. The visions within his mind blurred and grew less fearsome.

Grace's heartstrings pulled away from Uncle Richard and leaped across the room, and darted unnoticed back through the door's opening, and embraced Lyndsey through Grace. Lyndsey waited and listened for the voice of Uncle Richard to break its spell of silence. She sensed the wait would not be a long one.

Uncle Richard stared out through glazed eyes at a worried but composed Sadie. He made his first semi-coherent attempt to speak.

"S…S…ad…ie."

"Yes! Yes! Relax Richard. You're home. You're safe. John and I will care for and protect you from the harm." She paused, turned back towards John, and said to her husband, "He's come back, John! He's come back."

A smile burst forth on Sadie's face. She tipped the mug further upward and emptied its contents into the mouth of Uncle Richard. Suddenly Uncle Richard coughed—gagged on the rum. Standing up in the nick of time, Sadie avoided the spittle from Uncle Richard's mouth. She stooped down, leaned forward, and startled Uncle Richard by wrapping her arms fully about him. Instinct and a need to nurture Uncle Richard's soul drew her arms tighter and pulled him firmly against her bosom. Tears now poured freely down the cheeks of Sadie and Uncle Richard.

John moved silently but quickly over to them, reached out and wrapped his arms around Sadie and Uncle Richard. Tears burst forth and flowed down his cheeks. He babbled, "I'm sorry brother. I…I never thought. I'm truly sorry. Please. Forgive me!"

Sadie cast a sideways glance at John. Her look left little doubt in John's mind. He knew Sadie expected and would demand explanations before they extinguished the candle and retired for the night. He returned the blank expression of a condemned man.

Sadie released her grasp on Uncle Richard, and passed the empty mug to John.

John stepped back, turned around and placed the mug on the kitchen table. He picked up the rum jug and poured a healthy portion into the mug. Without hesitation, he leaned forward and topped up his own mug that sat on the opposite side of the table. Quickly, he set the jug back on the table, picked up Uncle Richard's mug, and passed it to Sadie. At this point, he wisely decided to sit at the table and left the nursing of Uncle Richard to Sadie.

Sadie again raised the mug to Uncle Richard's lips.

This time, Uncle Richard responded, raised his hands, and placed them about Sadie's and the mug. He nodded his head and indicated to Sadie his intention to take control of the mug and its contents.

Sadie slowly eased her hands off the mug and allowed Uncle Richard to exert his control.

Uncle Richard smiled at Sadie. He tipped the mug upward and allowed a healthy dose of rum to enter his mouth. The rum flowed smoothly through his mouth, entered his throat, and then continued its downward path. The soothing effects were reflected on his face. Uncle Richard moved the mug away from his lips and placed it on his lap. He looked directly into Sadie's eyes and in a slow but steady voice said, "Don't be blaming John for what we've done—where we've been. We did it together...willing brothers and fools."

Sadie interrupted, "No blame of that, I promise Richard. No need for you to speak unless you feel up to what you believe must be told." She paused, then continued, "No need to rush, Richard. Take the night and rest on it, dear brother-in-law. We can talk of what has been in the light of the morning sun. Let me prepare some food for you."

A stern Uncle Richard spoke, "It must be told. Telling will ease my mind...set the demons to rest."

Uncle Richard stood up and walked over to the kitchen table. Though slow, his steps were steady and sure. He pulled a chair out from the table and set himself down on it. His glance and smile beckoned Sadie—called her to join them at the table.

Sadie stood up and walked over to the table and sat down on a chair beside John and directly across from Uncle Richard. She grasped the silver crucifix that hung from a chain about her neck and said, "Lord be with us. Protect us from the evil that has fallen upon our path." She paused and made a quick sign of the cross, then said to Uncle Richard, "Unburden your soul, brother-in-law...the Lord is with us."

Uncle Richard echoed Sadie's summons of her faith and Lord with a slow deliberate sign of the cross of his own. He then said, "I'll speak of what and where we've been. I'll reveal what we've seen, but I will not be interrupted until I've had my say. No questions, Sadie. No denials, John." At that point, he paused and awaited acknowledgment and acceptance of the terms he'd stated.

Sadie and John nodded their heads to signal their acceptance of Uncle Richard's demands. They settled back on their chairs and waited for Uncle Richard to speak. Sadie grasped John's hand and held it tightly in hers.

On the other side of the closed bedroom door, a stunned Lyndsey stared out through Grace's eyes and the opening in the door at the proceedings as they unfolded. Her heart pounded rapidly. Anxiously, she waited along with Grace's Mother and Father for Uncle Richard to speak. The hairs on her forearm stood rigid and upright. Every pore of her skin tingled. She did not suffer through a long wait.

Uncle Richard raised his mug and took a slow drink of its contents. He returned the mug to the tabletop, wrapped his fingers firmly around it, and then in a slow but steady voice spoke the words so anxiously awaited by all present.

Uncle Richard's Words

> *I no longer fear Hell's Gates. I have stared directly into the eyes of its Master. I pray no other ever comes to stare onto that fearsome and terrifying sight. However first let me speak of the events that led up to my current state.*
>
> *John, you and I just this morning set out about our usual morning chores. We prepared the jigging lines, sharpened hooks, and finally cast off from shore aboard your boat. A red sun poked itself above the horizon to the east. Soon we both felt its welcomed and warming rays. We did not know how quickly our lives would change in the day just past.*
>
> *We sailed out past the large island and Mi'kmaq summer fishing grounds and in no time at all we found ourselves approaching the shores of Sinner's Island.*
>
> *The receding tide had assisted us as we sailed the boat towards our usual fishing haunt. We arrived there in less than our usual three hour journey. The sea was so quiet and serene, its smoothness like the glass of a mirror. We dropped the sail and rowed to our usual haunt. The swirling morning mist on the sea's surface kept us cooled from the sweat of our rowing.*

A short time later we were both hauling in a goodly catch of fish. I did not notice how quickly we had drifted towards the shore of the island. You must recall our shock at hearing voices drifting out towards us from its mist covered shoreline. I recall how you suggested then demanded that we stop our fishing and row over towards the leeward sheltered cove. It was from that protected spot that we listened and heard the fateful words spoken by persons we never did espy. At the time, we felt ourselves blessed for having been privy to the secrets we overheard. There remains no doubt in my mind, however that the voices truly belonged to long dead pirates of the worst kind.

At your insistence we departed quietly from the leeward cove. We rowed for a stretch till we were well clear of Sinner's Island then raised our sail. An hour later, we sailed cautiously near to the large mist shrouded island of which those voices had spoken. The sea no longer resembled the surface of a mirror, but as I now recall, it was not rough. We dropped our sail and rowed up to the island's shore and quickly disembarked from the boat setting our feet upon welcomed grounds, or so we thought. Together, we secured the boat with ropes to pine trees on the shore of the sheltered cove.

We walked side by side across the island and sought out the place the voices had revealed to our ears. Soon we found ourselves standing beneath an ancient maple tree. If only it had been able to speak. I believe it would have sent us scurrying off to safety with our tails tucked between our legs. Alas, trees do not speak. My words hence must be spoken. John, it was you that first spotted the disturbed earth beneath the outspread branches of the old maple. At first we dug into the earth using our bare hands and large flat rocks. At your insistence, I returned to the boat and retrieved a hammer, metal bucket, several pieces of our fishing gear and our spare oar blades that became our shovels.

I returned as quickly as possible and was short of breath. Together we used the collection of tools we had at hand. In no time at all it seems we'd dug down almost three, maybe four, feet into that accursed ground. The earth worked easily considering the sorry state of implements with which we worked it. We paused briefly then resumed the task that stood before us. When we reached a depth of five feet, we uncovered a scattering of gold coins and glittering precious gems. Your greed surfaced and you pocketed the coins and gems. Hell's Gates opened. The wretched-evil soul we uncovered in gathering those gems reached out and damned our souls! Buried alive I swear, he must have been, throat partly slit but no sign of blood lost. His eyes reached out from the grave, and I swear, sought to possess our souls. You and your greed spotted the glittering jeweled rosary held so tightly in its hand. All would have been well had we done right! Returned the earth to where it belonged ... firmly packed above that demon from Hell. But no! You'd have nothing to do with that John.

No, you grabbed his hand and bashed his fingers trying to get your hands on that rosary. The Demon screamed and howled while seeking to protect the rosary and the treasure it had been charged with protecting by those whose voices had unknowingly revealed the treasure's location to us. You should have abided my pleas, John! The minute you secured that rosary...all Hell broke loose.

CHAPTER 5

LYNDSEY'S EYES FLICKERED THEN POPPED OPEN. HER HANDS LEAPED upward to shield her eyes from a bright morning sun. A natural morning person, Lyndsey lowered her legs off the loveseat and placed her feet firmly down on the carpeted den floor. She stood up and started to walk across the den. The diary slipped and tumbled towards the floor. Lyndsey reacted quickly; her left hand swung downward and saved the diary before it passed her knees. She stopped, raised the diary, and looked with surprise at the pages open to her view. Her eyes caught the words at the bottom of the page *'The minute you secured that rosary…all Hell broke loose.'* The old kitchen of her dream flashed before her eyes. Lyndsey blinked, shook her head, and stood frozen for a second. In that brief second, memory of her adventure in dreamland faded and took refuge in the depths of her mind, eager to reenergize future adventures that awaited the Sandman's return. She shook her head, looked at the diary, and then just as quickly flipped its pages and cover over closing the diary. Lyndsey smiled then proceeded to walk toward the den's entrance.

On exiting the den, Lyndsey turned and walked down the hallway towards the kitchen. At the door, she stopped and a smile appeared on her face. She inspected Richard's clean up of the previous night and thought, *If only John could be as thoughtful and willing to participate and share our household chores.* Every dish and cooking utensil had been washed, dried and returned to its place in the cupboards. She continued into the kitchen and dropped the diary on the kitchen table. At the counter, she retrieved the glass pot from the drip coffee maker and proceeded to lose herself in the chores of preparing the morning coffee and breakfast.

Richard, awakened by the aroma of freshly brewed coffee, arose, grabbed his clothes, and walked briskly off to the bathroom. After a quick shower and shave, he dressed and followed his nose downstairs towards the much-anticipated coffee pot. He stopped at the den entrance and called out a hearty good morning to a slowly awakening John. The call of the coffee pot was too great. Richard stepped off towards the kitchen while calling out to John, "Up and at it…coffee awaits the early bird."

He entered the kitchen after a brief stop to admire Lyndsey as she stood before the stove, putting the finishing touches on a great-looking mushroom omelette. To Lyndsey, he sang out, "Good morning, Sunshine." Not waiting for her reply, he followed his nose to the coffee pot. He grabbed a mug from the cupboard and poured out his morning dose of caffeine. With coffee in hand, he walked over to the kitchen table and sat down to enjoy his morning brew.

The coffee performed its job well. Richard's senses became more alert with each sip taken of his mug's aromatic contents. From its place of rest on the table, the old diary caught Richard's attention. He reached over to retrieve it.

Lyndsey interrupted Richard's thoughts and actions. Her appearance tableside, offering up a fully dressed breakfast plate, demanded his full attention. He glanced down at the plate Lyndsey had set before him: a perfect omelette, golden-yellow, folded back over itself but exposing the edges of butter-fried mushrooms held within its centre. Strips of melted cheddar cheese accented the omelette's surface. Richard's taste buds raced about excitedly and caused his mouth to water. A slice of fresh red tomato and two thick slabs of Texas-style toast topped off Lyndsey's masterpiece. Richard's eyes moved upward away from the plate and locked onto Lyndsey's matching set of baby-blues. He uttered a quick, "Wo…oow."

Their eyes remained locked together until Lyndsey broke the deadlock with a blink. Her left hand appeared from its hiding place behind her hip. She offered up its contents to Richard, "A knife and fork perhaps would be of some use?"

Richard reached out and accepted Lyndsey's offering with his left hand. Humbly, he said, "Thanks. You've prepared a meal to tempt any man's palate. Trust me I'm not accustomed to this royal treatment. Being a bachelor and all...coffee and a nicotine patch is my normal fare of late."

Lyndsey smiled. She shrugged her shoulders and said, "Eat hardy Rich, We have a busy schedule ahead of us today, what with the reading of the wills. It's scary really. Makes all that's happened of late seem too final." Before Richard could respond to her words, Lyndsey turned away from the table, walked over to the kitchen counter and retrieved a second plate. It held her breakfast. On it sat a cereal bowl, filled with assorted fresh cut fruit. She carried it over to the table and sat down across from Richard.

Richard had already made a sizable dent into his omelette. Overhead, the sound of running water broke the silence of the house. Lyndsey tilted her head upwards and said, "John will be joining us shortly. Before he arrives I must ask a favour of you Rich."

"Fire away Lyndsey. Your wish shall be my command...as always," Richard answered.

Lyndsey frowned back at Richard, then said, "No time for your wish my wish games today." She continued to speak, "I'm really concerned about John. He's been under a heavy burden of stress lately. We all feel the pain of our losses, but John's burden, I fear, may be greater than ours. He really wanted this family reunion to happen. He believed it would patch up the differences that had built up between himself and Dad. Now he'll never know—never have the opportunity to patch up their silly differences."

"No!" Richard declared. "We both know where those differences came from: John's insistence on fighting Dad's strong will and beliefs on all but the smallest of issues. Let him live with it. Dad was no man's fool."

"Just think about it…is all I ask, Rich." Lyndsey pleaded, and then finished with, "Both your parents and grandparents are gone. Their sudden deaths robbed John and you of their love." Lyndsey sobbed and burst into tears. "I loved them too. A little compassion wouldn't hurt any one of us."

Richard and Lyndsey stood, he walked to Lyndsey and embraced her. Slowly her tears abated. Overhead, the running water continued to tell them that the privacy of their conversation would not be interrupted by John.

Lyndsey pulled away from Richard, with a pout, then broke into a smile. She changed the topic of conversation and said, "I read more of the diary last night."

Richard glanced at the table and his empty breakfast plate. He walked to the table and picked up the old diary. A quick flip through the pages brought him to the page now marked by his old sales receipt. "Wow! You really poured yourself into this last night." With the diary in hand, he returned to his chair and sat down. Richard asked, "Discover any new family secrets?"

Lyndsey's face paled. She answered, "Yes, one could say I lost myself inside those pages last night. I believe young Grace's words reveal some eerie family secrets. We're Ramsays, our families are somehow connected. We all need to read a great deal more of young Grace's diary. Something drastic happened to her; something that upset her life and the world in which she lived!"

"Get real!" Richard declared.

"Believe me Rich…I'm for real. The words that I read in the diary were real." She stood up, picked up their breakfast dishes, and added, "Trust me that young girl's words will step forward and they will affect our world." After a pause for effect, she added, "Call it a woman's intuition. Call it what you like. It will happen!" With those words, Lyndsey turned and walked to the kitchen sink.

John walked through the kitchen doorway. "What's all this talk of a woman's intuition?" He walked across the kitchen and sat down opposite Richard at the table.

Richard and Lyndsey remained silent. Neither one offered up an explanation to John.

John broke the silence and asked. "Would a quickie breakfast be out of line? We do have that appointment at the attorney's office set for ten o'clock this morning: Disclosure of our Parents' and Grandparents' wills."

"I'll fix you an omelette," Lyndsey offered up. She turned and carried a mug of black coffee over to John. After placing the mug on the table in front of him, she bent over and gave him a good-morning peck on the cheek. She then stood up, turned about, and set off to prepare John's breakfast.

John eyed Richard looking for an answer to his question. His eyes settled on the old diary, which appeared to hold Richard captive. He shouted out, "Boo!" He continued in jest, "Cat got your tongue, Bro?" Richard did not answer. John tried again to draw his younger brother's attention away from the diary, "Hello! Good morning to you."

Richard looked up from the diary and quickly closed it, then set it down on the table. "Sorry, John." He smiled and said, "Good morning to you too. It's the old history buff in me. Never could pass up words written describing or revealing places and times long past. What makes it more intriguing, John; I believe this is our history, our family."

"See! I told you so!" Lyndsey chirped out in triumph. She now stood beside John with his breakfast plate. A broad, all-knowing smile covered her face from ear to ear. She set John's breakfast on the table before him. With a perky twist, she turned away from the table and pranced off towards the kitchen doorway. To John, she said, "Enjoy your breakfast, dear." On passing through the doorway, to John and Richard she called back, "Sure hope you two left a little hot water for little old me. I'm off to freshen up. A quick shower and change of clothes sounds like a great idea. I'll be back in a jiffy." She disappeared from their sight.

John said, "We'd best give her at least an hour."

He directed his full attention to the breakfast plate that sat before him on the table. His stomach's gnawing hunger pains lessened with each helping it received. John remained silent and listened in earnest as Richard revealed more of the secrets uncovered in the old diary.

Richard's mind raced over the details they had discovered in the diary. To John, he spoke his thoughts aloud. "Grace most definitely had to be at least our great-great, and then a great some, grandmother or aunt. Her Uncle Richard, the one whose hair turned snowy-white in a flash, no less than a great, great and then a greater some uncle. It all makes more sense as one reads each new passage of her diary." He paused, gathered more of his thoughts, and then continued to talk aloud. "Ever wonder where our family's wealth came from, John? Will this diary reveal the source to us? Remember those tales Dad and Grandfather read to us at bedtime? Perhaps the pirates and ne'er-do-goods they spoke of were real!"

"Get real!" John injected. Before Richard could reply he continued, "Sorry, but I don't recall those bedtime stories in such a dramatic vein. God! Both you and Lyndsey are hopeless dreamers and wanderlusts."

Richard shrugged off his brother's pinpoint analysis of both his and Lyndsey's characteristics. He recalled vividly the tales and the colourful dreams that had followed a much younger version of himself to dreamland on many a night. A smile broke out on his face. A picture of both himself and John snapped to the forefront of his mind. In it, the characteristics John had spoken of burst forth on the face of a much younger Richard. At his side, a puzzled looking John posed another of his never-ending questions. Truly, nothing much had changed over the years. He much preferred the labels of dreamer or wanderlust to the reality of a predictable, logical, and stone-faced John. *Details…details…details*, he thought. To John he said, "Lighten up big brother. We're all going through a stressful time together. A year, heck ten years from now, I'll undoubtedly still be in a state of denial. Maybe I've taken this old diary too much to heart. I'll promise to back off if you'll but lighten up a degree or two. OK?"

"OK!" John answered with a smile. However I've given it a little thought. The diary that is! 1796 is a year after those young lads ventured out onto Oak Island and discovered the *'Money Pit'*. Could it be our Grace Ramsay is naught but an adventurous wanderlust and storyteller, a true forerunner possessing all the creative juices and imagination of my baby bro?"

"Not a chance John. The detail reveals the events too clearly to have been just a tall tale scribed by our great-great, and then a great some, grandmother. Trust me, her words will reveal our family's past!"

John chuckled and declared, "Next you'll be telling me Captain Kidd was in fact akin to our Clan Ramsay!"

Richard snickered and replied, "Could be!" He paused and said, "Now don't you feel a great deal better?"

"Ask me that question after we've wrapped up this morning's business with Roger," John replied. Before Richard could speak, he continued, "I keep expecting the four of them to come walking through that door. Today is just too final for me. I had hoped to score some points with Dad at this year's family reunion. Make peace. Hopefully heal a wound or two. Now that'll never come to pass."

Richard paused and recalled several of the workplace actions John had enacted during their Parents' and Grandparents' recent travels. Delaying the payment of overtime and refusing to approve vacation request had definitely not enhanced the workplace environment. Bill, their marine engine team leader had actually walked off the job after an angry and emotional exchange of words with John. News that his vacation request had been canned set off the fiery exchange. Bill had booked and paid for a family Caribbean Cruise. Bill went straight to Granddad who intervened and overruled John's actions. Richard brushed the recollections aside and reached across the table. He clasped both of John's hands firmly and spoke solemnly. "They were business wounds, John, inflicted on the battlefield of business. They healed quickly. Dad never held them against you. To him, business was business. Family was family. Above all else, family is love. Dad never loved you or me more or less than each other."

John squeezed Richard's hands then pulled himself free of Richard's grasp. He wiped away the tears that had trickled down his cheeks. He said, "Thanks Rich. Let's keep it that way, Dad's way."

"Let's move it!" Lyndsey sang out as she re-entered the kitchen. She walked over and stood beside John at the kitchen table.

Richard stood up. He picked the remaining breakfast dishes up from the table as Lyndsey hugged John and kissed his cheek. He said, "It's 9 o'clock. You two head off to Roger's office. I'll straighten up here and will meet up with you there no later than 9:45. Okay?" Neither Lyndsey nor John offered up a protest. Richard, now at the kitchen sink, deposited the dishes, then waved his hands at the couple and shooed them off.

John and Lyndsey turned and walked towards the front door. Lyndsey held the diary in hand. John called back to Richard. "That's 9:45 sharp Rich!"

Richard laughed aloud and answered back, "Trust me…I'll be there." He then removed his sports jacket, placed it on the back of a chair, and set about cleaning up the aftermath of the morning's breakfast. The task took next to no time. He finished it off by hanging the dishtowel on the oven door handle. He walked over picked up his tweed sports jacket and set off to their appointed rendezvous. The grandfather clock in the living room struck on the half hour as Richard closed and locked the front door. Plenty of time remained. He whistled aloud and thought, *Maybe for once I'll arrive somewhere on time.*

CHAPTER 6

THE DRIVE TO ROGER'S OFFICE PROVED UNEVENTFUL. RICHARD flipped on the right-turn signal and touched the brake pedal; his black SUV slowed in response to the braking action. He turned the steering wheel and directed the vehicle into the parking lot. Business appeared light: only five parking spots were occupied. He parked the SUV next to John and Lyndsey's Honda Civic. After switching the ignition off and applying the parking brake, Richard stepped out of the vehicle onto the paved parking lot. The mid-morning sun felt good. He locked the vehicle and then set off towards the building's main door. Halfway across the parking lot, Richard stopped dead in his tracks, looked to his left then broke into a fit of laughter. Sitting next to Roger's Caddie stood the strangest looking pickup truck he'd ever laid eyes on. He walked over towards the truck to afford himself a closer look. Unable to determine its vintage, Richard, assigned it to the early sixties. No classic, it had been hand painted a bright purple with a brush. The brush strokes were evident everywhere. Lettering in brilliant yellow paint on the pickup's passenger door declared 'LOBSTER CAPITAL OF THE WORLD...WE CATCHES THEM...WE COOKS THEM... WE EATS THEM.'

Richard's laughter lost the battle to a hoarse cough. He almost choked on it, but quickly recovered. The truck's side panel drew his full attention. He stepped forward and took a closer look. On the side panel, a deep red lobster smiled back at him. Below the lobster, gold letters spelled out the vehicle's home port: East River Nova Scotia. A flush fever broke out on his face. The opening entry of the old diary flashed before his eyes: "Diary of Grace Ramsay… East River Nova Scotia 1796." Richard pondered the possibilities he chuckled anew then stepped away from the old pickup truck. He stood silent in the parking lot. After what seemed a lifetime, but was at most a minute or two, his heartbeat slowed, Richard's thoughts returned him back to the present. He glanced across the parking lot to the front doors of Roger's office and wondered if John and Lyndsey had also seen the truck, and if the truck was connected to the family of the diary's author? Cautiously, he started to walk towards the office door. At no time did his eyes return to the truck. He reached the office door, pulled it open, and stepped inside. John and Lyndsey sat on a sofa across from the receptionist's desk. Richard walked over and joined them. He sat down beside Lyndsey.

"Have you been waiting long?" Richard asked.

"Maybe…twenty minutes," John answered then added, "Roger is with another client. He shouldn't be much longer."

Richard picked up a sports magazine from the end table. He slowly flipped through its pages. Both John and Lyndsey appeared calm enough to him, he assumed they'd arrived before the other client…the truck's owner…or they'd not noticed the truck. He settled on their early arrival. John's casual mention of another client reinforced Richard's conclusion. A quick glance at his watch told him it was 9:50 am. Richard recalled Roger's habit of meticulously adhering to the clock. A meeting scheduled to start at 10:00 am would start at 10:00 am: not 9:59 am and definitely not 10:01 am. He settled back on the sofa, and awaited Roger's 10:00 am summons.

CHAPTER 7

"ROGER IS READY FOR YOU NOW."

John, Lyndsey, and Richard looked up and in the direction the voice had come from. They stood up together, and set off down the hallway towards Roger's private office. At the office door, they nodded a silent good morning to Tessa, Roger's personal legal assistant.

Tessa greeted them. "Good morning John, Richard, Lyndsey." She then offered them her condolences, "So very sorry to hear of the terrible accident—such a great loss. They'll all be missed dearly."

Richard couldn't help but notice that Tessa's words addressed the trio but her eyes never left John's face. He also couldn't help but notice her appearance. Tessa was definitely overdressed for a Saturday meeting between business associates, even though it was a *business* meeting. Her black dress stopped well above Tessa's two attractive knees and exposed the lower portion of two very nice thighs. It also clung closely to every curve of her body. The low neckline drew Richard's eye to Tessa's breasts. The tight fitting dress thrust them upward and outward. Dark, black shoulder-length hair topped off Tessa's slim figure. Richard forced himself to look up and directly at Tessa's face. It was petite and slightly oval. Her full, deep-red lips moved as she spoke to John. Richard never heard a word she spoke. Definitely not his type, Richard told himself. He did not like the way she openly ignored the presence of both Lyndsey and himself.

Tessa turned about and said, "Roger is ready so we'd best not keep him waiting." She stepped forward and walked into the conference room ahead of the trio. Silently, she longed to once again share her bed sheets with John. In her heart, she longed to see the shocked looks that would soon adorn the face of pristine little Lyndsey and that of goodie—goodie Richard. Yes. Tessa looked forward to seeing their superior attitudes trashed. She stepped off to the side and left Roger to greet the trio. Quietly, she moved over to the conference table and sat down on the swivel chair that her dress's matching jacket rested on. She settled in and waited anxiously for the fire-works to begin.

Roger stepped forward and greeted his clients, his friends, "Good morning Richard, John, Lyndsey." He reached out and shook hands with Richard, then John. A step forward and to the side placed Roger eye to eye with Lyndsey. He swung his arms out and pulled her tightly to himself and gave her a trademark Roger hug, then kissed Lyndsey on the cheek and whispered, "How's my little angel? How are my angel's charges holding out?" Roger released Lyndsey then stepped back. He looked at the three and said, "Before we get underway. Some introductions are in order."

Richard froze. What introduction could Roger possibly mean? A picture of the old pickup truck flashed before his eyes. He looked first to John, then to Lyndsey to see their reactions. They appeared startled just like him. His eyes turned back to Roger as he waited for him to speak.

Roger smiled. After a moment had passed, three individuals walked into the room. Roger then offered up his introductions, "Richard, John, Lyndsey I'd like you to meet Mr. Lizards, Gilbert McClaken and his niece, Hope McDonald."

John, Richard, and Lyndsey's eyes turned from Roger to the individuals Roger had introduced. Their eyes locked onto the pair. Together they watched in silence as Gilbert McClaken and Hope McDonald walked over and stood by Roger's side. An eerie silence took over the room.

Richard stared wide eyed at the strangers. Gilbert was a giant. He stood at least six foot two in height, was broad of shoulder, and had a muscular frame. Richard estimated Gilbert's weight to be 275 pounds. Long, black hair speckled with a touch of gray topped the giant's head. It was tied in a ponytail, which reached his shoulder blades. Matching sideburns ran down the sides of his face. Richard's eyes were drawn to the man's sparkling blue eyes. Somehow he found comfort in those eyes and sensed kindness. A friendly smile was returned to him.

Lyndsey caught Gilbert's friendly smile. Somehow, the smile seemed very familiar to her but she couldn't grasp the why. Had she met him through her work? Could he be a family member of a resident at the Retirement Villas? No she reasoned, his size alone would connect me to his person. Lyndsey searched her mind pondering why Gilbert's smile felt so familiar.

Richard blinked then moved his eyes away from the giant and looked at Hope who stood by his side.

She was nineteen, he reasoned, twenty-one at the most. It wasn't her age that startled Richard. The girl was a strawberry blonde likeness to a photo of a man in the old photo album in his Grandparents' attic. No, this couldn't be, Richard reasoned. However a photo in the album's last few pages, stood out in his mind. She stood maybe five feet four inches tall at most—short compared to Lyndsey's five foot six height. Looking into her face, Richard momentarily lost himself gazing into her blue eyes. Hope smiled back at him. Her reddish freckles added a unique energy to her person. Slightly embarrassed he looked down from her face and viewed a firm and well-curved chassis. A flush rose over his face.

The giant spoke, "It's Gilbert, but you can call me Gil."

"Roger, what the hell is going on," John growled. He took a step toward Roger.

Richard grabbed John's left arm and refrained him from attacking Roger. "John, back off, give Roger some space and time to explain." He moved to John's side, relaxed his grasp on John's arm, and then wrapped his right arm over John's shoulder. He said, "It's going to be OK, John. We'll listen to Roger, and it'll be OK."

"Thanks Richard. If we can all take a seat…we can get the proceedings underway," Roger offered.

John said, "You'd best be good and get to the point real quick!"

"Trust me John. I will," Roger replied.

Richard relaxed his hold on John, and guided him over to the meeting table. He waited for John to be seated and then sat down in the chair beside him. Together, they sat silent while Lyndsey, Roger, Gilbert, and Hope walked over and seated themselves. Lyndsey sat down beside John. Roger took his place beside Tessa. Gilbert sat down next to Roger, and Hope sat down next to her uncle. Mr. Lizards sat in a chair distanced from everyone else. He placed his briefcase on the floor at his side, retrieved a file folder and placed it in front of himself on the conference table. The room stood silent.

Roger shuffled the notes that lay on the table before him. After a pause, he broke the silence.

"First things first John, I'm not trying to pull anything off. You should know that better than anyone. I like you and everyone at this table, was totally unprepared for what has happened. We're all deeply shocked and saddened by that tragic accident back in April. Your parents—I grew up with them."

John broke in and apologized, "Sorry Roger. It just startled me. I expected this to be a simple meeting—the three of us, you, and Tessa. These three strangers sent me for a loop."

Roger nodded and continued, "As I said, it has been a total surprise and shock to me."

He then continued with his explanation.

"Your grandparents, they practically raised me. I loved them like a second set of parents. I next to grew up in the old homestead and spent more time there than in my own home. Your Grandfather bankrolled my education. He made me what I am. There's nothing I wouldn't do for him. Furthermore, I am the family's business attorney. William, your Grandfather, set me up in my practice and saw to it that I survived those harried days of my early practice. However, he never hired me for any of his personal affairs. His family credo: business was business, family was family. Mr. Lizards of Lizards, Rose and Rose, has always handled your Grandfather's personal affairs. He is here today to handle William's last wishes. As for Mr. McClaken and his niece, I, like you, met them for the first time this morning."

After a short pause, Roger said, "I think it best that we hand things over to Mr. Lizards at this point."

Mr. Lizards said, "Thank you, Roger. I would prefer Walter, a touch friendlier." He flipped open the file folder that he'd placed on the table. From it, he retrieved a letter. He offered up his personal condolences to everyone at the table, and then closed with, "First off, I'll read this opening letter, written by William Ramsay to his son Bill, your father John, Richard. He requested it of me."

The room fell silent. Everyone present collected their thoughts and waited for Mr. Lizards, Walter, to speak.

CHAPTER 8

William C. Ramsay
RR#1
Newmarket, Ontario
December 21, 1968

BILL,

Time's passage stands still for no man. Its path forever etches a trail deep in each man's memory; a trail that the wise man oft times returns to while seeking to relive the cherished footprints along its path. Tonight I find myself standing over those footprints and recalling a step I once took. Christmas 1954 burns brighter tonight than it did for me on its first passage. It is a moment I now gladly offer up to you.

December 21, 1954, I sat in my favourite recliner, a leather La-Z-Boy. Off to my left, out of the corner of my eye, you sat before the Christmas tree. The sparkle in your eyes as you gazed over the many multi-coloured presents took me back to a time when I had sat there and my Father sat in my place. I now know the contentment that Dad promised would one day settle upon my soul. Four days later you awoke to the merriment of a Christmas morn.

Someday I pray you will likewise come to know the contentment and joy I felt and your son will after you. Time knows no bounds.

Blink and it will leave you gazing with wonder into its path. Grasp it and you will be rewarded by the ecstasy of its presence and its passage. We know not how much or how little of this precious gift will be ours. We can but cherish each and every passing day, hour, minute, and second. Someday, this gift will bring another sparkle to your eye; one which no brightly wrapped box beneath a Christmas tree ever will. Better than any toy, it's yours to give and share with those you love, in the hope that they will but share with you a day, an hour, a minute, and a second, of theirs.

I love you dearly, son. It hurts to know that once you've learned of this letter's existence; my time will have come to an end. Find peace in the memories of times we spent together sharing our precious gifts. Carry those memories forward and share them freely with those you love and whose love befalls you. Shortly, at this letter's end, you will come to know the words and wishes spelled out in my last will and testament. Some of the people I call upon will be well known to you. Others will come to you out of what seems to be thin air; as a total surprise one could say. Trust me, for this is the way in which I also came to know of our family's past. Only this time, true to my Father's wishes, I will set the past right and bring our family back together at last. Trust me son. I did not leave you alone.

John roared, "Enough already!"

Walter lowered the letter then said, "Please, Sir. I must read your Grandfather's letter. It is his expressed wish that it be done in this manner."

"The Lizard speaks!" John injected with disgust. He stood up and continued to vent his rage, "So the vultures and lizards have descended. Let the feast begin!"

Richard stood and turned to his brother. He said, "John…please let Walter continue. We're all hurting. It's a heavy burden we all carry. Please John, sit down again by my side. Hear Walter out. We need you."

John pushed Richard hard. Lyndsey started to stand up, but stopped when she saw the look on John's face.

She pleaded, "Please dear, listen to Richard. We must allow Mr. Lizards, Walter, to do his job." The John she now looked upon was not the one she'd grown to love. She just wanted this horrible day to end. She wanted the healing to begin. Lyndsey lowered her head. Tears trickled down her cheeks. John made no effort to console his wife.

John looked down at Lyndsey and said, "Good one Lyndsey, put on a crying jag. Poor little Lyndsey a beacon of innocence." He threw his hands up in disgust. "Look at them, vultures each and every one. They'll pick what's left of our family to pieces. Pluck every inch of flesh off Grandfather's bones…dollar by dollar." With a twist, he turned about, kicked his chair, and sent it flying out of his path. He then stepped forward and made his way towards the door. Without looking back, he spat out a parting shot. "I'm out of here. I'll not stand witness to this charade. This is not my Grandfather's wish. I'll not be party to it!" On reaching the door, he grabbed the knob, twisted it, and pulled the door open. John then stomped through the doorway. He did not look back. The door swung back from the office wall. John grabbed the handle and slammed it shut.

The office stood silent in the wake of John's abrupt departure. Richard sat back down in his chair. After a moment, he stood up, moved to his right, and retrieved John's chair. He moved it to Lyndsey's side then sat down.

Tears flowed freely down Lyndsey's flushed cheeks. Richard leaned towards her and whispered, "Say the word and I'll go after him."

Lyndsey coughed lightly and replied, "No, Richard. Not now. Give him some time—some space." In the background, the sound of squealing tires broke the room's silence.

Walter spoke, "Perhaps we should all take a breather, step outside and collect our thoughts before going on?" He closed his folder, picked it up and placed it inside his briefcase. With a snap of the clasps, he locked the papers inside. He stood up, looked at Roger, and said, "On second thought, Roger, would you lock up this office after we've all stepped outside. It's 10:45 am now. I suggest we all meet back here in 30 minutes."

Each person in the room took Walter's cue. Quietly they each stood up in turn and moved silently towards the door. Roger exited last behind Walter. He locked the door, turned, and walked down the hallway. After everyone had exited the building, Roger locked the door. Walter suggested an hour would be more appropriate.

Richard said, "So we'll all meet back here at 11:45 am?"

"Yes," Walter answered.

Roger walked over to his Caddie. After unlocking the door, he opened the driver's door and slid into the driver's seat. He started the engine then drove out of the parking lot.

Walter entered his rental vehicle, started the engine and followed Roger's lead.

Richard walked across the parking lot at Lyndsey's side. Gilbert and Hope walked along slowly behind. Gilbert called to Richard, "Suggestion! Could we four stop in at the coffee shop down the road? It's but a short walk, and I could use a java fix."

Lyndsey twisted about and answered. "Yes. That would be nice."

Gilbert and Hope quickened their pace. At the sidewalk, Gilbert pointed out the coffee shop that stood on the next block. The foursome walked along the sidewalk in silence towards their destination.

Tessa watched them disappear from sight. She got into her Oldsmobile and drove out of the parking lot. At the street, she turned left and drove off towards her apartment. She hoped to find it occupied. John needed support now. Who better to give it, and more, than Tessa!

CHAPTER 9

GILBERT REACHED FORWARD AND PULLED THE DOOR OPEN. HE held it while Hope, Lyndsey, and Richard entered the coffee shop. He then followed them through the doorway. Gilbert asked, "Any preference to seating, a window, or a cozy corner?"

"Let's make it a window perch," Lyndsey suggested.

"OK by me!" Gilbert answered then asked, "Any objections?"

No objections were expressed. Hope led the way to the only window booth that stood unoccupied. She sat down and slid over the bench until she sat next to the window. Lyndsey did the same and ended up sitting across from Hope. Gilbert sat down beside Hope; Richard sat down next to Lyndsey. The foursome sat in silence.

"Good morning all," their waitress offered up. She then asked, "Coffee all around, regular, dark roast or decaf? We also have a nice almond flavour on brew."

Hope spoke first, "I'll try your almond, black."

"Make that two," Lyndsey added.

Richard smiled and placed his order, "One more makes three. But add a dash of sugar to mine, and add on a chocolate dipped donut. No, make that two."

"Best make mine decaf, no additives," Gilbert said. He then asked, "Would you have a cranberry muffin per chance?"

"Sorry, can't help you there," the waitress replied. She added, "How about a freshly-baked blueberry delight? The berries are really big."

"Sold," A smiling Gilbert answered.

The waitress repeated their orders, "Four coffees, three almond, all black, one with a dash of sugar, one decaf no additives. Two chocolate-dipped donuts and one blueberry delight." She turned and before walking away said, "Thank you and enjoy."

"Thank you…Wendy," Gilbert said. He'd caught her name tag on her blouse.

Gilbert turned and faced Richard and Lyndsey. He said, "Maybe now would be a good time to tell you who we are and how Hope and I came to be here today." Before either could respond, he started his proper introductions and explanations.

"First off, I would really prefer Gil to Gilbert. Hope here is my niece. More like a daughter though. My wife and I raised her after her parents had their tragic accident, seems so long ago. She was a mere babe in arms when her parents' tragedy blessed us with a genuine bundle of joy and rewarded us with Hope. Hope has been tending to moi, her dear uncle, since the passing of my wife Karyn a year ago June. There's nothing special about us Bluenosers…Nova Scotians through and true." He stopped speaking when Wendy returned with their orders but quickly continued as she walked away.

"I'm a part-time lobster fisherman. The calling of the sea runs in the family. We've always been fishers of the sea. I said part-time and best explain. Grandfather and Dad envisioned the troubles of the fishery years ago. Not like our trusted bureaucrats who have next to shut it down, while laying the blame on everyone and everything but themselves. Grandfather and Dad insisted that I tend to my education. I rebelled at first. It was a battle short lived. Grandfather… God bless him, was a feisty old soul. Dad still is."

He took a breather and a couple of sips from his coffee mug then continued.

"The long and short of it, Gilbert M. McClaken: part-time lobster-fisherman, part-time Professor of English, jack of all trades… and an all around happy camper." Another coffee pause, a sheepish smile, and then he continued anew.

"I have two brothers, no sisters."

"Three!" injected Hope. She explained. "We mustn't forget Uncle Jeffrey."

"My apologies," Gilbert answered, then clarified, "Three brothers Paul, Morgan, and Jeffrey." He winked at Hope and continued, "Paul and Morgan left the home scene years ago; last saw them ten years ago. I attended a seminar out in BC. They're well situated out there. Don't expect them to return home anytime soon, however, a visit for Dad's sake would be nice. He's getting on, BC isn't a day trip, but it would be nice."

Gilbert paused. He took a sip of his coffee and explained, "They run a marine maintenance business. Between the fleet of west coast recreational boats, yachts and the commercial fishing fleet, there's a big demand for their services out there. Personally, I feel they're too committed to work. Need to learn to take care of their inner beings. Life's too short."

"No need to explain that one," Richard interjected.

Gilbert added, "I agree. Roger explained earlier that your family's business is also centred on marine maintenance along with sales of new and used recreational boats."

Richard added the focus of his line of work, "That and a growing interest in the maintenance of heavy duty equipment on board the commercial fleets of Great Lakes and Seaway shipping vessels, which at times keeps me away from home at the many ports of call on the Great Lakes and the Seaway"

Gilbert grinned then replied, "If not for my part-time Professor of English status, it appears our families are focused on reaping their livelihoods from the sea."

Hope hugged her uncle and declared, "Uncle Gilbert! You are a part-time lobster-fisherman of renown on Mahone Bay."

Gilbert chuckled and boasted, "Thanks Hope I've been redeemed and declared worthy of the calling of the sea." Gilbert set his coffee down then explained how the McClakens had come into contact with Richard's Grandfather. "First met your Grandfather when he dropped in on my other Grandfather—Mother's side: Grampa Ramsay. He was on vacation and doing a little family research. I was but a young lad when that first visit happened. He returned many times after that. Mother never said much about those visits, and I was only present for three. No, it must have been five or six of them."

He stopped for another helping of coffee, smiled, and continued. "After Grampa Ramsay and then Mother passed away, the visits stopped. One night Dad and I enjoyed a heart-to-heart chat in the good company of some fine white rum."

"A fine seaman's companion "Richard replied.

"Aye! How true," Gil replied then added, "Your Grandfather had in his possession a diary."

Both Richard and Lyndsey's faces perked up with interest. Gil picked up on their reaction.

"I take from your reactions you've both seen or heard of its existence?"

"We have a diary Lyndsey discovered it in Grandmother's old trunk. It could be the diary Grandfather possessed. Or it could simply belong to Grandma. What makes the diary in Grandfather's possession unique?"

Gilbert replied, "Grandfather Ramsay—Isaac often boasted that it was dated 1796 and from the hand of a Grace Ramsay."

"Yes," Richard answered and thought to himself, *sure helps put John's theory on creativity and imagination to rest.*

"Grace is a gifted storyteller, or recorder of life's special moments," Lyndsey added.

Richard and Lyndsey's faces and words confirmed Gilbert's suspicion. The diary he sought existed. "I'd love to see it and read it someday if I may," Gil asked.

Neither Lyndsey nor Richard answered Gil's request. Their minds raced through the old yellowed pages. Their wanderlust relished the idea that the words of young Grace, the diary's author, did indeed speak of times, places, and things...that had really happened.

Gil picked away at the blueberry delight and finished the last of his coffee. He glanced at his watch and said, "Time sure does fly. We'd best finish up here and head back down to Roger's office."

Richard set a ten-dollar bill on the table and said, "My treat."

Wendy walked over to their table and presented their tab. Richard passed her the ten spot and thanked her for her great service.

"You were right," Gil said, "The blueberry delight was everything you promised."

They all rose up from the booth and made their way towards the front door. Lyndsey and Hope excused themselves and stepped off to the lady's washroom.

Richard watched them walk away. He concluded that twenty or twenty-one best reflected Hope's age. From the rear, their walks were near identical: Lyndsey's hips swayed smoothly and were a touch heavier. A good thing, for Hope definitely required a touch more weight. It would, Richard reasoned, add a more gentle sway to her hips.

Gilbert held the door open and Richard stepped outside, then Gilbert joined him. Together they waited for the girls to rejoin them. Once outside, Gilbert pulled out his pipe and lit it up.

"I'd best take a pull or two on my vice before Hope and Lyndsey return. Needless to say, Hope does not approve." Gilbert commented.

Richard reached in his jacket and pulled out a package of gum. He smiled and said, "It's my quit smoking crutch. It has definitely been a tough road to travel."

"How are you coping?" Gilbert asked.

"It's been a tough six months, but it is getting easier."

They stood together in silence and awaited the return of Hope and Lyndsey. The cafe door opened and the girls stepped out onto the sidewalk. Gilbert moved quickly to tuck his pipe away. If Hope noticed, she did not comment or chide her uncle. The foursome set off anew and walked back to Roger's office.

Hope and Lyndsey trailed the men. In idle chit-chat Lyndsey explained to Hope briefly the struggles she was battling with in returning to work full time at Daylily Meadows Retirement Villas, where she held the position of Financial Administrator / Bookkeeper. The hurt and sudden loss of her in-laws, echoed in her heart each workday. Daily encounters with the residents reminded her of the loss their family continued to deny and accept on a daily basis. However on a positive side the abundant hugs and blessing they gave her each day was definitely adding positivity to her life.

....

Tessa inserted her key into the lock. She twisted it and unlocked her apartment door. Once inside, she flicked on the vestibule light then walked into the living room. John sat slouched on the sofa, an open bottle of scotch in his hand.

"I'll not have my family's fortune picked apart by that bald-headed little lizard and the friendly giant!" he screamed at Tessa.

"Spare me the detail. I was there."

"Then fill in the details."

"Simple; you blew it."

"Spare me!"

"Oh really, then what was the point of your outburst?"

"I stood my ground. God knows little Richie won't."

"Well you'll get a second go at it. We're to reconvene at 11:45"

Tessa walked over and sat herself down on the sofa. She sat on her knees and faced John.

John eyed Tessa's thighs. Her short skirt slid slowly up and exposed more of them to John's eye. He reached out and offered Tessa his bottle of scotch.

Tessa accepted. She raised the bottle to her lips and took a healthy swig. A tingle ran up her inner thighs. Finished with the bottle, she set it down between her thighs. It stopped John's fingers from continuing their journey. Tessa smiled seductively then pushed the bottle into his hands. She said, "No time to spare, my dear." She glanced at her watch then added, "We're all to meet back at Roger's office in half an hour."

"Not I," John proclaimed.

"What? Are we afraid to face the music?"

"No music."

"Tell me about it. Just who was that raging madman back at the office?"

"Damn it all! I'm the eldest Ramsay now. I get to call the shots. The Lizard and his companions, just who the hell are they?"

Tessa frowned and shook her head.

John smirked then said, "Stress will explain all, given time. No! I'll stay away for a bit and then a little bit more."

Tessa leaned forward and kissed John. She brushed John's hands away from her buttocks and pulled herself free from his grasp. She said, "You're right. It would be better for you to stay away for now. Let the proceedings play out." She stood up and pulled her skirt down to its full length: that being halfway down or up her thighs. She laughed, turned away from John, and walked towards the doorway. At the dining room, she picked her purse up off the table. *If Lyndsey only knew the half of it*, she thought. *Not to worry*, she reassured herself. *Love was good if one had the time. Sex was best.* She smiled to herself and walked on towards the door. She forced an extra sway into her hips. Best to give a man a little appetizer, she reasoned.

John eyed Tessa's swaying hips. "Don't be late, Junior likes the view."

Tessa called back, "Then don't be drinking his master into a stupor. I'll be back and Junior had best be up to the task he's set in motion."

John whispered, "Trust me, Junior needs no prompting. It's been a week and some since last he did the deed."

Tessa did not hear his words. She let the apartment door swing shut as she walked out into the hallway. She could still feel the heat of John's eyes burning on her buttocks. It felt good.

....

Roger drove down Main Street. Ahead, he spotted his destination: the entrance to Heavenly Gates Cemetery. He flipped on the left-turn signal and touched his foot to the brake pedal. Traffic was light for a Saturday. The Caddie turned into the cemetery. It passed under the wrought-iron entrance gateway and drove slowly along the dirt roadway. After a left turn and two right turns, the Caddie pulled up short in front of four recently worked gravesites then stopped. Roger stepped out of the Caddie. He swung the driver's door shut and walked over to the gravesite. The sun shone down on him and warmed his face. He stopped in front of the four grave plots.

A tear ran down his cheek. Roger looked up from the plots at the two headstones. He whispered, "I'm sorry, Will. If only you'd forewarned me. I could have better prepared John." He reached inside his sports jacket and retrieved a silver flask. Roger removed the topper and raised the flask to his lips. He drew a healthy splash of rye whisky. It flowed smoothly through his mouth and warmed his throat on its downward journey.

Roger read the names inscribed on the stones. The first stone a light grey marble, read 'William Ramsay Died April 6th, 1996 Aged 74 and His Beloved Wife Maureen (Nee Doyle) Ramsay, Died April 6th, 1996 Aged 72.' The second stone a light reddish marble, read 'William 'Bill' Ramsay Died April 6th, 1996 Aged 50 and His Beloved Wife Mary (Nee Tucker) Ramsay, Died April 6th, 1996 Aged 48.' His eyes returned to the grey stone. Roger spoke directly to it.

"I don't know what to say. True we both always knew John to be a bit of a hot head. Not in a bad way. It even helped us close a deal or two over the years. But where do I go from here? I will stand by the boys and bring John back into the picture. I trust your letter and the directions you placed in Walter's hands will provide the closure needed. Without question I will stand tall and firm on all the family's business needs. I owe you big time, Will. I'm going to miss your good character and companionship." He replaced the flask's topper and slipped it back into his inner jacket pocket, then turned and walked away from the gravesite. Another tear ran down his cheek as he walked back towards the Caddie. A glance at his watch quickened his pace. The session would resume in fifteen minutes. Roger got into his Caddie, switched on the ignition, and started its engine. The Caddie exited through the cemetery gate and slipped easily into the flow of traffic.

....

Mr. Lizards, Walter, eased off the gas and touched the brake pedal. He flicked on the right-turn signal and turned into the parking lot of the Blue Buzzard Tavern. After the goings on he'd just experienced, the tavern's smiling Blue Buzzard sign looked like a welcomed source of relief. He parked next to the tavern beside the only other car in the lot, a silver eightyish Honda Civic. Quickly, he slipped out from behind the wheel, locked the doors, and walked across the parking lot to the tavern's side entrance. On stepping inside the tavern, the dim lighting cast a calming hand over his frustrated mind, he relaxed. The only other patron appeared to be a gentleman of sorts. The dim lights confused Walter's attempt to place an age to the man. He walked across the tavern floor and sat down on a barstool. The bartender turned to face her newly-arrived customer. She smiled and Walter smiled back.

"Welcome to the Blue Buzzard"

Walter liked her voice; liked the warm kindness that touched his ears. He smiled again. Before she could ask what pleasure he wanted, Walter pointed to a bottle of white rum and said, "Best make it a double…no, after this morning a triple would be best."

"Home troubles?" the gentleman four seats down the bar asked.

"No," Walter replied. He chuckled and said, "Though after what I've been through that would be a welcomed alternative."

"Must be a gender situation of another stripe," the stranger said with a laugh. "What else could summon up the power of a triple? Not to fret, the white rum soothes all who call upon its counsel."

"I'll toast you on that one," Walter offered. He raised his glass and introduced himself, "Walter D. Lizards at your service."

The stranger smiled anew and introduced himself. "Uncle Wayne at your service: philosopher, manipulator of words, and would be author at your disposal. Keylyn put a topper to Walter's half-full glass on my tab please." He stood up and walked over to the barstool next to Walter and sat down.

"Thank you Wayne," Walter offered up to his new-found companion.

"I'd prefer Uncle Wayne. Not a royalty title, but one of which I'm proud."

"Then thank you, Uncle Wayne. Are you from this neck of the woods?"

"No. But I've got family here. Truth is I'm just wandering about."

"Your accent reveals a hint of the valley, the Ottawa Valley to be precise."

"I plead guilty as charged. Born and raised there I must confess."

Walter chuckled lightly and asked "Born and raised there. But not from there…right?"

"Right ag'in my friend. Born and raised there. But refined and matured on the pristine shores by the sea."

"Then the buggy with the Nova Scotia plates outside would be yours?"

"Right ag'in my friend."

"Strange. I just met a gentleman from there this morning. A McClaken," Walter stated.

"What? Not Bugshit McClaken…I trust."

"No. Actually his name was Gil…I mean Gilbert McClaken."

"No kidding. He's Bugsh…I mean Jeffrey's older brother."

"Strange, really strange," Walter said.

"No kidding. You met Gilbert this morning?"

"Strange but true, he's from…East River, Nova Scotia I was told."

"Well. I'll be."

"You've intrigued me. Gilbert seems a level-headed, good man. Why did you refer to his brother as Bug…Bugshit McClaken, instead of Jeffrey?"

"Oh. He's OK really. Best described as one of the jewels every family has in their midst, whether they admits it or denies it. In truth he's a real gem and a charmer."

Walter chuckled anew along with Uncle Wayne. He'd never set a foot down by the pristine shores of Nova Scotia but he'd often thought of heading out that way. Good God they're a friendly lot! Yes, someday he would do just that. He glanced down at his watch and frowned on realizing it was time to cut loose and head back to the office. His job seemed less ominous. The rum had counseled well. Walter raised his glass and drank its remaining contents. He retrieved his wallet and attempted to make payment.

The reprimand came swiftly. "I'll have none of that my friend. My tab will do just fine."

"But," Walter tried to protest.

Uncle Wayne pulled out a business card and offered it to Walter. He said, "Next time it will be on you."

Walter withdrew a business card from his wallet and offered it up. The card was readily accepted. He said, "Next time it will be on me." He stood up and the two shook hands before Walter and his new-found friend parted company.

"Pass my greet'in along to Gil," Uncle Wayne called out to Walter just before he reached the tavern's side entrance.

"I'll do that for sure," Walter called back. He stepped out through the doorway and walked over to his rental car. His step was much lighter. The session ahead seemed less burdensome now.

CHAPTER 10

ROGER PULLED INTO THE OFFICE PARKING LOT. HE EASED THE Caddie across the lot and guided it into his parking spot. On stepping out of the Caddie, he turned and waved at the foursome of Richard, Lyndsey, Gilbert, and Hope. They were walking together through the parking lot. Roger felt relieved. This had to be a good sign. Perhaps the session would go easier than he had feared. Tessa's Oldsmobile pulled into the parking lot: that left only Mr. Lizards and John missing. Roger did not expect John to put in an appearance. He turned and walked towards the office door. Tessa stepped out of her car and followed him. The foursome remained outside in the parking lot. Roger unlocked the door and stepped inside. He glanced back outside and observed Richard and Gilbert in the midst of what seemed a friendly conversation. He walked down the hallway towards his private office. Tessa walked over to the receptionist desk where she sat down and waited for the others to arrive.

The office door opened. Tessa watched Gilbert and Hope, then Richard and Lyndsey, enter the office. Through the door, she watched Mr. Lizards step out of his car and walk towards the office. She stood up and walked towards the door. Mr. Lizards opened the door and stepped inside. Tessa smiled and said, "Roger and the others are waiting in his office. I'll lock the door and we can get proceedings underway anew, sir."

"Please drop the sir, Tessa. Walter is just fine…really."

"Then Walter it is, Mr. Lizards."

Walter smiled at her reply.

Tessa shrugged her shoulders and apologized, "Walter, right?"

"Yes. Just think Water then add an L."

"OK," Tessa said with a coy smile.

Walter turned and walked down the hallway towards Roger's private office.

Tessa quickly locked the door. Her eyebrows frowned then relaxed. The scent of rum revealed Walter's most recent activities. *The only water he'd seen lately*, Tessa thought, *had come in the form of a rum chaser. Possibly the King's Pub, most likely the Blue Buzzard,* she reasoned. *Walter,* she reassured herself, *was definitely a Blue Buzzard man.* She stepped away from the door and watched Walter walk down the hallway. His walk reminded her of a duck's waddle. Yes, Walter was a strange little duck. Tessa walked down the hallway in Walter's footsteps. Her hips swung left then right in a non-seductive duck-like wiggle-waddle. Ahead of her, Walter pulled up short in front of the conference room. Roger and the others met up with him. Tessa reined in her wiggle-waddle and walked forward to re-join the group.

Roger stepped up to the conference room door and inserted his key in the lock. A twist of his wrist unlocked the door. He withdrew the key and returned it to his pocket, then opened the door, stepped aside, and waited for the others to enter. After Tessa had passed through the doorway, he entered the room. Once inside, he followed the others, walked over, and took up his former seat at the table. After everyone had seated themselves, Roger said, "Mr. Lizards, Walter, if there're no objections I suggest we pick up where you left off."

The room fell silent. Walter withdrew the file folder from his briefcase. He set it on the table and flipped it open. Walter then shuffled through the papers in the folder as six sets of eyes watched. They relaxed when he stopped and picked up the letter of William Ramsay. Walter smiled and said, "In view of what's taken place and John's continued absence, I'll start up where we left off. Richard,

Lyndsey, I trust time will aide John in his recovery. Your loss is great. Should the three of you wish to meet later, for John's benefit, I'm at your disposal."

"Thank you," Lyndsey said.

Richard accepted the attorney's offer with a nod of his head and said, "Yes. Given a little time, it would help if we could all sit down with you for a recap and review." He paused then asked all present to overlook his brother's untimely emotional breakdown. All parties signaled their acceptance of his apology.

Mr. Lizards scanned over the letter line by line, until he'd reached the last lines revealed to the parties present. After a pause, he reviewed the facts aloud. "William wrote this letter to his son Bill. In its opening he revealed to us his deep inner thoughts and recalled memories of his Father. I will start anew by rereading the last five lines."

William Ramsay's Letter (Continued)

Shortly, at this letter's end, you will come to know the words and wishes spelled out in my last will and testament. Some of the people I call upon will be well known to you. Others will come to you out of what seems to be thin air: as a total surprise one could say. Trust me, for this is the way in which I also came to know of our family's past. Only this time, true to my Father's wishes, I will set the past right and bring our family back together at last. Trust me son. I did not leave you alone.

Shortly after you were born, your Grandfather sat me down. He presented to me our family history. The facts revealed that day startled me. Our family's background and the fact our family stretched well beyond the old homestead here just north of Newmarket came as a total shock to me. I set out determined to prove my Father wrong. To my Father's credit, I failed. However, I did make contact with our forefathers' descendants. I hold that accomplishment high among the list of worthy deeds completed in my lifetime. Our forefathers arrived from Scotland in the late 1700's. Their ship set anchor in New Scotland, and they stepped ashore to a new life in a barren land. A land today called Nova Scotia. Their first footsteps landed on the shores of Halifax Harbour.

Ramsays, never known as city folk, stayed but a short time in their new surroundings. Within a year, they purchased land outside of Halifax in an area known today as Nova Scotia's South Shore. Together, brothers John and Richard traveled south and took possession of their land they worked the land in earnest. Their family traditions and work ethics which had been honed in Scotland rewarded them over the years. John married Sarah soon a daughter Grace was born. A son named Thomas rounded out their happy household. Richard never married. The Ramsay homestead built by brothers John and Richard endured the passage of time.

Bill a hunger to walk in the footsteps once taken by his forefathers called out to your Grandfather. In 1954 your Grandfather and I visited East River, Nova Scotia. The visit energized Dad's interest, but sadly, it did not answer all his questions. Your Grandfather passed away a short time later in 1958. It would be ten years later before I again found myself back in East River.

Fortune stood at my side on that trip. Armed with ten years of research and an old family diary, I located the old homestead. Your Mother approved of my visits to East River. However she only accompanied me on two of my trips. Blessings upon her, to her those trips were a time of personal discovery for me. She remained here at home and took care of you and the business in my absence. The diary, once in your hands, will disclose the source of our family's original wealth. Sadly, that wealth brought about the breakup of our forefather's family. It denied us the companionship of good people.

I spent many a pleasant hour with Isaac Ramsay and his daughter Helen McClaken. Isaac, a lobster fisherman, came from a long line of seafarers. Our forefathers, John and Richard, started that tradition. John Ramsay split the family apart. He fled their East River home and traveled inland, where he established our branch of the family in Upper Canada (Ontario). His brother Richard remained in East River. He supported John's wife Sarah and their children Grace and Tom. Today, our families in East River and elsewhere consists of Robert McClaken, his sons, Gilbert, Paul, Morgan, and Jeffrey, along with our Newmarket Ramsays. John Ramsay on fleeing East River ended up in Newmarket. He remarried. Technically he never divorced Sarah, hence my desire to share our family's wealth and success and reconnect our families, once torn apart by greed and principles.

In my will, retribution is set out to return a portion of our wealth to the McClakens. Our family should have set things right in their time. They did not but I have to. Do not begrudge these fine people their rightful due, son. My will corrects past wrongs. Please take the time to re-unite at last with the descendants of our forefathers. Like us, they are good people. Make it right.

Good-bye, Love Dad

Walter set the letter down. The room fell silent. He reached towards his file folder, but stopped short.

Richard broke the silence. He smiled, then looked across the table at Gilbert and asked, "Gilbert how are we related?"

"I don't know, Richard. Hopefully I'm not my own grandpa."

Walter interrupted. He asked, "Roger, could we have some fresh coffee brewed, take a quick break and allow the Ramsays and McClakens time to talk."

"Not a problem."

Roger stood up and walked towards the door. Tessa followed his cue. Together, they exited the room and set off to prepare the coffee.

Walter gathered up his file folder and placed it inside his briefcase. He snapped the lock in place, then stood up and walked out of the room, briefcase in hand.

CHAPTER 11

RICHARD AND LYNDSEY STOOD UP. THEY STARTED TO WALK AROUND the table to where their newest family members sat. Gilbert and Hope caught sight of their intentions. They too arose and moved to meet Richard and Lyndsey. The two couples stopped four feet apart. Richard spoke first.

He said, "Gilbert, I do not know what Grandfather and Father's wills hold in store for our families. I do know our loss has been great. Today's meeting for me signaled a hope for closure; a time for our family of three to accept and move forward, but not forget." Richard frowned.

Gilbert listened and nodded his agreement with Richard's words. After Richard stopped speaking, he said, "Time is a great healer. I struggle to imagine the extent and pain of your losses."

Richard replied, "But there is another need. There is something I must know."

"Ask. If it's within my power…I'll answer truthfully."

"I do not doubt that Gilbert."

"In what way can I help you?"

"Our ancestors parted ways. The old diary Grandfather referred to has shed some light on how the parting unfolded."

"Someday, if allowed I'd love to read that diary."

"No need to ask. We'll gladly share it with you. I'm a confessed wanderlust at heart. I willingly admit the diary has ignited my imagination and a need to rediscover our family's heritage."

Gilbert sighed.

Richard continued, "There's something I've never had—never known. Hope has it."

Hope looked bewildered. She asked, "I have it?"

"Yes, you do."

"Could I say the same of you?" Hope asked.

Richard frowned. He rolled the possibilities through his mind, then answered, "In a round-about way, maybe." His eyes turned directly to Gilbert. The question was asked.

"What are we? Related, yes, but how?"

Gilbert smirked then said, "In all honesty Richard. I do not know."

"Could you be…my …"

Lyndsey picked up Richard's difficult question and finished it, "What, Richard needs to know is… could would you be our uncle?"

Gilbert chuckled aloud. "It's a title not easily earned. Most become through no actions of their owner."

"I know."

"Others, like you Uncle Gilbert, are naturals at it," a beaming Hope blurted out.

"Why thank you Hope. I am truly honoured you would think that of me," Gilbert replied.

"So?" Lyndsey asked.

Gilbert flushed and took on an unnatural and bashful look, then offered his reply, "If asked I'd be honoured."

Richard grinned. He stepped towards Gilbert. "Consider it asked and your answer embraced."

The foursome moved together, and with outstretched arms, clasped each other in a joyful group hug. Richard sobbed. Lyndsey kissed his cheek.

Hope asked, "Am I? Are we…cousins?"

The group hug drew tighter. First Lyndsey then Richard answered, "Yes."

The door to the room opened. Roger stepped inside. He started to turn back towards the door. Gilbert stopped him.

He called out, "Don't go, Roger. We're ready. Just finishing—I mean starting a family reunion."

Tessa poked her head through the door. The foursome had separated. She said, "I'll get Walter if it's OK."

Roger said, "Give us a couple of minutes Tessa." Tessa closed the door and returned to her reception desk.

Everyone looked to Roger.

He explained, "I lied to John. It wasn't all a total surprise to me."

The room fell silent.

Roger said, "I knew there was a Maritime connection. Until today I never met any of the individuals involved. I simply knew there was a tragic accident that happened on one of your Grandfather's visits down east. He made arrangements to handle the legal details through the firm that handled his personal affairs, that being Mr. Lizards, Walter's firm. Beyond that I never anticipated meeting Gilbert and Hope today. I did anticipate Walter's participation."A knock on the door caught everyone's attention. Roger opened the door and nodded his approval that they were ready to proceed. Tessa stepped into the room. Gilbert, Hope, then Richard and Lyndsey took up their old seats. Tessa followed their lead and returned to her chair and sat down. Relieved, Roger turned about, then moved across the room and took up his seat at the table. Walter walked into the conference room with his briefcase and a coffee mug in hand. He returned to his place at the table, looked around the table and said, "If there's no objection it would be most convenient to get down to the main purpose of today's meeting. Before we get underway, would anyone else like a coffee?"

Nobody replied to the coffee offer or raised their voice in protest. Walter set his briefcase atop the table and withdrew the Ramsay folder from it. He set the folder down before himself and flipped it open once more. From the folder, he withdrew the last will and testament of William Ramsay senior. He glanced around the table, surmised that all parties were prepared to proceed, then held the document out at an easy eye's distance and proceeded to read its contents aloud.

Last Will and Testament
of
William C. Ramsay
October 22, 1973

> I, William C. Ramsay, being of sound mind and body, decree this to be my Last Will and Testament. I assign the legal duties of processing my instructions contained herein to my dear friend Mr. Walter Lizards, the president of the law firm Lizards, Rose, and Rose.

Richard settled back and waited for Walter to dispense with the legal mumble-jumble of Grandpa Ramsay's will. The process lasted just over an hour and a half, and the end result Richard understood clearly. A ten percent share of the business went directly to the Ramsays/McClakens: Gilbert, Hope, and their down-east family connections. The balance of the company had been bequeathed to his son, Bill Ramsay. All personal properties, bank accounts, and investments had been bequeathed to William's wife Maureen Ramsay. Upon the death of Maureen Ramsay those personal properties were in turn bequeathed to Bill Ramsay. Richard had been surprised to learn that the life insurance policies in place on the lives of both grandparents had named himself as sole benefactor. He accepted the policies when Mr. Lizards personally handed them to him, but had refrained from opening them up in the presence of the others. He did not feel it appropriate.

Next, Walter worked through the details of the will set out by Bill and Mary Ramsay.

With the death of both parents, the directives of his Father's will held precedence; the employees had been given a fifteen percent share, and Roger had received a five percent share. A ten percent share had been placed in a trust fund with Roger appointed as trustee. In time, the trust fund would go to the children of John and Richard. The balance of the business went directly to John, Richard, and their spouses. Each son received a twenty percent share. Lyndsey and Richard's future spouse would each receive a ten percent share. Walter again surprised Richard. He handed him the life insurance policies of his Father and Mother. To Richard's surprise, he had again been named the sole benefactor. Silently, he resolved to share any sums of money received from the insurance policies equally with John.

Walter then handed out sealed packages to Richard, Lyndsey, Gilbert, and Roger. Roger received two packages, one for himself and a second one that had John's name on it. Mr. Lizards explained at length the value of the business. Prior to the accident, assets had exceeded the business's liabilities by two million dollars. Business insurance in effect on both Richard's Grandfather and Dad had increased the sum to four million. The personal properties and all other assets fell equally to John and Richard. Richard, unclear on all the details, had requested a meeting with Walter, John, Lyndsey and himself.

Tessa sat silently. Numbers flashed through her mind, concern about her maxed out credit cards vanished. She glanced at Lyndsey then shifted her gaze towards Roger and the package with John's name on it. A sense of satisfaction accelerated the greed in her heart. Eager to exit the office and celebrate her new found wealth Tessa turned and stared hard at Lyndsey. Silently in contempt she gloated. *You lose bitch, your man and that package are mine!*

Walter passed Richard a business card and told him to contact him once things had settled down. Richard agreed and committed to arranging a time that would be mutually agreeable for all parties. Walter promptly left the meeting. Tessa spoke quietly to Roger then fled on Walter's heels eager to update her man on the outcome of the meeting.

Roger, more of a family member than a friend and business associate, had remained behind to answer questions with Lyndsey, Gilbert, Hope, and Richard. He left with them twenty minutes later.

The sealed packages contained personal copies of all the legal documents. Roger retained John's copy. He would pass it to him later when they could sit down and fully discuss the details.

"I don't feel the closure I had anticipated this process would bring," Lyndsey said to Richard, than added "I hope once John cools off and is brought up to date it will finally come."

Richard frowned. He sensed a hostile work environment taking shape at the family's business. The actions of John and the loss of Grandfather and Dad's control over John's hunger for power concerned him.

Gilbert asked, "I'd like that. I mean. I'd like to meet John under better conditions."

"I'll set that up," Richard assured Gilbert. He then suggested they leave the office. It had been a long, trying day filled with personal stress for all of them.

Lyndsey took the lead and walked towards the office door. Hope followed her lead. Gilbert and Richard walked side by side behind the girls. The hallway stood empty. Richard slipped over to Roger's personal office and informed him of their departure.

"Ring me up later this evening, Rich."

"Thanks Roger. I'll be sure to do that."

Richard stepped out of the office. He stopped and added, "I'll be staying over at the house tonight. If John should call…"

"Not a problem. I'll let him know."

Richard joined the others down at the front entrance to the building. He opened the door and stepped aside. This allowed Lyndsey, Hope, and Gilbert to exit. He then walked out into the parking lot behind them. They walked over to Richard's vehicle. Richard opened the driver's door, deposited the papers he held on the seat, and closed the door. All four stood there in silence, each waiting for the other to speak.

Roger stepped out of the building. He locked the door and walked over to where the others stood. After he'd exchanged handshakes and a personal good-bye with each, he went to his Caddie.

All four watched the Caddie move out of the parking lot. They followed it until Roger turned at the corner and disappeared from sight. The time of their departure had arrived.

CHAPTER 12

GILBERT SHOOK RICHARD'S HAND, THEN STEPPED OVER TO LYNDSEY and wrapped his arms about her in a brief but emotional hug. A tear trickled down his cheek. He released Lyndsey and stepped back from her.

Richard waited for the right moment. It came when Hope and Lyndsey embraced. He stepped up to Gilbert and held out a piece of paper to him.

"My home, the homestead, the business, and cell phone numbers are on the bottom. I drew a quick road map to the homestead above them."

Gilbert accepted Richard's offering. He passed Richard one of his business cards. It read, 'Gilbert M. McClaken, English Professor, BA, MBA, and Doctorate English Literature.' The reverse side read, 'Lobster Fisherman RR#1 East River, Nova Scotia.' Below that, Gilbert had added his hotel phone, room numbers, and personal email address.

Richard pulled out his wallet and stored Gilbert's card safely inside and handed Gilbert one of his business cards. He returned the wallet to his pocket. A glance over to Lyndsey revealed they were still engaged in serious girl talk.

Gilbert signalled Richard to step aside with him. They walked over and stood beside Gilbert's pickup truck.

"I'm overwhelmed by all that's befallen us today, Richard."

"Say no more Gilbert."

"Do what's best. I'm best when standing in front of my students… or out tending to our lobster traps."

He tapped the side of his truck lightly.

"I understand. But I do not want to lose what we rediscovered today: our family roots."

"Nor do I Richard."

"When do you plan on returning home?"

"It's open right now. I think it best we take a day or two and mull it all over."

"Good. Give me a day or two. Stay over until next weekend."

"That might make it tight. I'll call home and let Jeffrey know."

"Great. That will give me time to sit down with John."

"He'll be OK with everything?"

Richard hesitated then replied, "Don't worry. We'll give him the time he needs."

"Yes. Each of us must deal with it in our own way and our own time."

Hope and Lyndsey finished their girl talk. They walked over and joined the men.

Richard and Gilbert fell silent.

Lyndsey said, "I've invited Hope and Gilbert out to the homestead for supper." She added, "Tomorrow night."

Richard frowned and replied, "Maybe Tuesday would be better. It'll give us time alone with John."

"Right, I got caught up in all the excitement."

"I know the feeling. But let's give John the time to deal with it first."

"OK," Lyndsey answered with a smile.

The foursome exchanged parting gestures. Gilbert stepped back then walked around to the driver's side of his truck. Richard and Lyndsey stepped away from the truck. Both Gilbert and Hope climbed into the truck sat down and engaged their seat belts. The truck roared to life then dropped back to a smooth idle. Parting waves were exchanged and the truck, under Gilbert's direction, backed up then moved forward towards the street. Lyndsey stepped in front of Richard and embraced him. She stepped back, smirked and apologized, "I needed that."

"Not a problem."

"What's next Richard?"

"We go back to the house. If John's there we sit down and work things out. Explain."

"And if he's not there?"

"We find him."

They walked over to Richard's SUV. Richard opened the passenger door and Lyndsey stepped inside. Once she'd settled into the passenger seat, Richard closed the door. Lyndsey picked up his bundle of legal documents from the driver's seat. He walked around the vehicle got in behind the steering wheel and started the engine. Richard made a detour on their drive back to the homestead. He stopped by John and Lyndsey's house. The driveway stood empty. He got out, accepted a key from Lyndsey, and walked up to the side door. It was locked. He inserted Lyndsey's key opened the door and stepped inside.

"John. John, are you here?"

John did not answer Richard's call. Richard made a quick walk through the house: a two-storey brick Victorian. Upstairs, he paused a second inside the door of the master bedroom. He looked longingly at the large four-poster bed then stepped back out into the upstairs hallway. John was nowhere to be found. Back downstairs, Richard took a sheet of paper from a pad sitting on the kitchen counter. He wrote a quick note to John. 'It's Rich, John. Call me at Grandma's or on my cell phone. Lyndsey's with me. I will drop her off after we have a bite to eat.' *The note placed on the kitchen table stood out. John, will have no trouble finding it* thought Richard. He turned and walked back to the side entrance. Outside, he locked the door and joined Lyndsey in the SUV.

"No John?"

"No. I left a note. He'll call us at the house or on my cell."

"I'm worried Rich."

"It'll be OK, Lyndsey. John will be okay."

The SUV backed out of the driveway and they set off anew to the family homestead. Neither Richard nor Lyndsey spoke until they arrived at the house. John's car was nowhere to be seen. At the front door, Richard used the spare key he'd taken from the kitchen key rack earlier. Back inside, Lyndsey entered the kitchen.

"I'll fix a light meal; I'm hungry."

"OK. I'll try to contact John on his cell phone."

"Try the office if that doesn't work."

"Right, he might be there working things out for himself."

Lyndsey worked her way through the cupboards and fridge then settled on a package of sausages, a can of creamed-corn, potatoes, and a bag of frozen peas/carrots. She set about preparing their meal. The motions were automatic. Her mind was not on the work at hand. Since her graduation from university, she'd lost contact with most of her close friends. John had swept her up the aisle and away from the arms of Richard. They had a good marriage, she assured herself. They had a few problems, not unlike any other married couple. The sex had been good. She wanted a child and had made her wishes known to John…six months ago. That had been the start of their problems. John had lost his spontaneity. He'd been spending much more time at the office. "Big project," he'd explained. Grandfather Ramsay had backed up John's explanation. She had resented Richard's intrusion into the attic yesterday afternoon; it had been the closest she'd come to sex in over three months. The accident had turned John's faltering sex drive to ice. The hug with Richard in Roger's parking lot brought back memories of a sexual urge from her past. After all, they'd been sandbox and high-school sweethearts.

"No sign of the man yet," Richard reported. He then walked through the kitchen and retrieved a jug of milk from the refrigerator and a glass from the overhead cupboard.

"I'm starting to worry, Richard."

Richard tore off a piece of paper towel and wiped off the counter. He'd over-filled his glass with milk.

Lyndsey took his paper towel and chased him from the counter. "Go sit down. You're in my way."

Richard obeyed and sat down at the table.

Lyndsey gave him a partial look and suppressed an urge to hug him.

Richard covered his eyes in jest. He pleaded, "No. Not the…"

"Really, Men are so..."

"Sorry."

Lyndsey smiled; she then set out two dinner place settings at the table.

"I'll try the marina in a bit." Richard then added, "Right now din-din looks good."

"It's nothing fancy."

"Mmm it does smell good."

Peace had been restored. Lyndsey served directly from the pot. She filled Richard's plate with six sausages, a healthy portion of mashed potatoes, topped it off with a scoop of peas-n-carrots and one of creamed-corn. Her plate received much less. Concern over John had dampened her appetite. She sat down across from Richard. They ate in silence.

Richard chewed the last of his sausages. He stood up and started to clear the table.

Lyndsey stopped him in his tracks. She said, "No," and motioned to Richard with a wave that he should sit back down. Richard complied.

Richard looked straight at Lyndsey and said, "He'll come around. It's John's way of working things through."

"I've never seen him this way before. It scares me."

"Trust me. John has always had a temper. You've been good for him. You've held him in check."

Lyndsey wiped away a tear. She asked, "Will he accept Grandpa and Dad's wills?"

After a thoughtful pause Richard, replied, "In his time and with our support yes he will. Meanwhile, I'll go chase him down. I'll try the marina first. You can brew up a pot of tea and stop worrying! It'll soothe your nerves."

"OK. Rich."

Richard stood up again, turned, and walked out of the kitchen. Lyndsey stood up, she engaged the drain plug in the sink, gathered up their meal dishes, and deposited them along with the pots in the sink. She filled the kettle with water and plugged it in. Next, she turned on the hot water, and added a dash of dish detergent. From the tea canister she took two tea bags. A twist of her wrist turned off the hot water tap. The kettle hit its boiling point and switched off. Lyndsey took the china teapot, deposited the tea bags inside, and filled it with boiled water. From the cupboard, she picked two mugs and the sugar bowl. She placed them on the table along with the steeping pot of tea. Richard had not returned to the kitchen. Lyndsey washed and dried the meal dishes and cookware then sat down at the table and waited for Richard to return.

Grandpa Ramsay and Dad's wills played on her mind. She recalled the decrees as spoken by Mr. Lizards...Walter. 'All personal property, bank accounts, RRSP funds etc., and real estate go to John and Richard in equal shares. All life insurance in effect at the time of the deaths go directly to Richard.' This bothered Lyndsey. She knew John had differences with both his Dad and Grandfather. The reunion had been John's hope of resolving those problems. This, more than the other stipulations, would cause resentment to simmer in John's mind between himself and Richard. On the up side, she reasoned Richard's easy nature would dissolve any resentment John might harbor over the insurance issue.

Lyndsey poured herself a mug of tea. Richard had not returned. She hoped this signalled progress in his search for John. The first sip of tea soothed and eased Lyndsey's tension, just as Richard had predicted. Her mind drifted back to the wills and focused on the ten-percent share that was entrusted to Roger for John's and Richard's future children. Doubts twisted through her inner thoughts. John had avoided physical contact with her, following mention of a desire to start a family. A gentle sob cast aside a recalled image of a blonde, blue eyed Richard in short pants and a tee shirt staring at her from a sandbox shared in their youth. Through the tears that followed, Lyndsey felt the joys of her anticipated motherhood vanish. The ten-percent shares Lyndsey and Richard's future spouse would receive overwhelmed her.

Lyndsey had not come from a wealthy family background. On graduation from university, she'd considered herself wealthy to escape diploma in hand…debt free. The idea of owning a ten percent stake in the family's business frightened her. Walter had stated the business assets stood at four million dollars in excess of its liabilities. She wondered, shouldn't I feel better than this?

Richard stepped through the kitchen doorway. He said, "Sorry Lyndsey, no sign of John yet."

"Did you try the house again?"

"Yes."

Richard sat down across the table from Lyndsey. He poured himself a mug of tea and added a dash of sugar. The first sip dampened his dried mouth. Ten phone calls and he was no closer to identifying John's whereabouts.

"I'll drive you back over to your place. John's sure to show up."

"I…I want you to be there Rich."

"I will, tomorrow morning bright and early. Just have one of your omelettes ready for me."

"Please promise."

"Cross my—"

Lyndsey interrupted Richard. She said, "Thanks Rich. John needs you now. So do...I."

They emptied their mugs and the teapot in silence. Richard stood up and cleared the table. He walked back over to the table and took Lyndsey's hand. He said, "Your chariot awaits its princess."

Lyndsey smiled and stood up. They left the house together. Richard locked the door after stepping out behind Lyndsey. On reaching his vehicle, he opened the passenger door and Lyndsey stepped inside. She sat down and strapped up her seat-belt, then waited for Richard to slip into the driver's seat. Richard closed the passenger door. He walked around and stepped inside the SUV. The sun had started its descent. Overhead, clouds showed promise for an eye-catching sunset.

Lyndsey asked, "Why don't I feel like a princess?"

"You will. First I'll get you home. Then your prince will return to sweep you off your feet."

"Right, sure hope the feeling hits me soon!"

The ride took less time than Lyndsey expected or wanted it to. Richard slowed down on approaching John and Lyndsey's house. All the lights were out. He pulled into the driveway and stopped. Lyndsey stepped out onto the driveway. Richard followed suit and walked her to the side door. She opened her purse and retrieved her set of house keys. She unlocked the door, stepped inside, and flipped on a light. Richard remained outside. Lyndsey turned around, leaned out the door, and kissed Richard on the cheek.

"Goodnight Rich. Remember. Be here bright and early."

"Trust me."

He then turned and walked back to his vehicle. The drive back to the homestead took longer. Richard drove around the downtown area and stopped at several of Main Street's watering holes-eateries he'd often frequented with John. The diversion did not lead him to John's whereabouts. Discouraged, he left the downtown area and drove back out to the homestead. Darkness had settled in before he arrived at the house. Inside again, he turned on the hall light then walked through to the kitchen and flipped on the kitchen light switch.

"Meow."

A hungry looking Bailey welcomed Richard home. The old feline looked hungry. Richard opened the pantry door and picked out a can of cat food. Bailey followed him over to the can opener.

"Meow!"

"Burrrr…Burrrr." Bailey rubbed himself up against Richard's legs.

"Easy fella. Din-din is almost ready."

"Meow...meow...meo..."

Richard took a plate out of the sink and wiped it off with paper towel. He took a fork from the utensil drawer and scooped the cat food out of the can and onto the plate. Bailey stood up on his hind feet and pawed Richard's knees.

"OK. OK. Big-Guy, here you go."

Richard stooped down and placed Bailey's plate on the floor. Bailey wasted little time in attacking the food set before him. Richard had made a friend for life. He stood up, retrieved a bowl from the cupboard, and filled it with water. A look down at Bailey and Richard realized how hungry Bailey had been. Half the cat food had been devoured. He set the bowl of water down on the floor by Bailey, then stood up and walked across the kitchen. Tired, he opted to tackle the kitchen cleanup in the morning. He switched off the kitchen lights. Before turning in for the night, he turned and called to Bailey, "Goodnight Big-Guy."

"Meow."

Richard walked down the hallway towards the staircase. It had been a long day. Too much had happened. Once his head hit the pillow, the Sandman rushed forward and whisked Richard off to dreamland.

CHAPTER 13

"YES. I'LL TRY YOUR CRANBERRY SURPRISE," GILBERT ANSWERED THE waitress. He looked across the table at Hope.

"So, do you think they'll come?" Hope asked.

"I'd like to. But I'm worried about the brother: Lyndsey's husband, John."

"If he's anything like Richard, you'll have no need."

"I'm hoping. He did not react well to Roger's counsel when we first met. His reaction to Walter's reading…"

Hope jumped in, "But the wills of William and Bill made everything much clearer."

"To those of us who remained to hear them, yes they did."

"So, why are you worried?"

"Call me an old maid but—"

"But what, what other concerns have you fretting like an old maid?" a puzzled Hope asked.

"I sensed a deep kindred connection concealed beneath the surface between Richard and Lyndsey. They're a natural team. What stopped them from seeing it? What made her take the long walk down the aisle with John?"

"Duh, like maybe she loved him? Like maybe he's everything you think he's not."

"Please, Hope. Give me credit. It's just a gut feeling I have."

"Boy, is this what I've got to look forward to?"

The waitress returned with their dessert orders. Gilbert and Hope took a time out and set to work on their selections. Hope had opted to go the safe route; she'd ordered a tried and true favourite: apple pie and ice cream. Gilbert's love of sweets had led him to a cranberry-orange crisp covered in whipped cream and topped off with a tempting scoop of hot melted chocolate. He wasted little time in clearing his plate. Hope picked at her apple pie then pushed it aside half finished. She asked, "So. What do my suitors-to-be have in store?"

"Not to worry. I'm a sheep in wolf's clothing."

"And they'll know?"

"Trust me. You'll tell the right one."

"OK. I could live with that. What's next?"

Gilbert mulled over Hope's question then answered, "Hopefully you're right about John."

"Which would make you?"

"Wiser."

Hope laughed and blurted, "No way, did I really hear you right?"

Gilbert laughed aloud, then said, "Yes, Hope, really."

Hope smiled, reached across the table and picked up her uncle's hand. She raised it to her lips and kissed it. Satisfied that she'd succeeded in embarrassing him, she pleaded, "So. Spill the teapot. Why are you so uptight when it comes to John?"

Gilbert responded, "In early April John, along with Richard and Lyndsey, lost their family. That alone is a hard bridge to cross. You never knew their Grandfather. William Ramsay was a good man. His letter said a lot about the nature of what he was and the values he held and lived by."

Gilbert took a sip from his coffee mug then continued, "Richard and John each receive half of all the family's personal property, bank accounts, RRSP funds etc., and real-estate. However Richard receives all the proceeds from the insurance policies carried by their parents and grandparents. Upon his marriage, he holds a thirty percent control of the family business."

"So what's the hitch?"

"Why wasn't John named on at least one or two of those insurance policies? He is the eldest, the first-born son. How will he react to not being named on at least one of those insurance policies?"

"It's a simple oversight. Richard is a giver he'll willingly share proceeds of the policies with John"

Gilbert paused then added, "The employees—he could live with that. They helped make the business into what it is today, Roger—also acceptable and he holds family status. The ten percent given to total strangers us that one will be a hard sell."

Their waitress returned, took away the dessert dishes, and refilled Gilbert's coffee mug. Hope declined her offer of a refill. She presented the tab to Gilbert. He looked it over briefly and signed it over to his room account. Gilbert sipped away at his refilled coffee mug. Hope waited for him to speak. Finally, Gilbert pushed aside his half-full coffee mug and stood up. Hope followed suit. They walked out of the hotel dining room side by side. At the hotel elevator, Gilbert said, "I really hope my concerns are off base."

"They are."

"Hopefully then, our invite to supper will stand."

"It will."

The elevator doors opened. Hope stepped inside. Gilbert followed.

"You do have a personal motive: the diary."

"It is family history, theirs…ours."

"And not related to your passion for things from the past."

Gilbert pressed the button for the eighth floor. He chuckled, then put his arm around Hope and squeezed her. An elderly couple stepped into the elevator and looked at him disapprovingly. Gilbert whispered to Hope, "You know your old uncle better than he knows himself."

Hope hugged her uncle and whispered back, "And I love him just a tad more."

The elevator stopped on the sixth floor. Hope and Gilbert ended their embrace. The elderly couple stepped out of the elevator. The woman looked back into the elevator. Gilbert bore the brunt of her disapproving stare. The doors closed.

Hope laughed and said, "If only Uncle Jeffrey could see you now."

"Don't even think it, missy."

At the eighth floor, they stepped out of the elevator and walked down the hallway to their room. At the door, Gilbert handed Hope a key for the adjacent room. "It's Lyndsey's gift. She insisted," Gilbert explained.

Hope recalled a conversation with Lyndsey and how she'd played up the intensity and prolific nature of Gilbert's snoring. The thought of enjoying a stretch of me time, suppressed any regrets over her exaggeration of Uncle Gilbert's storied snoring reputation.

"She's a sweetheart. Goodnight Uncle Gilbert."

"Goodnight Hope."

Gilbert waited until Hope had entered her room. He then stepped inside their old shared room. He grabbed the TV converter and flicked it, turning the TV onto the news channel. On reaching the far side of the room, he turned on a desk lamp, sat down, and waited for Hope to come collect her travel bag and clothes. He never heard Hope enter or leave the room. The day's events had taken their toll on him. He fell quickly into a sound sleep on the sofa chair. Hope would not miss his snoring that night.

CHAPTER 14

LYNDSEY PASSED QUICKLY THROUGH THE DOWNSTAIRS FLOOR. Upstairs, she entered the master bedroom. There, she stripped, tossed her clothes into the clothes hamper and walked into the adjoining bathroom. A quick shower refreshed her. Back in the bedroom, she slipped into a nightgown, blow-dried her hair and crawled under the covers. Sleep did not come easy. She tossed and turned for an hour. First, she struggled with a mild frustration over John's behaviour earlier that day. Next, she fretted and worried over his failure to return. Finally, she curled up into a ball and slipped into a light sleep. Slowly, she entered a dream state.

The dream carried her back into Grandpa Ramsay's attic. In it, she relived the romantic interlude she and John had enjoyed twenty-four hours earlier. Just prior to the arrival of Bailey, the colour of John's eyes changed from hazel to blue. His face faded then another reappeared. It was Richard's. Bailey never did manage to make his grandstand appearance. The dream peaked around 5 am as Richard slid his fingers under the elastic band of her panties. This time, the panties slid over her hips and down her thighs. Her hands slid from his buttocks and fumbled with the belt of his pants. The belt yielded to her fingers. In a motion, she unsnapped the button of his pants and pulled his zipper down. The pants slid over Richard's hips and down his thighs. She reached inside his briefs and sought out Richard's...

Bang! A loud crunching sound and the house shook. Lyndsey jumped up and sat wide eyed on the bed. Startled, she leaped off the bed and ran over to the window. Outside, she spotted John staggering out of their Honda Civic. The car was parked half in, half out of their attached garage. The unopened garage door had given way to the nose of the car. Lyndsey ran out of the bedroom and down the stairs. She arrived in the kitchen to see John stagger through the side door. Blood trickled down John's forehead. Lyndsey grabbed a dishtowel and ran over to him. She wiped his forehead. John staggered away from her. He ended up leaning against the fridge door.

"Are you hurt, Honey?"

"I think...I'm drunk."

Lyndsey looked into John's face. A cold chill ran up her spine. John's forehead, cheeks, lips, and neck were smeared with deep red lipstick. Her heart sank.

"What's du mata Lynssy?"

"Where've you been? Everyone's been worried sick about you."

"An you?"

"And me! What about her, John, who have you been with?"

"Nobody, I've been consoling mysssyself."

"Mysssyself sure likes her lipstick with a whore-like twist! I tossed and turned trying to sleep, worried sick about you."

"So whe...ere is he—Richie?"

"He's over at Grandpa Ramsay's."

"Count'n up all his inssur...ce checks I bet."

"You've talked to him?"

"Nope. Didn't hav to."

"Roger?"

"Wrong agin."

Lyndsey walked over and sat down at the kitchen table. John staggered over and sat down across the table from her. Tears started to flow down Lyndsey's cheeks.

"Tessa told me all the gruesome details."

"You slept with that—"

"Spare me. We had sex. Good sex."

Lyndsey collapsed on the tabletop. She sobbed, and a multitude of tears flowed freely.

"I want your share, Lyndsey!"

"You want! You want! What about me?

"You want kids. I want sex."

"Get out of my sight. You make me sick!"

"Wrong...bitch. Noo...body taks ta me like that!"

Lyndsey stared through tear-blurred eyes straight across the table into John's face. What was happening to her world? She watched John stagger to his feet. He walked around the table and stood in front of her.

John grabbed Lyndsey by the arm and pulled her up out of the chair. He stared hard into her eyes.

"I said nobody talks to me like that. Apologize!"

"No. I'll never apologize to you in the state you're in!"

John stepped sideways, pulled hard on Lyndsey's arm, and flung her across the room. She landed hard against the counter then fell to the floor. Her nightgown flew up and exposed Lyndsey's hips and buttocks.

"Wow, ya ass looks reall...ly good!"

Lyndsey pulled the gown back down over her hips. She cowered on the floor in fear.

"To bad it only makes looove...an don't do sex."

Lyndsey sobbed.

"I want your shares, Lyndsey. I'll not leave without them."

John staggered towards her. He reached down for her arm. She ducked, then crawled terrified across the floor. He laughed hard and watched Lyndsey work her way to the side door. Lyndsey, terrified, grabbed the doorknob and pulled herself upright. John staggered towards her.

Lyndsey screamed, "Stay away from me, John. Don't you dare touch me!"

John wavered then continued to advance towards Lyndsey. She twisted the doorknob, stepped aside and pulled the door open. She ran out onto the doorstep and down the stairs.

John called after her, "Git yur ass back in here bitch! I want my money! They had no right to die. No right to give you a share of my family's business."

Lyndsey did not answer. She ran towards the front of the house. Barefoot and nearly naked, she approached the driveway. She just wanted to escape—get away from the man she'd married: a man she no longer knew or wanted to know. John had left the car's engine running. Lyndsey ran over to it. She pulled the driver's door open and climbed inside. Without thinking, she pressed her foot against the clutch then grabbed the shift-stick. An abandoned goal, learning to drive and then not taking the test for her driver's license, triggered a bout of regret. Why had she not followed Richie's advice and topped the lessons off with a driving school. The lessons she'd received from Richard in high school paid off. She shifted the transmission into reverse. The car jerked, almost stalled, and then pulled quickly away from the garage.

John fell down the side doorstep. He got up and ran after Lyndsey and the car. He screamed, "You stupid bitch. Git outta my car. You can't drive!"

Lyndsey never heard his words. At the end of the driveway, she turned the steering wheel hard left. The car backed out onto the street, turned, and jumped up over the curb onto their lawn. Her foot hit the brake pedal. The car stopped. Its engine stuttered. She engaged the clutch, pulled the stick shift out of reverse gear and rammed it into a forward gear. Her left foot released the clutch, the right hit the gas pedal, and the car lurched forward, jumped off the lawn, and headed down the street. Lyndsey found each ensuing clutch/gear-shift maneuver easier. After running the first two stop signs, she calmed down and regained control of her senses. The steering part came easy. She followed the instructions of Richard's voice that flowed through her head. It was a younger Richard that spoke. The loving tone in his voice guided Lyndsey and the Honda Civic closer to the Ramsay homestead and Richard, where she longed to be. The dash clock revealed the hour to be 6:05 am. Morning traffic volume had increased in line with morning's embrace of daylight.

Ahead, she spotted a familiar road sign. It guided her onto the highway and closer to Richard. The images of John and their kitchen confrontation faded to the background of her mind. Suddenly it hit her. A giggle broke out deep in her throat. It erupted into a hysterical laugh. The laughter subsided and a smile slowly added a touch of confidence to her face. She was driving down the highway: next to naked, no purse, and no driver's license. An urge to hug Richard and thank him for those high school era driving lessons in his Volkswagen Beetle hit home. Regrets surfaced over her youthful refusal to take the driver's road test, Lyndsey whispered a prayer, "Lord, please give the boys in blue an extra Java…donut fix. Let me pass this driver's test and reach Grandpa Ramsay's house. Ten minutes later, she spotted the sign to Ramsay Lane, slowed down, and made the turn onto it. The two-kilometre drive to the homestead took forever. Finally, Lyndsey spotted the house. She downshifted and turned into the yard. The Honda came to rest behind Richard's vehicle.

Lyndsey opened the door and jumped out onto the gravel driveway. The stones hurt her feet. She hopped gingerly over to the lawn, looked up at the house, and called out, "Richie! Richie! Help me please!" Lyndsey collapsed onto the grass. She waited for the front door to fly open.

Upstairs in the guest bedroom, Richard stirred. Sunlight had started to shine through the window and caused his eyes to flutter. The second "Richie" jarred him out of bed. He sat up on the side of the bed and rubbed his eyes.

"Richie. Richie. I need you."

Richard stood up and grabbed his jeans off the bureau. He managed to get one leg into them, then fully awake, heard the voice again.

"Richie. Please...pleaasssse I need you now!"

He panicked and ran out of the bedroom and down the staircase. Twice, the jeans almost tripped him up. At the base of the staircase, he stopped, stepped fully into his jeans, pulled them up, snapped the button in place, and pulled up the zipper.

"Richie."

Richard raced down the hallway. He stopped at the front door, unlocked its dead bolt and whipped the door open. Stunned, he stepped out onto the doorstep and stared at a Lyndsey clad only in a nightgown and crouched down on the lawn weeping and calling out to him.

"Richie I…I need you."

Richard rubbed his eyes. He jumped down off the doorstep and ran across the driveway towards Lyndsey. Her beauty caught and held his gaze he spotted Lyndsey's bruised arm and cheek, and burst forward, dropped down on the grass and stared in shock at her. Richard reached out to her, "Lynd…sey what happened?"

Lyndsey did not answer. She leaned forward and wrapped her arms about Richard, then burst into tears once again.

CHAPTER 15

"HE'S BACK RICHIE."

"Who, who is back, Lyndsey?"

"John. John did this. He's crazed."

Stunned, Richard wrapped his arms about Lyndsey and drew her hard against his bare chest. He ran a hand slowly over her head and whispered, "It's OK. It's OK. I'm here. I'll take care of you."

"I'm not going back."

"Don't talk. Just relax."

"He slept with that bitch Tessa. Called it sex…good sex."

"Don't think. Don't talk. Just relax."

"OK, OK. I'll try."

Richard continued to run his hand over Lyndsey's head. He felt her wet tears run down his chest. They remained there for what seemed a lifetime, when in fact, it was a mere five minutes. Richard stood up and pulled Lyndsey up with him. He placed an arm behind her back and another at the back of her thighs. In one motion, he lifted her up in his arms. Lyndsey's head rested against his chest. She sobbed gently as Richard carried her across the driveway and into the house. Inside, Richard proceeded down the hallway and into the den. He set Lyndsey down on the loveseat then knelt down in front of her.

"He's drunk. He's…"

"No. Not now, just rest. Close your eyes."

Lyndsey obeyed. Richard kissed her cheek. He looked down over her bosom and further to her legs. The hem of Lyndsey's nightgown had slipped up and exposed Lyndsey to Richard's eyes. He pulled the gown down over her thighs and quietly watched her until she sobbed herself to sleep.

Richard stood up, turned about, and departed the den. He returned a few minutes later with a comforter in hand. After spreading the comforter over Lyndsey, he stepped out of the den and entered the kitchen. Frustrated, Richard paced restlessly about the kitchen. At the counter, he stopped and set up the drip-coffee maker. The pacing resumed. Suddenly, Richard headed to the front door, closed it and engaged the deadbolt lock. Next he walked past the den a glance into it confirmed Lyndsey was ok. He walked upstairs to his Grandparents' bedroom. There, he opened the closet and looked over Grandma Ramsay's wardrobe. He reasoned both Lyndsey and grandma to be a close match in height, build, and weight. From the closet, he picked three pairs of slacks and two cotton dresses, along with several blouses and set them down on the bed. From the dresser, he picked out several pairs of cotton briefs and two bras. He set the briefs on the bed, realized the bras were a mismatch, and returned them to the dresser drawer. If needed, they could pick some up at the mall later.

Richard made a quick trip back to the guest bedroom and slipped on a polo shirt, his socks and shoes. He stood in front of the dresser mirror, picked a brush up off the dresser and ran it through his hair. Satisfied with his appearance, Richard returned to his Grandparents' bedroom. He picked up the clothes off the bed, carried them down to the den, and laid them out on the coffee table for Lyndsey. Satisfied with his selection of clothes, he took a loving but worried look at Lyndsey then returned to the kitchen. There, he poured himself a mug of coffee and took it over to the wall phone. A call to John's number proved fruitless. Next, he tried Roger's home. Noreen answered and asked Richard how he was managing. After a short, friendly exchange she passed the phone over to her husband.

Richard explained to Roger the situation as he now understood it.

"Get her out of the house, Richard. You can bring her over here. She'll be safe."

"She's sleeping now. I can't wake her up, Roger."

"OK. Stay there. I'll drive over and pick her up."

"Don't tell Noreen."

"Just stay put. Give me half an hour."

"OK."

The phone line fell silent. Roger recalled stories of Lyndsey and burnt clutches.

"Roger? Are you still there?"

"I'm here Rich, just recalling tale or two out of the past and the reek of burnt clutches."

"Those driving lessons in my Beetle sure paid off. Lyndsey never went for her driver's license."

"Then they definitely turned into a blessing from above. Keep an eye out for John. I'll be there shortly."

"Thanks, Rog."

"Not a problem."

Richard hung up the phone. He tried John's cell number without success. A trip back to the coffee pot, refilled his mug. Hungry, he decided to put the toaster to work. Four slices of white toast later, he sat down at the table. Armed with a jar of his favourite garnish, Richard applied a thick layer of peanut butter to each slice of toast.

The toast disappeared and left Richard sitting at the table with his mug of coffee. He pondered over the events of the morning. John had held all his emotions intact since the fatal accident. Yes, he'd expressed a regret at not closing the door on differences between himself and their Grandfather and Father. But that was business, Richard reasoned. Richard had accepted John and Lyndsey's marriage—didn't like it but accepted it fully. Lyndsey had been a radiant bride. Her love of John glowed in her face and in her actions. Why? Why, would John risk that love to romp between the bed sheets with Tessa?

Tessa, he frowned. Now there was an item best avoided. Richard had taken to her like fire to water. She'd joined Roger's law firm just prior to John and Lyndsey's marriage. What Roger had seen in her, Richard couldn't fathom. Two former husbands had failed to meet Tessa's needs. Why did John think he could succeed? Richard uttered a mild, "Damn." He sipped more coffee and tried to come to some resolution. The initial damn escalated. Richard clenched his fist and his knuckles whitened, in response to his growing anger. In his mind Richard screamed, *"you really screwed up this time John,"* while his fist unleashed an angered relay of punches that repeatedly hit the image of his brother's fading face. The fact that Lyndsey had actually fled the house barely clothed and driven a vehicle with a standard transmission ten miles to the homestead amazed Richard and magnified John's transgressions in his mind.

He recalled the feel of Lyndsey's body and their shared embrace on the front lawn. His anger vanished and suddenly he found himself sitting in the passenger seat of his old Volkswagen Beetle. It was a Sunday morning. They were in high school grade 10—no 11. Lyndsey sat in the driver's seat, and the mall parking lot stood vacant except for Richard's Blue Volkswagen Beetle. The interior of the car reeked of burnt clutch.

"I'll never get the hang of it, Richie."

"Trust me. You will."

"What's that smell?"

"They call it a clutch, Lyndsey."

"Right, that's the pedal over on the left."

"You got it."

"Shall we?"

"Go for it. Just remember, clutch in—shift into first, clutch out—accelerate, clutch in—shift into second and accelerate, clutch in…"

The sound of a car approaching the house interrupted Richard's daydream. He jumped up and ran to the front door unlocked it, then stepped outside. The sight of Roger's Caddie eased Richard's concern. Roger pulled up and parked directly in front of the house.

Roger quickly joined Richard on the doorstep. He asked, "How is she, Richard?"

"Sleeping, she was in really bad shape when she first got here."

"I swung by the house. No sign of life there. The garage door is banged in pretty good."

"God, what possessed John to…"

"Tessa, my apologies, She's gone the minute I step foot back into the office."

"But…John? It takes two."

"No pun, Richard. But John always had it in him. Your Dad and Grandpa tried to—"

Richard interrupted, "I know. But they loved each other, John and Lyndsey. I stepped aside—accepted Lyndsey's wishes and their love."

"I wish…"

Lyndsey stepped through the doorway and said, "Hi, Roger."

Richard turned about and wrapped his arms around her. He kissed her forehead then asked, "Feeling any better?"

Lyndsey stepped away from Richard. She replied, "If you mean… am I prepared to forgive and forget...no."

"OK."

"You weren't there, Rich."

Roger held his arms out and suggested that they all step inside the house.

Lyndsey turned and led the way back into the house.

Back inside, Richard pointed Lyndsey towards the den. He said, "Roger, I'll join you in the kitchen. Help yourself to a coffee. Lyndsey, I laid out some of Grandma Ramsay's clothes. They're on the coffee table in the den."

"I know."

"If you need more, you know where to find them."

Lyndsey walked off to the den. Richard watched her go. After she'd entered the den, he turned and joined Roger in the kitchen.

Roger was on his cell phone. Richard overheard him telling his partner Jack Robertson, "Just do as I asked, Jack. Get the office locks changed now. Call me when it's done." Roger then terminated his call. He helped himself to a mug and Richard's offer of coffee. The two men sat down at the table.

Richard spoke first, "The bruises look to be worse."

"But she's safe," Roger answered. He continued, "I had an idea on the drive over, and now that I've seen Lyndsey…I don't think we have a choice."

"Go on. I'm open to suggestions, Roger."

"First, I called my brother over in Port Perry. He jumped at the chance to help out. I'll drive up to Uxbridge with Lyndsey and meet Mike there."

"And I'll?"

"Stay here. John may show up. Hopefully, not before Gilbert gets here," Roger continued, "I've had John's business credit cards temporarily revoked. It'll curtail his activities and hopefully, help bring him back to reason quicker."

"You've been busy."

"I've seen you kids grow up, Rich. Your Grandfather..."

Richard smiled and said, "Say no more Roger."

"Gilbert agreed to help. You will drive John's car back home. Gilbert will follow and get you back here. Hope will go with me. She will step in and help Mike, adding a woman's touch. You know... what with Mike being a widower. It will be a great match both ways. Mike is still struggling to recover from Chloe's passing. It's been a year however with everything that we've been through lately, it feels like it happened yesterday. The girls will add a dash of sunshine into Mike's day and he's a sweetheart. They'll love him."

Richard jumped up. He walked to the front door and watched Gilbert's truck pull up onto the lawn. Hope leapt out of the truck and raced up to the house. Richard pointed her down the hallway to the den. Gilbert joined Richard on the doorstep. He wrapped his arms around him in an embrace. Richard almost sobbed.

Gilbert squeezed hard and said, "It's OK Richard. We're family."

When Roger, Hope, and Lyndsey appeared at the door, Gilbert released Richard.

Roger led the two women down to his Caddie. He waited until both had slipped into the back seat, then said to Gilbert, "You've got my number? Call me if anything goes awry."

Gilbert nodded his agreement to Roger. Gilbert and Richard watched Roger's Caddie pull ahead then complete the loop before disappearing down the lane to the highway. Gilbert put his arm on Richard's shoulder and said, "I sure could use a coffee."

Richard laughed and then sobbed. He let Gilbert lead him back inside the house. In the kitchen, Richard handed Gilbert a mug. He then filled it with coffee and topped up his mug.

Gilbert frowned and said, "Relax. She's in good hands with Hope."

They sat down at the table. Richard looked across the table at Gilbert and surrendered to a feeling of hope. *Yes*, He thought, *everything will be OK.*

CHAPTER 16

JOHN KICKED A SHRUB BESIDE THE DRIVEWAY. HE WATCHED HIS car and Lyndsey drive down the street then disappear from sight. He cursed, "Stupid bitch. She'll never get away with it. None of them will." A glance up and down the street showed all the neighbours' lights were still off. He turned and staggered back into the house. At the fridge, he stopped and pulled out a can of beer, went into the living room, and sat down on the sofa next to the telephone. He snapped the can's pull-tab open and raised the can to his mouth. The beer tasted good. John set the beer down next to himself on the sofa. He picked the phone up from the end table, then set it on his lap and picked up the receiver. He pressed the buttons, and the phone at the other end rang.

Ring…Ring… Before the third ring Tessa rolled over and picked up the receiver.

"Hello."

"She knows. Lyndsey knows."

Tessa sat up and the bed sheet fell down onto her lap. She looked quickly around the bedroom and brushed the hair back away from her eyes. Naked from the waist up, she turned towards the nightstand and poked her feet over the side of the bed.

"Where the hell are you?"

Tessa stood up. The bed sheet fell away from her body. From a high-rise window across the way, a baldish little man stared through his pair of binoculars. He liked what the binoculars presented to his eyes.

Unaware she was being observed, Tessa paced back and forth across the bedroom.

"I'm home."

"Christ, are you stupid?"

"Frig you, bit…"

"Excuse me. I just woke up to an empty bed."

"But, I."

"But, you what? You had great sex last night—cried yourself to sleep babbling away facedown in my breasts—begging little, old Tessa to make things right and to screw the bastards that were stealing your money."

"You've got to do it."

"Honey, I don't got to do nothing."

"She took my car. Stupid bitch can't drive, but she stole my wheels."

"Good one."

"Just haul your ass over here. I need your whee…I need you."

Tessa bit her tongue. She'd wanted to tell John to bend over and kiss his ass goodbye, but refrained herself. She said, "Keep your shorts on. I'll be there in twenty minutes." The idea of romping around in little Miss Prissy's bed turned Tessa on.

"The address is three …"

"Don't bother, I know the house. Stay put. I'm on my way."

Tessa hung up the phone. Things weren't so bad after all, she reasoned. After all, hadn't John just inherited well over a million dollars if not two? Not all cash, much of it tied up in property, but nonetheless, little Tessa could force herself to get by on a paltry sum like that. She walked to the closet and selected a short, green skirt, a beige pullover sweater and a pair of black pumps. The sweater slid down over her head and ample breasts. She pulled the skirt up over her hips. She tucked the sweater in under the skirt and buttoned the skirt. Tessa didn't trouble herself with panties and bra. They didn't figure in her plans. Across the way, a disappointed admirer started to scan the windows above and below Tessa's apartment.

Satisfied with a quick curl and hair brushing, Tessa stepped out of the bedroom. Next stop, she smiled, is pay dirt and my new home. In the living room, she stopped and picked up her keys and purse. Tessa exited her apartment and took the elevator down to the underground parking. Her Oldsmobile started up and Tessa set off towards her destiny. Lyndsey had saved Tessa the trouble of a messy breakup. She'd abandoned the prize.

On the drive over to John's, Tessa reviewed her situation. After dumping her two ex-husbands and cleaning out their bank accounts, she was ready for a new investment. *Third time lucky,* she thought. The first two divorce judges had alluded to the value of parenthood. Their paltry court orders reflected on the fact that no children were involved. Not this time. Unknown to John, Tessa's period was running late. Welcome to the real world, Jonathan Ramsay. Call it good sex. Call it lovemaking. It's your choice. But what could be growing inside of little, old Tessa is called payday.

The Oldsmobile slowed on approaching its destination. Tessa steered into the driveway. She pulled up short of the crumpled garage door. *Wow. The little bitch really can't drive.* On stepping out of the car, Tessa walked up to the side entrance and entered the house. Inside, she passed through the kitchen into the living room. The only sign of John was an abandoned beer can on the sofa. Tessa proceeded upstairs and quickly located the master bedroom. Inside it, she found John passed out—sprawled across the bed. She set herself to work. First, she stripped off her clothes. Next she removed John's pants, underwear, and shirt then slid onto the bed beside him.

Slowly, Tessa worked an unconscious John into a state of sexual arousal. Satisfied with her work, Tessa mounted John and rode him hard. John's eyes blinked then opened. Tessa smiled and hastened her ride. John exploded inside Tessa. She collapsed onto John's body.

John pushed her off and over to his side. He uttered, "About time you got your little ass over here."

He rolled off the bed and stood up.

"Get up, Tessa."

"But I like it here."

"Get dressed and get me out of here."

Tessa shrugged and sat up on the bed. John had tossed her clothes onto the bed. She slid the sweater over her head and down over her breasts once again, then sat and watched John get dressed.

"Move it," John ordered.

Tessa frowned and then complied. Dressed, she took a look back at the bed, smiled, and whispered, "You're mine." She then followed John back downstairs to the kitchen.

John smiled and said, "Get me over to Roger's office. I want my papers and money now."

"Could we at least stop for a bite to eat? I'm hungry."

"Hit a drive-through. I want them now!"

Tessa followed John out the side door. Once inside the car, the pair grew silent. The Oldsmobile backed out of the driveway then moved down the street. At the first stop sign, Tessa made a right turn and headed towards the downtown and her breakfast. At the first fast-food restaurant, she pulled into its parking lot and stepped out.

John relented and followed suit. The first signs of hunger had taken hold of his stomach. They walked side by side across the parking lot and into the restaurant. *After all,* John thought, *I can wait another thirty minutes, before setting things straight with the Lizard and his band of thieves.*

CHAPTER 17

RICHARD ALERTED BY A FRESH SERVING OF TOAST POPPING UP IN the toaster asked, "Will a peanut butter topping work for you Gilbert?"

Gilbert chuckled lightly and replied, "Top it off with a healthy serving of jam and I'll be dining on a gift from heaven!"

"You're definitely easy to please."

"And then some provided a dash of sweetness is added to the offering."

Richard joined Gilbert at the table with a plate of peanut buttered toast, topped off with homemade raspberry jam. He then topped up their coffee mugs with the last of the coffee. The toast quickly vanished from its plate.

On the first ring Richard answered his cell phone. Roger's voice greeted him with a welcomed update, "Lyndsey is fine, she and Hope are talking up a storm. We will be meeting up with Mike shortly."

"Good," Richard sighed.

He added, "Oh, Rich…don't bother trying to call through to my cell. I expect it will be in overload mode for the duration. I will call you with updates."

Richard laughed then replied, "Thanks Roger, still no word from John. We'll head out shortly and return his car to the house. Oh, thanks again Roger. I don't know what we'd do without you."

"Trust me. Your Dad and Grandfather have been my second family throughout life. I will be there for you, Lyndsey and John down the stretch and for the long haul. I'm at a lost to explain John's actions. I won't condone what he's done. I will call him to task and work to get him back and connected to our family."

The phone line fell silent.

"Later Richard I'm at Uxbridge and see Mike's truck up ahead in the church parking lot."

"Thanks Rog...," Richard answered as the call disconnected from Roger's end.

He turned to Gilbert and said, "The girls are good. Roger is at Uxbridge and meeting up with his brother Mike. I'll do a quick walk-about the house before we head out."

Gilbert polished off his coffee then stepped outside and waited for Richard to join him. In the kitchen, Richard turned off the lights, and unplugged the coffee maker. Satisfied, he stepped back out onto the front doorstep, closed the door and locked it.

Gilbert had wandered down by John's car. He eyed the interior, in particular the old diary that sat on the front passenger seat. Richard joined Gilbert beside John's car. A glance inside revealed the object of Gilbert's attention.

Richard laughed and said, "Follow me to John's in your truck."

"At John's, remind me to take the diary with us."

"Not a problem," Gilbert grinned and answered.

Richard smiled, turned, and stepped into John's car. He waited while Gilbert walked over to his truck. He recalled how twenty-four hours earlier the same truck had brought tears of laughter to his face. Once Gilbert drove up behind him in his truck, Richard started the engine, shifted into gear and headed out. On reaching the main road, Richard led and Gilbert followed. Twenty minutes later, they arrived at John and Lyndsey's home. Richard parked in the driveway. Gilbert parked his truck on the street. Richard stepped out of the car with the old diary in hand. He walked over to the truck and handed Gilbert the diary then suggested, "Best you remain outside for now. I just don't know what to expect from John.

He's my brother. I love the guy, but…this morning he stepped over the line. Give me a little time alone with him."

"I understand. Richard, if you need me…"

"Trust me. You'll know."

Gilbert's focus turned to the diary Richard had handed him. Richard went up to the side door and knocked. Nobody answered the door. He tried the doorknob; it turned and he opened the door. Inside the kitchen, Richard called out, "John are you here?" In the living room, the words were repeated, "It's Rich, John are you here?" Richard climbed the stairs and took a quick look in each room. He stopped inside the master bedroom. The bed sheets and covers were in disarray—half on and half off the bed. He felt satisfied that John had left the house. A glance at a framed photo of Lyndsey's parents caught his eye. Memories of the joyful times shared with them throughout his childhood and teen years gladdened, then saddened Richard. He stared at the photo and vowed, "I'll make things right for your—our Lyndsey. Liam—Lettie, I will make things right!" Richard picked up the photo and gazed into the loving eyes of Lyndsey's parents. Tears dampened his cheeks. He added a few outfits and personal items from the bedroom closet and dresser for Lyndsey.

Richard left the master bedroom returned to the main floor. In the kitchen, he spotted the note he'd left John Saturday afternoon. Scrawled across the note in pencil were the words 'F u c k You.' Richard picked up the note, crumpled it up into a ball then stuffed it into his back pocket. He left the keys to John's car on the table. A shopping bag he found in the kitchen pantry provided privacy for Lyndsey's cloths and personal items. The photo of her parents Richard held in his right hand helped him battle the anger and frustration he felt towards John. The love in Liam and Lettie's eyes eased his anger. On the side doorstep, he stopped long enough to lock and close the door then walked out to Gilbert's truck. There, he spotted Gilbert reading the old diary. The passenger door was locked. Richard knocked on the window.

Gilbert almost jumped through the roof. He dropped the diary, reached over, and unlocked the door. Richard opened the door and stepped up into the passenger seat. He closed the door, looked at Gilbert, smiled, and joked, "Reached the part about ghosts and demons I see."

"No. No. I just started reading. So far it's happy, joyful little girl things. Ghosts you say?"

"Yuppers."

"Care to drive?"

"Not really."

Gilbert shrugged and said, "I tried," and then started the engine. The photo Richard held caught his eye. He asked, "Would they be Lyndsey's parents?"

"Yes. I thought seeing Liam and Lettie would reconnect her with love's touch. Her parents' love touched many. It's helping me sort through my anger towards John's actions. Gilbert nodded giving Richard his approval and understanding. Richard surveyed the truck's interior. It amazed him. The interior was in showroom condition. Gilbert suggested they stop at the hotel for a meal. Richard first directed Gilbert to Roger's home. There he talked briefly with Roger's wife Noreen, they hugged. He passed her the bag with Lyndsey's clothing and her parents' photo. They hugged once more, then Richard returned to the truck. Gilbert followed Richard's directions. Talk centred on Richard giving Gilbert directions to the hotel. The last turn placed them half a block away from the hotel. From there, Gilbert took them into the hotel parking lot then proceeded around to the hotel's back lot. Gilbert parked at the far end of the lot. They stepped out together. Gilbert locked up the truck and carried the diary. They entered the hotel's rear doors and took the elevator up to Gilbert's room. Inside the room, Richard sat on the chair by the desk. Gilbert put the diary on the bed.

Gilbert asked, "Are we ready for that meal I suggested? I'm hungry"

"You bet. I'll give Roger's cell a try. Then we can head downstairs for a bite."

"OK."

Roger's cell phone—surprise—rang through to the message centre. "*The client you have reached is unable to take your call at this time... if you wi —*" Richard hung up. No need to leave Roger a message. Roger had stepped in from the minute he'd answered Richard's call for help and taken control of the situation.

"Let's go get that bite to eat. I'm really hungry all of a sudden."

"Great," Gilbert replied.

In the dining room, the waitress started to read off the daily specials. Richard interrupted her, "Does that steak with eggs come complete with all the dressings?"

"Yes sir, along with your choice of a breakfast dessert."

"Then I'm sold, I'll take it medium-well done with the eggs sunny side up."

"Me too," Gilbert added.

The waitress poured them each a cup of coffee, then headed off to place their orders with the chef.

Richard relaxed and said, "Not the morning I expected."

"I totally agree on that one."

"She's safe."

"Thank God."

"And Roger: he's a saint—a knight in shining armor."

"Tell you what. Let's —"

Richard interrupted, "Try changing the subject? OK."

"Tell me a little about yourself."

"Not much to say really."

Gilbert took a sip of his coffee. He laughed and chided, "Sorry. I don't buy it."

Both men fell silent. Richard drank half his coffee before finding the right thing to say. Then he never got his words out. The waitress had returned with their main course. Their hunger further delayed Richard's words. Over the course of the meal, Gilbert and Richard exchanged idle chitchat. Richard learned more facts about Nova Scotia than he'd ever imagined existed. Gilbert left small gaps in his recital for Richard to ask questions, which he answered with great detail. It became obvious to Richard that Gilbert was a true Bluenoser and loved his land of birth deeply.

Dessert arrived, and finally Richard got an opening to speak about himself. He'd quickly learned that Gilbert was a man in love with the dessert tray. Richard had abstained from the offer of sweets and opted for a coffee refill. Gilbert had talked their waitress into upgrading his breakfast dessert to a double-chocolate cheesecake.

Richard started to recite his life story. He explained how he'd grown up in Newmarket, Ontario then added specifics that covered his education from grade school through to university. "Left home and attended Queen's in Kingston."

"Yes. A fine university," Gilbert injected.

"It was there I earned my degree in…" A tear rolled down Richard's check.

"Rich. Are you OK?" Gilbert asked.

"No. Not really. But I'll continue. Just give me a minute."

"Take all the time you need."

Gilbert finished off the last of his double-chocolate cheesecake.

Richard picked up where he'd left off. "It was there in my third year I learned about John and Lyndsey."

"Do you want to go there?"

"Have to."

"OK."

"Lyndsey and I grew up together—started out as sand-box sweethearts. Grew up and were actually king and queen of the high-school prom. Queen's accepted me into their engineering program. Lyndsey, she stayed closer to home. Business Administration at U of T. Make a short story shorter: absence didn't work in my favour."

"Did John also attend Queen's?"

"Yes and he graduated at the end of my second year at Queen's. He was here. I was there. I should have opted for a university closer to home—closer to Lyndsey."

Gilbert pondered Richard's words then replied, "Absence often puts a relationship to a test. Did a sibling rivalry exist between you and John?"

"Not really. We were brothers, and on occasion, we pushed each other's buttons. I've always believed we had a great brother to brother connection."

"She loved him?"

"I've always believed it started out innocent enough: a movie here, a dinner there.

Yes, Lyndsey loved John. We talked things out. I thought I saw the love between them. I did the right thing and stepped aside—actually stood as best man at their wedding."

"It must have been tough. No doubts?"

Richard slammed his fist down on the table and in anger uttered, "Damn you John! You really screwed up this time!"

Gilbert frowned then said, "He's still family Rich. Messed up—absolutely! But he's still family."

Richard gazed down at the table and replied, "Before today I had no doubts. Yes he's my brother. Yes, he screwed up big time! Can I forgive him? Just yesterday in their presence I sensed a distance between them at times. Today, I ask myself, were there any warning signs? What were they? What was I thinking? How did I miss them?"

Gilbert reached over and took Richard's clenched fists in his hands. After a pause he committed his support, "We'll see this through Rich. Lyndsey, Hope, you, me and John."

A moment or two passed then Richard broke the silence, "You asked if there was a sibling rivalry between John and me. Now that I look back yes I can see it."

"Serious?"

"Didn't think so, John liked money, would kill for control. There were many disagreements between him, Grandfather and Dad. John brokered many good business deals. However, the tensions I believe centred on his unauthorized diggings into company files and employee records. Dad and Grandfather were dealing with his indiscretions in a manner he resented. On second thought a rivalry could have existed in John's mind. He resented my grades through school and university: straight A's to his C's and B's."

"Did he date through those years?"

"One could call it that. Tessa represents the type John always ended up with."

"I see."

"You don't think…"

Gilbert jumped in, "Don't go there Rich. At least not now."

The waitress returned with their bill. Gilbert signed it over to his room. First Richard and then Gilbert stood up. They exited the dining room and returned to Gilbert's room.

Gilbert called the front desk for messages. There were none recorded. He thanked the receptionist and hung up the phone.

"Should we call through to Roger's cell phone again?"

"No. He's fully in charge of the situation. I trust him." Richard then asked, "Mind if I borrow one of your beds?"

"Mind if I browse through little Grace Ramsay's diary?"

"Here's my cell phone. Wake me if Roger calls."

"Double guaranteed!"

Richard removed his shoes and stretched out on one of the double beds. Gilbert sat down on the sofa with the diary in hand. He flipped it open to the last page he'd read and started to read again. Richard quickly dosed off into a deep sleep.

CHAPTER 18

JOHN AND TESSA FINISHED THEIR BREAKFAST AT 10:00 AM. THEY departed the restaurant and drove over to Roger's office. The parking lot stood empty. Tessa and John breathed a sigh of relief. They'd feared Lyndsey might have gone to Richard or Roger. The vacant parking lot eased that fear. Tessa parked close to the building.

John said, "Crazy bitch probably pulled off and fell asleep in a park somewhere."

Tessa shrugged her shoulders and stepped out of the car. John had not related Lyndsey's exit wardrobe to her, otherwise she would have questioned his explanation. At the office door she started to unlock the door. Her key would not fit into the lock. Frustrated, she looked over the key ring, tried another key then returned to the original when that one failed. The original did not work the second time. Tessa slowly realized that they were too late. She tossed her keys at the windshield of her car.

She screamed at a startled John, "Son of a bitch has changed the locks. My fucking key doesn't work."

John jumped out of the car. He asked, "Did you use the right one?"

Tessa gave John a look he'd never seen from her before. He did not push the issue. Tessa picked up the keys off the car's hood. She stomped around the car then jumped into the driver's seat. John sheepishly opened the passenger door and sat down beside her. He closed the door. Neither one uttered a word. Tessa hit the accelerator and engaged the starter. The engine started with a scream. She shifted into reverse squealed her tires in backing up then pasted the accelerator to the floorboards. The rear tires spun and left a trail of burnt rubber. At the curb, oncoming traffic screeched to a halt as Tessa's Oldsmobile shot out onto the street. She jumped in and out of lanes avoiding traffic. Three blocks later she began to calm down a level or two. The light turned red and Tessa brought the car to a full stop.

John asked, "Should I call Rog—"

Tessa roared, "Go for it, shithead. Just who do you think changed the fucking locks?"

John took his cell phone and called Roger. The call fast tracked into Roger's voice mail. John cursed, "Son of a bitch has my papers, my fucking money. The bastard will pay big time for fucking with John Ramsay!"

The light turned green. Tessa hit the accelerator hard. The rear tires let out a chirp, then took hold. Ahead, the next traffic light turned yellow. Tessa stomped the accelerator and burned the light. She cranked the steering wheel hard right and moved into the mall entry lane. Inside the mall parking lot, she pulled up into a handicap spot near the mall's front entrance. Tessa reached across and popped the glove compartment open. She retrieved a counterfeit handicap-parking permit and slapped it down on the dash, opened the door and stepped out into the parking lot.

John followed Tessa's lead. They walked off together to the mall's entrance. Inside the mall, Tessa led and John followed. They stopped in front of the bank's ATM.

Tessa tapped John's shoulder and said, "Go for it, Maestro."

"Say what?"

Tessa raised her eyebrows and suggested, "Let's just say they're onto us." She explained, "Office locks changed. Just maybe you'd be wise to try out your company cards."

"Credit cards?"

Tessa stood at his side and silently fumed.

John withdrew his wallet and stepped up to the ATM machine. He inserted the card. When prompted, he entered his PIN number. The ATM paused then flashed up a message: "Please contact Your Branch. Your card authorization has been revoked." The ATM's motors whirled, then swallowed John's card. A dumbfounded John stared wide eyed at the ATM screen.

Tessa walked up to John and asked, "So?"

"It ate my card!"

"Son of a bitch, what's our child going to live on?"

"Our...what?"

Tessa spun around and walked away from John and the ATM. Enraged at her stupidity, she mumbled, "God! I let that one out premature."

John stepped off and chased Tessa. "Pardon me?"

Tessa ignored him and continued to walk down the mall towards the food-court. She stopped dead in her tracks. John almost ran into her. Tessa whipped around and demanded, "Get me a coffee. We have to talk."

"You got that one right. I don't do kids. I do sex."

"Right, forget the coffee. Let's go back to the car."

Tessa set off in the direction of the mall entrance. John followed. Outside the mall and back inside the car, John erupted, "How could you be so stupid? Haven't you heard about the pill?"

"Fuck you."

"No. It's not mine. Find another sucker."

"Hello? I supplied the egg. It was your zip-pity du dahs that turned the trick."

"Abortion, we'll get an abortion."

"Over my dead body, this is my ticket."

John reached for the door handle. He froze when Tessa slapped his face hard.

Tessa ragged, "You bastard. You're all the same. Six-stroke wonders. Bimb-boom-bam, thank you ma'am!"

"I'll fight it all the way. I'm infertile! Lyndsey tried this one on me. It didn't work."

"Get out of the car now, you bastard!"

"Gladly, and you best give abortion another thought!!"

John opened the door and stepped out of the car. He slammed the door and walked off in a rage.

Tessa slammed her hands against the steering wheel. Tears watered her eyes. She brushed the tears away. Enraged at John's pompous attitude, she slammed the key into the ignition and started the engine. There was no way Tessa would ever submit to an abortion. No child of hers would ever be labeled a bastard. Its father might be one, but not her child. Composed, Tessa shifted the car into reverse and backed out of the parking spot. A touch of the brake slowed the car. She shifted into drive and moved forward through the parking lot. At the mall exit, she turned left and headed back to her apartment. Traffic stopped and Tessa picked up her cell phone off the center console. She dialed her doctor's office, got the answering service, and left a message, "Tessa Rozener calling. I need an appointment ASAP. I need to know how to do a personal DNA test on my baby. Call me." Traffic started to move. Tessa dropped the cell phone onto the seat. Ten minutes later, she pulled off the street and entered the ramp to her apartment's underground parking lot.

John walked across the mall parking lot. At Davis Drive, the walk signal changed. John crossed the intersection and set off towards the downtown of Newmarket. Thirty minutes later, he stood in front of the Blue Buzzard Tavern. It took only a second for John to make up his mind. He stepped forward and walked in the front door of the Blue Buzzard. Inside, he took a side booth. A barmaid took his order. She returned quickly with his double rum and cola.

He took a gulp of his drink then set it back down on the table. Fifteen minutes passed before John took a second drink from the glass. Abortion seemed the only solution to his problems. He convinced himself that once Tessa came to her senses, she'd see things his way. The thought of Tessa's body deformed and stretched out of shape repulsed him. With Tessa's problem solved, he pondered over his other problem…Lyndsey. What approach would work best? *Perhaps,* he thought, *the time of remorse had arrived.* John decided he needed some help…Roger's help. He took the cell phone out of his jacket pocket and called Roger's cell number. The line rang once then by divine intervention, Roger answered.

"Hello. Roger here."

"I've screwed up big time, Rog."

"John is that you?"

The connection fell silent. John struggled to find the right words. He spoke, "Help me, Roger."

"Where are you John? We need to talk."

"I screwed up."

"Tell me where you are. I'll meet you. Lyndsey's OK."

"Thank God, I really messed up!"

"Have I ever lied to you, John?"

"She's really OK?"

"Yes. Now tell me where we can meet."

"Is Rich pissed?"

"He's worried. We all are."

Again the connection fell silent.

"John. Please let us help. Where are you?"

A sob erupted in Roger's ear. He pleaded, "John. Let me help."

"OK."

"Where are you?"

"I'm at The Blue Buzzard. On Dav—"

Roger interrupted, "Stay there. I'll be there in fifteen minutes."

"She's OK?"

"Yes."

The line disconnected. Roger pressed the accelerator down. The Caddie lurched forward. Roger made a lane change and sped off back towards Newmarket and the Blue Buzzard Tavern.

John gulped down the last of his drink. He ordered a refill. Best to get it before Roger arrived and cut off his medicine. Let them worry…it would work wonders for John's remorseful scheme. Best to take care of the worried family, then he'd be free to adjust Tessa's attitude.

CHAPTER 19

GILBERT STOOD UP AND WALKED OVER TO THE MINI-BAR. HE opened it with his key. He selected a can of cola with a rum chaser. On returning to his chair, he mixed the two into a glass that sat on the table. Satisfied, he picked up the diary and started to read anew from page one.

Diary of Grace Ramsay
East River Nova Scotia
1796

> *Mother and Father presented me with this diary today, November 22, 1796 ... my 11th birthday. I feel at a loss for words, tongue tied really. I do not know what to write into the pages of my treasured gift. My dear friend and companion Alice told me to keep my entries short and to the point. She said I must never enter a hurtful thought or word. For one day, they may come to be. My teacher, Miss Cruthers, said to write of things that came my way...feelings of what happened and why ... of how I felt ... and lastly good things I wish to come my way.*

Gilbert paused. Hope—his Hope—floated to the forefront of his mind. *Ironic,* he thought that a family member out of their past named Grace appeared to be reaching out and touching the lives of her modern day family. Not a blood relation—his Hope was definitely a true kindred member of the Ramsay/McClaken Clan. The daughter he and Karyn never conceived. What would happen now? Twenty-one years had passed since the fatal accident that had robbed him of his life-long friends, Allan and Sandy McDonald. Had an emergency caesarean section not been performed on Sandy at the accident scene, his Hope—the joy of his life would never hav—. Tears trickled down his cheek. Though he'd not witnessed the accident, he had later heard the gruesome details spoken of by the couple that had been on the scene. Would the discovery of Grace Ramsay's Diary, destroy his family, or bless him with renewed hope.

Sandy had passed on before the ambulance arrived. The man, a doctor on the scene, had acted of his own accord and removed the child Sandy bore from her womb. There had been an investigation. The man was a well-respected doctor. Therefore, the investigation had not resulted in charges being laid. On the contrary, he had been hailed a hero. Gilbert sobbed. He recalled how happy he and Karyn had been upon being granted custody of that child. Yes, his Hope was truly a gift from God. He fretted over the pros and cons of the Ramsay/McClaken family reunification. Would his Hope one day learn all of the details surrounding her parents' accident that he had concealed from her fearing the loss of her love.

Ring…ring.

"Hello, Gilbert here."

"Hi, Gilbert, it's Roger."

"Where are you, Roger? What's been happening? How are Lyndsey and Hope?"

"Whoa. Slow down. The girls are fine. Mike, my brother, will see to their needs."

"OK."

"How's Richard doing?"

"He's sleeping. It's been a trying situation."

Richard sat upright on the bed. He looked over to Gilbert and asked, "Who's on the line Gilbert? Is it Roger?"

Gilbert spoke into the phone, "I'll put him on for you." He waved Richard over to the phone.

Richard took the receiver from Gilbert and spoke into it, "Is Lyndsey OK? What's happening?"

"Whoa! Slow down Richard. As I told Gilbert, she's fine all things considered."

"When can I see her?"

"Not now. Hope and Mike are seeing to her needs."

"Then when?"

"Later. First…first I need a favour. I've located John."

"Are you with him?"

"No. I'm on my way."

"I want to see him. I should be fit to kill. But he is my brother."

"Yes, he is. Richard, give me a chance to sit down with him. He didn't sound good."

"Then he realizes what he's done?"

"Just let me sit down with him. When the timing's right I'll suggest bringing you into it."

"Is that a promise?"

"Have I eve—"

Richard interrupted, "No Rog you've never lied to me. Take care of John. Let him know we care."

"That's my intention Richard. I'd better hang up now. I'm almost there. Bye. I'll call, Rich."

Richard hung up the receiver. He turned to Gilbert and said, "Roger has located John. He's meeting him now."

"Anything I can do?"

"No. It's best we remain here until Roger calls back."

"Then help yourself to the mini-bar," Gilbert replied. He tossed the key to Richard.

Richard caught the key. He went to the bar and withdrew a duplicate of Gilbert's earlier order less the rum.

Gilbert sat down on the chair he'd been reading from and waved Richard over to the chair opposite him. After Richard had seated himself Gilbert asked, "Roger mention where he's meeting up with John?"

"No. I'm hoping he'll smooth things over. Then after a bit, convince John to let me sit in."

"Smart move on his part; you boys are really fortunate to have Roger."

"Can't remember when we didn't. He grew up with Dad—has always been a part of the family."

Gilbert changed the subject. He held out the diary and stated, "Care to bring me up to date? I've only managed to work my way through the early entries. My God, she reminds me a lot of my Hope."

"Good idea. I could use a diversion right now."

"Great."

"You can set the diary down. The section I'm most familiar with is well etched in my mind. Trust me."

Gilbert set the diary down on the table.

Richard started his summarization of the diary's contents, "Strange as it may seem, it all started out with another John and Richard Ramsay…many years ago."

Gilbert's eyebrows twitched and he settled back to listen.

Richard explained. "John had a wife, Sadie. It could be short for Sarah. Grace and Tom were their children. Both John and Richard were fishermen and part-time farmers. They all lived in the same house."

"That would be the old homestead. Jeffrey and Pappy now live in it," Gilbert interjected excitedly.

"The same house Grace once lived in, the one from the diary?"

"The same, the home has had some additions, but…yes, it's the one."

"Fascinating," Richard commented. He continued the summarization. "Seems one morning the two men set out on their regular fishing trip. They ended up out on the bay near some islands. The islands were shrouded in an eerie, early-morning mist. Grace referred to them as the ominous Floating Islands."

Gilbert turned ashen.

Richard asked, "Are you OK Gilbert?"

"I will be. You're sure about the islands?"

"Yes. She mentioned them several times."

"Mmm. Not good."

Richard said, "OK, your turn. Care to explain?"

Gilbert gave Richard his explanation, "I know them well. Can't say I've ever set foot on them. The truth be told. I wouldn't wan—"

Ring…Ring. Richard picked up the receiver, "Hi Roger, how's it going?"

"Good. John would like to see you."

"Ok, where?"

"We're at the Blue Buzzard."

"I'll be there in ten."

"Bring Gilbert along with you. I've explained things to John. He's ready and willing to meet Gilbert again."

"OK. Can I speak to him?"

"He'd rather see you in person."

"Understood, we're on our way."

Richard hung up the receiver. He stood up and said, "Let's go, Gilbert. John and Roger are at the Blue Buzzard Tavern."

"Good."

They walked out of the room together. At the elevator Richard said, "Before this morning John could, at times be, an irritant. I never felt him capable of what has unfolded. This will be a tough one to ever forgive."

"Then we'd best listen to John's side."

The elevator doors opened. Richard stepped inside. Gilbert followed. They exited the elevator on the main floor.

Out in the parking lot, Gilbert handed Richard his truck keys.

"Best you drive Richard. We'll get there quicker."

Richard unlocked the truck and they both got in. He started the engine and drove off towards the Blue Buzzard, hesitant but eager to see John—eager to find out what went wrong.

CHAPTER 20

RICHARD DROVE INTO THE PARKING LOT OF THE BLUE BUZZARD Tavern and pulled into the empty parking spot adjacent to Roger's Caddie. Both Richard and Gilbert remained inside the truck. They took a time-out to gather their thoughts and emotions. Richard felt anger towards John rise again. He struggled hard to understand and wondered if he could forgive John for his treatment of Lyndsey. He reasoned *John is my brother. I only have one and there'll never be another. But why?*

"Ready, Richard?"

"Yes and no."

"Well spoken. It must be extremely difficult for you."

"That it is. If you think I step out of line please help me. I don't want to lose my only brother."

"Stay calm, listen and remember, if needed, Roger and I will be there. Are you ready?"

Richard opened his door. He stepped out into the parking lot. Gilbert followed his lead. They entered the Blue Buzzard through its side entrance. The lighting inside was dim. Richard scanned the room. He spotted Roger and John sitting in a booth off to the far side. Roger waved at him. Richard led the way across the floor.

John stood up. His eyes stared down at the tabletop. He looked ashen, and his hair stood in disarray. Richard held his right hand out to John. At first John hesitated then he took Richard's hand and shook it meekly.

"I'm sorry. I really screwed up this time, Rich. I'm so sorry."

Richard remained silent.

John broke the silence, "I don't deserve you—or Roger for that matter."

Richard replied, "We're brothers John, You screwed up big time. Today, I won't talk forgiveness, I cannot go there today. You, Lyndsey we're family. I need you."

John started to sit down. Richard stopped him. "John. I have someone I want you to meet." He stepped aside, and Gilbert moved forward. Gilbert held his hand out to John. John accepted it and the two shook.

"Gilbert…Gilbert McClaken. I knew your Grandfather: a good man."

"Yes, he was so much better than I."

"Don't sell yourself short, John. We all make mistakes. We become a better person once we recognize and correct our errors."

"I want that."

Gilbert and Richard answered, "So do we."

The three men sat down. Roger spoke up. "John and I have had a good chat. We're both drinking cola. I'll order up another round and we can hash things out."

Their waiter delivered the fresh round of cola that Roger had requested. John took a sip from his, then spoke out. "First, I'm eternally grateful and fortunate that my irresponsible actions did not result in graver results. I regret their having taken place at all. I did what I did. I was wrong."

"Why?" Richard asked.

"It started after your return from Kingston."

"What, John? Did I do something to set all this in motion?"

"No, Richard. It started with my having stolen Lyndsey's heart. She had been your companion since the day we all met in the sandbox. I envied you and the positive connections you had with her, Mom, Dad and Grandfather. Grandma loved you but not like she loved me. I wanted your life. I wanted Lyndsey. I worked at helping her overcome your absence: a burger here, a movie once a week, and then the odd dinner out. Before she knew what had taken place she'd had fallen in love...deeply in love with me."

Richard shook his head in disbelief. He stared directly at John and said, "I never doubted that she loved you John. Did I not stand up as best man at your wedding?"

"Yes, Richard, you did."

"She loved you John. Had any doubt existed I never would have stepped aside."

"Our first year and a half of marriage was great. Then she started the *'I want to be a Mommy, it is baby time honey.'* talk. I found myself shutting Lyndsey out of my love life. After six months the baby thing turned me impotent. There was no way I was going to be trapped or tricked into becoming a father."

John paused, took a long swallow of cola, and continued, "About that time, Tessa came onto the scene. I had been working long, intense hours on a major business proposal. There is nothing maternal about her and she aroused me sexually. It was wrong. I knew it, but we became lovers."

"Did Lyndsey suspect anythi—"

"Not that I knew. I believe her love remained undaunted until early this morning." John sobbed.

Richard stared at him in disbelief.

John recovered and continued his explanation, "Sex with Tessa possessed me. It was raw, hard, and seemed unending. I could not get enough of it or her. Lyndsey stuck to her talk about starting a family and I wanted no part of it. The more the topic came up the more I ran to Tessa."

"Did you find what you were looking for?"

"In the end, no, definitely no, next along came the accident. It couldn't have happened at a worse time—right in front of my eyes. I was totally powerless."

"We all were, John."

"Yes. But again, Tessa provided the diversion my body and mind craved. The finality of yesterday's session at Roger's office terrified me. It had to be dealt with, then all the new faces."

Gilbert spoke up, "My apologies, John. Up until three days ago I didn't know about the accident, nor expect to find myself summoned to Newmarket."

"I realize that now and apologize for my actions."

"No need to explain. The tragic accident must have been a massive strain on you," Gilbert injected.

"Yes. But not an excuse for my actions," John answered. He carried on his explanation; "I fled Roger's office after making a total ass of myself. I couldn't bring myself to return. I ran off in panic to Tessa's apartment. There, I proceeded to drink away my shame. I passed out for a few hours. When I woke up the drink continued to flow freely. The sex reached intense levels, I passed out—collapsed. Next thing I remember was standing in my driveway screaming obscenities at Lyndsey the woman who, two years earlier I'd professed my love to."

"John, I'll not condone your actions or their reasons. It happened. Let time take its course and heal everyone," Richard offered. He continued, "I cannot speak for Lyndsey. Only she can decide what path lies ahead. She too will need time. I can only offer to be there if and when needed or called upon." Richard paused then said, "I'm angry and definitely need time to grasp everything that has played out in our lives."

"Rich, I wish there were no more pieces to be picked up. Unfortunately there's more. Tessa is pregnant. She claims it's mine!"

Richard and Gilbert sighed. They had never figured on this scenario.

Roger spoke out, "Leave it with me John. For the time being, I suggest we not inform Lyndsey. I'll see what can be arranged before going that route."

"When can I see her, Roger?" Richard asked.

"Give me a couple of days to work on the Tessa situation. That will give Lyndsey time to heal. Also, by then we'll know better where things stand."

Richard and John said, "OK."

The table fell silent. Finally, John spoke, "I really screwed up. Someday I hope yo—"

Richard cut John off. "Yes, this time you screwed up big time, hit the jackpot. But you're my brother. I'm not ready to give up on you, but it will take some time."

John expressed his gratitude, "Thanks, Rich. I don't deserve it. But I need it."

Roger took control and said, "I have a request, no, more of an order to make." He waited for a comment; it did not come. Roger stated his order, "Both you boys need a break. I've spoken to Ralph at the office. You're both officially on a short term hiatus from work." Nobody protested, so Roger continued, "It'll be with full pay. You'll need it until everything settles with the estate. Meanwhile, just take this time and work things out for yourselves."

"How long is our hiatus?" Richard asked.

"We'd best give it a month," Roger answered.

"That's a long time."

"Let's just try it. I'll keep in touch, and if appropriate we can look at a shortened timeline."

"OK. I'll give it a chance," Richard conceded.

John accepted the terms. He said, "Yes. It sounds good. Let's give it a chance."

"Then it's settled," Roger proclaimed. He continued, "John I'll run you back over to your place. It might prove wise to spend a day or two in reflection. You're OK in running Gilbert back to his hotel, Richard?

"Not a problem. Roger, when can we see Lyndsey?"

"Take the day or two I've suggested and relax. She's OK. But, like all of us, will benefit from a short break."

"Well, OK. You'll keep in touch?"

"Yes. I'll touch base with everyone daily."

Richard said, "Thanks Roger. We appreciate everything you've done for us, really."

Roger smiled, stood up and said, "I think it best we get you home John. Ready?"

"Yes. Again Richard, Gil...Gilbert, I'm truly sorry. I should have reached out for help quicker, than I did."

Gilbert responded, "Fact is, you did. Now we'll take Roger's advice and allow the healing to begin."

Roger stepped out of the booth; John stood up and followed his lead. Next Gilbert and Richard rose up and joined them. Roger withdrew his wallet and placed a twenty-dollar bill on the table.

Richard stepped up to John and embraced him. No words were spoken. They separated, and Gilbert looked over to John. The two men stepped up and exchanged handshakes then Gilbert gave John a short embrace. Gilbert said, "Take care. Call if you need us."

"I will. Trust me I will," John answered.

Roger stepped off, and John followed him. Gilbert and Richard watched them walk out the side entrance. They allowed Roger time to depart the parking lot then made their own exit. On the drive back to the hotel, both expressed their concerns and satisfaction with the meeting. Richard expressed guilt over not having spotted John's problems. Gilbert listened then counseled him on controlling his feelings of guilt. He then told him, "John wasn't ready. In all probability he didn't see it as a problem at the time. Besides it may have been construed as interference."

Richard turned into the hotel parking lot. He chose a parking spot in the front lot. On getting out of the truck, Richard thanked Gilbert for his council. He said, "I know you're right. I just can't help wondering…"

They walked up to the hotel's front entrance. At the door, Gilbert said, "I am right. In time you'll see it. Meanwhile, I have that diary upstairs. Could I twist your arm into picking up our discussion where we left off? I find the whole matter intriguing."

"I'd like that. I'll not lie. The diary has captured my imagination."

Richard pulled the door open and held it until Gilbert had entered the hotel, then he followed Gilbert into the lobby. To their surprise the afternoon had slipped away. Gilbert grinned after a glance at the lobby clock revealed the hour to be 4:30 pm. He suggested they enjoy an early supper and offered to drive Richard back over to the homestead after they'd eaten. Richard accepted. He found himself drawn to Gilbert and enjoying his companionship.

CHAPTER 21

HOPE HUNG UP THE PHONE. SHE TURNED, FACED LYNDSEY, AND SAID, "Still no answer in Uncle Gilbert's room. I left a message at the front desk. He's sure to call when he gets back in."

"Thanks Hope. You've been like a sister to me. I feel so stupid. Your Uncle Gilbert sure has a sweet smile"

"Uncle Gilbert's smile and sweetness, now there is a definite matched pair. However, right now I'll settle for you relaxing and me discovering the special person I see in you." In an effort to divert Lyndsey's mind from her troubles, Hope proceeded to give Lyndsey a verbal guided tour of her home. She started at the old homestead, "It is currently occupied by Gilbert's father Pappy McClaken and his brother Uncle Jeffrey. Pappy can be a bit cantankerous at times, but most times proved to be a lovable, old soul. He misses Grammie a great deal." Hope explained how she spent hour upon hour listening to Pappy spin tales about his days spent out at sea. "However," she explained, "Uncle Jeffrey is the real sweetheart of the family."

Lyndsey asked, "Uncle Jeffrey...he'd be the brother Gilbert mentioned at the coffee shop?"

"The one and only," Hope confirmed. She paused and said, "Both Uncle Morgan and Uncle Paul reside out in BC. I can only recall meeting them once. That must have been at least ten years past."

Lyndsey said, "Tell me about the house. The old homestead."

"It's quaint."

"Has it changed much over the years?"

"It has got running water and indoor plumbing now. Jeffrey and Pappy built on an addition the summer Paul and Morgan came home. I remember that well. I got into trouble more than once for exploring the construction site."

Lyndsey laughed and exclaimed, "Not a fitting place for a young woman…I'd wager."

"Right, it must be a *'man'* thing."

Lyndsey pounded her chest and called out, "Me mighty hunter and provider—you a frail damsel—you stay home—you wash my dishes, my clothes, clean my house…." Tears bust forth from her eyes as she sobbed.

Hope reached over and embraced Lyndsey.

Lyndsey pulled Hope closer to herself. Slowly, she recovered from her fit of tears. She said, "Sorry Hope. I'm a big sissy at heart."

"Give it time. Give it time," Hope counseled, and said, "Maybe, we should change the subject."

"No. No, I need to know more about the homestead."

"Only if you are absolutely sure it's what you want?"

Lyndsey pulled herself away from Hope and said, "Yes. I'll be OK. I really want to know."

"Then I'll try to concentrate on the old house and forget the men-folk."

Lyndsey said, "Thanks." She explained her passion and need to know more about the old house, "The night we discovered the old diary, I fell asleep reading from its pages. That night, I had a dream. In it the world of Grace Ramsay and her words triggered my imagination and I felt connected to her world her time. It was almost like her spirit possessed me."

"Really? That's eerie."

"Yes, but it didn't feel eerie. I felt connected."

"Gad," Hope exclaimed. She grinned and asked, "You wouldn't be a Maritimer per chance? You spin a really good ghost tale."

Lyndsey chuckled. She brushed her hair back and said, "It's true. I've never had a dream so vivid and life-like. It felt like I'd stood right there in Grace's bedroom."

"That would be Uncle Jeffrey's room now," Hope explained.

"It's a small room right?"

Hope explained the original parts of the house in detail, "Yes, by today's standards very small. It is set off what must have been the main room, kitchen, and living or sitting room. A window has been added to the bedroom. The walls are old. Real old there must be at least ten layers of wallpaper on them." *In her mind boastful claims and tales of questionable repute swirled about.* Grammie she recalled could spin ghostly tales that others swore to be factual and true. An image of lovable Uncle Jeffery popped up and reached out to hug her. Hope held back on hearing Uncle Jeffery's oft asked words echo in her head, *"Have yee seens mes wee little one dearriie. Me Gooods Neeighbour Faeiry?"* A glance into Lyndsey eyes revealed the extent of the girl's interest. Hope continued, "The living room still has small windows, but they are the new kind. Floorboards are original. Big, very wide boar..."

Lyndsey jumped in, "When the wind blows at nigh—"

Hope anticipated the question and answered, "Do the walls shudder and shake? Let me tell you, girl. As a youngster I spent many a night curled up in Grammie and Pappy's bed. Scar't stiff I was."

Lyndsey shuddered. In her mind, she felt the walls tremble and heard the howl of the wind whipping about the house. "Hope—Is the old homestead haunted?" The kitchen of 1797 flashed before her eyes.

Hope laughed loudly. "Dang it all girl! You must have a Maritimer's blood flowing in yer veins! Her laugh vanished and she answered, No! Absolutely no Uncle Jeffrey's house is not haunted." She took Lyndsey's hands in hers and made her sales pitch; "You absolutely must come and visit us in East River, Lyndsey. You'd love it. Nothing quite like the big cities you're accustomed to."

"Newmarket is a town."

"Right, our towns are just a tad smaller, girl. Take ten to twenty homes and toss in a liquor store and we call it a town. If the population grows and they add a pub, toss in a second liquor store and we call it a city."

The girls burst into laughter. Although from two different backgrounds and surroundings, they felt a deep kindred connection.

Mike knocked on the door and drew the girls' attention. He asked, "Care for a bite to eat girls? I have some soup and crackers on the go. Be ready in ten minutes."

Lyndsey responded, "Yes, that would be nice. We'll be out shortly. Thanks."

Mike smiled and said, "No problem at all, whenever you're ready. I'll be in the kitchen."

"They should all be so kind," Hope opined.

Lyndsey added, "Too bad about Mike's wife. He must miss her a great deal."

They stood up and started to walk off towards the kitchen. At the bathroom, both girls stepped inside and freshened up before going to the kitchen. In the hallway Lyndsey excused herself. She whispered to Hope, "Give me 10 minutes. I'd best call my office and update them on my status."

Hope continued on into the kitchen, where Mike had set out two place settings. He placed the serving bowl of vegetable soup on the table. Next, he set a container of crackers and a jug of milk down beside the soup.

He asked, "Is Lyndsey OK, Hope?"

"She fine, Mike. Thank you so much for taking us in on such short notice."

"It's my pleasure. On the rare occasion when Roger calls asking for help I jump at the opportunity to lend a helping hand."

Lyndsey joined them in the kitchen.

"Besides, I get rewarded with the company of two beautiful, charming young ladies. Enjoy." Mike turned and walked out of the kitchen.

Hope smirked after Mike had departed she whispered, "Mike is such a sweetheart. It must be the Grampa in him."

Tears trickled down Lyndsey's cheeks.

Hope spotted them, reached out and embraced her. "Lyndsey I'm so sorry, I can't imagine the heartache that accident cast on your family."

"I was like a daughter to their parents, a granddaughter to Grampa and Grandma Ramsay. They lived the essence of love and shared it willingly. They were more than in-laws—they were family."

Once Lyndsey recovered the girls sat down at kitchen table to a meal of vegetable soup and crackers that awaited them.

Hope described the grounds about the McClaken/Ramsay homestead. The property now had two houses. The original and the one Gilbert had built fifteen years past. From the front lawn of Gilbert's house, one could look out over a beautiful hedge of old-fashioned roses. The view above the rose hedge and out over the bay was spectacular, an absolute must see, and an artist's haven. Early-summer brought the rose hedge into full bloom. In a good year, one could barely see the green leaves. The pink roses would almost cover them completely. Down a well traveled path from Gilbert's stood Jeffrey and Pappy's house: the original homestead. A narrow dirt trail ran from there down to the seaside and the dock. Gilbert and Jeffrey's lobster boats docked there. Hope finished her description of the homestead by describing a typical sunset viewed from the end of the dock.

Lyndsey could feel herself standing on that dock and gazing out over a glittering sea. Overhead, seagulls called out to her. Before her, the sea's surface, calm and not unlike a mirror, changed colours from blue-green to a deep orange and then glowed a reddish-pink. Just before the sun dipped below the horizon it changed to a pale, enhancing pink.

Dreamily Lyndsey stated, "I absolutely must see the seaside glitter you dangle before the palette of my mind."

Hope leaped out of her chair. "Yes! Yes! You must...you absolutely must! However I best bees a warning ye girl, Uncle Jeffrey may speak of one he calls his *Gooods Neeighbour Faeiry.* Don't let it frightens ya. It's just his friendly ways."

CHAPTER 22

LYNDSEY AND HOPE BONDED A SOLID FRIENDSHIP IN THE TIME they spent together at Mike's home in Port Perry. On discovering Mike was a semiretired chartered accountant Lyndsey connected to him through their professional backgrounds and experiences. Lyndsey encouraged Mike to commit more time to his profession. Both girls felt it would help him accept the passing of his wife, Chloe. Two days—then five—passed before Roger arranged a reunion among the parties involved. Roger drove up to Port Perry and stole the girls away from Mike. Hugs were shared by all before Roger headed back to Newmarket with Hope and Lyndsey. Along the way Roger explained to Lyndsey that their advice to Mike had already paid dividends. Roger had met up with Lyndsey's employer Daylily Meadows Retirement Villas and advised them of the situation. "Fantine your manager agreed that a hiatus from work would be the best solution for you at this time."

"But, but I need to get caught up. I've already missed too much time," Lyndsey protested.

Roger smiled into the rear-view mirror. He replied, "The problem is solved Lyndsey. You and Hope solved it in your chats with Mike. Fantine on learning Mike was a chartered accountant open to volunteering his time in your absence jumped at the opportunity. She contacted the Retirement Villas's owners and they concurred with her. Mike agreed to step in and be a volunteer-temp replacement during your time away from the office. Actually a volunteer in kind. His wages will be donated to the Villa's Residents' Social Club."

Lyndsey reach forward and squeezed Roger's shoulder. A tear trickled down her cheek. "Noreen is one luck lady to have you Rog... you're a keeper."

"And I'm double lucky girl. Mike has agreed to stay at our home while he filled in for you. A double bonus! It's been years since Mike and I spent any real quality time together."

"Thanks Rog. You are a sweetheart," Lyndsey added with another squeeze of Roger's shoulder.

Everyone, John, Gilbert and Richard had been instructed to meet at the family homestead. Richard arrived first at 2 pm. A short time later, John pulled into the driveway. Richard made a pot of coffee. The two brothers sat down across the table and talked. Richard related to John his plans to travel down to the east coast. John expressed concerns that he might be jumping too quickly.

"No. I believe the timing of Roger's imposed hiatus to be perfect," Richard countered.

"It's the wanderlust in you, Rich. I suppose you've memorized every word of that diary by now."

"No. But Gilbert's descriptions of the original homestead; well, I have no choice."

"Are you really sure?" John asked. He chuckled and added, "The creative minds and imaginative ideals of our ancestors is definitely alive and thriving in you bro!"

Richard missed John's attempted humour and stated, "The house young Grace lived in still stands."

"A broken down piece of history no doubt," John commented.

"No. Actually Jeffrey and their Father live in it."

Richard stood up went to the counter and refilled his coffee cup. John declined the offer of a refill. The subject of Lyndsey and John's dilemma with Tessa was not broached. Richard, excited about the prospect of a trip to Nova Scotia, tried to convince John to join him. His efforts fell on deaf ears. John would not consider taking part in such folly. Richard remained standing at the counter.

"Will Lyndsey be going with you?" John asked.

"I haven't..."

"Should she decide to accompany you, it's OK by me."

John's comment took Richard off-guard.

"Believe me, Rich, I'd be OK with it. She's going to need some time. And the trip would give her that."

"We'd best let her decide."

John closed the subject by stating, "Fair enough, Rich. But please go. It's obvious that for you the trip is a must do. I'm sorry, but I do not feel as passionate on the matter as you do. Let's face it, I'm simply good old steady-as-she-goes John and definitely not a wanderlust at heart. I'll serve my period of exile from work, but the minute Roger lifts the order...I'm there. Work is what I do best."

Richard accepted John's line of reasoning. He did not confer with the reasons John employed in defense of his position, but he did accept John's decision.

Their discussion ended when a vehicle pulled up into the yard. Richard went to the front door and greeted Gilbert at the doorstep. They exchanged a handshake then embraced each other. Next Roger's Caddie drove up the driveway. They remained on the doorstep and waited for Roger and the girls. Richard's eyes locked onto Lyndsey as she and Hope stepped out of the car. He sensed the time they'd shared together at Mike's had cemented a bond and friendship between the pair. Seeing them stand side-by-side he smiled on catching a glimpse of positive aura glowing outwardly on both their faces. Lyndsey appeared to have recaptured an essence of the positivity that had drawn him to her side at their first encounter in the sandbox and onward throughout their teen years. Lyndsey reached the foot of the doorstep and distracted Richard's thoughts, "Hi, Rich."

Richard started towards Lyndsey, but Gilbert held him back. He stepped aside and allowed the girls and Roger to make their way up the doorstep and into the house. After Gilbert had stepped inside, Richard followed suit. Inside, John stepped out of the kitchen and made his appearance.

He addressed Lyndsey, "I'm sorry. I won't ask your forgiveness. I don't have that right."

Lyndsey started to tremble, then pulled herself together and said, "We both need time John. I'm hurt. I need time."

"I understand. I'll respect your needs," John answered.

Roger spoke out. "Perhaps it would be best if we went into the living room. It'll provide a relaxed atmosphere."

He stepped aside and Richard led the procession into the living room. John joined the procession behind Lyndsey and followed her into the living room. Roger claimed the leather recliner. Richard sat on a small sofa. Hope sat on the centre of the large sofa, and Gilbert took the spot to her left. Lyndsey joined Gilbert and Hope on the large sofa. She sat down next to Hope. John walked into the living room. He sat down next to Richard.

Roger broke the silence. He stated, "I wanted everyone together in order to review the events of the past week." He continued, "I've spoken to each of you individually and believe each of you understand the state of William and Bill Ramsay's estate. John and Richard have agreed to and accepted the terms of the wills. The employees have willingly stepped forward and assumed the task of running the daily affairs of the family business. John and Richard, I appreciate your stepping aside and taking a time out. So much has happened it's hard to firmly grasp the realities of it all. Richard, your time out will start next week, on completion of that heavy engine overhaul you've been working."

Richard chuckled, "Best make that 10 days maybe two weeks Roger. It's a major overhaul—I'll push to make it 10 days."

Roger nodded his approval to Richard.

"I appreciate all you've done, Roger. But when can I get back to work?" John asked.

"John, you may feel you need that to see yourself over everything. Trust me. You'll thank me later."

"Thanks Roger."

Roger presented an offer made by Gilbert earlier, "Gilbert has kindly offered up accommodations to any of you who have displayed a desire to travel to Nova Scotia and visit the family's original homestead. I believe it to be an excellent opportunity, John would you care to take Gilbert up on his offer?"

John hesitated then said, "No offense intended, Gilbert, but I'm just not ready for that right now."

"Understood," Roger said.

Gilbert smiled and said, "The offer is open, John. If not now—whenever you feel ready."

"Appreciated, Gilbert, I will take you up on that offer one day," John replied.

Roger then took over the meeting. He asked for and received signed authority to oversee the estate's affairs in partnership with Walter Lizards and the business's financial activities. Talk then shifted towards Gilbert and Hope's travel plans.

Gilbert expressed regret then explained that personal commitments called on him to return home. He had an extra credit Shakespeare course underway and didn't want to extend his time away beyond a reasonable time line.

This was against Hope's wishes; she was enjoying her time with her new family in Newmarket. It was determined that they would head back east in one or two days time.

Roger, satisfied that he had served his purpose, excused himself. He stood up and bade his farewell. Lyndsey followed Roger. At the front door she embraced him and thanked him profusely. They separated then she hugged him anew briefly. Roger opened the door.

Lyndsey smiled and said, "Pass that one along to Mike. He's a sweetheart."

Roger nodded and stepped outside, then closed the door. In the living room John followed Roger's lead. He claimed there were some private matters that required his attention and headed towards the front door in the hallway he stopped on encountering Lyndsey.

He whispered into Lyndsey's ear, "I suppose you'll be playing house with Rich before long."

Lyndsey pulled away from John and stared at him in disbelief. She slapped John's face in anger at his taunt. Then in a stern lowered voice she asked, "What? Did I hear you right?" She continued, "You have your nerve. Playing house more aptly describes what you did with Tessa, while I foolishly stayed home and kept our home together."

John shrugged his shoulders, grinned and replied, "I like it. You've finally got style that resonates! Out of view from the others, John rotated his hips then quickly thrust them back and forth in a lewd motion. He winked and mockingly suggested, "We did SEX. Not exactly my idea of playing house."

Lyndsey turned away from John in disgust.

Before she moved back towards the living room John snickered and whispered lowly, "You just don't get it. Well, no hard feelings. Keep your share. I need cash. Next time you're riding Richie's bones…tell him half the insurance money is mine."

Lyndsey blocked out John's words. She walked away from him and rejoined Richard, Gilbert, and Hope in the living room. John grinned then left the house.

In the living room Lyndsey rejoined Gilbert and Hope on the sofa. She smiled and listened in on the ongoing conversation.

"You brought it with you, Gilbert?" Richard asked.

Gilbert nodded and said, "Out in the truck."

Hope jumped up and offered, "I'll go bring the diary in, Uncle Gilbert."

Gilbert laughed and stood up. He said, "That coffee still fresh? No matter. I'll take a chance."

He went to the kitchen in search of his coffee. In truth, it was a good excuse to allow Lyndsey and Richard some time together.

"So?"

"I'm good Rich, really."

"Then smile."

Lyndsey determined to not allow John's negativities to destroy her positive life views frowned then said, "I'd really like to go with you, to Nova Scotia…I mean."

Richard hesitated then asked, "You're sure about this?"

Lyndsey hugged herself. A smile burst out on her face. She boasted, "I'm on hiatus! Roger came through for me too. He came through big time. His brother Mike, is a chartered accountant. He offered to be a volunteer-temp at the Villas in my absence. Fantine agreed. Pleeeease take me Richie—to Nova Scotia."

Lyndsey pleaded, Richard gazed into her eyes. He asked, "Really?"

"Absolutely, Hope has worked on me endlessly the last five days."

"Did I hear my name?" Hope asked cheerily and walked back into the living room carrying the old diary.

Nobody answered. Finally Lyndsey stared at Richard and said, "Say yes, please!"

Richard grinned and whispered to Lyndsey, "Yes. Yes, I'll take you with me."

Lyndsey leaped up and bounce around the coffee table. She stopped in front of Richard and hugged him.

Hope shouted, "Hello. Would someone let me in on what the hippity hoppities are all about?"

Lyndsey released Richard turned to Hope and boasted, "Richie's taking me with him to Nova Scotia!"

The girls hugged. Hope gleefully boasted, "Girl, you're gon'na love de sunsets."

Gilbert rejoined the gathering with his coffee in hand and looked questioningly at Hope.

The room fell silent.

Lyndsey broke the silence. She suggested, "Shall we return to the place of discovery, the attic? It would give the reading a proper setting."

Richard looked at Lyndsey and asked, "Maybe we should stick with the living room. It has a relaxed atmosphere.

Lyndsey simply shook her head at Richard and rejected his suggestion.

He stood up and said, "I'll grab the last of the coffee and join you up there."

She stood and directed Gilbert and Hope towards the attic. Along the way, she gave a guided tour of the old house. The tour and conversations quickly pushed thoughts of her earlier encounter with John aside. They paused at the doorway to the attic. When Richard didn't show after a short wait, she opened the door. A yellow ball of fur flew between their legs and raced up into the attic.

Gilbert chuckled and said, "Master of the house I presume?"

"The one and only," Lyndsey answered.

Gilbert led the way up the stairs. Lyndsey switched on the attic lights then followed Hope up the stairs. Richard entered the staircase just as Lyndsey stepped off the top step into the attic. He thought to himself, *now the secrets of the old diary will be revealed to a truly willing audience.*

CHAPTER 23

RICHARD REACHED THE TOP STEP AND WALKED INTO THE ATTIC. Lyndsey had started Gilbert and Hope on a guided tour of the attic. He walked over to his Grandfather's desk, where Gilbert and Hope were standing. Lyndsey had stooped down and started to pick up Grandfather Ramsay's prized picture of the unknown seashore. Gilbert crouched down and took the picture from Lyndsey.

He rose up smiled and boasted, "Look, Hope. It's a photo taken from the lawn looking out over Grammy's rose hedge."

He set the picture down on the desk and picked off the broken shards of glass. The other three gathered around.

"It must have been taken in the Fall," Hope declared. "Look, you can see the rosehips on the branches. Too bad it's not a colour print."

The centre of the picture had been cut by the broken glass. Lyndsey carefully turned the frame over and removed the photograph from its frame. A yellowed piece of folded paper fell out from between the photograph and its cardboard backing. Lyndsey picked it up and unfolded it. She laid it out next to the photograph. She said, "Look, it's a map of some sort."

Gilbert looked at it cautiously. The drawing resembled a crude drawing of East River Bay and Mahone Bay. It extended, he thought, eastward beyond the Big Tancook Island and out past East Ironbound, Flat and Pearl Islands into the Atlantic. The upper section looked very familiar. It included what had to be the entrance to East River. The two islands far out beyond Big Tancook were drawn out of proportion to the rest of the map. One he figured had to be Sinner's Island. The other he preferred not to dwell upon, just as he always steered his lobster boat well to the leeward side of it when out on the Atlantic beyond Mahone Bay.

"Look," Lyndsey proclaimed, then explained, "Both of the islands have strange markings on them."

She pointed to the island Gilbert recognized as Sinner's Island and said, "That marking and the larger island's marking look like skulls with crossed bones."

Richard opened the desk drawer and withdrew a magnifying glass. He placed it over the spot Lyndsey had pointed out. The marking on Sinner's Island on closer inspection turned out to be a simple 'X', but next to it in small print they read *'Pirates' voices changed our lives forever'*. Richard moved the magnifying glass over to the other marked island. Close to its seaward side, someone had drawn a circle with an X in its centre. On closer examination, he found that 'X' to be a crude rendering of a skull and crossbones, positioned close to what appeared to be a large tree. It had been aptly described by Lyndsey. Below the skull, in a faint pencil, was written, *'Hell's Gateway—Satan's Doorway.'* Nobody spoke. Several squiggles could, he thought, represent trees or rocks.

Gilbert spoke out, "Perhaps we'd best leave this alone for now and return to the diary."

Richard, enthralled, exclaimed, "What! Not study what must be a map to the family's original wealth?"

"Those two islands—more precisely the one with the circled X it is evil, and you'd be well advised to stay clear of its shores."

"Get out'ta here."

"No, trust me on this Richard. I grew up amidst many good, honest men—men who to this day counsel any who will listen to their wisdom. Both of those islands are known as the Floating Islands. If you had grown up in our neck of the woods, you'd be well aware of it. Rumour is the islands float eerily in an evil swirling sea mist. They've been sighted in more than one location. Heed those words printed on the map. I've been told death would be a treasured alternative to being cast away on the Floating Islands. It's the other undiscovered Treasure Island and reported *'Gateway to Hell's feared doorway to the Eternity awaiting Sinners.'* I'm not referring to 'Oak Island' and its buried treasure."

Richard scoffed and said, "No disrespect, Gilbert. I've heard tell of Oak Island, but you're a man of the sea and from a family of hardy seafarers. The tale you spin would be better saved for tourists and those possessing a fainter heart." He frowned then added, "You're surely referring to the tales of the *'Money Pit'* and its buried treasure, never uncovered on Oak Island. It's protected by underground tunnels to the sea that have flooded it out and hindered every attempt to recover its buried treasures. Many a fool has parted company with his money in attempting to solve its mystery. They were the fortunate ones. Others I've heard paid a greater price; their lives. Besides, this could set us free to walk once more in the footsteps of our ancestors."

Gilbert pointed to the island with the circled X and retorted, "Then you'll walk those footsteps alone. For I'll not step foot upon that hellish place."

Lyndsey stepped in and mediated. She said, "Perhaps Gilbert is right. We set out to study the diary. Now might be a good time to return to it."

Gilbert sighed and said, "Thank you, Lyndsey. You've spoken wisely."

Richard shrugged his shoulders and surrendered.

Lyndsey folded the map up and stuffed it into her front jeans pocket. She picked up the photograph and asked, "Is this photo really taken from your front lawn, Gilbert?"

"Yes, but it must have been taken when I was very young. The rose hedge has grown much larger."

Lyndsey walked over to the old trunk. The others followed her lead. She sat down on the floor. Richard sat down next to her. Hope and Gilbert chose a spot three feet in front of them and likewise sat down on the floor. Lyndsey noticed the old photo album on the floor and picked it up.

Richard said, "Give it to Gilbert, Lyndsey. He may recognize some of the scenery in the pictures. I took a quick look the other night, but nothing looked familiar."

Gilbert accepted the photo album from Lyndsey. He placed it on his and Hope's laps. Lyndsey and Richard slid across the floor. Lyndsey ended up at Hope's side, Richard at Gilbert's. Gilbert opened the album. The first pictures did not look familiar to him. After looking at several pages, he commented on some of the people. Some of their features he felt resembled those of his grandparents or great aunts and uncles. Lyndsey and Richard slid closer for a better view. Gilbert, and then Hope, recognized the pictures of the original homestead. Gilbert described the changes that had been made to the house. When they turned to pictures of the seaside, he indicated where his Grandfather and Father had built the dock that both he and Jeffrey still used to this day.

Hope pointed to a photo on the last page. She smiled and softly said, "Oh, look, it's a picture of my Dad. He looks so young."

The attic fell silent. Gilbert hugged Hope and sighed. He said, "Yes he is, sweetheart and Allan was young. We were in high school when that photo was taken. Damn I miss my Karyn, Sandy and Allan" He turned over the back cover and closed the album then set it down on the floor. Gilbert rose up onto his knees. The others followed his lead. They formed a circle and shared a group hug and melted together. Two long-separated branches of their family's tree came together as one.

They separated and sat back down on the floor. Lyndsey glanced at her watch, surprised at how quickly time had passed. She suggested they break for a bite to eat. She asked, "Hope, would you give me a hand in the kitchen? We'll leave these two together and pray they don't misbehave."

Lyndsey and Hope stood up and walked off towards the staircase. Bailey appeared out of nowhere and joined them. The old feline sensed the possibility of a meal. He followed the girls downstairs and into the kitchen.

Gilbert turned to Richard and said, "My apologies if I seemed a bit uptight earlier. I had my reasons."

"No need to explain."

"Yes. I believe I must. I reacted as I did because of a personal experience."

"Are you sure?"

Gilbert sighed and explained, "Both Hope and I are ecstatic at the prospect of having both you and Lyndsey show up at our doorstep for a visit. When you get there, you'll meet the rest of our family: Pappy McClaken, my father, and Jeffrey, my youngest brother. Pappy can be cantankerous, but is generally an easy-going, fun person to have about. He'll talk your ears off if you allow him too."

"So he has a tale or two to tell."

Gilbert laughed, "More like a library and then some."

Richard chuckled and said, "I'm going to like him."

"You will, I can assure you." Gilbert then continued to explain the cause of his reaction. "Jeffrey is a good-hearted soul; he'd give you the shirt off his back. When you meet him, you may think him a bit eccentric or maybe even slow. His manner of speech will definitely stand out and catch your attention. I'm not saying this just to defend him, as he is my brother. Others who live nearby may comment of him in jest. There have been occasions when he's managed to frustrate us beyond reason. His nickname back home is Bugshit McClaken."

"Say. What?"

"Bugshit McClaken."

"Bugshit McClaken?" Richard asked.

Gilbert nodded and said, "Yes." He then elaborated. "Years ago, Grandfather Ramsay and Pappy took little Jeffy...Jeffrey out on one of their lobster runs. That's where we go out and pull up our traps, remove our catch, bait the traps, and then send them back down hopefully for more. Once they'd finished hauling their traps they set out on a course that carried them out beyond Big Tancook Island towards the islands, the Floating Islands. The same islands I'll never set foot on and I encourage you to heed my stance. Jeffrey took to fussing and driving Pappy and Grandfather Ramsay around the bend. Even though it went against Pappy's better judgment, they set ashore on the bigger of the two islands."

"The one with the circled X?" Richard asked.

"Yes," Gilbert answered. He then continued, "Before that day Jeffrey spoke as clearly and fluently as you or I."

"Come and get it," Hope hollered up the staircase.

Richard jumped and Gilbert laughed.

Gilbert apologized he said, "Sorry I don't mean to leave you dangling. But this old boy is one hungry camper."

"No need to apologize. I had some toast earlier but that's all I've eaten today."

Gilbert stood up and Richard followed suit. They walked off together, eager for anything that resembled food. On the way down, Gilbert promised to fill Richard in with all the details later that night. Once in the kitchen, they were treated to a meal of pork chops complete with all the trimmings. During the meal conversation touched on the travel plans of Gilbert and Hope. The highlight centered on news that Lyndsey would be Richard's traveling companion on his visit to Nova Scotia and its famed East River.

Hope served dessert then stood behind Lyndsey. The glow on her face burst into a smile. She then sat at the table and picked at her dessert. Over dessert, a determined Hope attempted to alter their travel plans. An offered second dessert was accepted, but it failed to alter their departure plan. With reluctance, Hope accepted Gilbert's set in stone plan to hit the road and head back home to Nova Scotia the next day.

Gilbert softened the impact of their agreed departure. He stressed to Hope, "Give yourself two weeks, and we'll all be gathered together back home."

In an attempt to shorten Richard and Lyndsey's departure Hope asked, "Isn't there another employee that can stand in for you, Rich? Two weeks feels like a lifetime."

Richard grinned and said, "Hope, your concern is noted. I'll keep you in mind and try to cut it down to 12 days."

"That would be great!" Hope exclaimed.

"No promises! It could go the other way. It's a major engine overhaul."

A short period of silence fell over the kitchen then Gilbert and Richard did the honourable thing and performed the after-dinner cleanup. Lyndsey and Hope retired to the den and engaged in friendly chit-chat. During their cleanup, Gilbert hinted a desire to spend the night at the house. Richard was quick to pick up on Gilbert's hint and suggested that they consider spending the night.

Gilbert accepted. He said, "Love to. It'll give me an opportunity to finish our earlier discussion after the girls have turned in for the night."

Richard thought this a great plan as he dried the last of the dishes and returned them to the cupboards. Gilbert rinsed out the sink, and they both set off to rejoin the girls in the den. The kitchen clock ticked away. Its hands set the hour at 8:30 pm.

Richard and Gilbert walked into the den. The girls stopped talking and looked up at them.

"Girl talk," Hope declared.

"No, surely you jest?" Gilbert chided.

Both Richard and Gilbert sat down on the large sofa across from Lyndsey and Hope, who sat cross-legged on the loveseat.

Richard made an announcement, "In view of our photographic diversion this afternoon...Gilbert has accepted my offer to spend the night here at the house. Do I have the approval of you girls?"

Hope uttered an affirmative, "Yup."

Lyndsey looked at Hope, smiled, and nodded her head up and down.

"I'll take that 'Yup' and Lyndsey's dippity-do head nod as a yes."

Lyndsey smirked then got up off the loveseat. She signaled Hope to follow her. She turned to Richard and said, "I'll set Hope and me up in Grandma Ramsay's bedroom, if it's OK with you, Richard?"

"Sure. It has the queen-sized bed. I'll use the guest bedroom, and Gilbert can bunk out in Grandma's sewing room. There's that big pullout sofa bed in it."

Hope followed Lyndsey out of the den. They disappeared down the hallway.

Richard stood up walked over to the liquor cabinet in the corner. He pulled out a bottle of white rum. A glance Gilbert's way saved him the trouble of seeking approval of his choice. Richard closed the cabinet. He walked over to the coffee table and placed the bottle on it.

"Hold steady, Gilbert. I'll get some ice and cola and we can start to relax."

"Sounds like a plan. Anything I can do?"

"Relax."

Richard went to the kitchen and returned shortly. He bore a load of cola, ice, a saucer, and two large tumblers.

Gilbert stood up. He assisted Richard with his load. The two sat down on the sofa. Gilbert twisted the cap off the bottle of rum.

Richard popped ice into their tumblers.

Gilbert poured a healthy portion of rum into the glasses. He set the bottle down and watched Richard add a dash of cola to the tumblers. They then raised their glasses in a toast to each other. He grinned and watched Richard pour a healthy serving of rum into the saucer. Nonchalantly, Bailey strutted into the den. He walked directly to Richard. Once there, he proceeded to rub himself against Richard's legs. Richard picked the saucer up off the coffee table. Bailey started to meow in anticipation.

Gilbert set his tumbler down. He laughed heartily and said, "Get out'ta here! Does that old feline really want a serving of rum?"

"Straight up," Richard proclaimed. He explained, "Grandpa never was one to dilute his medicine. Bailey, being Grandpa's true comrade in arms, never argued, though he's been known to sneak a lick or two from an unattended glass. The fact it may have been tainted with cola never deterred this old feline. He rubbed Bailey's head and set the saucer down on the floor. Bailey quickly lost interest in Richard's legs.

The first serving vanished quickly from their tumblers. A refill followed.

Gilbert revisited their earlier conversation. He broached the subject and said, "As I was saying before we were interrupted for that splendid supper…before the day Pappy, Grandfather Ramsay, and Jeffrey set foot on that island, he spoke just as clearly and fluently as you and I."

"But! But you're an English Professor. Well schooled and all. Surely, you don't buy into—"

"Gilbert interrupted, "All that hocus-pocus?"

"Right, all that hocus-pocus!"

"If I hadn't lived it, then you're right; I'd dismiss it totally. But, I did live it."

"OK. Explain."

Gilbert refilled their glasses, topped off Bailey's saucer, and started his explanation. "I've always felt a handsome dose of guilt over the events of that day. To be truthful, it should have been me out there—not Jeffrey. I took off early that morning...shirked my duties...opted for a day of play with friends. Pappy, well, he was fit to be tied. He let me know in no uncertain terms upon their return."

Richard laughed and said, "Don't tell me the old hickory stick?"

"No. The old wood shed and a tanning rod." Gilbert shuddered. He continued, "Jeffrey never recovered from that day. You'll see when you meet him. Hope thinks there's some kind of animosity between us. She couldn't be any further from the truth." He sighed and explained, "In truth, it is pure unadulterated guilt. If not for the events of that day, our roles in life could easily be—would be reversed."

"And Jeffrey, does he feel this guilt?"

"Not a shred. He has no reason to—doesn't remember a thing about it."

This time, Richard performed the bartender's duties. He topped up the two tumblers and Bailey's saucer.

Gilbert continued, "Pappy pulled me aside after Mother had passed on and begged my forgiveness for the beating he'd set upon me. It must have been his way of dealing with Mother's death. He finally broke down and talked about their fateful visit to the island. Anyway, the shortest way to explain it: ghosts—demonic souls from the other side."

Richard's face went blank. He asked, "Ghosts?"

"Yes, ghosts! Grandfather Ramsay pulled the boat up into an inlet on the island and tied the boat off. The three stepped off onto the island. Jeffrey had to relieve himself. The little blighter took off into the woods. Pappy and Grandfather called out in vain after him. They let what they figured was five or ten minutes pass before they set off in search of Jeffrey. Where could he go? It was an island. Then, if Pappy is to be believed, a dense mist set in over the island, completely out of nowhere on a bright, sunny day."

Richard stated, "It's a phenomenon known to happen on occasion."

"The mist, yes not the rest of their misadventure. Pappy and Grandfather called out after Jeffrey. They walked deeper into the woods and towards the island's centre. On the seaward side they spotted Jeffrey. He had entered a clearing. They broke into a run and continued to call out to him. Jeffrey stopped. He looked back at them. Then it happened."

Gilbert paused and refilled the two tumblers along with Bailey's saucer. This time, the ice and cola were omitted.

Richard raised his tumbler. Gilbert followed suit. A toast was made. Then Gilbert resumed his recital of Pappy's confession.

"Just behind Jeffrey, something rose up out of the light but thickening mist. Pappy and Grandfather stopped dead in their tracks. At first they thought it was nothing more than a small tree an alder perhaps. A bone-chilling scream erupted from behind Jeffrey. Pappy and Grandfather froze there…he claims. Jeffrey was the first to turn around and face the apparition. Two icy hands straight from hell stretched out and attempted to grab him. Pappy leaped forward. He crawled over rocky ground in an attempt to reach Jeffrey. The creature roared in a blood-curdling voice, *'Get away from it! I'll suck you into the depths of hell and beyond!'* Its eyes flashed red and burned a tattoo like scar etched onto Jeffrey's arm. He bears that mark to this day. Grandfather Ramsay hurled himself past Pappy, grabbed Jeffrey by the collar, and pulled him away to safety. In a flash, Pappy jumped up and raced madly after Grandfather, who had picked up Jeffrey and fled back towards the boat, neither dared to look back over their shoulder. They arrived back at the boat. Both had suffered deep scratches to their faces from tree branches that tried to impede their escape. Grandfather threw Jeffrey onto the boat and leaped in after him. Pappy withdrew his knife, sliced the rope that tied the boat to shore, and dove feet first into the chilly water. The boat had drifted away from the island, and Pappy swam out to it. Grandfather started the engine and helped Pappy back into the boat. The creature continued its unearthly screeching. Jeffrey sat in a corner of the boat and trembled like a child in an epileptic seizure. Within ten minutes of fleeing the island the screeching ceased. Upon their arrival back at the dock, they took Jeffrey up to the house. Days passed before Jeffrey spoke a word. He's not spoken a proper sentence since that day."

Richard looked puzzled. He said, "No disrespect Gilbert, but that's one hell of a tale. Perchance, does Pappy subscribe to the same medicine that we now administer?"

"On a good day, Pappy can drink many a good man under the table, including yours truly. However, on the day he made this confession to me, I swear the man had been stone sober for days."

"OK. But…"

Gilbert interrupted, "No buts. I know what kind of toddler Jeffrey had been before that day. Many a day since then I had to step forward and defend my kid brother from others. People can be cruel."

Richard tried to reason, "Could it be he caught a virus or something that impeded his development?"

"No. Old Doc Rose would have picked up on it. Mother took Jeffrey to him often. Every possible diagnosis and cure has been attempted to remedy Jeffrey's problems."

Gilbert poured the last of the bottle into the two tumblers. After a glance down at Bailey, Gilbert decided to pass on the saucer. The old feline had passed out on the floor. He started to laugh when Bailey let out a volley of snorts, followed by a gassy eruption that lifted his tail off the floor.

Hope popped her head around the corner of the doorway. She frowned at Gilbert.

Gilbert, in an attempt to cover up the topic of their conversation, entered into one of his famed Shakespearean debates with

Richard. He declared, "It's pointless to argue the merits of Macbeth in those terms!"

Hope walked into the den followed by Lyndsey. They looked like a pair of young Grannies, dressed as they were in near-matching nightgowns from Grandma Ramsay's closet. Hope looked sternly at Gilbert and scolded him. She asked, "Uncle Gilbert…you're not thrusting another of your Shakespearean debates on poor Richard?"

"Me? I would never." Gilbert protested.

"Meoow." Bailey opened his eyes but did not attempt to sit up.

"My God! What have you done to that poor cat? He's drunk! Look at the poor thing's eyes!" Hope exclaimed.

"Relax Hope," Lyndsey said. She crouched down by Bailey, rubbed the feline's head and explained, "They didn't do anything that you would object to, right Bailey?"

"Meeoow."

"Sorry Bailey," Richard said. He held up the empty bottle and waved it for Bailey to see. "Iiit's empptie."

Bailey dropped his head back down onto the floor.

Hope folded her arms, looked down at the watch on her arm, and asked, "Wouldest thou know the hour it would be?"

Gilbert looked guiltily at the bar clock. He did not answer. There was no need. The clock showed 4:00 am. Gilbert and Richard raised their tumblers and emptied them with one last swallow.

Lyndsey stood up, walked over, and stood by Hope's side. She frowned then broke into a slight snicker. Hope tried to frown but couldn't. Together they gave the two men the look.

"Oh, oh," Richard whispered to Gilbert. "We've been had by double trouble." Through his blurred eyes, he looked back at the girls struggling to suppress their laughter. He stood up and Gilbert followed his lead. The girls turned and walked out of the room ahead of them. Richard stepped forward gingerly; in a step or two he gained his bearings and followed the girls out into the hallway. Gilbert staggered along at his side and the two followed the girls up to the bedroom level.

On the second level, Hope stepped into Grandma Ramsay's bedroom. Lyndsey walked further down the hallway then stood by the door of Grandma's sewing room. She waited for Gilbert to arrive and directed him into the room. The sofa bed had been pulled out and made up. A night-light guided Gilbert to the bed. She glanced down the hallway at Richard and said, "Good morning… Richie." She walked back to Grandma's room.

Richard called out, "Gad night go…ils." He slipped into the guest room and staggered over to the bed. There he sat down, started to remove his pullover sweatshirt, and then simply collapsed back onto the bed. He did not manage to get undressed.

CHAPTER 24

LESS THAN FOUR HOURS LATER, LYNDSEY AND HOPE WERE UP, showered, and dressed. At nine o'clock in the morning, they were eating breakfast and on their second cups of coffee. The bedroom level remained silent.

Hope suggested they drive over to the house and pick up some of Lyndsey's clothes and personal items. Lyndsey remained uncommitted. Hope continued to pitch her suggestion to Lyndsey over a breakfast of coffee and fruit salad. Sensing Hope's determination, Lyndsey relented and agreed to the suggestion.

Lyndsey stood up, went over to the kitchen phone, and picked up the receiver. It felt strange calling her home phone number.

John picked up on the second ring.

"Morning, John here."

"John. It's Lyndsey."

"Ah! It's the lady with newly discovered attitude. Care to give me a demo?"

"Go to Hell! We will be there within the hour…to pick up a change of clothes."

John cut her off, "Come alone. You won't need them—the clothes!"

"Damn you! We'll be over within the hour. Don't be there!"

"Why? Is Richie coming with you?"

"No. No Hope and I will make it on our own. Rich is still sleeping."

"So you took my advice. Treated my baby brother to a little bump and grind. Did he agree to give me half the insurance money? You know—my half?"

The phone line fell silent.

"Well? Lyndsey…I really need that money. It's mine too! They were my parents and grandparents, not just his!"

Lyndsey remained silent. John's words and demands had taken her off guard.

John asked, "Still there Lyndsey? Got my needs straight in your head? No. Don't say anything. Just do what I ask. I'll give you your freedom or whatever it is you want. Just do whatever it takes to convince Richard."

"I can't—I won't do your dirty work, John."

"You can and will if you want things to stay friendly. Meanwhile, I'll set out your luggage."

"No."

"You'll need it for the trip. The trip will give you a chance to get me what I want."

"No. You want it so you take care of it and John, I've decided what I want."

"Have a good trip. Enjoy. Bye, got'ta go. I'm hungry. Get my money." John hung up the receiver.

Lyndsey hung up her end of the line.

"Is everything OK?" Hope asked.

Lyndsey returned to the table and sat down. "No we're done. We never should have been!"

Silence took possession of the room. Lyndsey pondered the casual social outings she'd shared with John during Richard's extended absence while he attended Queen's in Kingston. Yes, she had been lonely. Love letters via snail mail and email, topped off with long distance phone calls don't replace the passion of physical presence. John was physically present, Richard was not. John had pursued her with that physical presence, her physical needs had responded. A tear drop reached her lips. Its salty essence sent a shiver through her body. In her mind she recaptured a passionate embrace she's shared with Richie in their teens. In her heart she rued her rejection of

Richie's sexual advances. If only she pondered, if only I could relive that precious moment.

Hope went to Lyndsey and massaged her neck. She asked, "Can I help?"

Lyndsey failed to respond. Concerned, Hope slapped Lyndsey's shoulder and said, "OK, Girl. Let's get moving."

The drive over to the house in Gilbert's truck passed in silence except for Lyndsey's directions to Hope. Fifteen minutes later, Hope parked the truck in the driveway at the house. A neighbour out cutting his grass did a double take on spotting Gilbert's truck, but relaxed when Lyndsey stepped out of the passenger side.

Lyndsey exchanged greetings and introduced Hope as family from Nova Scotia. She thanked him for his expressed sympathy over the deaths of John's parents and grandparents. Lyndsey asked him to keep an eye out for John and the house, as she would be traveling to Nova Scotia on a short visit. The neighbour wished her a pleasant trip, restarted the lawnmower and set off focused on completing the job at hand, giving his weedless lawn a perfect trim, mowing it to perfection.

Hope followed Lyndsey up to the side door. After Lyndsey had unlocked the door, they stepped inside. The house had been cleaned and looked nothing like it had the night Lyndsey had fled in terror. Upstairs in the master bedroom, John had set out their set of luggage. Lyndsey worked her way through the closets and then the dressers. She picked out a wide variety of clothes and followed Hope's suggestions on several choices. The luggage quickly filled to capacity. Satisfied with her selection, Lyndsey zipped up the compartments. She picked up the biggest piece of luggage. Hope took the smaller one and the overnight bag. They made their way back downstairs and out to the truck. Lyndsey locked the side door then started her return to the truck. A flash of blonde hair and a smiling face caught her eye. Lyndsey stopped as Rebecca her energetic three year old neighbour, popped up and cast Lyndsey's worries aside.

"Missed you Lynds. Where you been hiding?"

Lyndsey sat on the doorstep and greeted Rebecca, "I missed you too Beckie. I've been visiting family at Grandma Ramsay's house."

"Oh. I like Gama Maureeeen."

Lyndsey smiled at her inquisitive and charming neighbour. In her heart she silently admitted that seeing her busily dashing about outside and chatting with inquisitive little Beckie had triggered her thoughts of motherhood. Beckie crawled up on Lyndsey's knee and hugged her. Lyndsey returned the hug and kissed Beckie's cheek.

Beckie slid off Lyndsey's knee and ran back into her yard. She happily shouted, "Got to go, Mommy is baking cookies!"

Lyndsey stood up smiled as she waved goodbye to Beckie. She walked back to the truck where Hope awaited her. The engine was running and the luggage had been loaded into the truck's box. She got in and pulled the door shut.

Hope backed out of the driveway and said, "Sweet little neighbour and I'd say a typical bundle of joy."

Lyndsey laughed lightly and replied, "That and an almost never ending bundle of energy." On the drive back, Lyndsey tried to visualize how she'd ever managed to drive the same route. She couldn't, and if asked to repeat the feat felt certain her death would be the outcome. Silently she admitted the time had arrived to correct a mistake from her past. She resolved to get her driver's license. Their return trip took twenty minutes. They arrived back shortly after 11:00 am.

On entering the house, Lyndsey soon realized both Gilbert and Richard had not yet re-joined the world of the up-and-abouts. It surprised her. Richard had long been labeled the family's legendary early riser and the brunt of many a jovial ribbing.

Hope entered the front door carrying Lyndsey's bags. She asked, "Where do you want these put Lyns?"

"Oh. Let me help."

Lyndsey took the overnight bag that Hope handed to her. She led the way back to the master bedroom. They stopped at the guest room and looked in on Richard. Lyndsey and Hope shook their heads and laughed lightly in response to Richard's robust snoring.

Hope followed Lyndsey into the master bedroom with Lyndsey's luggage. She set them down on the bed and walked out of the room. Lyndsey joined her and they walked to the sewing room. Hope entered the room quietly and whispered, "Time to awaken the sleeping professor."

"Don't do it," Lyndsey pleaded.

Her words reached Hope's ears a second too late. Hope's fingers had reached Gilbert's feet. They flickered up and down the arches.

Hope's sleeping professor reacted to her tickling fingers. He twisted, turned, then lept free of the Sandman's domain. He bolted up and sat on the sofa bed. Both arms swung about wildly in the air around him. In a flash, Gilbert's eyes popped open, and a smile took possession of his face. He dropped his arms down to his side and said, "What? What? Oh. Oh. Good morning princess…what time is it?"

Hope laughed and proclaimed, "He just won't wake up a grouch no matter what I do."

"Morning Princess. And the hour would be?"

"It's now 11:20 am. Time all good men and boys were up and about."

"It can't be. I won't let it."

"Sorry." Hope walked out of the room. In parting, she said, "Bathroom is down the hallway. See you downstairs for breakfast—I mean lunch—shortly."

Lyndsey followed Hope downstairs to the kitchen. Twenty minutes passed before Gilbert joined them in the kitchen. Gilbert had polished off two servings of pancakes and syrup before Richard made an appearance. Together, the men bore the brunt of Hope's friendly, verbal tongue-lashing. Lyndsey kept herself busy over the stove producing what appeared to be a never-ending supply of pancakes. After the last of the pancakes had vanished, she left the stove and joined the others at the table. Their showers, combined with Lyndsey's feed of pancakes, worked a miracle on Gilbert and Richard. Neither one displayed any signs of a hangover.

Gilbert had Hope retrieve his copy of the Nova Scotia *Doers' & Dreamers' Travel Guide* and maps from the truck. They covered Ontario, Quebec, New York State, Vermont, New Hampshire, Maine, and Atlantic Canada. He spent the next half hour working out a travel itinerary for Richard and Lyndsey. Using a highlighter, he marked out the route they should take.

Richard questioned the necessity of taking a ferry across the Bay of Fundy, but Lyndsey over-ruled him. The idea of sailing across the bay from Saint John, New Brunswick to Digby, Nova Scotia appealed to her. This pattern continued through the balance of Gilbert's recommended travel itinerary. He would recommend a must-see tourist attraction, Richard would question the delay then Lyndsey would approve it. Gilbert flipped through the *Doers' & Dreamers' Travel Guide* from cover to cover then closed it. He refolded the maps then handed the guide and maps over to Lyndsey for safe keeping.

Finally, the taboo subject was broached. Gilbert crossed the line and said, "It's been a great time. Hate to be a party-pooper, but unfortunately we don't want to overstay our welcome."

Hope turned pale. She stood up and walked away from the table. Lyndsey joined her. Following a long hug and a burst of tears, they released their embrace of each other and stared at each other through tear filled grieving eyes. Hope wiped away her tears, as did Lyndsey.

Lyndsey said, "Cheer up. Rich and I will be on the road in 12 days. Following Gilbert's directions, we'll be on your doorstep in another two days."

Hope smiled and said, "I know."

Richard and Gilbert left the kitchen and walked out to the front yard. After what seemed an eternity, the two girls joined them out by the truck. Gilbert went to Lyndsey and wrapped his arms around her. This time, Gilbert tried to hide a sob and an accompanying tear, but Lyndsey detected it. She kissed Gilbert's neck and they separated. Then Lyndsey popped up on her tiptoes and kissed his cheek.

She said, "See you real soon…Gilbert."

Gilbert smiled. He did not speak. He went over to Richard and they exchanged a hearty handshake. Again, no words were spoken. He stepped away from Richard. They acknowledged each other with head nods. Gilbert then stepped into the truck and slid behind the steering wheel. Hope sat opposite him in the passenger seat. The engine started. Gilbert slipped the transmission into drive and released the brake and the truck moved forward. He extended his left arm out of the window and waved to Richard and Lyndsey, but did not look back at them. Each had their own thoughts on how difficult it was to leave their family. Even though they were newly-acquainted family members, the hurt ran deep and pulled at their heartstrings.

Hope did not wave. She sat beside Gilbert and stared straight ahead. Gilbert stopped and filled the gas tank at a self-serve station, then drove to the hotel, picked up their luggage, and checked out of their rooms. The hotel bill had been paid in full prior to their checkout. Silently, Gilbert thanked Richard. Hope had remained in the truck while Gilbert checked out. From the hotel parking lot, he drove across town and caught the express highway to Toronto. Traffic was light and soon they were on the 401 eastbound towards Oshawa.

After the truck had disappeared from sight, Lyndsey went into the house and disappeared up into the attic. Richard did not see her again until she re-emerged, composed, an hour later. Neither Richard nor Lyndsey spoke. She picked up the *Doers' & Dreamers' Travel Guide* and went into the den. There, she mentally followed Gilbert's purple pickup truck along its route. Richard stepped outside, retrieved the Garden Claw from the shed and busied himself working the soil in Grandma Ramsay's flower beds. An hour later, he responded to Lyndsey's call to dinner. *Yes*, he thought, *staying behind is always hardest.*

CHAPTER 25

NEXT DAY LYNDSEY PASSED TIME WORKING IN THE FLOWER gardens around the house. Richard drove into town and met John for breakfast. There, he tried to work out his pent up anger over John's actions. He updated John on the pending trip to Nova Scotia. John updated him on the latest details concerning Tessa. Her attorney had met with Roger and served papers that initiated a paternity suit. Money played a large part, but John did not reveal the amounts to Richard. He did allude to a possible solution; a solution that required up-front money. Money John sorrowfully confessed he had no means of accessing. Roger froze my business credit cards. I never bothered getting personal cards. Access to funds we inherited will take a while to work through the processing stages required.

"It's ironic Rich. I lost Lyndsey because I refused to discuss her desire to start a family."

"Give it some time."

"No. I've been offered a way out; a solution."

"What? What could Tessa want of us now?" Richard asked.

"Not us, me, marriage."

"That's bigamy. You have a wife!"

"She…Tessa isn't the evil bitch you might think. For God's sake Rich, it's my child."

"You've seen her?"

"No. But we've talked. She'll drop the paternity suit and marry me." He added, "If I come up with a hundred thousand. No, Rich. It's—not what you think. It's a trust fund for my son or daughter."

Richard frowned and shrugged his shoulders. He said, "So you trust her and you're just going to toss Lyndsey aside?"

"The minute she learns about Tessa's condition, it's over. I can't fool myself. I blew it. What else can I do?"

"Hold off till I get that overhaul done. Help me work it through then come with us. Get away from this place and let Roger handle things."

John frowned. Meekly, he confessed, "Can't do it Rich. You know me. I need to be in control, at the helm."

Richard thought to himself *it doesn't sound like you're in total control here, Bro.* He pulled out one of Gilbert's business cards. He said, "Here's where we'll be staying at Gilbert's." On the back, he wrote, 'Call me…Rich.' He passed the card to John.

John read Gilbert's credentials. He smiled and said, "Impressive."

"He's a good man John, been a godsend for me. Give him a try."

John pulled out his wallet and slipped Gilbert's card into the billfold. "Go," he urged Richard. "Get that overhaul done and go. Enjoy your trip, if things should take a turn for the better, then…maybe. But, just maybe."

"That's all I'm asking. John, please talk to Roger. Review your options. Let Rog take care of things. It's what he does!"

"Get out'ta here, Rich."

"Talk to Roger, John."

Richard stood up. The two brothers exchanged a firm handshake. A thought popped up in Richard's mind. *Why demand a trust fund? A five percent trust fund was provided for both his and John's future children?* He held the thought in silence, turned and walked out of the restaurant. From there, Richard drove over to the marina and lost himself in the engine overhaul job. Time slipped by quickly.

Over supper on the third day Lyndsey took a step towards achieving her new goal. She asked a favour of Richard, "Rich, while you're in town tomorrow would you..." Her determination stumbled.

"Would I what?" Richard asked.

A silent pause passed then Lyndsey ask, "I'm going to go for my driver's licence. Would you pick up a driver's handbook for me?"

Richard smiled and said, "Done!"

"I want to review the dos and don'ts of the road, then get my beginner's permit before we head down east. Maybe take a lesson or two before we leave."

"Fantastic!" Richard answered. "I will pick it up tomorrow."

True to his word Richard handed Lyndsey her handbook on returning to the house the next evening. Three days later, he drove Lyndsey to the Ministry of Transportation Office; she passed her exam and received her beginner's permit. Each day while Richard worked Lyndsey booked sessions with a driving instructor. Burnt clutches faded from Lyndsey's memories of lessons in Richard's Volkswagen Beetle. She opted to bypass the clutch option and go with an automatic transmission.

On day twelve Richard left the marina and drove to his townhouse. There, he packed a set of luggage to take on the trip to Nova Scotia. He called Lyndsey at the house and explained his whereabouts. She reviewed the contents of his luggage. Richard answered, "Yes" to every question Lyndsey asked. He laughingly said, "Goodbye." Then unzipped the luggage, went back to the dresser, and pulled out extra underwear and socks to add to his traveling wardrobe. Richard listened to Lyndsey's voice replay itself in his head. He followed her instructions fully. In the bathroom, he picked out a razor, replacement blades, shaving cream, hair brush, shampoo and a deodorant stick. He laughed then added a toothbrush and paste to his collection of personal care items.

Back in the bedroom, he placed the items in his overnight bag. Satisfied that he'd followed Lyndsey's motherly suggestions to a T, he closed the bags and carried them down to the front door. A quick walk about placed him in front of his exotic goldfish aquarium. Duty and guilt called out and he fed them. Two quick phone calls later, Richard found himself back on the road. One call informed the local police of his pending absence. The second extended the job of the neighbourhood's house sitter. He had hired young Jenny the day after the accident. Since then, she had been house-sitting the townhouse and tending to the needs of Richard's exotic goldfish. Richard stepped on the gas and raced back to the house and Lyndsey. Richard finally started to feel the excitement of the trip take hold.

Lyndsey walked towards the door to the attic. Some would call it a woman's intuition. However to Lyndsey the words of Grace Ramsay's Uncle Richard and memories of kind words often shared with Grandfather Ramsay—William were calling out to her. She answered the calls. Suddenly Lyndsey found herself standing in front of Grandfather Ramsay's old desk in the attic. In her mind Uncle Richard's words echoed, '*All would have been well had we done right! Returned the earth to where it belonged ... firmly packed above that demon from Hell. But no! You'd have nothing to do with that John. No, you grabbed his hand and bashed his fingers trying to get your hands on that rosary. The Demon screamed and howled while seeking to protect the rosary and the treasure it had been charged with protecting.*' Lyndsey froze. A moment then two passed. She relaxed as William Ramsay's voice spoke in her mind to a youthful preteen Lyndsey, '*Sweetheart one day this special rosary will be yours. A gift untarnished by the passages of time. A gift that one day will touch you with a love beyond your wildest expectations. A gift that wi...*' Lyndsey watched her hands reach out and open the desk drawer. Her hands extended to the back left corner of the drawer. They hesitated then her fingers touched and picked up a jeweled rosary. A love held within the rosary touched her heart. Tears trickled down her cheeks. Suddenly Lyndsey found herself standing in the kitchen on the main floor surrounded by the aroma of a roasted chicken dinner.

Within minutes Richard arrived back at the house. He entered the house and walked into the kitchen. Quickly the aromas of dinner were topped when Lyndsey embraced him and pressed her tear stained cheeks to his chest. The embrace ended. Lyndsey pulled away from Richard. She chided, "Dinner will be on the table in five minutes. You'd best wash up, while I set the table. No further words were exchanged. Richard headed to the bathroom, he returned washed and ready to treat his taste buds to the source of the kitchen's pleasing aromas. Over dinner, Lyndsey reviewed their travel plans aided by a highway map and her *Nova Scotia Doers' & Dreamers' Travel Guide*. The evening passed quickly. Richard simply listened and nodded approval to all questions surrounding their travel plans.

The anticipated excitement of an early morning departure greeted Lyndsey and Richard with the morning's sunrise. He claimed the shower first. After a quick shower the aroma of freshly brewed coffee drew him to the kitchen. He relaxed and savored his first coffee of the morning. Overhead, he heard the water stop running and the shower doors slide open. An image of Lyndsey stepping out of the shower jumped to the forefront of his mind. Droplets of hot water trickled down her breasts. Richard reacted. A tingle ran through his groin. He blinked then sighed. The Lyndsey in his mind had grabbed a towel and wrapped it firmly about herself. The images played with Richard's imagination.

"Boo!" Lyndsey exclaimed as she walked into the kitchen.

"Good morning, Sunshine. Are we ready?"

Lyndsey simply answered with a smile. Both opted for a light breakfast. Richard relaxed with a second coffee while Lyndsey rushed about clearing off the last items on her pre departure *To-do List*. With her last item completed. Lyndsey stood in the kitchen doorway and watched Richard finish off a quick clean up of the kitchen as he turned towards her, Lyndsey smiled and exclaimed, "I'm ready! Let's hit the road."

On passing Lyndsey in the doorway Richard hugged her lightly then grinned sheepishly on spotting her luggage stacked neatly near the front door. Bailey eyed them casually from the den. Bailey then strutted into the kitchen glanced back at Richard and hit him up for a meal.

"Meow—Meow."

Richard watched Bailey make short work of the offering: a can of chunky tuna. It suddenly dawned on him. Who would take care of Bailey in his absence? Unable to find a long-term solution to the problem, he decided on the quick fix. Bailey would accompany them on the trip. After all, Grandpa Ramsay would never approve of a pet hotel.

He went out to the hallway and picked up Lyndsey's luggage. From there, he carried it out and deposited it in the back of his SUV. He wanted to make sure that he arranged his and Lyndsey's luggage to allow space for Bailey.

Ring...ring.

"Hi John, What's up? Have you decided to accept Gilbert's offer.?"

"No. Not now bro. I just wanted to touch base before you head off down the road. A lot has happened to us, to our family over a very short time. I called to apologize. Lyndsey won't talk to me. I cannot blame her. I've been a total ass! I screwed up our lives and hurt the people who loved me."

"Yes, John. You did. But don't burden yourself with all the blame. I coul..."

"No Rich I really screwed up. After breakfast this morning, I visited Mom, Dad, Grandmother and Granddad at their gravesides. Had a soul searching talk and with their blessings I'm ready to move on. Accept my actions and take ownership. I swear bro I'll make things right."

Richard hesitated than replied, "The horror you lived through at the accident, John don't take all the blame on yourself. I should have be..."

No Rich. I was and I own it. I just want to say. Relax enjoy your visit with our extended family. Give them my blessings, and I'll see you soon back at work. See you soon little Bro."

The line disconnected. Richard returned his cell phone to his jersey pocket and returned to the house. Bailey did not greet him. He walked back into the kitchen and caught Lyndsey snacking on a fistful of chocolate chip cookies.

"The…y're go…good. Want some?"

Richard laughed and declined. He said, "No," then asked, "If they're so good, why the guilty look?"

Lyndsey stuffed the last cookie into her mouth. She chewed it quickly then in a series of gulps swallowed the evidence. With a grin, she said, "It's the cookie jar syndrome."

"Which is?"

Lyndsey walked up to Richard and kissed his cheek. She boldly stated, "The old hand in the cookie jar. Don't tell me you've never been caught?"

Richard stared blankly back at Lyndsey.

She retorted, "OK. So maybe I was a little bit slower than you." Then Lyndsey smirked on recalling the cookie jar of Richie's youth and its unrestricted access.

Richard did not answer. He too recalled how the cookie jar of his youth had never been off-limits. He had never experienced the *'cookie jar syndrome'* Lyndsey had offered in her defence. Instead of prolonging Lyndsey's guilt, Richard changed the subject entirely. It seemed an opportune time to spring on her the news of Bailey's travel plans.

"I put your bags in the SUV."

"Give me five minutes and we'll be on our way."

"OK. That'll give me time to get Bailey settled in."

"Say what?"

"Bailey. He's coming along for the ride."

"Richard W. Ramsay! Have you ever traveled with a cat in the car?"

"No. But...but, Grandpa would want it. So you see...there's no choice. We'll have to take Bailey along. Besides, the old boy will make a great chaperone."

"And we wouldn't want him to go hungry."

"I would never deny Grampa Ramsay's buddy a hankering or a need!"

Lyndsey shrugged her shoulders. At this point, she was not about to risk delaying their departure any longer. With a grin and a twinkle in her eye, she accepted Richard's decision and simply said, "OK!" She went up to the bedroom and grabbed her jacket off the bed. Then she stopped in the bathroom, gave her hair one last fix up, and rejoined Richard at the front door.

Richard held Bailey in his arms. He passed Lyndsey the house keys and asked her to lockup after they'd stepped outside. He walked into the dining room and opened the drawer of the dining hutch. On spotting the drawer's well organized contents Richard grinned. In the back corner he spotted his Grandparents' passports.

Underneath them he found Bailey's Veterinarian's papers and stuffed them in the hip pocket of his jeans. Silently, he resolved to working towards downsizing the contents of his townhome's catch all hutch drawer. Confident that they were ready to hit the road, Richard joined Lyndsey by the front door. He smiled at her then stepped outside.

Lyndsey followed Richard outside and locked the door. She met him at the SUV and slid into the passenger seat. Silently, she watched Richard get into the driver's seat with Bailey. The driver's door closed and the three occupants of the SUV sat in silence.

Richard twisted around and set Bailey down in the spot he'd prepared for him earlier. He then started the engine. "MEEEEoow." It started. "Meoow...Meeeeow." Richard bit his lip and held a straight face.

Lyndsey quietly picked up the *Doers' Dreamers' Travel Guide* and flipped through its pages. The SUV started to move. Bailey's cries grew deeper and more desperate. Lyndsey glanced up into the rear view mirror. This time she bit her lip, but couldn't suppress her laughter. The look on Bailey's face was priceless. A flood of childhood memories added energy to her laughter. She recalled sitting in the back seat of her Dad's 85 Volkswagen Jetta. They were on their way to the family cottage. Mitsy, the family's black and white cat, clung fiercely to the top of the back seat above her head. Mitsy's face displayed the same distraught look that now adorned the face of Bailey. "MEEEEoow." Lyndsey snapped back to the present.

With a straight face, she recalled for Richard the advice her Dad had freely shared over the years with fellow travelers and cat owners, "Accelerate quickly. Hold a constant speed, and sooner or later he'll settle down. Or, you'll arrive at your destination."

"Thank you, Lyndsey. Your Dad was a very wise man."

Lyndsey broke down anew in laughter. She recovered and said, "Wise, yes. But...I could never count the number of times he threatened to toss Mitsy out the car window. Thank God for Mom."

Traffic thinned out shortly before they reached Oshawa. Richard never once threatened to toss Bailey out the window. Somewhere between Oshawa and Trenton, Bailey dozed off into a peaceful sleep. At Cornwall, Richard crossed over into the USA. Richard handed their passports and Bailey's papers to the border guard who checked them over. On viewing Bailey's Veterinarian's papers the guard grinned on spotting Bailey meowing loudly and feverously with a look of pure anguish on his face. He handed their passports and Bailey's papers back to Richard and welcomed them to the USA. Lyndsey looked in the rear-view mirror as they drove away from the guard's quarters. The reflection revealed a guard doubled over in a fit of laughter.

At the Vermont border, Richard pulled into a service station/ restaurant. Bailey did not budge. He had embraced the sandman in the depths of a euphoric catnap, having been treated to a healthy ration of rum in New York State. Richard filled the SUV's gas tank then waited with Bailey until Lyndsey returned with their take-out meals. He removed Bailey from the SUV and they shared Bailey sitting duties while they dined at a picnic table in the grassy park like setting by the parking lot. The sandman's captive slept contentedly during their dining experience. Before heading out anew, he purchased several cans of cat food, a package of catnip and several bottles of chilled water. Lyndsey frowned on not spotting a can opener among his purchases. She slipped back into the service station/restaurant and returned with a camper's utility multipurpose can opener. Bailey awoke on their return to the SUV. He refused to eat, but did eagerly welcome a second rum ration. Fifteen hours after leaving Newmarket, they re-entered Canada, passing from Calais, Maine into St. Stephen's, New Brunswick. Ahead lay the city of Saint John and the ferry to Digby, Nova Scotia.

CHAPTER 26

RICHARD DROVE AHEAD AND JOINED THE LINE OF VEHICLES QUEUED up for the next ferry. At the registration centre, the gentleman had been very friendly, and on confirming Richard's plate number, had referred to him by his name, then handed him a prepaid passage voucher Gilbert had arranged on his trip home. Bailey slept soundly in the back of the vehicle. The only sounds he made were the occasional snore.

Richard returned to the vehicle. Lyndsey had joined Bailey and fallen into a deep sleep. The gentleman parked in front of Richard joined him.

"Nice chariot you're riding there. What part of O'tario do you hail from?"

"Newmarket. It's north of…"

"Taranta...Been there. Uncle Wayne's the name and yours?"

"Richard. Richard Ramsay."

"Mmmm. Visiting family?"

"Yes. Matter of fact we are."

Uncle Wayne peeked inside Richard's vehicle at a napping Lyndsey. "Little lady all tuckered out?"

Richard smiled. He said, "Yes. It's been a long day."

"Live in Newmarket long?"

"Born and raised there."

"Then you must know The Blue Buz—"

"The Blue Buzzard! Yes. Good food. Good company."

"That's the one. Stopped in there last week for a chow-down and met an interesting chap, a Walter Lizards."

Could it be, Richard pondered then asked, "A short, balding, friendly chap?"

Uncle Wayne laughed. He said, "Sure'nuff did, a strange little duck or should I say lizard, a man with woman problems I figured."

Richard grew more curious. He asked, "What makes you say that?"

"Any man tossing back triple doses of the rum. Well, let's just say it showed."

"Mr. Lizards...Walter is our family's lawyer."

"Now, that accounts for that black briefcase he kept by his side. He stood out because of a friend we have in common. Gilbert McClaken."

"No wa—"

"Got'ta go laddie. Ferry's loading up, maybe later, on board. We'll strike her up anew."

Richard watched Uncle Wayne climb into his rust spotted 80ish Honda Civic. He jumped back into his vehicle and started up the engine, then followed Uncle Wayne's Civic and their line of cued cars up into the ferry. Lyndsey stirred but did not wake up. Bailey let out a series of snorts and a fart then settled back down. Richard followed his line of cued vehicles and boarded the ferry. Richard touched the brake, then came to a full stop when directed to do so. He ended up parked at the front of the second row of vehicles. The 80ish Honda Civic and its driver ended up parked at the tail end of the first row of vehicles. Richard hoped to meet up again with the gentleman. He'd enjoyed their short chat before they'd boarded the ferry to Digby. In a strange way he felt drawn to the man. In less time than Richard thought it would take, the Princess of Acadia's staff directed its passengers and cued vehicles on board.

Lyndsey stirred then opened her eyes.

"Time to wake up, sleepy head. We're safely aboard the ferry."

"Why didn't you wake me?"

"No time. Besides I got to chatting with an interesting chap in the parking lot."

Lyndsey stretched her arms then rubbed the sleep out of her eyes. She asked, "How's Bailey?"

"Shhh! The beast is out, hopefully, for the duration."

"I warned you."

"Did your Dad ever make good on his promise?"

"No. Dad loved that cat!"

Richard picked up the old diary off the dash and placed it under the driver's seat. He'd resolved himself to living in the moment on the ferry crossing to Digby. That resolve included a desire to embrace Lyndsey's excitement over their trip and their reconnection to family through Gilbert and Hope. He felt a connection to Gilbert and Hope had definitely bonded with Lyndsey. He gently released the latch of his door and signaled Lyndsey to follow suit. First, he stepped out onto the deck of the ferry then after he'd closed his door, Lyndsey joined him. Bailey remained comatose in the back of the vehicle. Richard wondered if the old feline needed attention. Bam! The driver of a vehicle behind them closed a door with a thunderous slam! Bailey's eyes popped open and he stood up and started to plead loudly to Richard. Lyndsey spotted a sign and pointed it out to Richard, 'DO NOT LEAVE YOUR PETS in YOUR VEHICLE during CROSSINGS'; she smiled on spotting Bailey calling out for attention. Richard rescued Bailey. Soon they found themselves up in the lounge. Hungry, Richard decided to grab a bite to eat. Lyndsey passed on the offer of real food and settled for an ice-cream cone. She rescued Richard by taking Bailey while he set off in search of food and ice-cream. After Richard had finished eating all but a few chunks of the haddock in his order of fish and chips, he purchased Lyndsey's ice cream cone and returned to the lounge. He sat down on a bench next to Lyndsey. Bailey deserted Lyndsey. The aroma of fish and ice cream drew him affectionately to Richard's lap where he purred contentedly in anticipation of the meal his taste buds anticipated. Lyndsey stood to distract Bailey and accepted her ice cream cone from Richard. The fish overpowered Bailey's love of ice cream. Each piece of chunky haddock Richard offered up quickly vanished. Bailey savored the last bite before swallowing it. He vigorously rubbed his head on Richard's chest confirming Bailey's kinship and commitment to a lifelong admiration of Richard.

Lyndsey sat back down next to Richard. She reached over and affectionately rubbed Bailey's head. Bailey ignored her until he spotted the half eaten ice cream cone that held Lyndsey's attention. Bailey quickly moved over to Lyndsey's lap and purred affectionately while eying the ice cream cone. She managed to enjoy one last bite before ceding ownership of the cone to Bailey. Like the fish, the cone and its ice cream quickly vanished. Lyndsey looked at her watch and with a smile said, "We'll be entering the Gut within the half hour."

Richard remained speechless and stared into Lyndsey's blue eyes. Inside he fought an urge to reach out and embrace the woman his childhood sweetheart had become. Memories of holding her in his arms and floating over countless dance floors raised the intensity of his urges. He glanced down at her rosette coloured lips and started to move his lips towards the desire and passion burning within him. Lyndsey reached out and passed Bailey back to his master, then stood and walked over to the lounge windows.

Richard froze, accepted Bailey, and stared longingly over at Lyndsey standing by the window. He stood and secured Bailey in his arms, then joined Lyndsey at the window. Looking out of the ferry's window, he asked, "What's the Gut?"

"Oh. Its proper name is the Digby Gut, the entrance to the Annapolis Basin. You should check out our Nova Scotia *Doers' & Dreamers' Travel Guide*; it's loaded with local names and places and great details. We'll be arriving at the ferry terminal real soon."

"OK."

"What? We're this close and it's just an OK? You will soon return home to your family's roots?" Lyndsey questioned. She continued, "We'll be setting foot in the land of your ancestors…and all you can say is 'OK?'"

Richard looked anew into Lyndsey's eyes, then stepped forward and hugged her. He whispered, "It's weird. I should be elated. But

I feel strange, uncertain of what awaits us, yet excited and eager to reconnect with Gilbert. I feel drawn to him. Could he be the Uncle I never ha..."

Lyndsey embraced Richard, Bailey caught in their embrace struggled to escape. She released Richard and pulled away. Lightly, she chided him, "Lighten up, Rich. We'll be sitting down with Gilbert and Hope for supper tonight. It's great. I can hardly wait."

"You're right. We should've put that diary back in Grandma's trunk and left it there."

"No. It ended up in our hands for a reason."

"Ah, a reason for everything, and everything in its time has a reason."

"So true, and a positive serving of life's energies awaits each of us!"

Richard stepped up to Lyndsey. He placed his arm over her shoulder and said, "Let's go catch a glimpse of the Digby Gut and forget this discussion."

Lyndsey did not respond. She followed Richard's lead and walked with him out onto the outside deck where passengers had gathered to take in the view. The water had changed from a dark blackish-blue to a mystic-green. The ferry sent a frothy white spray out over the water. In the background, cameras clicked and captured images of the time and place for their owners. Lyndsey sighed. She had left her camera below, under the front seat. Richard spotted his companion from the ferry dock in Saint John. He raised his hand and waved in his direction. Uncle Wayne caught sight of them, walked over, and joined Lyndsey and Richard.

"Hi. I'll presume you've both enjoyed your Bay of Fundy crossing. It's Richard, right?" He then reached out scratched and massaged Bailey's head then commented, "Your furry traveling companion travels well."

Richard nodded, smiled to acknowledge the praise of Bailey's traveling poise. Richard spotted the camera and asked, "Could you snap a picture of us? You could drop it off at Gilbert's. We'll be staying there on our visit." He pulled Lyndsey over against the ferry's railing. There, he placed his hand around her hip and pulled her snugly up against his side. Richard smirked. Lyndsey reached up and tickled his lower chin. A smile broke out on both their faces and coincided with a series of camera clicks. Lyndsey stepped away from Richard and started to thank the cameraman, but the overhead speakers interrupted her. The voice requested all passengers return to their vehicles for disembarking. In a flash, their photographer vanished. Lyndsey took Richard's hand and said, "It's time we joined the others and followed them down to the vehicle."

Lyndsey walked at Richard's side. Soon they stood by Richard's SUV. The ferry trip from Saint John to Digby neared its conclusion. Richard offered no protest. Lyndsey looked about and smiled at an elderly couple also returning to their vehicle. A tingle ran up her spine. Strangely, it almost felt like a homecoming. Gilbert and Hope had spoken highly and at great length of Nova Scotia's beauty. Her first look upon its land had just passed. The view from the ferry had filled the expectations set out by Gilbert. Those same expectations would later be exceeded when they drove off the ferry and officially entered Nova Scotia.

Richard unlocked Lyndsey's door. She opened it and quietly slipped into her seat. Richard pushed against the door. It closed without disturbing Bailey. Bailey purred contentedly in Richard's arms and showed no signs of an exit from dreamland he had re-entered. Richard patted Bailey and waved to Lyndsey. She responded, reached over and unlocked the driver's door, and then sat back upright in the passenger seat. Once successfully inside, Richard passed Bailey to Lyndsey, then engaged his seat belt. Each had their own thoughts and remained silent as they sat in the SUV. After a short time had passed, the SUV jerked lightly sideways. Lyndsey turned and smiled at Richard. It signaled the docking of the Princess of Acadia at her Nova Scotia destination. "MEEEEoow. Meoow…Meeeeow." The gig had expired. Bailey moved. The old feline stood up on Lyndsey's lap. He looked at Richard ... Meow... meow...meo... Bailey called out to Richard for sympathy. Richard picked him up and rubbed his head.

Ahead, the bow of the ferry opened, and the ferry's crew engaged the exit ramps. Sunshine hit the SUV's windshield and those of the vehicles parked beside and to the rear of them. He reached for the ignition and engaged the starter. The SUV's engine roared to life along with its neighbours. He passed Bailey over to Lyndsey. Akin to a finely tuned timepiece, each vehicle in turn accelerated and drove towards daylight and the exit ramp. The 72 km ferry run had come to another successful conclusion. Richard flipped his sun visor down and blocked out the sun's bright rays. On leaving the ferry, the procession of vehicles exited the ferry compound and headed down the highway.

With bright seawater to their left and tall ancient pine trees to their right, the SUV carried Lyndsey and Richard closer to their destination. Digby Pines Resort appeared on Lyndsey's side of the highway. A short distance later, they turned and proceeded towards the town of Digby. On entering the town, a brightly painted array of businesses and homes greeted their eyes. The site of a main street waterfront park caught Richard's eye. He tapped the brake pedal and signaled his intentions to turn into one of the angled Main Street parking spots. Traffic cleared, Richard turned the SUV hard left, and guided it into a vacant parking spot.

Lyndsey passed Bailey back to Richard. She opened her door then jumped out. She looked to Richard, smiled, and then slammed her door shut. She ran over to the gazebo that stood in the park and overlooked the water then walked over to the handrail that looked out over the waterfront. She sighed. The water was crystal clear, no algae or pollution in this water. Off to her left, a large dock extended out into the basin. The watermarks on its pilings indicated the tide to be midway between a high and low state.

Bailey delayed Richard's exit. Once successfully outside with Bailey secure in his arms, he walked up behind Lyndsey. Lyndsey's father had earned Richard's respect over the past twenty-four hours. Pet ownership had taken on a new meaning.

He stepped aside, then forward, and side-by-side they looked out over the glistening water. Several small fishing and pleasure boats dotted the water's surface. They bobbed gently on the water. Tied securely to their mooring lines, they did not move. Alongside the dock, the larger fishing boats lay at rest.

"Look at the water marks on those pilings, Richard."

"Yes. I read about these Fundy tides, they're the highest tides in the world."

"It should be illegal for a province so small to possess so much of our country's natural beauty."

"It puts a new spin on the term 'have not.' These riches don't know the meaning of a price tag."

"Gilbert warned us about this."

Bailey contentedly gazed out over the water and smiled into the gentle sea breezes that embraced the threesome.

"Yes, he did. It's amazing. Those large boats—I mean, the trawlers look at the high water mark the trawlers are at least twenty feet below the high tide water markings.

"Yes! There are so many breathtaking scenes to take in and too short a time in which to enjoy it all.

Richard turned away from the rail. He looked over at the small building attached to the gazebo by a wooden walkway.

"Look Lyndsey, a tourist bureau. Let's take a look inside."

Lyndsey walked over to his side and together they crossed the walkway then entered the tourist bureau. Once inside, they were greeted by a friendly guide. Richard signed both their names in the guest book and added Bailey's in printed form. It made him feel good. He liked its look: *'Richard and Lyndsey Ramsay— with chaperone aka Bailey Ramsay, Newmarket, Ontario'* Richard explained their destination to the guide.

The guide asked, "Visiting family?"

"Yes," Richard answered. He explained, "Here to spend time with an uncle and his family. They live in East River near Chester."

She reached over and patted-fluffed Bailey's head, then guided them to a section of pamphlets and information that covered the area known locally as the South Shore. She then suggested, "We have several very nice bed and breakfasts, which you may find to your liking. That is, if you plan to spend the day in our charming little town?"

Lyndsey answered first, "Yes. That would give us a nice break."

Richard added, "We'd best call Uncle Gilbert before we commit."

Lyndsey pulled her cell phone out of her shoulder bag then stepped outside the tourist bureau for privacy.

Richard shrugged, turned to their guide, and said, "Problem solved, any recommendations?" He pause smirked then added "Oops! We're traveling with a chaperone, Bailey Grandpa's cat. Are pets ...?"

She replied, "Best to look at the brochures. Each one is unique and offers different features and amenities. Some may be more to your liking and needs." A smile ensued then she added, "Several welcome pets of exemplary character."

Lyndsey returned with a smile on her face. She said, "He's a little disappointed, but has suggested a route to follow after we've had a good night's rest."

"OK. Here are some brochures of some local bed and breakfast establishments. I'm a little partial to these two."

Richard passed the brochures to Lyndsey. She glanced over the top two and passed the others back to Richard. She said, "Looks good to me. I'll call the *Ocean Hillside Bed & Breakfast* first and see if they have a vacancy and would welcome our traveling companion."

Richard placed the brochures back into the wall rack in their appropriate places. He walked over to the counter and struck up a short conversation with the guide. The conversation did not last long. Lyndsey's first phone call secured their accommodations for the night. She smiled and announced, "We're booked at the *Ocean Hillside Bed & Breakfast.* They had a cancellation 10 minutes before I called. Perfect timing and meant to be."

The guide replied, "The extensive flower gardens, view of the water…well, you'll see. You'll love it, Mr. and Mrs Ramsay."

Richard and Lyndsey bid their farewells, gave thanks to their friendly guide, and parted company. The drive up to Shore Road passed quickly, too quickly for Richard. The parting words of the tourist bureau guide echoed in Richard's mind and heart, 'The extensive flower gardens, view of the water…well, you'll see. You'll love it, Mr. and Mrs Ramsay.' They arrived at their destination quicker than anticipated. Richard's thoughts lingered on the guide's words. Their guide had understated the beauty of the gardens. On driving up to the house, both Richard and Lyndsey wasted little time in stepping out of the vehicle. They took a short walk about the grounds and its beautiful gardens, but inevitably both their eyes would wander off towards the blue-green waters of Annapolis Basin below. Fifteen minutes later, they stood outside the front door and their hosts greeted them. The host helped Richard retrieve their overnight bags and luggage. Bailey introduced himself to the host, who insisted that Richard bring Bailey up to the house. Richard and Lyndsey settled into an upstairs room. Bailey settled in quickly; he claimed a perch on their bedroom window ledge. Richard made a quick side trip back to the SUV and retrieved Bailey's toiletry—litter box. The room presented them with a breath-taking view of the grounds below, back dropped by a blue-green sea and a cloudless, blue Scotian sky.

Following an evening spent in the company of their host, Richard and Lyndsey settled into their room for the night. Lyndsey took the bed at Richard's insistence. She tossed about for a moment or two then she entered dreamland. He opted to spend the night in a large billowy sofa chair set in front of the window. Sleep eluded him. Having just driven 12 hours with the woman who'd once been his teenage sweetheart at his side, his emotions raced between anger, regrets and amorous turmoil. He fought off an urge to turn and catch a glimpse of Lyndsey asleep on the bed. The day's journey eased his emotional battle. The journey had taken its toll. Richard's eyes blinked but quickly lost their battle with fatigue. Next morning, both awoke refreshed and eager to begin their journey anew. After separate trips to the bathroom for showers, a shave for Richard and a blow dry for Lyndsey's hair, they descended the staircase. The scent of freshly brewed coffee drew them towards the kitchen.

At the entrance to the kitchen, their hostess called out a hearty greeting, "Good morning all. Coffee is on the counter. Mugs are in the cupboard overhead. Help yourselves. My husband is out tending to the gardens. Feel free to take your coffee out on the porch."

"Thank you. And good morning, too," Richard answered.

Lyndsey busied herself at the counter. She turned about with two mugs of fresh coffee, one in each hand, and asked, "Which way to the porch? Sounds like a great way to start off the morning."

"Straight down the hallway. You can't miss it. We have fresh fruit salad and omelettes for breakfast. If you prefer your eggs another way...the choice be yours."

"Fruit salad is great for me," Lyndsey answered.

Richard asked, "Cheese and mushrooms included in the omelet?"

"If they weren't they are now," the hostess answered. She continued, "Enjoy your coffee out on the porch. The view will captivate you. Breakfast will be ready in fifteen minutes."

Richard followed Lyndsey down the hallway. At the doorway, he opened it, stepped aside, and waited for Lyndsey to pass through. He followed her out onto the porch. Lyndsey sat down on a loveseat. Richard accepted the coffee mug Lyndsey held out to him then sat down at her side. They sat in silence. Both stared out over the yard and beyond to the blue-green waters on the basin. The fifteen minutes passed by too quickly. The breakfast exceeded their expectations. Bailey received a personal invite and joined them for breakfast. He wasted little time in clearing off the plate of fresh fish presented to him. On its conclusion, Richard retrieved their overnight bags and luggage from their room and Lyndsey settled their bill for lodgings. On thanking their evening's host and hostess, they set off fresh on the last leg of their journey to East River, Nova Scotia.

Lyndsey relayed Gilbert's directions, and Richard followed them to a tee. Outside Digby, they caught the 101 and proceeded past Smith's Cove, Bear River, Clementsport, and Upper Clements to the junction of Hwy 8. There, they exited onto Hwy 8 and headed cross country to Liverpool. At Caledonia, they stopped. Richard gassed up the SUV and purchased several postcards. Lyndsey did a short walkabout to stretch her legs. The stop lasted ten minutes. The next destination was to be Liverpool, *'The Port of Privateers'* government-sanctioned pirates, however, at Highway 103 Lyndsey directed Richard towards Hope's must see point of interest a secluded beach along the less popular stretches of the South Shore south and west of Liverpool. She then returned to reading the diary's last pages.

The pages held her captive. Through tears that flowed freely she stared at Grace Ramsay's last entry dated August 18th, 1798—the day young Grace's entries abruptly stopped. She would have been on the cusp of experiencing and embracing her womanhood and the physical development of her body. Young Grace's writing pined on the loss of her Father. He had deserted his family, leaving Grace, her brother Tom and mother Sarah in the care of his brother Richard. Sarah never remarried. Richard willingly supported them in the role of a loving uncle. His white hair soft, straight and flowing never regained the robust, flowing black curls that Grace had so dearly loved. A closing entry was written by her brother young Tom Ramsay. Lyndsey sensed Tom had been deeply saddened in writing the words. The words now leaped forward through the ages and savagely pulled on Lyndsey's heartstrings. Tom told of Grace's foolish actions that had suddenly ended his sister's life. Saddened over the loss of their Father, she had stolen away in the family's boat and headed out in search of the island that had destroyed their family and deprived her of their Father's presence and love. The boat had been recovered overturned in East River Bay. Grace's body had washed ashore days later.

Determined to embrace happiness and the reconnection of their families, Lyndsey closed the diary and slid it under her seat. With a handful of tissues she wiped away her tears. Determined to stave off her sadness, Lyndsey closed her eyes and called up memories of happier times. Flashes of times spent in the care and companionship of her parents Liam and Letitia, quickly added a smile to her face. Next she embraced images of her and a youthful Richie in the sandbox. Beckie, her little blonde next door neighbour, dashed through her thoughts shouting, *'Lyndssi—Lynssie come plays wit me!'* Hope's laughter echoed loudly followed by a hearty laugh from Gilbert's jovial smiling face. Her eyes popped open, and she pondered asking Richard to turn back and head straight to East River.

However, Lyndsey's passion for curiosities and tales based on history were ignited and it silenced her urge. In anticipation of their trip, Lyndsey had sought out books written about Nova Scotia's past. The librarian, a Maritimer, had recommended several. Not one to dwell strictly on facts and figures, Lyndsey had chosen several books by noted authors that the librarian highly recommended. They were works of fiction steeped in history, and told through the eyes of authors who had lived, known, and loved the land of which they'd written. From the librarian's recommendations, Lyndsey had selected and read two books and the books had ignited Lyndsey's wanderlust. Spotting name-places Hope had mentioned in selling her must see point of interest she had amended it to Gilbert's lists of must-sees.

Richard questioned Lyndsey's directions but quickly accepted her explanation. He recalled Lyndsey mentioning a need to stop at Hope's one suggested point of interest, a secluded beach along the less popular stretches of the South Shore. He understood Lyndsey's desire to visit Hope's point of interest, but he questioned the need to visit it today. In drawing closer to the home of his family's ancestors a nervous excitement was growing within him. In silence he listened to Lyndsey entertain him with a series of abbreviated adventures weaved by the authors in the books she had read. Personally he preferred books based on facts, which he would inevitably weave into fictional adventures whilst reading the author's accounts of the facts.

They drove past various points of interest, while Richard listened to Lyndsey warning him that their turn off was just up the road a wee bit. Silently he chuckled and thought, she's starting to talk like a Maritimer, more specifically a Bluenoser. Lyndsey picked up the *Doers' & Dreamers' Travel Guide* and flipped through its pages. She stopped at a page that mentioned East River and started to read.

CHAPTER 27

LYNDSEY SIGHED AND SAID, "WHAT A BEAUTIFUL PLACE. FIRST THE ferry passage across the Bay of Fundy, the rolling forested hills, the rugged rocks and coastline, the many secluded bays and inlets with their fishing boats and seaside homes."

"Yes," Richard answered. He eased off of the gas and continued, "It destroys all the images that years of textbook learning erected in my mind." He grinned and said, "Perhaps we Upper-Canadians have it all backwards. Could it be we're the have-nots of the country? That these Bluenosers in their wisdom have been silently suffering an age-old nation's misconception of have...and have-not?"

"Beauty is in the eye of the beholder."

Richard did not answer. He touched his foot to the brake and slowed the vehicle down. Up ahead he'd spotted a sign highlighting the turnoff Lyndsey had mentioned. On taking the turnoff, they drove much further than expected before they arrived at the next turnoff. It took them down a dirt and gravel road that ended at a large graveled parking area. He tapped the brake pedal. He drove into a parking spot another braking action brought the SUV to a standstill. The lot stood empty. There, he switched off the ignition and stepped out of the vehicle.

Lyndsey remained inside. She reached back behind the seat and retrieved a pair of shorts. The belt on her jeans held her up briefly.

Once she'd managed to unfasten it and undo the button, she pulled the zipper down in one motion. Her hands grasped the top of the jeans, and quickly she wiggled them down over her knees. In less than a minute, Lyndsey had flipped off her sandals and slid out of her jeans. Outside, Richard had walked over to a graveled pathway leading into the forest that surrounded them. Lyndsey stared out the window at his back. Both of her hands slowly moved up and down her exposed thighs, their fingers massaged her thighs and aroused a need. Sex had been denied her for months. Richard turned back and waved to her. He beckoned her to join him. She picked up the shorts and slipped her legs into them. They slid easily up over her thighs. A quick butt lift and they rose up over her hips. She pulled the zipper up, snapped the button into place and fastened the belt. She picked up her jeans, paused then reached into a pocket and retrieved the jeweled rosary. After holding it in the clasped palms of her hands a moment then two, Lyndsey placed the rosary in the SUV's glove compartment and tossed her jeans back towards Bailey. Lyndsey opened her door, hesitated, then grabbed her sandals and stepped out into the parking lot. She swung the door shut; put on her sandals, smiled on seeing Bailey strutting about inside the vehicle and calling out to her.

"Meow ... meow!"

Bailey's ploy worked, Lyndsey opened the door and picked him up and he coyly snuggled up to her. Together they set off and joined Richard.

Richard frowned on spotting Bailey. Lyndsey defended her companion, "I couldn't leave him alone in the car he'd suffocate or be roasted alive if left alone inside your black car on a day like today!"

Richard's disagreement exposed itself in his facial expressions. He suppressed his opinion and boasted. "It's an SUV not a car Lyns!"

She cuddled Bailey tighter and gently rubbed his head. Her facial expressions revealed disagreement. Together they walked side by side down the path. It took them through a thickening evergreen forest. Just when both thought it would never end, they walked into a large grassy opening. In its middle stood an old decrepit abandoned house and shed. Beyond the house, they spotted another pathway into the forest. The forest quickly closed in on them again. They caught a faint echo of a distant pounding of the sea's surf, and Richard broke into a light jogger's sprint.

Lyndsey watched him disappear around a twist in the path and frowned anew on hearing him call out.

"If he pulls a Bailey and escapes with a leap to freedom, I'll happily chase our charmer—*with you at my side*!"

Following in Richard's footsteps Lyndsey felt the silence of the forest fade away and the sound of the sea's pounding surf call out to her. She pondered the opportunity Richard had shouted out. Sunshine from a brilliant blue sky caressed her face and arms. Bailey purred softly and contentedly, he snuggled up tighter to Lyndsey's bosom. She rubbed the contented feline's head thoughtfully. A short wooden walkway appeared. Lyndsey stepped onto it and walked forward. The sound of the pounding surf increased. At the end of the walkway, she looked out over a sandy beach and its lone occupant Richard.

Lyndsey ran towards the beach. She slowed her pace on drawing close to Richard then stopped 10 yards short of him. He stared out over the sea, unaware of her presence. Richard's frame silhouetted against the deep-blue sky, and the sea stirred Lyndsey's inner being. They both stood in silence then Richard stepped forward and ran across the sand away from Lyndsey. He veered right and ran towards the water. Lyndsey called out. "Wait for me, Richie."

In that split second, Lyndsey lost herself in time. Memories carried her back to the playground of her childhood. No longer a troubled young wife, she stumbled on the grass in the playground. With both hands flung outward, she fell forward and flew through the air. First, her knees hit the grass, then her outstretched hands hit. Six-year-old Lyndsey Melville slid forward over the grass. Her dimples firmed and a trademark pout took hold. Thump. Lyndsey's chin hit the ground hard. Tears streamed down her cheeks. Frightened and hurt, she called out, "Richie!" Time stood still.

"Hey Lyn...sdie, you OK?"

"No. Look at my chin."

"Don't be silly"

Little Lyndsey sat up. Richie, her playmate, crouched down at her side. In a serious voice, he said, “Gee Lyndsey, you bumped you…r self up real good.”

“Duh”

“No really. Want me to get my Mom?”

“No!”

“Then what do you want?”

Little Lyndsey raised her left hand and tapped her bruised chin. She turned a pair of baby-blue eyes up to Richie and whispered, “No dumb...dumb! Kiss me all better.”

Richie leaned forward, puckered up his lips, and planted a kiss on her chin. “There now you’re all better.”

“No!”

He shrugged his shoulders, puckered up anew, and this time… kissed Lyndsey squarely on her lips. It lasted all of three seconds. Richie looked deep into Lyndsey’s blue eyes. “Now?”

“Maybe.”

Back on the beach, Richard stopped, twisted about, and called back to Lyndsey. “Hey slow poke. Move it. The sand is great.”

The playground faded from Lyndsey’s mind. She kicked off her sandals, stooped down, and picked them up. Lyndsey looked down the beach at Richard and called out. “Don’t move. I’m coming.” Her right leg stepped out and Lyndsey dashed forward. She ran towards Richard in a zig zagging pattern. The warm sand felt great. Her blonde hair swayed to and fro in the wind. Lyndsey’s feet slid in the fine beach sand. She fell forward towards Richard, Bailey sensed freedom and leaped free of Lyndsey’s grasp. He tumbled, then landed in the sand. A glance towards Lyndsey assured him he wasn’t the focus of her attention. Off to his right in the wet surf washed sand rapid movements caught and held Bailey’s attention.

The sand gave way beneath her and Lyndsey slid to a spot off to Richard’s side.

“Bout time, slow poke. You okay?”

Lyndsey smiled up at Richard. She bit her lip and suppressed a *“No dumb dumb. Kiss me all better.”* An image of John flashed in the back of her mind.

Richard held out a hand to Lyndsey. She took it and pulled herself back up onto her feet. He opened his hand and released hers. Lyndsey placed the sandals between her knees and patted both legs and then her shorts. The fine beach sand fell and blew away in the sea breezes.

"Look, Lyndsey a rocky mini mountain. Let's check it out and see what's on the other side of our mountain." Together they walked towards the mini mountain of rocks.

"OK. But we'd best check out Bailey first!"

Ten energized sandpipers captured and held Bailey's attention. Their rapid synchronized movements both entertained Bailey and triggered his hunter instincts. Stealthily Bailey crouched down onto the warmth of the sun kissed beach. He tensed and prepared to leap upon the returning sandpipers. Taste buds heightened Bailey's focus on the sandpipers. His travel companions faded from his mind. Instinct overpowered him. With front paws extended outward in a predatory greeting, Bailey leapt towards his anticipated dining pleasures. Dinner took flight and soared to freedom in the salty sea air. Thud! Bailey landed unceremoniously on the wet sea washed beach. A fresh wave raced up the beach and embraced a shocked Bailey. He twisted about and leapt free of the chilled seawater. Bailey braced himself and landed on four paws. He shivered and shook attempting to shake off the icy embrace of the sea. A sour faced Bailey stared out defensively at the blue-green sea.

Lyndsey shuddered and laughed on spotting the wet and shivering Bailey staring out with distain at the ocean. Lyndsey then frowned and stated, "Later Rich. Bailey needs us!" A smile captured Lyndsey's thoughts, she walked towards every artisan's vision of a perfect sour puss. Bailey twisted his head sideways and hunger pangs flared anew. Dinner flew past him then landed on the beach off to his left. The sandpipers ignored Bailey.

Lyndsey crouch down smiled at Bailey she called out, "Bailey... Bailey, come to Lyndsey sweetie, come to Lyndsey."

Bailey stared hesitantly at Lyndsey then took several steps towards her. Suddenly his attention shifted eagerly to a blue green delight that skittered along the wet beach unaware of the potential danger Bailey posed to it.

Lyndsey stood up and stared amusedly at the attentive Bailey. She vanished from his attentive eye, instead Bailey walked stealthily towards the sea and his new prey a blue crab. She turned about and walked back to Richard's side. The warm sun kissed sea breezes assured her Bailey would survive his introduction to the Atlantic Ocean's watery caress.

Richard pointed to the rocks and said, "Watch your step, those rocks look slippery. We'd best stick to the dry ones over there." He walked towards the dry rocks. Lyndsey followed his lead then gingerly climbed up on the rocks. On reaching the peak, Richard stopped and offered his hand to Lyndsey. She waved him off, took four steps upward and stood by his side. Richard stepped forward and started his descent down the other side.

He pointed out over the newly discovered beach. "Look Lyndsey, it's a whole new beach. Our private beach. Shall I lead the way?"

Lyndsey remained at the peak. She shielded her eyes and looked longingly out over the sea. Her hair twisted and turned with the sea breezes. A faint voice sang out to her from the sea. It sounded weirdly familiar and gently touched her heartstrings. She started her descent down the rocks. At the base, she accepted Richard's hand and stepped off the last rock back into the soft sand. He then stepped away and walked towards the water. A glance ahead and down the beach revealed to Lyndsey a never-ending horizon. Swirling eddies of sand whisked freely down the beach's length to its end and beyond.

Richard turned about and yelled aloud, "It's great! I love it, the sand, the sea breezes…let's try out the water." He spun away from Lyndsey and kicked off his shoes. Lyndsey watched Richard raise one foot and hop about the sand trying to remove his socks. She burst into laughter and ran forward to help him. The first sock came free of his foot and Richard flung it off back towards his shoes. He then changed feet and entered battle with the other sock.

Each hop brought Richard closer to the water. Lyndsey fought a losing battle against her fits of laughter as she remained close at hand. Finally, Richard's sock came loose and his foot landed in the water.

"OH MY GAA…D! It's freezing."

He spun about hopped away from the water and wet sand, then fell back towards Lyndsey and the beach. Thud their bodies met and he tumbled downward and landed on top of a laughing Lyndsey, her body cushioned his fall. Above them, a pair of seagulls soared freely. Their lonesome song of the sea echoed in the ears of Richard and Lyndsey. Richard pressed his hands into the sand and lifted his chest up off of Lyndsey's. "Sorry Lyndsey. You okay?"

His question remained unanswered. Richard looked down on the face of Lyndsey. She no longer laughed. He looked longingly at her lips, her closed eyes, and her trademark pout. Beneath him, Lyndsey's legs wiggled, then slipped free of his weight. Richard slid and landed firmly between Lyndsey's thighs.

"Lyndsey."

No reply.

"You okay?"

"No dumb, dumb kiss me all better."

Richard stared down at Lyndsey's lips. He blinked and replayed the words in his mind '*No dumb, dumb kiss me all better.*'

He lowered his face towards Lyndsey's slowly—very slowly. Five years had passed since he'd last tasted the sweetness of her kiss. The time seemed right. An image of John flashed through his mind. The replay button struck up her words anew, *No dumb, dumb kiss me all better.* Closer and closer he moved. Lyndsey's scent rose up and filled his senses. His lips touched gently on hers. He fought the urge to press hard, thought better of it and started to pull away from her.

Lyndsey reached out to Richard and pulled him to her. She ran her fingers through his hair and heightened the passion of their kiss. Her hands eased down onto his back, then slipped up under his polo shirt. They massaged and pulled Richard against her body. She lifted the shirt upward as their lips parted.

"No Lyndsey. It's wrong. John."

"He's got Tessa. I want you."

She lifted the shirt up and over Richard's head. A tug pulled it off, and she tossed it aside while staring up at his chest. Slowly, her fingers worked their way over it inch by inch. Her lips reached up and kissed his chest, then returned longingly to his mouth. Overhead, the seagulls called out to the lovers below.

Richard's resistance failed quickly. The memory of so many teen-aged Saturday nights spent in Lyndsey's arms raced though his mind. He stopped waiting for Lyndsey to pull away. Their lips moved apart and each moved slowly over the other's face and neck. The heat of their bodies rose a degree with each kiss given and received. Richard felt Lyndsey's hands tugging at his belt. He offered no resistance. The belt released. Lyndsey gave it a quick deliberate tug and pulled it free of Richard's pants. Her hands undid the button and tugged at his zipper pulling it down. In one move, she pushed him away, grabbed hold of his pants and underwear, and pulled them down over his hips. She paused and smiled on seeing Richard's passion exposed. Sea breezes raced over Richard's exposed buttocks and through his thighs. Lyndsey smirked on spotting Richard looking sheepishly, first to the right and then to the left. Nothing but sand and beach surrounded them, to the right stood the mini rock mountain. She almost chuckled on spotting him seeking out signs of approaching voices and unwanted footsteps in the sand, none were detected. Richard's hips swayed. They reacted to Lyndsey's fingers touching him and driving his passion skyward. He pulled back and away from her. Their eyes locked. Lyndsey's knees rose up to his hips. Her toes remained firmly on the sand. Richard's fingers slowly moved up and down Lyndsey's inner thighs. Her hips shifted in response to Richard's sensual touch.

Richard's eyes looked down on Lyndsey's midsection. Her tank top had moved upwards and exposed the soft whiteness of her belly. He reached out and his fingers gently drew a pattern of never-ending circles on her belly.

"What are you waiting for, Richie?"

He did not answer. The silence continued. Doubts and desires raced through their aroused minds. He took Lyndsey's hands in his and pulled her up towards himself. Facing each other eye to eye on their knees, their lips moved forward and gently touched each others. The kiss lingered. Lyndsey's reached down and playfully squeezed Richard's exposed buttocks. His hands moved down and sought out the top of her shorts. They stopped at the belt and released it. At the button he fumbled with it.

Flashbacks to happy moments once shared in John's loving arms injected guilty feelings in Lyndsey's heart. She struggled and teetered on the edge of rejecting Richard's advances and denying her body its ignited hungers. Recollection of the humiliation, terrors and rejections John in his drunken rage had exposed her to sent a rippling wave of sadness though her body. Richard heightened the passion of his kiss. Lyndsey surrendered to her body's desires. She released her hold on Richard and moved to the button. Their lips parted.

She whispered, "Need some help?"

"No."

Lyndsey's fingers popped the button open and slipped her zipper downward. Her shorts fell down to her knees.

"That's more like it," she whispered anew.

Richard's hands moved to Lyndsey's buttocks and started a slow sensual massage of her cotton panties, they renewed their kiss and their passions soared. Time slipped past the entwined lovers. Lyndsey pulled away from Richard, she shifted her weight and stood upright. Richard remained down on his knees, he gazed up at Lyndsey. She reached down pulled her peach tank top up over her head and tossed it aside, then reached to her back and pulled at her bra. The hooks released and the bra fell forward and down onto Richard's face, he inhaled its aura of Lyndsey's body then tossed the bra aside. His eyes looked upward to Lyndsey's breasts. They stood full; their temptation quickly drew his full attention. His hands fell away from her panties. Lyndsey started to kneel down, but Richard stood up first.

"So…so beautiful, it should have been us from day one Lyndsey. Not John."

"Not now Richie. Let this be our day one. I need you. I want you now."

Richard's fingers gently rubbed and circled her nipples. Lyndsey reached down and pulled at the elastic of her panties. Little effort was needed to pull them down over her hips. Once past her hips, they fell freely down to her feet. Her left foot rose up and out of the panties. It returned to the sand. The right foot kicked sideways and flicked the panties aside. Overhead, the two seagulls had been joined by two more and then another two. Their lonesome song of the sea fell down upon the two lovers on the beach. Richard's lips met Lyndsey's. His arms encircled her and pulled her body closer. Lyndsey responded; she placed her hands firmly on Richard's back and pulled him closer. The kiss continued. Their body temperatures raced skyward. Lyndsey's hands slipped off of his back. She pulled her hips away from Richard's, then reached for and grabbed hold of his passion. Richard shuddered and uttered a deep, guttural moan. He attempted to escape from Lyndsey's grasp. His knees buckled and he fell backwards onto the beach. Lyndsey squeezed her fingers tighter around Richard's need and tumbled forward. In midair, she twisted her torso and her knees slipped apart. She landed atop Richard. Their hips met, Lyndsey shifted her weight and guided Richard toward her need. She drove her hips hard to his and sighed. He entered her. They lay frozen in ecstasy and time. Richard's thighs trembled. Every nerve in his body twitched. He reached out to Lyndsey's breasts and treasured their touch with his hands. Lyndsey opened her eyes and sighed. She braced herself and slowly worked her hips with a rhythmic sway. Each sway of their young hips drove the sexual desire of the other higher. Time raced on, leaping beyond all boundaries; it paused, stood still, and then froze the two lovers inside an erotic time capsule. Richard made one final thrust and their hips locked. Tears of joy trickled down Lyndsey's cheeks. Richard and Lyndsey drifted off into a dream like state embracing each other's euphoria. Gentle sea breezes and the sun's rays massaged and warmed their sated bodies. Their lovemaking had transcended the bounds of sex and together they had discovered the joys of each other's love.

CHAPTER 28

RICHARD'S EYES FLUTTERED THEN OPENED. THEY STARED INTO the golden strands of Lyndsey's hair. He picked her hand up off his shoulder and kissed each of its fingertips. Lyndsey stirred. She opened her eyes and smiled at Richard. Their lips touched softly then parted.

Lyndsey pulled herself up then rolled away from Richard. Sitting on the hot sand, she looked wantonly over the length of Richard's naked body. She stood up on her knees, then jumped up onto her feet. Teasingly she said, "Come play with me...and I'll play with you." Before Richard could answer, Lyndsey stepped away and proceeded to retrieve her scattered pieces of clothing.

Richard eyed Lyndsey's naked body walking about the beach in search of its clothing. He propped himself up to get a better view.

Mission accomplished. Lyndsey stooped down one last time and retrieved Richard's polo shirt. She walked back to Richard, took a quick glance at her watch, tossed the shirt down to him and said, "Time's a wasting, Love. We'd best get back on the road. Gilbert and Hope are expecting us to arrive in time for supper."

"Don't need it."

"Need what?"

"Supper, it is standing right in front of me."

"Don't tempt me, Rich. I've never made love before today. Had sex…but today." She moaned and stated, "Today love-making and its gentle touch embraced my heart forever."

"Me too."

"So move before I'm forced to pig-out on the dessert plate."

Richard laughed. He jumped up and pulled the polo shirt down over his head. Voices rose up in the distance beyond the rocky mini-mountain.

Richard hurried his pace and soon had all his clothes in hand.

Lyndsey quickly dressed, then sat down and watched Richard scramble to get back into his clothes. Silently she thanked Hope for the amazing must see, that had opened the floodgates to an amazing world of love. A world that they had previously been wrongly denied.

After he had slipped his belt back through its loops and snapped its buckle back in place, Richard walked over to Lyndsey and kissed her nose.

"Love you."

Lyndsey smiled and replied, "In my heart, I always have."

He took her hand and they set off back towards the mini-mountain. They crossed over the rock pile then walked together hand in hand down the beach towards the parking lot. Halfway down the beach they spotted a middle-aged couple sitting on the beach. On nearing the couple they smiled on seeing Bailey stretched out contentedly on the lady's lap, his belly swayed in tune with the massaging fingers and hand of the lady.

"Bailey!" Lyndsey chided. You are definitely a charmer. Who are your new found friends?"

The lady smiled holding Bailey she stood and said, "Danica, I am Dannie Rhymes and Stephan is my husband." She passed Bailey over to Lyndsey. Stephan stood up and reached out to shake Richard's hand.

They shook hands, Richard said, "I'm Richard Ramsay and this is Lyndsey. And this charming ball of fluff is our charming traveling companion, Bailey."

Dannie, answered, “Yes I suspect your Bailey is a graduate of Miss Kitty’s Charm School 101.”

Everyone smiled and laughed in response to Dannie’s comments on Bailey’s demeanor. The woman glanced at the logo on Richard’s polo shirt *‘Newmarket, Ontario’* then offered up a welcome. “Enjoy your stay in the Maritimes. It’s a Lover’s Paradise.”

Lyndsey and Richard smirked. Together they said, “We are, and we will. It’s the best”. Conversations shifted to introductions of each couples’ travels and their points of origin. Danica and Stephan declared Stewiacke, West St Andrews, Nova Scotia as their home digs and stated they were on a mini vacation that would land them in Bar Harbor, Maine in three days time. Danica being a Chester girl added in series of recommendations that highlighted a must do stop at Chester’s Lobster Pot Pub & Eatery. Stephan and Richard exchanged business cards and the couples parted ways.

A minute later Stephan smiled and called back to Lyndsey and Richard, “Beautiful day…for the beach.”

Lyndsey smirked and answered, “The best, the absolute best!”

They continued along the beach hand in hand, until out of hearing range. Lyndsey turned to Richard and said, “They’ve been over the mountain.”

“They’re going back.”

Lyndsey smiled then said, “Yes.”

“The beach is good.”

Lyndsey simply smiled and squeezed Richard’s hand. They kissed, turned, and walked the last stretch of beach. They walked off the beach and onto the wooden walkway. Richard took one last longing look down the beach towards the mini-mountain. A sense of contentment touched him. He gently squeezed Lyndsey’s hand in his. They paused and shared a lingering kiss.

“Meow ... meow.” Bailey called out for attention. Their lips parted and they set off along the pathway towards the parking area. Once there, Richard held the passenger door open for Lyndsey. She slid onto the passenger seat. Bailey snuggled up to Lyndsey and purred contentedly on her lap. Richard closed the door and walked around to the driver's side. Once inside, he put on his seat belt and started the engine.

Bailey greeted the engine's roar, "Meow...meow, MEEEEoow!" Bailey stood up, stretched, expressed his opinion, frowned then settled back down. Richard rubbed Bailey's head then slipped the transmission into reverse. He backed up, stopped, shifted into drive and headed back down the roadway towards the highway. The return run back to Highway 103 appeared much shorter. Back at Highway 103 he turned right and set off towards Liverpool, *'Port of Privateers.'* On approaching Liverpool, he took the first exit for Liverpool. The town appealed to both Richard and Lyndsey. Its periodic and well-maintained homes stood out in their minds. A drive across the Mersey River took them past the Hank Snow museum and into Brooklyn. From there, Highway 331 carried them towards Gilbert's next 'must see' LaHave and the LaHave Bakery.

CHAPTER 29

GILBERT SET THE OVEN FOR 375 DEGREES, THEN PICKED UP THE casserole pan and walked over to the counter. Hope smiled, then asked, "What time do you expect Lyndsey and Richard to arrive, Uncle?"

"Not to fret, it's ten past two now. Provided they left Digby before noon and depending on how many stops they make along the way, they should pull into the yard no later than six or seven tonight."

Gilbert took a mug from the cupboard and poured himself a java fix. "Care for one?" he asked.

"Nah. I'll pass, but thanks for asking."

"That's no, Hope."

"I know, I'm just teasing. Not everyone has an English Professor for an uncle."

"So true, only the chosen can make that claim."

"And you'd never let me forget."

"Correct, I would never deny you the honour."

"I'm really looking forward to seeing Lyndsey again."

"Yes. You two really took to each other well."

"She's just a really nice person. If I were to have a sister and could pick, Lyndsey would be it."

Gilbert gulped and swallowed a mouthful of coffee. He coughed hoarsely then recovered.

"You okay, Uncle Gilbert?"

"I will be. You threw me off, with the thought that there could be two of you."

"Really, uncle, you can't handle what you've got!"

Hope walked out of the kitchen, through the living room, opened the front door, and walked out. Once outside, she walked towards the old homestead and glanced across the lawn at her Grandmother's treasured rose hedge. Hope followed her eyes and walked over to the rose hedge. It had started to bloom early this year. The dainty rose flowers filled the air with sweetness and promises of more treasures in store for tomorrow and beyond. Hope stooped towards a cluster of pink roses and inhaled deeply. Her cheeks flushed. The rose hedge always reminded her of Grandmother. Her eyes watered. "God I miss you Grammy." She rubbed her eyes. The watery haze washed away on her hands.

"Grammy miss...es you too, wees alls shor'nuff looves hour Hope."

She spun about and smiled. Before her stood Uncle Jeffrey.

"Didn't spect me dis herly…did'ya."

Hope stepped forward and wrapped her arms about Jeffrey.

"Yuk!"

She jumped back. Her face grew stern. She scolded her uncle, "Fish guts and juice. Really! Uncle Jeffrey it's icky!"

"Cannot help it dearie. Your dear...iest an sweeteeest uncle is a fisherman true and blu."

"And a good one to boot, I might add."

"I'll not deny it, dearie."

"Good haul today?"

"Oh ya, reeal good."

"We'll be needing some, Uncle Gilbert is fixing a—"

Jeffrey interrupted, "He's up toos de hoose den?"

Hope pouted and looked hard at her uncle.

"Gad. I looves yer pout. Dem dimplees makes ya looks so cute."

"I don't want cute."

"Den don't pout."

Hope smiled. She asked, "What is it between you and Uncle Gilbert?"

"I looves to bug h'im. He looves it too. Jest too sop'isticated ta k'now it."

"He's a fisherman too."

"Part-timer."

"But a fisherman all the same."

Jeffrey laughed aloud. He countered, "Jest has a funny way of go'n bout it."

"How many ways can you go about setting and hauling lobster traps?"

"Wells. He's de only one bout heres that dooes it quot'n Rome'o en Juile't, or dat King Leery guy."

"Adds a touch of class."

"Oh sure you'd say dat. You does it wit hi'm."

"Yes."

Jeffrey smiled. He performed his rendition of a curtsy/bow and added. "You does it wit class."

"Thank you."

"So how many lobst'rs is Gilbert look'n fer."

"Five or six should do. He's doing up McClaken...lobster lasagna."

"Isn I invoted?"

"Yes, of course you're invited." Hope grinned, stepped forward, and kissed her uncle. She whispered, "Go down to your place, run the bathwater, get bathed, put on a change of clothes, bring the lobsters, and I'll put in a good word for you."

"Gad. I looves you Hope."

Hope watched Jeffrey walk off towards his house, the original Ramsay homestead, and sighed. *Yes,* she thought, *I love you too Uncle Jeffrey.* Her focus returned to the rose hedge. Its fragrance cleared the last traces of Uncle Jeffrey's fish-stained clothing.. A glance above the hedge presented a majestic view of the sea. After a quick scan of the water, Hope turned and walked back to the house and Uncle Gilbert. On the walk back, Hope wished time would fly by faster and hasten the arrival of Lyndsey and Richard.

She reached the house, paused briefly, then opened the door and stepped back inside.

"Good. You're back. Thought for a minute I'd scared you off."

"You could never pull that one off!" Hope then asked, "Need any help preparing dinner?

"No. Not really. Bread is in the oven along with dessert."

"And it would be?"

"Simply stated, a very special surprise."

"Then all we need is our guests."

"Well it would be nice to have some fresh lobsters."

"Problem solved."

Gilbert smiled then asked, "How many?"

Hope smiled and boasted, "Enough."

"Really, and what is enough? Did he have a good haul? How many do I get?"

"Uncle Jeffrey is freshening up and plans to bring at least five or six good ones."

Gilbert set the paper he was grading down on the end table. He stood up and walked over to Hope. The two eyed each other then Gilbert put his arms about Hope and hugged her. He stepped back.

"Is there a chance of getting a few more?"

"Call him! And you best be quick about it, he's headed for the tub to freshen up."

Gilbert headed for the phone. He called and caught Jeffrey just in time. A smile broke out on his face, Gilbert hung up the phone. He said, "We're good to go. Jeff said Pappy is feeling a tad better, but not up to joining us for supper, maybe tomorrow."

"Yes. I hate to deny them Pappy's company, but he has been a tad under the weather lately. It's going to be great having them here with us. You, me, Jeffrey, Richard and Lyndsey together reunited into an extra special family. Hopefully, tomorrow Pappy will be up to jumping into our family's reunion. Jeffrey is really excited about meeting Lyndsey and Richard. Pappy at times gets Richard confused with William, Richard's Grandfather." She paused then added, "A time or two he snapped and called them, those other Ramsays, de ones that comes from aways."

Hope leaned forward and kissed Gilbert on the cheek.

"The delay will sweeten him up. They'll love him."

"Ring, Ring." Hope turned and raced into the kitchen. She grabbed the oven mitts from the wall rack and opened the oven door. The smell of fresh baked bread filled the kitchen. She tugged at the oven rack and it moved. Another tug and it slid outward towards Hope. Four loaves of homemade bread surrounded a large blueberry pie. Hope picked up each bread pan in turn and placed them on the stovetop. The blueberry pie ended up on the side counter. She turned the timer and oven controls off and stood there eying the bread.

Gilbert walked up behind her. He scolded, "Don't even think it."

"What?"

"You know."

"Peanut butter is good."

"Very."

"I would say, five adults, a melt in your mouth McClaken Lobster Lasagna and blueberry pie. Three loaves will do."

"Are you absolutely sure?"

"Yes."

"Then peanut butter it is."

Gilbert retrieved the peanut butter from the pantry. Hope selected the smallest loaf, flipped its pan over, and placed the loaf on the side counter atop a cutting board. She pulled a bread knife out of its rack and started to slice the bread.

"Crust. Please," Gilbert pleaded.

"But only one, the other is mine!"

"OK."

They each took a butter knife from the drawer then dipped into the peanut butter jar. After they'd each covered three slabs of bread in a thick coating of peanut butter, Hope took out the milk pitcher and poured two tall glasses. She carried them over to the table. Gilbert followed behind with peanut-buttered bread in hand. Gilbert and Hope sat down on opposite sides of the table. Their feast began.

CHAPTER 30

JEFFREY WALKED AWAY FROM HIS HOUSE. HE STOPPED IN FRONT OF the outdoor shed for a moment then stepped inside. Cautiously, he stepped around the lobster bins spread randomly about the floor. At the back of the shed, he picked out an appropriate-sized dinner basket, turned and walked back to the lobster bins. He set the basket down and eyed the lobster bins for apt dinner selections.

The first selection took awhile as Jeffrey gazed down into the bin and admired his catch of the day. He reached down and picked up a two pounder.

He said, "Comes here's me beauty. Aye. A fine choice you are."

Each candidate in turn received Jeffrey's personal praise before it landed in Jeffrey's dinner basket. The selection process completed, he carried the basket over to the side counter and set it down.

He said, "Waits he're me pretties. Uncle Jeffrey will be back in a flicker."

Jeffrey stepped away from the counter and exited the shed. Outside the shed, he turned and called to the selected ones, "Gots to get prettied up. Little Jeffy is a goi'n ta dinner wid he's darl'n niece."

He scratched his beard then set off to the house. Once inside, he removed his jacket and hung it on a wall hook. He looked over to the mantel and eyed the pictures lined up along its length. When his eyes fell on Gilbert's picture, he paused.

"Yer little brudder wont disap'oint. Truth be tol't he'd kill fer a feed of McClaken lobster lason'i."

"It's about time you showed up. I was starting to get worried."

"Sorry Pappy. Stopped to chat wid our young Hope."

"Not a problem. She stopped in the other day for a visit."

"I kin see dat."

Pappy McClaken entered the living room. He stopped to catch his breath, then walked slowly over and sat down in the room's only sofa chair. The senior McClaken lifted his cane then set it down across his knees. He looked proudly about the living room/kitchen and smiled. In a show of pride, he turned to Jeffrey. He poked his chin, with its silvered beard, out in Jeffrey's direction.

Pappy McClaken declared, "Cleaned more than the house this time. Hope trimmed my beard right nice."

"Did a good job'a it too I sees. But no womo'n will git he'r snipp'rs dat close tad Jeffrey's pride-n-joy."

"The right one will change that song-n-dance in a hurry."

"I's me own man Pappy. I sings me own song."

"Trust me. Duets always sound sweeter."

"Gott'a go Pappy. Hope's giv'n me de ward."

"The what?"

"Gott'a git spruc'd up'n bathed. Eati'n at the big house ta'night."

"I'm not hungry, son. Still a tad under the weather."

Jeffrey waved off his Father and walked across the living room. At the hallway he turned, walked past the bedrooms and into the bathroom. A look about the room revealed Hope's touch had passed through recently. Jeffrey moved over to the four-legged antique bathtub and inserted the stopper into its drain. He turned on the hot and cold water taps then walked over to the sink. In the mirror above the sink, a smiling, bearded Jeffrey smiled back at the real thing. The real Jeffrey ran a hand over the top of his brush-cut head. The Jeffrey in the mirror followed suit.

"Oh you han'dsim dev'l."

The other Jeffrey moved his lips miming Jeffrey word for word. Jeffrey turned away from the mirror and stripped off his clothes. He set them down on the floor, thought better of it, and picked them up off the floor. He carried them across the bathroom and tossed them into the clothesbasket, which Hope had set out for just that purpose. A sideways glance at the mirror told him his friend had departed. Jeffrey turned the hot and cold water taps off. He raised his left leg and dipped it into the tub's steamy hot water. The urge to yank his toes out of the tub of hot purifying water abated. Jeffrey grabbed onto the far side of the tub. Determination and the aroma of Gilbert's McClaken lobster lason'i fortified his resolve. He plunged his left leg into the tub then followed up with his right leg Jeffrey felt invigorated! He sucked in a deep breath of steamy hot mist, then uttered a subdued, *"Jerone…moooo!"*

The water parted and welcomed him butt first.

"Eee…ooowww. Bou'ys she be ho't."

Jeffrey sat silently. Slowly, his body adjusted to the water's temperature. He shuddered then picked up a bar of soap from the dish.

"Goo'd tin a lobster only gott'a do dis once."

Soap in hand, Jeffrey started on his arms and worked up a thick, soapy lather. He dunked his arms under the water and rinsed the soap off them. With soap in hand, he stood up and worked the soap over the rest of his body. Finished, Jeffrey sat back down, then slowly slid forward until only his head remained above the water. He shook his legs and torso and cleansed himself of the soapy lather. Next, Jeffrey pinched his nose and plunged his head below the water. Splash he emerged anew from the depths of the tub.

"Whoa. Rifresh'n or what!"

After working a thick lather into his hair and beard, Jeffrey pinched his nose once more, inhaled a deep breath, and then dove again to the depths of the tub. Beneath the surface, he shook his head and cleared the lather from both hair and beard. Splash! Jeffrey emerged completely rinsed from head to toe. He stood up and grabbed a bath towel from the rack. Jeffrey towel-dried himself vigorously from head to knees, then reached down and pulled the plug out of the drain hole. He stepped out of the tub and dried his feet, then completed one more pass of the towel over his body. Satisfied, he tossed the towel into the clothesbasket.

A short stint in front of the mirror completed the next step in Jeffrey's makeover. He ran a brush back over the top of his crew-cut hair, then passed it through the black curls that ran from the side of his head down to his shoulders. Next the scissors were deployed, a quick snip here, then there and Jeffrey's beard stood trimmed to perfection in his mind. The beard over two feet long had garnered many an encouragement to enter the local contest held in town every fall. Jeffrey's shy nature amongst strangers held him back from accepting the challenge. Finished with stage one, he put on his bathrobe and walked towards the bathroom door. He stopped abruptly, turned about, walked to the tub, and turned on both taps; he grabbed a face cloth, knelt down, and cleaned the tub stem to stern. With this task completed, Jeffrey stood up turned off the taps, tossed the face cloth in the clothesbasket and walked out of the bathroom.

Pappy grinned and called out to Jeffery from the kitchen in jest, "Mmmm. Looking spiffy."

Jeffrey ignored Pappy McClaken's jibe. He walked down the hallway and entered his bedroom. A trip to the closet produced a pair of clean jeans and a sports jacket. In the dresser drawers he found a pair of socks, underwear, and a golf shirt. Jeffrey removed his bathrobe, tossed it on the bed, and proceeded to dress himself.

"Ye be looking like a gentleman stepping out to woo a lady, young lad."

Jeffrey twisted about on seeing Grace, his Good Neighbour Faiery, he smiled broadly at her.

"Cann...nary be a wasting me time wee lassie. Kin foolks frooms aways bees a'comin soon. Grace did not reply. She merely nodded and smiled at Jeffery. Happy and eager to spend the evening with Hope, Jeffrey turned and walked out of his room. He hummed a seaside melody to himself.

CHAPTER 31

THE ROADSIDE SIGN CALLED OUT ITS GREETING: 'WELCOME TO LaHave.' Traffic slowed upon entering the town's 50 km speed zone. Ahead, Richard spotted a build up of traffic. Couldn't be a traffic jam…they'd left those behind in Ontario. Richard recalled Gilbert's words. *In Lahave you absolutely must stop in at the Lahave Bakery*. His mouth watered.

"Care for a rest stop?"

"Do we have time to spare?" Lyndsey asked.

"I'm starving, got me a real hunger. It must be all the sunshine and fresh sea air."

"Men, feed them and they're putty in your hand!"

"No not me. Right now I'm just, a very hungry one. There's an energizing zing in the air. It's like there's an alluring, haunting kiss in every sea breeze. Besides, I think this is the hometown of Gilbert's beloved LaHave Bakery."

"OK! But we'd best make it a short pit stop. I'm growing anxious to reach East River by dinner. Oh! You'd best leave windows open. Bailey's lost in kitty-kat dreamland. I suspect the beach wore him out."

Richard smiled on recalling their time on the beach. He opened all four windows after he'd eased the SUV into a vacant parking spot. Then he stepped out of the vehicle. The building stood on the waterfront. The smell of freshly-baked goods called out to him. He followed his nose and quickly reached the bakery door.

Lyndsey left Bailey sleeping on her passenger seat. She arrived at the bakery's doorway, but not before Richard had stepped inside and observed every dieter's worst nightmare. Inside the bakery, Richard was confronted with wall-to-wall delights.

Lyndsey joined him, and after much deliberation, a difficult decision was resolved; they settled on two large chunks...pieces of carrot cake along with a cup of tea for Lyndsey and coffee for Richard. Richard paid the bill. Lyndsey carried their tray over to a vacant table by the front window.

"Care for another ferry ride?" Richard asked. He explained. "It's a short one. Fifteen minutes, a cable ferry across the river."

"OK."

"You're easy to please."

"Must be the salt water, could be the beach."

Richard blushed. He ate his carrot cake in silence then looked up at Lyndsey. She held her tea mug in both hands. Her carrot cake had not been touched. The look on Lyndsey's face scared and excited Richard. He had never seen this side of her before today. Sure, they'd been sand-box playmates...high-school sweethearts. They'd shared more than one passionate kiss through their teens, but never anything like today. He recalled how university had separated them. John had befriended her halfway through his third year away. Time had worked against them. Time had worked in John's favour.

Lyndsey interrupted Richard's thoughts. She whispered to him over her teacup, "I love you, Richard. I'm never going back to him. Never should have allowed my love of you to falter."

"I was gone a long time."

"Way too long."

"He loved you?"

"In his way yes he did and I loved him, but not completely."

"But you're still his wife."

"One of my life's not-so-little tragedies, but one that Mr. Lizards' associate, Thomas Rose, has agreed to handle."

"You did love him. He loved you. He is my brother and I don't want to lose him."

"You won't. Trust me. Besides, he has Tessa."

"One mistake, one transgression and it's over?"

"No. After John's reaction to Grandfather's letter and will and by John's actions that have followed, I've done some in-depth soul-searching."

Richard began to pick away at Lyndsey's untouched carrot cake. She did not object.

Lyndsey explained, "Our bed turned cold months before the accident took place. I never stopped wanting or needing him. He just turned cold to me in ways I could not understand. We never displayed the fact openly to the world, but I did feel abandoned and unwanted."

"But why didn't you…"

"No. I couldn't seek out your counsel. You were my brother-in-law and ex-sweetheart on top of that."

"Ferry departs in ten minutes, friends."

Richard and Lyndsey turned to the woman behind the bakery cash register.

"Where do we catch it? Do we have time?" Richard asked.

"Not to worry sir! The ramp is less than a country block away. You've got plenty of time."

"Thanks for the warning. It's very much appreciated," Richard replied.

"Not local right?"

"No."

"Come from away…I'd wager, but not Toront'o, right?"

Richard stood up. Lyndsey followed his lead. Both smiled sheepishly.

"No. Not Toronto," Richard answered. He explained, "Town of Newmarket. About an hour's drive North of Toronto."

"Oh. Then you'd be closer to Peterborough and Ottaw'a."

Richard grinned and said, "In-betwixt Toronto and the two. However a town that stands alone."

"Gott'cha. Enjoy your honeymoon."

Richard bit his tongue and did not answer. He held the door open for Lyndsey then followed her out of the bakery. At the SUV they found Bailey awake and leisurely enjoying the scenery. He stood on the seat with both front paws on the door and his head extended out into the fresh sea air. Back in the vehicle Lyndsey set Bailey on her lap.

The country block was much shorter than he had anticipated. Richard quickly spotted the ferry ramp. He turned and drove up to the ramp. Only one other vehicle had preceded their arrival, and it was already on board the ferry. He followed the ferry operator's signals and drove up onto the small cable ferry. No below deck parking here, they occupied the ferry's only deck. Their journey across the LaHave River was over almost before it started. The trip lasted ten, maybe fifteen minutes. The scenery took hold of Richard's eye and held on firmly. The sighting of what had to be a navy ship distracted him momentarily, but the slight bump of the ferry pulling up to the dock and ramp jolted him back to his immediate surroundings.

Lyndsey sat silent through the entire trip. The bakery woman's words replayed themselves in her mind: *'Gott'cha. Enjoy your honeymoon.'* The trip so far had been everything a maiden could imagine and hope for on her honeymoon. A tingle ran up through her inner thighs. She trembled as their day at the beach flashed before her eyes. A song echoed in her ears. Seagulls soared freely in her mind's eye. Their song of the sea echoed in Lyndsey heart. Sex for sex's sake would never again fill her womanly needs. Those deep sensual needs now would demand the total giving of herself unto her mate in the act of love-making and that she be in the arms of a giver and that the giver must be her soul-mate…Richard.

"Hello"

Lyndsey blinked. Her eyes stared ahead at a winding stretch of paved highway.

"Oops. Sorry Rich. I must have nodded off."

"Yes. It has been a half hour plus since we left the bakery."

"No way, you're joking?"

"Guess again girl, we're actually ahead of schedule."

"So where are we?"

Richard grinned then said, "On our way to Lunenburg."

"Lune...Lunenburg?"

"Yes."

"OK. I remember. It's on Gilbert's list of absolutely must sees." Lyndsey paused smiled and said, "I sure hope we get there soon, I feel a craving for an ice-cream fix!"

"Well Gilbert gave this one a triple-A rating. There's a fish museum down on the waterfront."

"And ice-cream I trust."

"If we're really lucky, the Bluenose will be in town."

"Get outt'a here."

"Never, Lunenburg is her home port."

"The Bluenose, the ship; no I mean the schooner on the dime?"

"Yes, the one and only Bluenose."

Richard pressed the accelerator and upped their speed. He shook his head and declared, "I can't believe it."

"Believe what?"

"My whole life has been centred around boats and boating. Our family business was built up around pleasure boats. Most of our work takes place around the Great Lakes, Lake Simcoe and now... now I'm on a highway driving towards one of the greatest ship-building towns known to man."

Lyndsey sat silent and took in Richard's enthusiastic musing. She'd not seen him this excited about the family business for a long time.

"How could I have missed it? Lunenburg, home of the master ship builders who built the Bluenose, the Bounty, and countless more—along with a rum runner or two, I'd safely wager."

Lyndsey laughed aloud then exclaimed, "Richard! Slow down. There are the exhibition grounds."

Richard eased off the accelerator and tapped the brake pedal.

Lyndsey continued to give Richard, Gilbert's directions, "At the stop sign ahead, turn left."

"OK."

"Then at the lights go right."

At the stop sign Richard brought the SUV to a full stop. He turned left then completed Lyndsey's instructions by making the right turn at the traffic light.

"Where to now?" he asked

"Here, turn right. The museum and waterfront is down along this street."

Richard completed Lyndsey's new instruction and turned right, then headed down the street in search of Lunenburg's waterfront and the Fishery Museum. The water appeared to their right. Ahead, also to the right, stood a large, bright, red building, a sign proclaimed it to be *The Fishery's Museum of the Atlantic*. Richard turned into the museum's parking lot at the end of the building. He opted for a parking spot that pointed towards the water.

The SUV's third occupant, Bailey, stirred on Lyndsey's lap then called out, "Meoow…meeoow." Richard and Lyndsey turned and faced each other. Lyndsey acted first. She smiled and carefully opened her door, then stepped out into the parking lot. Richard spent several minutes with Bailey; he opened all the windows to give Bailey access to fresh air, set up a dish of water for him on Lyndsey's seat then joined Lyndsey. Together, they surveyed their surroundings. Lyndsey turned and looked back at the tall, brightly painted buildings across the street from the museum. They appeared to be restaurants, taverns, pubs, and artisan/souvenir shops.

Richard's attention fell directly on the large schooner positioned along the museum's dock. Next, his eyes leaped over to the vessel's nameplate. It read, "Bluenose II." His heart skipped a beat. He called out to Lyndsey, "Look. She's in port."

Lyndsey turned back to Richard. Except for the missing blond curls, for his hair had turned a light sandy brown, and the extra height, the Richard she saw greatly resembled the Richard of their sandbox days. Unable to deny the enthusiasm that radiated from Richard's face, Lyndsey demanded, "Go. Live the dream. I'll visit the museum gift shop."

Richard stepped up to Lyndsey, leaned forward, kissed her, and then declared, "Love ya Lyndsey."

He stepped back, turned, and raced off towards the museum entrance.

Bailey on the driver's seat stood up and poked his head out of the window. Seeking attention he called out, "Meow...meoew...meeeow."

Lyndsey walked around the SUV and casually rubbed the old feline's head. A boy and girl raced over and joined her and Bailey.

"Can we? Can we pet the kittie?" They sang out to Lyndsey.

A lady joined them and admonished the pair for bothering the lady and her kittie-cat.

Lyndsey smiled and defended the young ones, "Not to worry. Bailey loves the extra attention. Oh, I'm Lyndsey. And you are?"

"Maria, Maria Lamont. Taylor and Megan are my grandchildren. True blessing they be."

"Gramm, Gramms can we pet Bailey. He likes me!" Megan shouted out.

Maria smiled then replied, "Sorry Meg, Lyndsey here wants to go visit the museum. We'd best let her be on her way."

Taylor continued to rub Bailey's head. Megan pleaded her case, "But Gramma, we've been to the museum. Maybe we can kittie-sit while Lyndsey visits the museum?"

Maria grinned fondly at Megan and Taylor. She replied, "Sorry but we must be heading over to Ice Cream Heaven, iff'in you two want a treat before we head home."

Lyndsey aided the pair in rubbing a contented Bailey's head. She asked, "Maria, if you're not in a hurry to head home, I'd be happy to hire these two eager kittie-sitters to entertain Bailey while I visit the museum. It will be a short visit. We're meeting up with family for a dinner—supper-get together?"

"Please... pleeeese Gramms", Taylor and Megan pleaded.

Lyndsey reached into her purse retrieved one of Richard's business cards and gave it to Maria. "I'll pay with a trip to Ice Cream Heaven. I hear it calling out my name. I'm Lyndsey—Lyndsey Ramsay."

Maria relented, "Ok. Ok. Lordie what we grammas will do for our wee grandkids."

Lyndsey thanked Maria and promised to return in a half hour and a bit. She glanced at Maria's wee ones and wondered—could they be twins. She guessed them to be five or six years old.

Maria whispered to Lyndsey, "Taylor-Butterscotch ripple, Megan-Heavenly Hash."

Lyndsey nodded and thanked her then headed off towards the museum entrance. Inside the museum, Lyndsey entered the gift shop. A quick glance about confirmed that Richard had entered the museum and by now was walking the planks of Bluenose II's deck. Half an hour later, Lyndsey paid the cashier for her purchases: Richard's gifts included a video of Bluenose II, a book written on the same subject, a sweatshirt with the Bluenose II on it, another depicting Lunenburg's waterfront, and a heavy cotton T-shirt with three wooden dories painted beneath the words 'The Dory Shop… Lunenburg Nova Scotia.' Finally, for herself, she'd selected a collection of postcards. She stepped back out into the parking lot and walked towards the SUV. A quick look to the waterfront revealed that Richard had departed Bluenose II and now stood aboard another floating exhibit, a smaller schooner named the Theresa E. Connor.

Calculating at least another half hour wait, Lyndsey walked across the street to the welcoming sign above the windows of Ice Cream Heaven's shop. She purchased four small cones and laughed on seeing they came with double scoops of ice cream. With the cones in a carrying tray she returned to the SUV and joined Maria and Bailey's kittie-sitters Megan, Taylor. With payment in hand Maria, Taylor and Megan thanked Lyndsey and parted. She placed her purchases on the SUV's back seat and waited for Richard to return. Bailey eagerly licked her hands free of the ice cream that dripped onto them.

Richard cut his odyssey aboard the museum's floating exhibits short. He walked back through the museum then entered the gift shop. There, he selected an assortment of pink, blue and green tops, their fronts highlighted with beach scenes and sea gulls. One was a fleece pullover, its warm snuggly look drew Richard eye to it. On exiting the museum, he scanned the parking lot for Lyndsey. He spotted her standing beside the SUV driver's door with a rapidly melting ice-cream cone in hand. After catching her attention with a wave, Richard walked over to the SUV. He asked, "Is it good ice-cream?"

"Yup, it's mmm…mmm blueberry."

"You're addicted."

"Guilty."

Richard opened Lyndsey's door. She almost claimed her seat, spotted Bailey's water dish, set it on the floor then stepped inside and slid into her seat. Richard, once inside and behind the wheel, started the engine and drove out of the parking lot. Their drive back through the Town of Lunenburg took them through the older downtown area. The bright colours of the buildings and steep hills made an impression on both Richard and Lyndsey silently they bid the quaint colourful town farewell.

The drive from Lunenburg through to Mahone Bay passed quickly. Lyndsey remained quiet and focused her attention on Bailey, who had climbed up onto her lap. She rubbed his head and soon had Bailey purring contentedly. Richard spoke nonstop the entire way. Everything revolved around the Bluenose II and the Teresa E. Connor, the museum's flagship schooner which was steeped in history being Canada's oldest Saltbank Schooner. Lyndsey received a history lesson centered on the Atlantic Salt Cod Fishery.

Lyndsey continued to take in all the scenery along the route. A small grin appeared on her face as they drove past the sandy shore of yet another Scotian beach in silence. Both looked with envy at the young couple that walked along the shore. Neither spoke. Further along, Lyndsey spotted a sign pointing to Oak Island. It felt familiar to her. Richard missed the sign and continued to relate to Lyndsey the memories of his visit aboard Bluenose II.

"Welcome to Chester," the roadside sign declared. Lyndsey picked up the *Doers' & Dreamers' Travel Guide*. She opened it up and found Chester on its map. Chester stood a mere eight km from East River. Lyndsey set the guide down, smiled, and said, "Ten minutes tops, Rich. Ten minutes and we'll be back to where it all started."

"I'm strangely excited but also sad," Richard answered. He explained, "I need to find the truth—find my family's roots. Sadly, I do not want our time alone with each other to end."

Lyndsey replied, "Trust me. It has no end."

She placed her hand on Richard's thigh, giving it a squeeze. Lyndsey then looked at Richard, puckered her lips, shifted closer to him, and kissed his cheek.

"Slow down, girl. We're almost there. The journey's almost over."

"Trust me, there's no chance of that happening in our lifetime."

CHAPTER 32

JEFFREY STEPPED OUT OF THE HOUSE. HE WALKED OVER TO THE shed. There, he picked up the dinner basket that contained the pre-selected lobsters and added the extras Gilbert had requested. Jeffrey could almost taste Gilbert's lasagna. He left the shed and headed up the trail to Gilbert's house.

Along the walk, Jeffrey tried to recall the names of Hope's friends—no, he remembered, they were family and were visiting from O'tario. Cusins, Hope had called them. He asked himself, "Now whot war dar nomes?" After a second or two, Jeffrey uttered aloud, "Lin…na. Lyn…dsie, yes dats it, Lyn…dsie. Now what be hes name? Rick…iee. Na. Rich? Ah. King Rich'rd. Dats it."

Jeffrey smiled; he'd realized anew that if Hope had new cousins, then Jeffrey also had a new niece and nephew or maybe two. She'd mentioned a third person, but hadn't dwelt much on him. Most of what Hope had talked about centred on the girl, the Lyn…dsie. Real nice, Hope had told him. Then she's said something about a business and something about them, the McClakens owning some of it. *No matter*, Jeffrey thought. *I's got me hands full jest taking care of what I's got.* However, the idea of being an uncle all over again appealed to Jeffrey. He emerged from the path and stepped onto the edge of Gilbert's lawn. He stopped dead in his tracks. The image of a childhood playmate reminded him of times past. In his heart Jeffrey prayed that he wouldn't reveal anything about the big family secret.

He walked across the lawn and stopped short at the front door of the house. A quick rat-a-tap-tap on the door brought forth an invite to step inside.

"Come on in, Uncle Jeffrey. We're in the kitchen."

Jeffrey opened the door and stepped inside. He walked across the living room and entered the kitchen. Gilbert sat at the table. Hope stood by the counter slicing up what remained of a homemade loaf of bread. Jeffrey looked first to Hope then switched to Gilbert. "Where dos ya wants dem?" Jeffrey asked.

Gilbert chuckled and wiped away the last traces of peanut butter from his face. He said, "Hi Jeff, good to see you."

Hope looked at Jeffrey and said, "Over here on the counter is fine, Uncle Jeffrey."

Jeffrey walked around the table and placed his basket of lobsters on the counter.

Hope peeked into the basket and uttered, "Nice. They'll fit the pot just fine."

She smiled at Jeffrey, then walked over and embraced him. The hug was warmly reciprocated. Hope stepped back and said, "Now that's more like the uncle I love so dearly."

Jeffrey brimmed with pride. He looked over to Gilbert and was about to crow.

Hope piped out. "Don't be flaunting me love, laddie. You know well I love the two of you equally."

"Nat evun a tinge more?" Jeffrey asked in jest.

"No equally. Now get over there and say hello to Gilbert."

"Oh wells. I trayed."

"That you did."

CHAPTER 33

RICHARD SLOWED DOWN ON THE DRIVE THROUGH CHESTER THEN accelerated after they'd passed through the village. The final stretch of their trip approached its end when a sign announced their arrival in East River. Richard tapped the brake pedal and slowed down. He'd expected to see a town filled with shops and a main street. The sign directed them right at the next turnoff. The business district turned out to be the combination of a convenience store and a fish and chip outlet. Richard turned right as directed. A short distance down the road, Lyndsey directed Richard to turn off onto a dirt road. He complied and drove slowly ahead. It took several more turns before Lyndsey pointed out a laneway ahead to Richard's left. He turned and drove along the lane. It narrowed and passed through a short stretch sided by birch trees. Beyond the birch trees, an opening appeared. Ahead stood a large cedar-sided house, Gilbert's purple pickup truck parked off to the side identified the house as their final destination. Richard pulled up beside Gilbert's truck and stopped.

Before Richard could step out onto the earth of his ancestors, Hope raced out the front door of the house. She almost tumbled off the porch, regained solid footing, dashed towards Richard and Lyndsey. On arrival Hope excitedly pulled Lyndsey's door open, leaped inside and wrapped her arms around Lyndsey then broke into tears. A yellow flash dashed out the passenger door. Bailey hit the ground and raced off towards a dense rose hedge. Once safely under the rose hedge, Bailey stopped, then turned around and peered back at Richard's SUV. It would be two days later before he resurfaced and accepted an offer of fresh, unprocessed fish.

Richard looked over at the girls and said, "Hi, Hope. It's nice to see you too."

Hope released Lyndsey and climbed over her to Richard. She grabbed his shoulders and pulled his face to hers. Her lips landed directly on Richard's and she gave him a welcome-home kiss. She released Richard and returned her attention to Lyndsey. Another emotional hug ensued. This time, Lyndsey joined Hope. Her eyes watered, and like Hope she started to sob. The girls fell silent. Hope felt relief on sensing and seeing sparkles of positive energies and confidence in Lyndsey. The time the girls had shared together following John's explosion and drunken outburst of anger towards Lyndsey had seeded and ignited an emotional bond. Lyndsey embraced Hope. It proved too emotional for Richard. He stepped out onto the ground and closed his door.

Gilbert rounded the corner then broke into a run on spotting Richard who braced himself for a hug. Instead, Gilbert thrust his hand out and grasped Richard's. He shook it hard, smiled, and said, "Welcome home. This is it. No palace, but home all the same." Before Richard could speak, Gilbert gave him the hug he'd been braced to receive. Gilbert's arms wrapped around Richard, he patted Richard's back then released him.

Richard relaxed. He turned and watched Gilbert step off towards Lyndsey. The girls had finally managed to separate and now stood beside the SUV. Lyndsey disappeared in Gilbert's embrace. Hope jumped forward and greeted Richard. Again she hugged him and planted kisses on his cheeks. Richard did not offer any resistance. It would have proven futile.

Hope dropped her head on Richard's shoulder then pulled him tight against herself. Her sobs of elation broke out anew. Gilbert and Lyndsey walked up to Hope and her captive, Richard. Gilbert hummed and hawed, then finally tapped Hope on the shoulder. At first, she did not respond. It took two more attempts by Gilbert before Hope turned and looked in Gilbert's direction. She planted one more kiss on Richard then released him from her grasp. She blushed, and said, "Sorry. It's only been a few days since we parted. A month ago we lived in two unconnected worlds." She paused then added, "Your family suffered a tragic loss. I cannot fathom the hurt and sorrow you've faced. However, it brought us together, and yes, I'm glad to finally have both of you here!"

"I believe you've made that point," Gilbert informed Hope. He then directed Richard and Lyndsey towards the front of the house. Hope walked along at Lyndsey's side.

At the front door, everyone stopped. Richard turned to Hope and jested, "Thanks Hope. That's absolutely the best homecoming I've ever received." He reached out and hugged Hope briefly then said, "Thank you."

Gilbert turned the doorknob and pushed the door open. He waved the others into the house then followed Richard inside.

Hope moved forward and assumed the role of hostess. She led Richard and Lyndsey on a thorough tour of the house that started in the living room, then proceeded to the upper level. At the top of the stairs, they turned down the hallway. She pointed out the rooms Gilbert had set aside for them. Lyndsey's room was next to Hope's, and Richard's was across the hallway from Hope's and beside the bathroom. Gilbert's was at the end of the hallway. It was the master bedroom, had a self-contained bath and over-looked the bay. The view from the bedroom's bay window held both Lyndsey and Richard in awe. The rose hedge continued its early bloom. Out beyond the hedge and its clusters of pink rose blossoms stood the blue-green waters of the bay. Hope gave them a moment to gaze out the window then led them to the bathroom they would use. With the upstairs completed, they returned to the main floor. Hope took them through the dining room and into the kitchen.

There, she proclaimed, "Saved the best for the last."

Gilbert stood in the kitchen and looked frustrated. At his side stood a much shorter man, but one who made a lasting impression on both Lyndsey and Richard. It appeared obvious that they'd walked into a heated discussion.

Gilbert displayed an unfamiliar frown, he yelled at Jeffrey, "Hello!"

Jeffrey looked directly back at Gilbert. He did not answer.

Gilbert, frustrated, lowered his voice and asked anew, "Care to offer up your explanation. I'd love to hear it."

Jeffrey smiled sheepishly. He said, "The Gooods Neeighbour Faieryiry."

Gilbert's face went blank. He replied, "I won't go there Jeff!"

"The Gooods Neeighbour Faieryiryry, you know, bees a sweet wee lassie, and she hass stood by me fer yeeaars."

"Get real Jeffy. There's no such ting asin a The Good Neighbour Fairy!"

"Don't be a calling me Jeffy bro."

"You just don't get it. It's simply been the shock of your island experience. In your mind only the Good Neighbour Fairy exists and shields you from the hand from Hell that tried to seize your soul that day! Besides, I'm the only good neighbour you have within a mile of you."

"Naw! Dat day ons th island wer but a stoop fer me ta pee. Nuting bad errver happon'd ta mee. Gillies, she bees buts a sweeet young un she bees. An onlees everrs ask't one ting of mee"

"Hope interrupted. She said, "Uncle Jeffrey. I know well your views on the Tooth Fairy, Fairy Godmothers, and Santa Claus. I have heard rumours, through Pappy and the chats we've often shared on occasion have alluded to your Good Neighbour Fairy. However if it...she were real, wouldn't the card and candy companies have launched a holiday campaign years ago?"

Gilbert interrupted. "Hope…enough please. Let it drop."

Lyndsey stared at Jeffery. Both Hope and Jeffery's words, '*Gooods Neeighbour Faieryiry*', echo in her head.

Jeffrey looked at young Hope and said, "It is Santie Claus not Santa Claus you know."

Hope nodded and accepted her uncle's correction. She shared with Lyndsey and Richard her uncle's oft told explanation of the two Santas, "Santa Claus, number two came on Christmas Eve to all good little boys and girls after he'd finished up his job at the local mall, where he took care of all the merchants' demands. He did not come to older boys and girls. He also had been known on occasion to miss a child or two in his rush to get the job at hand done. On the other hand, Santie Claus number one came Christmas Eve to all good boys and girls young and old who believed in him. Santie Claus did not discriminate on the basis of age. He simply swooshed in a flash down de chimney, zip...zap in a flash straight through closed doors, and never ever missed making any of his stops." Hope looked at Uncle Jeffery, nodded and said, "No Yes, Uncle. Admit it your little Hope got it right."

"Weells you sorta deed, de truth bees tolt. Ans trusts mees Hope. Ones nevvers sees Santie Claus. Wheere's dee wee lassie ders ting dooes good tings fers yers favourite uncle alls de times. And trusts yer unclie I sees heer and de lassie sees mees. Wes chatted a times or twoo fer shore."

Gilbert shrugged his shoulders. He turned from Jeffrey and faced Richard and Lyndsey. He said, "Richard, Lyndsey, this is my baby brother, Jeffrey. Jeffrey, you remember William…Mr. Ramsay? He stopped by the house to visit Mother when we were but young lads and numerous times over the years since. Richard here is one of his grandsons. Lyndsey is Richard's sister-in-law."

"Plased ta makes yur aquanances," Jeffrey said to Richard and Lyndsey. He looked puzzled and stared at Lyndsey. Something about her seemed familiar to him.

"Woow she bees a rite preety one fer shore," Jeffrey boasted about his new niece. He turned to Gilbert and said, "I's must'a bee'n but a wee tad ween yer Mr. Ram…say come a tap'n on'ta da doar dat first time."

"Yes come to think of it, you couldn't have been much more than nine or ten on his last visit," Gilbert replied.

Richard stepped forward and held his hand out to Jeffrey. Jeffrey responded. He reached out and gripped Richard's hand firmly. The two men shook hands, then released their grip on each other and stepped apart.

Jeffrey did a quick sidestep then stepped forward to greet Lyndsey. The two stood before each other. Jeffrey smiled and stared into her blue eyes. He did not speak. Lyndsey's blue eyes had captured him in their allure. Inside, his mind raced. Something about this young woman reminded him of someone or something. *But what,* he asked of himself.

Lyndsey broke the brief silence. She said, "Pleased to finally meet you, Mr. McClaken. Your brother has spoken—"

Lyndsey's words stopped in mid-sentence. Jeffrey had stepped forward and wrapped his arms about her. He hugged her tightly then added an extra squeeze and a friendly back pat. Just as quickly, he released her, stepped back, and said, "Welcome to de family, missy. An byes de way…Jeffrey is jest fine." He winked and said, "We'll have no mores of dat Mr. stuff. Rights?"

A shocked and relieved Lyndsey smiled at Jeffrey and said, "Right. Jeffrey it is then."

Gilbert looked across the room sternly at Jeffrey. He did not speak.

Jeffrey spoke before he could be corrected by Gilbert. He said, "It's okay, Gilbert. Sorry if I scar't you Ly…Lyndsie. Hope has tol't her favrit Uncle Jeffrey all aboot her trip up to Ontar'o. Well, almost every-ting." He paused then continued, "She didn't tell her dearest of dear uncles that we now had a famous beaut'y…full model lady in de family."

Lyndsey smiled at Jeffrey and said, "Sorry to disappoint. No model here, just me."

Jeffrey smiled back. He said, "No disappo…nmen't her's. I knows whats I sees."

Everyone broke into light laughter.

Gilbert recovered first; he looked at Richard and said, "Shall we step outside and retrieve your luggage? You will be setting up base camp here with us…right? We'd hear of nothing else…I assure you."

Hope broke away from the group and walked off to the kitchen. Once there, she busied herself by preparing a pot of tea for the guests. She giggled lightly at recalling Lyndsey's introduction and Uncle Jeffrey's greeting.

In the living room, Jeffrey broke away from the group and walked over to the front door. He opened it, then stood aside and waited until Gilbert, Richard, and Lyndsey had stepped outside before he followed them out. Lyndsey walked away from the others. She moved across the large, grassy lawn towards the yard's edge. At the edge, she stopped, before her stood a robust rose hedge. It was covered in many clusters of dainty, pink rose flowers. A breeze carried the rose hedge's aromatic scent straight to her face. She closed her eyes and deeply inhaled the intoxicating aromatic aura. Her eyes opened as she looked out over the rose hedge and locked onto a majestic seascape. She raised both hands and shielded the sun from her eyes. The blue-green swells of seawater rose and fell to the beat of the sea. Overhead, sea gulls soared and called out their song of the sea. Further out into the bay, Lyndsey spotted a small cape-island fishing boat. It bobbed up and down in tune with the waves beneath its keel. She stared out over the sea and watched the boat grow ever smaller then in a blink of her eye it disappeared from sight over the horizon. Off to the left, she spotted what appeared to be a pair of islands. A silver-grey mist surrounded the islands. In Lyndsey's eyes they appeared to float above the sea atop the slow swirling mist. The words of a once young Grace Ramsay echoed in Lyndsey's mind and carried her across the bridge of time.

> *A week has passed since last I guided my pencil upon these pages. Uncle Richard's once black and curly hair remains whiter than snow to this day. I have looked out upon the sea more than once this week past. Most days the fog possessed the bay. There was an occasion or two when I was blessed with sunshine and did lay my eyes upon what must be the island of which Father and Uncle Richard have spoken. I did on those occasions feel an eerie tingle run up and down my spine.*

Lyndsey shivered lightly. She pulled her hands down then wrapped her arms tightly about her bosom. Unsure and frightened by the words that had just echoed through her mind, she turned her eyes away from the sea and back upon the rose hedge. The pink rose flowers held her eyes. She pondered. Could Uncle Jeffrey's Good Neighbour Fairy be the ghostly spirit of the diary's—Grace Ramsay? Lyndsey resolved to chat with Jeffrey later and question the possibility.

Richard walked up behind Lyndsey. He stopped short, glanced briefly out at the sea, then reached out to Lyndsey and placed his sports jacket over her shoulders. Lyndsey jumped. The jacket almost fell from her shoulders. Richard caught the jacket before it could slide towards the ground. He placed it back over Lyndsey's shoulders.

She turned about smiled and said, "Sorry Rich. My mind was off yonder. It's a chilly but pleasant breeze blowing off the sea. Let's go back inside."

"OK! Hope I didn't scare you too badly. Gilbert suggested you might need the jacket."

"It's so beautiful Richard."

"Yes. I'm standing in the foreground of Grandfather's old seaside photo-picture. I feel totally reconnected to him"

They took one last look out over the rose hedge at the sea, then turned and walked side by side back to the house.

CHAPTER 34

GILBERT AND JEFFREY HAD UNLOADED THEIR LUGGAGE AND carried it into the house. Lyndsey entered the house first, followed closely by Richard. He closed the door and trailed Lyndsey across the living room into the kitchen, where the others had gathered about the small oak kitchen table.

"The rose hedge is unbelievable," Lyndsey declared.

"It was Grammy's favourite. Mine too," Hope answered.

"So many rose blooms, the scent, how did she ever get it to flourish so?"

"Grammy merely tended to its needs," Hope replied. She continued, "The hedge itself must be 200 plus years old. Its care is now a task I truly treasure. Though standing beside it, I swear Grammy still has a hand in its care. Since her passing, the rose buds have been far more profuse and seem to burst forth into bloom much earlier than in the past. Yes, Grammy mus—"

Gilbert interrupted, "Don't be spreading tales of ghosts to our guest, Hope. Give yourself a touch of credit."

Jeffrey added, "Yes sir…ree. Hope here. Well all the gard'n seen heres a'bout is her work'ns."

Hope blushed.

Gilbert stood up and walked over to the kitchen stove. He paused, then suggested, "The time has arrived to introduce you to a helping of our famed McClaken/Ramsay cooking. Hope, if you would take our guests to the dining room, I will retrieve our main course."

Nobody moved. They all stood and faced Gilbert and the oven. He donned a pair of oven mitts and pulled the oven door open. The arresting scent of McClaken Lobster Lasagna filled the kitchen. He stooped over and withdrew his masterpiece from the oven.

"Oh. I love lasagna," Lyndsey declared.

"Yer in fer a treet den," Jeffrey added.

Gilbert carried the pan of lasagna over to the side counter. "Okay Hope. The chef requires a moment alone. One must maintain the family recipe's secret ingredients and finishing touches."

Hope stepped off. She said, "Best follow me. Uncle Gilbert does not jest, at least not on this matter."

Lyndsey, Richard, and Jeffrey followed Hope out of the kitchen. She led them through a greenhouse kitchen nook and into a large, spacious dining room. Its centrepiece was a large cherry-wood dining table. Places were set for five. Two small baskets held fresh baked and sliced homemade bread. Candles flickered in a centrepiece made from driftwood and adorned with dried flowers from the seaside. Steam drifted up from the spout of a china tea pot. The teapot matched the *Blue Willow* plates and teacup setting. Hope directed everyone to their designated sittings. After they had all seated themselves, Hope raised her hands and started to applaud. The others joined her cue.

Gilbert walked into the dining room bearing his masterpiece. He carried it over to the table and set it down on a large porcelain hot-plate holder. Everyone sat in awe and waited for Gilbert to seat himself.

He broke the silence and said, "Before we start in…I believe a blessing and offering of thanks is in order."

"Nat a probl'm Gil," Jeffrey offered. "I be pleas'd tat do de honars."

Gilbert lowered his head and closed his eyes. Everyone followed suit and waited for Jeffrey to recite grace.

Jeffrey did not disappoint. He clasped his hands together and entwined his fingers, then spoke aloud to the Lord, "Lard, we tanks ye fer bring'n dis fam'ly backs toged'r. Little Hope done tolt her

Uncle Jeffrey...me...alls bout yer good workins up der in O'terio. You done good Lard. Deys sitt'n hir cross de table frem me. She be a right nice purty one at dat. De lad he be OK too. Tanks fer make'n old Jeffrey hir a triple uncle. A bless'n on Gilbert's fine cook'n set before us all would be a nice ting too Lard. Last'ly Lard, no disrispect but I's a hungr'y lad. Could'n we jest git to de good stuff? So iff'n yeu'd bless dis food and den all us good folks could git dow'n ta bless'n yer gid work'ns da honly ways we knows."

Jeffrey opened his left eye and looked upwards for a sign. A grumble erupted in his stomach. He closed his eye quickly and closed off conversation with the Lord.

"Tanks ye Lard. Amens."

All present at the table echoed the end of Jeffrey's grace. "Amen."

Gilbert opened his eyes, looked over to Jeffrey, and said, "Thank you Jeffrey. Your grace and call for blessings on our gathering is A-One and a tough one to top. We'll surely be truly blessed."

Jeffrey nodded to Gilbert his appreciation. He eyed the large bake tray that sat across the table from where he sat. Hope took advantage of the short break in conversation and served tea to everyone then returned to her place at the table.

Before Jeffrey started to reach for the tray, Gilbert said, "Richard. Would you do the honours and serve the first portions to the ladies?"

Richard smiled, picked up the spatula, and went to work on the lasagna. Lyndsey held out her plate to Richard. He placed a large portion on it. Lyndsey frowned but did not refuse. Next, he repeated the process when Hope held out her plate to him. The sweet aroma of lobster lasagna filled the dining room. Richard served himself a portion then passed the spatula to Gilbert.

Gilbert took one look at Jeffrey and passed the spatula to him. He helped himself to the Caesar's Salad and waited for Jeffrey to fill his plate.

Jeffrey did not disappoint his brother. He stopped just short of leaving the bake tray empty.

Gilbert accepted the spatula from Jeffrey and helped himself to the last of the lasagna.

"Mmm. This is very good Gilbert. I've never had seafood lasagna before," Lyndsey stated.

Jeffrey beamed and declared, "It's a Mar…itim'r sec'rete. Leas'n dis one is."

Gilbert stepped in and explained, "It's a legendary secret family recipe. Jeffrey kindly provided us with the star ingredient lobsters."

"Wow!" Lyndsey exclaimed then confessed, "I've never tried lobster before. I understand now…all the hubbub."

"Ah. I ner did," Jeffrey injected. He continued, "Eat'n lobbies be whot us Nov'ies dooes best'ta all."

Everybody laughed. The main meal disappeared, and an hour had passed before the diners realized the time. Hope excused herself, picked up the dinner plates, and carried them out to the kitchen. Lyndsey offered to help, but Hope would not hear of it. Five minutes later, Hope carried Gilbert's prized dessert into the dining room and placed it next to Gilbert. Another trip to the kitchen brought the dessert plates to the table.

Lyndsey begged off, then settled on a small piece of the blueberry pie. Hope accepted what Lyndsey thought to be a large piece. Richard's matched Hope's. Gilbert followed suit. Jeffrey eyed the pie that remained in the pie plate and licked his lips.

"Anyone for seconds?" Gilbert asked. Nobody spoke up. Gilbert passed the pie plate to Jeffrey. Jeffrey set the plate down in front of himself.

He said, "One mar'e chance at'it."

Again, nobody spoke up. Jeffrey picked up his fork and attacked the pie. In less time than it took the others to clear their dessert plates, Jeffrey had devoured the third of the pie left to him. He wiped away a splatter of blueberry droppings from his beard and belched.

"Scuse me."

"You're excused Jeffrey," Gilbert said.

He then asked everybody to step into the living room with him: everyone followed his lead except Jeffrey. He stayed back and cleared the table, started a pot of coffee, and then placed the dinner dishes and pots in the dishwasher. Hope joined him. She chased him out of the kitchen and tested the coffee to ensure it wasn't too strong. Satisfied, she placed five mugs, sugar, and the coffee pot on a serving cart. She wheeled it into the living room. Over coffee, Richard and Lyndsey described their trip and thanked Gilbert for his excellent guide service. Neither revealed their side trip south of Liverpool down to the secluded seaside beach. Lyndsey worried about Bailey, suggested they set a dish of food outside. She mentioned Bailey's destination on escaping the vehicle...the rose hedge.

Jeffrey jumped up and offered to handle the task.

After he'd stepped out of the room, Gilbert suggested they take a tour of the grounds and drop in on Pappy, who'd not been able to join them for dinner due to a touch of an early summer flu. He stood up and led the procession out to the front yard. They spotted Jeffrey over by the rose hedge with Bailey's dish in hand.

"Here, kitty kittty. Uncle Jeff'rey's got yer din din fer ya."

Bailey crouched down deep under the hedge and did not respond. Something about the stranger tempted him, but he refused to budge and risk being put back inside the black beast. The ride had lasted much longer than Bailey had expected. In the past, he'd only been subjected to vehicle travel for a trip to the vet's office. Bailey resolved himself to waiting it out. Once the stranger had placed the dish down beneath the hedge, Bailey sighed, relieved at having made the right choice. He watched the stranger turn and walk away. Over by the house, Bailey spotted Richard and Lyndsey along with two people that he found familiar. He watched the five people walk off together towards the far side of the lawn.

CHAPTER 35

LYNDSEY WALKED AT HOPE'S SIDE. EXCITEMENT RACED THROUGH her mind. Visions from a dream that had captured her imagination back in Newmarket flashed randomly in her mind's eye. One image held her captive. In it, she stood on the front lawn of the old homestead. At the lawn's edge, she stopped then entered the trail that stood before her. A short walk brought them to the shed. The old house stood off to the left. Lyndsey stopped dead in her tracks. She stared at the old homestead and blocked out the addition added to expand the homestead out into its back yard. An icy tingling sensation raced throughout her body. Lyndsey stood frozen and stared at an image straight out of her dream.

Hope nudged her. She asked, "Lyns...Lyndsey are you OK? You look like you've seen a ghost!"

Lyndsey recovered her thoughts. She answered, "I'm fine, Hope. The house it's the perfect image of every little girl's life-sized dollhouse." She stared at it. The front appeared to have been built many years past. The front windows were small and comprised of nine panes of glass.

Hope smiled and hugged Lyndsey, then coyly boasted, "And this little girl got to live many enchanted childhood days inside its magical world."

Lyndsey extended their hug, released Hope, then walked at her side and joined the others at the front door. Jeffrey did the honours and opened the door. Hope entered first. Lyndsey held herself back and waited until both Gilbert and Richard had entered. She then stepped through the door ahead of Jeffrey.

Pappy McClaken stood across the living room. A cane helped steady his fragile frame. He said, "Git yourselves in." Jeffrey stepped forward and made the introductions. He passed on Gilbert and Hope. Pappy made the trip across the living room and shook Richard's hand. Lyndsey made eye contact and held her hand out to him. Pappy passed on the offer, dropped his cane, stepped up to her and gave her a hug. He whispered, "Welcome home dearie. Bout time you got here."

Lyndsey kissed his cheek and thanked him. She said, "Thank you, Pappy. It really does feel like home."

Pappy accepted his cane from Richard who'd picked it up off the floor. Cane in hand, he made his way back across the living room to his chair.

Hope rescued Lyndsey and offered to take her on a tour of the house. She explained the current room layout, and compared it to what she believed had been its original floor plan. The living room had once been a one-room kitchen and living/family room. It was now a living/dining room. From there, they entered the open concept combined kitchen/hallway. It had been the original master bedroom. They paused in the kitchen and Hope boasted up the kitchen's oak cabinets. Across from the kitchen/hallway Hope stepped into Jeffery's bedroom and Lyndsey followed.

An icy-chill ran up her spine. *I've been here*, she thought. *This had been little Grace Ramsay's room, the room in which she'd once written her thoughts and dreams into the old diary.* She stared ahead past Hope to the figure of a petite girl about twelve years of age. A tear trickled down her cheek. She pondered so young to have died and been denied the gifts life holds in store for everyone touched by its magic.

The young girl smiled and greeted Lyndsey. She said, "Bout time you got here. Did you bring the rosary?"

Lyndsey answered back, "Yes. It's in the glove compartment of Richard's SUveee."

Hope jumped, looked at Lyndsey's ashen face, and asked, "You okay Lyndsey? You definitely look like someone who's seen a ghost!"

Lyndsey shuddered, then rubbed her arms vigorously and said, "I…I'm fine. A touch road weary maybe."

Hope accepted Lyndsey's explanation. She offered to cut short their tour. Lyndsey refused to hear of it. Hope led Lyndsey out of Jeffrey's bedroom back into the hallway.

On passing through the doorway, Lyndsey heard the voice softly call out, "Come back alone. Bring the rosary with you."

Lyndsey blocked the incident out of her mind. She followed Hope down the hallway. They paused and glanced into Pappy's bedroom, then she followed Hope into the bathroom and its four-legged antique bathtub. Running water, Hope explained, had been added fifteen years past, when the addition had been built. Outside the bathroom the tour continued into an enclosed sun-room. Instantly, Lyndsey fell in love with it. Hope sat down on one of the large, cushioned chairs. Lyndsey claimed the one next to it and curled up on it. She felt instant relief. Through the large, glass windows she stared out onto a view of East River Bay and the much larger Mahone Bay. The wind had disappeared, and the water took on the appearance of a large sheet of glass. To the west, the sun had started its descent. Its rays bounced off the water and caused Lyndsey to squint. She listened to Hope's voice in the background, but soon lost herself in the aura of a spectacular sunset. The sea turned from a silvery sheen into a blazon-red field of fire. The flames receded, and the sea turned into an enchanting pink, which glittered softly in Lyndsey's blue eyes. She sighed and whispered dreamily, "So beautiful. I feel sated and fulfilled. It's like sex on the beach."

"Lyndsey, you didn't!"

"What? Didn't what?" Lyndsey called out.

Hope laughed, grabbed Lyndsey's arm and said, "It is okay, girl. I've looked at his butt a time or two. Nice. Really nice, if you know what I mean."

Lyndsey blushed, looked back at Hope and made an attempt to deny Hope's allegation. The words never reached her lips. Instead, she listened to the gentle call of seagulls that soared through her mind. Lyndsey's insides tingled and she relived the joys and spontaneity she'd shared with Richard on the beach. She blinked.

"Not to worry. It'll be our secret," Hope blurted out.

Lyndsey did not reply. There were some things that one woman could never conceal from another. She conceded this to be one of them.

After a moment of silence had passed, Hope suggested they rejoin the others in the living room. Lyndsey accepted the suggestion, stood up after Hope had bounced up out of her chair, and followed her back into the living room. A cold chill passed through her as they walked past Jeffrey's bedroom. There, they were greeted and chided by Gilbert and Jeffrey for having taken so long.

Hope defended their tardiness. She explained, "Blame it on the sunset."

Gilbert and Jeffrey nodded their understanding. Sometime later, everyone bid goodnight to Pappy who was looking tired. Lyndsey had to promise to return early the next day with Hope. Jeffrey stood off to the side. Lyndsey walked over to him and treated him to a goodnight hug.

Jeffery whispered, "Didin ye sees me wee one. Me Gooods Neeighbour Faieryiryry? Shee's beeeen'a wee biits anxiooous, await'ng yer a'com'ings downs aur ways. A sweet ting shee bees." Lyndsey stiffened then relaxed in his embrace. He released Lyndsey and grinned on feeling Lyndsey's lips gently kiss his cheek. Lyndsey rejoined the others.

Gilbert, Richard, Hope, and Lyndsey stepped back outside into a front yard that rapidly grew darker under evening's tightening grip. Jeffrey remained inside with Pappy. Morning came early to those like himself who made their living from the sea. They walked quickly back along the pathway and were soon back at the edge of Gilbert's lawn with only a few mosquito bites inflicted on them. Hope raced over and checked out Bailey's dish. She met up with the others at the front door and reported that Bailey's appetite had not fully returned.

Back inside, Gilbert suggested they turn in for the night. Richard and Lyndsey gladly accepted his suggestion. Hope led Richard and Lyndsey up to their rooms. Richard bade the girls a good night and stepped into his room. Hope looked longingly at his butt as he passed through the doorway. Lyndsey looked at Hope and smirked. She did not speak.

Hope whispered, "Sweet dreams. Don't let the beach fleas bite. That's definitely one hot tomato you've hooked up with girl!"

They turned away from each other and walked into their bedrooms. Gilbert walked down the hallway a short time later and called out, "Good night all. Enjoy a sound and restful Nova Scotian night."

CHAPTER 36

LYNDSEY CLOSED THE BEDROOM DOOR AND WALKED OVER TO THE double, four-poster bed. She sat down on it and switched on the night table lamp. Her luggage and overnight bag had been set down beside an old four-drawer oak dresser. Tired after a long, eventful day, she pulled her tank top up over her head and removed it. She stood up, went to the dresser, and dropped her tank-top on it, then crouched down next to the overnight bag and pulled out a light, mini-length cotton nightgown. She stood up, released her belt buckle and popped the button on her shorts, then tugged on the zipper and the shorts fell to the floor. Lyndsey reached up her back and released the clips on her bra. Its straps fell off her shoulders and down her arms. She set it on top of the tank top. Next, she quickly removed her panty briefs. They joined the shorts on the floor. Lyndsey stood there naked and slapped off the minute grains of sand from her thighs and butt. She listened to the wind outside swirling and howling in the night's darkness. It had picked up since their return. The panoramic sunset shared earlier with Hope called out to her. She closed her eyes and for a second or two stood with Richard on the beach at sunset. Her hands ran up over her buttocks then reached out for Richard. Lyndsey opened her eyes and Richards naked body vanished. Lyndsey frowned, picked the nightgown off the dresser, and slid it down over her head. A quick trip to the bathroom refreshed her before turning in for the night. She walked over to the bed, pulled the cover and sheets down and turned the lamp off. The room turned pitch black. There were no streetlights to cast a glow in through the window. Next, she climbed up onto the bed and slid under the sheets and cover. The bed sheets were cold so Lyndsey grabbed the covers and pulled them up over her body, as she curled up into the fetal position. She laid there and stared out into the darkness of the room.

A hundred and one Richards floated before her eyes. She started to count them. At fifty-six or seven, her eyelids closed. Before falling into dreamland, Lyndsey fought off her frustration at having revealed to Hope her adventure on the beach. In her mind it had been an unconscious murmur—Hope had picked up on it the minute Lyndsey had whispered *'It's like sex on the beach'* and the words had left her lips. At that point, Lyndsey crossed the line and entered dreamland.

A breeze blew in gently from the sea and caressed her breasts. Beneath her, Richard lay on the sand. Inside, she felt him ebb, then swell up anew as she trembled against him. The sea breeze grew cold and chilled her naked body.

A soft voice called out, *"Come back alone. Bring the rosary with you."*

In a flash, Lyndsey's dream swept her into Jeffrey's bedroom. She stared at the ashen-faced ghost she'd encountered earlier on their visit to the old homestead. An eerie aura surrounded the ghostly spirit. It held out a candle to Lyndsey and beckoned her to approach. Afraid, Lyndsey stood frozen and did not move. The spirit persisted Lyndsey relented and walked towards her. A chilled and eerie wisp of wind extinguished the candle. Moonlight cast its beacon of light throughout the room.

"I knew you would come if I waited patiently for you. Thank you for bringing the rosary back to where it belongs. Back home to me."

"Who are you, really?" Lyndsey whispered. She continued, "A mere figment of my imagination perhaps?" The spirit did not reply. Lyndsey struggled within to fight off and repel the image that now possessed her mind. Her fear cast a shiver throughout her being. Curiosity drew her closer to the spirit. Hesitantly she stared at the spirit and whispered, "The Grace Ramsay from our diary is long dead. Her words were merely the imaginative adventures of a young girl in a new world. Her words describing it in the diary and alluding to its significance have simply been etched in my mind and have energized my creativity and imagination."

The spirit's hands reached outwards towards a frightened Lyndsey. Its face grew paler, "The diary is mine, not yours! Keep my foolish scribbling. The rosary is what I want. It is mine. My rosary was a gift Father gave me before he disappeared."

Lyndsey recoiled away from the spirit. Her body twisted and turned under her bed sheets. She struggled to escape the icy fingers of dreamland. In frustration she shouted out, "What is it you want of me?"

The ghostly figure pulled back from Lyndsey. It smiled, and a touch of colour returned to her cheeks. She said, "I want my rosary, Grace Ramsay's rosary! With it, I will appease the demonic beast that destroyed my family, deprived me and young Tom of Father's presence and love."

Lyndsey shuddered and grew cold. She asked, "What beast?"

"Don't act coy. You have Father's map and my diary. You must take me with you…out to the Floating Islands."

"How how can we possibly get there?"

"First, don't ask Gilbert. He'll not go. Pappy warned him of the island's evil. Go to Jeffrey. He's been there and is too simple to realize the dangers the island holds."

Lyndsey's face turned pale. From the moment Richard had first read young Grace's words and alluded to the possibility that the island had been the source of his ancestors' wealth, she had longed to return to the land and walk in their footsteps. Now, she felt a tingle of doubt and fear surfacing inside of her.

She asked, "Why? Why would you, a spirit from the past, seek out that rosary; it being but a trinket compared to the treasure your Father once held?"

"It'll release me from this prison in which I've remained a captive nigh on the past two hundred years. It'll gain my Father's attention.

Greed tore our family apart. Atonement will now serve to reunite it and will appease the beast."

Lyndsey suppressed a grin and said, "I'll talk to Richard. I'll ask him."

"Yes. But please...Make it quick."

"Excuse me? Just who do you think you are?"

"I am Grace Ramsay, author of the diary. I am also the spirit that could possess the child that grows inside of you if you do not do as I have kindly asked."

Lyndsey's hands sought out her belly. Her fingers caressed it. Her body tossed and turned. The bed sheets flew off of her. *She sat upright in the bed, her body trembling. She* screamed out, "*Frii...ig you!*"

Then, almost before the words had left her lips, Lyndsey felt a pang of sorrow for the spirit of young Grace Ramsay. Although it had once guided Grace's hand over the diary's pages with pencil in hand, it now appeared to be pleading with Lyndsey in its quest to become re-united with the Father whose greed had stolen his love from her. The night lamp snapped on. Lyndsey's eyes flashed open. She stared into the face of Hope. Drops of perspiration rolled down her temples.

"Lyndsey, Lyndsey, are you OK?" a frantic Hope called to her.

"Sorry Hope. I had a nightmare, a real spine tingling one!"

Hope sat at Lyndsey's side and embraced her. She whispered, "It was only a dream and will vanish from your mind in the blink of an eye." Her embrace pulled them closer. Hope kissed Lyndsey's forehead then said, "Don't move. I'll get you a drink of water. It will help you relax."

"OK."

Hope left the room to get Lyndsey the glass of water.

Lyndsey looked down at her watch and observed the hour to be 4:30 am. She tried to recall the details of her dream, pieces of it surfaced then faded stirring up the fears that had torn her away from a deep sleep and drawn Hope to her bedside. Frustrated, she sat there silently and waited for Hope to return. Hope's footsteps sent a thought racing through her mind, then it vanished, she pondered can one hear the footsteps of a ghost? She recalled Hope's reference to having heard rumours via Pappy of Jeffrey's Good Neighbour Fairy. Hope's steadfast denial that the old homestead could possibly be haunted cast a shadow of unease on her mind. Eager to remain connected to Hope, Lyndsey convinced herself that Hope simply lacked the paranormal powers needed that she now believed both Jeffery and she possessed. The bedroom door opened, and Hope walked into Lyndsey's bedroom. She held a large glass of water in her hand. Lyndsey felt a warm wave of relief pass through her being.

Hope arrived at Lyndsey's bedside and sat down. She held the glass to Lyndsey's lips and said, "Please drink. It'll make you feel better."

"Is that a promise?"

"Yes," Hope answered and laughed lightly.

Lyndsey took a sip. The cold water felt good, just like Hope had promised. She reached up and took the glass from Hope's hands. After a bit, she took another drink. In less than five minutes, she passed the empty glass back to her.

Hope removed the glass from Lyndsey's hands. The half hour they'd just shared had vanished in a flash. She placed her hand on Lyndsey's shoulder and urged her to relax and lay down. Lyndsey obeyed Hope's silent request. Hope pulled the sheet and covers up over Lyndsey. She said, "Best you try and rest now, catch a few more hours of sleep." Her hand passed over Lyndsey's forehead and hair; slowly, she gently brushed Lyndsey's hair.

Lyndsey sobbed, "It threatened to possess the child within me."

Hope continued to stroke Lyndsey's hair. She whispered, "Remember the secrets we shared at Mike's. You can't be pregnant. You haven't had sex in months if we don't count your little encounter on the beach. Relax girl. Don't fret I'm right here with you. I'll not allow harm to befall you."

Lyndsey sniffled and asked, "Really?"

"Yes. Now close your eyes. Silly, and toss your fears aside. Hope is here. You'll be safe."

Another half hour passed before Hope rose up from Lyndsey's side. Satisfied that Lyndsey had drifted off into a sound and peaceful sleep, she returned to her room and bed. There, it became her turn to fret and worry over Lyndsey's condition. Finally, reassured that it had been but a nightmare brought on by the long trip and recent stress endured by her friend, Hope too joined Lyndsey in a sound, restful sleep. The clock on her night table showed the hour to be six am. Another three hours would pass before Hope and Lyndsey arose to start their day anew.

CHAPTER 37

LYNDSEY'S EYES FLUTTERED THEN OPENED TO THE NEW MORNING. She sat up and tossed the cover aside, then turned and dropped her feet off the bed onto the hardwood floor. Her room in the light of morning took on greater appeal. All the furnishings were antique. The flowered wallpaper pulled the room together. It softened the dark oak dressers and doors. Lyndsey stood up and went to her overnight bag. There, she retrieved her toothbrush and toothpaste, soap, cleansing cream, shampoo, hairbrush and dryer. From her smaller traveling bag, she selected a pair of cut-off jeans and a fresh set of under garments. Out of the bag from the fisheries museum, she picked the medium sized pink top Richard had bought her. On holding it out to examine the front, she smiled. Three sea gulls soared in flight above a seaside beach that called out to her heart. A glance out into the hallway told her the bathroom stood vacant. With her clothes and personal items in hand, Lyndsey left the bedroom and entered the bathroom. The shower called out to her. She pulled her nightgown up over her head and dropped it onto the floor. Lyndsey stepped into the shower. The hot water felt invigorating. It held her captive in the shower longer than normal. Twenty minutes later, she emerged cleansed and shampooed from a refreshing shower. She fluff-dried her hair and dried her body with a towel taken from the rack then dropped the towel on the vanity.

Lyndsey stood naked before the bathroom mirror. She looked into the mirror. Suddenly, a terrible thought hit her—a recollection from her early morning nightmare. What if she did have a child growing inside of her? After the incident with John, she'd stopped taking the pill. Pregnancy had not been something she considered possible after their separation. The beach, Lyndsey recalled, had changed all of that. Not on the pill. The spontaneity of lovemaking on the beach had not allowed time to consider safe sex. *Oh My God,* Lyndsey thought. *What if I am pregnant with Richard's child?* She leaned forward and looked closely into the mirror. She searched for signs that her Mom had often claimed would reveal the state of a woman's body. First, she pulled her upper then lower eyelids open and stared hard into her eyes. What had Mother said about the signs of pregnancy, spots on the eyes? No spots. Next, she examined her breasts. They also revealed nothing that alleviated her concern. Still concerned, she leaned forward to get a closer and more personal confrontation with the mirror. She first pulled her upper, then lower lips out for inspection, then opened her mouth and shot her tongue out at the mirror again no spots. Worry grew to panic, and Lyndsey frantically started to examine the remainder of her body. She stopped then had to laugh out loud at her early morning thoughts and actions. Mom had, after all been a storyteller-embellisher of renown. Her tale of the seven signs of pregnancy that she claimed would reveal a young woman's condition through a series of spots on her body likely was just her way of dealing with the birds and the bees and a teenage daughter. Silently, she paused and recalled a flurry of special moments she treasured; special moments, once shared with her dearly departed Mom—Letitia...Lettie Melville. A tear touched her cheek and trickled down to her lips. She savored its salty taste and the precious moments just shared with her Mom. Mild anger touched her on recalling the dreaded c-word...cancer that had denied her extended moments, days and years of her Mother's loving presence in her life. She had not heard the bathroom door open.

Hope stood in the background and watched Lyndsey perform her frantic body examination. Hope did not realize what the poor girl was up to until Lyndsey uttered sheepishly, "What if I'm really pregnant? That spirit really could possess my child!" She gazed into the mirror. In her mind Richard's passions and loving embraces ignited tingling sensations within her body. She recalled childhood claims of her Mom's friend Mrs. Cullen—Jena, 'Lettie no word of a lie. I can recall and relive in the blink of an eye the exact moment of my precious Penelope's conception.'

Hope blurted out, "What in the name of Heaven are you going on about, girl?"

Lyndsey on hearing Hope speak grabbed her bath towel and wrapped herself inside its security. Then whipped around and stared frantically at Hope. She blurted out, "I'm pregnant. The spirit of Grace Ramsay is going to possess our child!"

"Say what?"

"Richard…me. We made love on the beach, I'm pregnant, our child's about to be possessed!"

Hope struggled to suppress a bout of giggles and said, "OK. So you made love. When? How often? Have you missed a period?"

"Yesterday, once, no!"

"Pardon me backwards down-east ways, girl; but if you did it once, that once occurred less than twenty-four hours ago, and you've not had time to miss a period, what makes you think you're with child?"

Lyndsey's face paled. She sobbed and whispered, "I want to be a Mom I want a daughter like little Beckie, Rebecca my neighbour back home."

Hope sighed. She pointed to Lyndsey's undergarments on the vanity and said, "It's unlikely you're pregnant. I need the bathroom. Relax, get dressed and we'll chat in a bit over breakfast.

Lyndsey looked sheepishly at Hope and asked, "Really?"

"Yes girl, really!" Are you really a 'Come from Away?' Dar's got'tta be a little Maritimer hidden inside of you girl—Ghosts and possessions? You ain't pregnant." She turned and walked towards the door.

Lyndsey paused then slipped into her bra and had her panties almost up over her hips when Hope twisted about faced Lyndsey and blurted out, "Oh my God, No! You got de mark. You're pregnant!"

Lyndsey almost passed out on the spot. She did not speak, but stared at Hope, then burst into laughter with Hope. Her hands pulled the panties up over her hips.

Hope stepped back out of the bathroom and said, "I'll give you ten minutes."

"Thanks, Hope. Sorry…but the nightmare seemed so real!"

"Ten minutes. OK? And trust me, you just ain't pregnant, girl.

Lyndsey smiled back and watched Hope depart and close the door on leaving the bathroom. Lyndsey quickly dressed, brushed her teeth, and fixed her hair. In less than ten minutes, Lyndsey stepped out of the bathroom. While walking back to her room, she knocked on Hope's door and called out, "It's all yours now." Back in her room, she removed yesterday's clothes from atop the oaken dresser then placed her personal care items there. She set the nightgown and soiled clothes on a wooden chair in a corner of the room. Lyndsey then went to the mirrored dresser. She looked into the mirror and started to laugh lightly at the stupidity of her bathroom antics. The shower started up anew. Lyndsey left the room and walked downstairs in search of Richard, Gilbert, and breakfast.

CHAPTER 38

GILBERT LOOKED UP AND SMILED AT LYNDSEY WHEN SHE ENTERED the kitchen. He greeted her, "Morning Sunshine. All set for another great day?"

"I'm ready and willing."

"Good. Richard raced the sun and won. He joined Jeffrey on his morning lobster run. Jeffrey hauls out a healthy catch each morning. Today, the weather's good, they should be back in at the dock nigh onto eleven-thirty or twelve. Care for a cheese omelette?"

"Mmm. Not really. Do you have any fresh fruit? A fruit salad would be nice."

Gilbert went to the refrigerator and opened the door. He waited until Lyndsey had seated herself at the table then read aloud the list of available fruit, "We have apples, oranges, grapefruit, apricots, a kiwi, and two pears. Will that fill your salad bowl?"

"That and more, is the grapefruit pink?"

"Only kind Hope will allow."

"Then perhaps I'll settle on a grapefruit breakfast. It's quick and easy."

"Salad's not a problem."

"Grapefruit will do just fine."

Gilbert removed a grapefruit from the bottom tray and closed the refrigerator door. He went to the counter and started to prepare the grapefruit for Lyndsey. Halfway through the preparation, he stopped, took a mug from the cupboard and poured Lyndsey a cup of fresh, hot coffee. He carried it over to the table and placed it before her. He returned to the grapefruit.

"Thanks Gilbert. I can really use a good coffee this morning."

Gilbert picked up the plate of grapefruit and carried it over to Lyndsey. He handed it to her, sat down across from her, and said, "You're quite welcome. I trust your coffee craving is caused by the bright morning sun. Did you sleep well last night?"

Lyndsey took a bite of grapefruit. Her lips puckered up. She pleaded, "Sugar…please," then lied and added, "Yes. I did sleep very well last night. Gone the minute my head hit the pillow."

Gilbert answered Lyndsey's plea for sugar. On returning to the table he sat and handed the sugar bowl to Lyndsey. He smiled and said, "Good," paused then added, "Hope and I will be running into Halifax. Care to join us?"

"No. Maybe I'd best stick around and wait for Richard and Jeffrey to return."

"You're more than welcome. We should be back before one or two."

"Thanks for the offer. I'll lay low here. Maybe go pay Pappy a visit."

"Sorry. Pappy hit the road early. He's off with a buddy. They swap tales down at the waterfront dock in town every Wednesday till two or three. Perhaps we could drop you off there. It's a beautiful spot to see. Besides, Pappy and old Lenny can be quite entertaining once they get on a roll."

Lyndsey shrugged, then declined Gilbert's offer. She said, "No, maybe next time. I'll take the morning to relax and pull myself together. The trip, though great, took its toll on me."

Gilbert nodded. He accepted Lyndsey's desire for a little private time. Finished with his coffee, Gilbert stood up and said, "Understood. I'll ask no more." He then went to the counter and placed his mug in the sink.

Hope walked into the kitchen. She sang out, "Morning Uncle Gilbert. Good, morning Lyndsey. Good morning Sunshine. Isn't it a great day we're into?" Gilbert smiled at her. Hope joined Lyndsey at the table. She accepted the second half of Lyndsey's grapefruit and Lyndsey's explanation that her eyes had proved to be bigger than her stomach. Hope started to eat her grapefruit then set into a session of girl talk with Lyndsey. They avoided their earlier bathroom exchange. Gilbert feared their girl talk could go on if uninterrupted forever. He reminded Hope of their morning plans. Hope laughed off Gilbert's chiding and finished off her grapefruit. She then left the table, placed the dish on the counter, and joined Gilbert at the door, where he patiently awaited her.

Gilbert called back to Lyndsey, "One last chance. It's not too late. We have room for you in the truck."

"No thanks. Go ahead. I'll be fine here until Richard and Jeffrey return."

The door closed and Lyndsey was left alone in the kitchen. She heard Gilbert's truck start then drive out of the yard. The kitchen clock showed the hour to be ten past ten. A minute or two passed by, then Lyndsey got up from the table and went to the sink. There, she washed and dried the morning's dishes. She returned the dishes to the proper cupboards and the utensils to their place in the counter drawer. Lyndsey stood in front of the sink and looked out the kitchen window. A shiver ran up her spine. Outside, she spotted Bailey stealthily creeping up on an unsuspecting robin out by the rose hedge. Further down the rose hedge the lawn ended. Off to the right of the hedge, she looked nervously at the entrance to the path that led to Jeffrey's home...the old homestead. Lyndsey decided that moment that she had to return to the old house—more specifically, to Jeffrey's bedroom, the same room that had once belonged to the diary's author...Grace Ramsay.

She looked for a key to Gilbert's house, but could not find one. Determined to visit the old house before Richard and Jeffrey returned, she stepped outside and headed towards the pathway. She left the door of Gilbert's house unlocked but closed. The pathway seemed shorter this time. Lyndsey reached the shed and then Jeffrey's front door before any self-doubt could challenge her resolve. She tried the front door. It had not been locked. Lyndsey opened the door and stepped inside. The only lighting came in the form of sunshine through the windows on the front wall of the house.

Lyndsey cautiously walked towards the hallway. Time seemed to stand still. A few steps down the hallway found her staring into the open doorway of Jeffrey's bedroom. She took in a deep breath then walked into Jeffrey's room. Guilt showed its presence, and Lyndsey almost decided to retreat back to Gilbert's kitchen. A voice called out. Lyndsey froze in time.

"Thank you for coming back so promptly. I had my doubts. I am pleased you have returned."

Lyndsey looked towards the voice. She spotted the speaker. It appeared to be the same young girl she'd encountered here yesterday and in her nightmare just hours earlier. The girl wore a simple cotton dress that appeared to float atop her eerie flesh, or what once had been her flesh. Her blue eyes sparkled. They displayed signs of inner warmth and calmed Lyndsey.

The girl, Grace Ramsay, pointed to Jeffrey's bed and beckoned Lyndsey to sit on it. Lyndsey obeyed. Grace Ramsay frowned. She said, "You did not bring the rosary."

Lyndsey blinked then replied, "I did not feel it necessary. Your request is echoing in my mind each word is etched solidly into my memory."

"It best be as you say. It may suffice. If not…I will simply remind you of your condition."

"My condition, what condition?"

"You are pregnant."

Lyndsey allowed Grace's words to echo in her heart, 'You are pregnant.' A glow and gentle smile brightened Lyndsey's face. In her mind she gazed upwards from the beach at seagulls soaring in a blue cloudless sky. Their love song of the sea echoed in her heart. Beckie, replaced by Lyndsey's daughter to be *Letitia* in her heart sang out, *'Mommie—Mommie come plays wit me!'* She sighed, "No. That will not be needed. I will bring the rosary."

Grace smiled and whispered, "That would make me happy. I do not wish to possess the child within you."

Lyndsey no longer feared Grace's spirit. She looked into the warmth of the spirit's blue eyes and said, "Tell me about your life. How did the rosary and diary end up in the hands of the Ramsays of Ontario—I mean Upper, or was it Lower Canada? Lastly, why is it you are so young? You appear to be not much older…than when you'd have been when writing your words into the diary."

"Upper, Lower Canada. It matters little. In my time, this place Canada you speak of did not exist. How did the diary get there? Suffice to say that after my death…Mother sent it to Father. She sought to cause him pain and throw blame his way for what befell my worldly being. Why the rosary? After Father ripped it from the grasp of the island's demonic beast, he claimed it to be a sign of his faith. Uncle Richard called it a sign of his shameless greed."

Lyndsey interrupted Grace. She said, "But she, your mother Sadie was such a God fearing woman. Surely she'd never seek to cause pain."

"I thought so myself. But upon my death, brought about by my foolish actions, mother turned bitter and remained so a long time. It took many years and Uncle Richard's undying efforts to nurture and restore Mother's loving nature back to life. My foolish actions and desire to seek out a piece of Father's treasure and the forgiveness of his greed brought about my early death. I drowned out in the bay. I set out seeking to plea to the beast on Father's behalf. If I succeeded, I believed Father would have returned from the place he had fled to in fear. I never reached the Floating Islands. I failed sadly and never came close enough to see them within my line of vision. I will succeed with your help."

Lyndsey sighed, "But what could the rosary possibly do for you today. You're dead, been so it seems for the past two hundred years or more."

"Father's greed, it drove him to flee and leave our care, Mother's, my brother Tom's, and mine in the hands of Uncle Richard. Richard cared dearly and provided the love and support we needed, but he never returned to the man he once had been. The islands destroyed his soul but not his capacity to provide for and love those in his care. Regardless of his good efforts…a father he was not. I needed my Father. I loved and missed him dearly. I died long before my time and never within sight of the accursed place that could have reunited us the Floating Islands. Take me there, I beg of you. With the rosary returned to the demonic beast's hand, the curse on Father will be lifted and Father will return for me! We will once again be reunited, and I will be freed from this solitary hell I've been cast into."

Lyndsey wiped away the tears that streamed down her cheeks. The young Grace's spirit had pulled and captured her heartstrings. She blurted out, "Yes. Yes. I will take you there." She looked across the room at the face of Grace's spirit. It smiled gently back at her and whispered, "Thank you. You will not regret your choice. God's speed and blessings be upon you and your child."

Lyndsey felt strangely peaceful. She watched with a touch of sadness the spirit of young Grace Ramsay vanish before her eyes. A glance down at her watch revealed the hour to be eleven-thirty. Lyndsey rose up from the bed and quickly walked out of the room. She glanced back one last time, but did not see any sign of the girl's spirit. A brisk pace took her to the front door. There, Lyndsey opened the door and stepped out into the bright sunlight. She closed the door and walked away from the little house. From there Lyndsey set off back towards Gilbert's house. She spotted another path and decided to explore it. It took her down a shaded trail, up over the crest of a small hill, and then, before her eyes, the water of East River and what had to be Gilbert's lobster boat appeared. The boat lay moored up to a long wooden dock. Lyndsey walked the final hundred metres to the bottom of the hill. She became determined to sit on the dock in wait of Richard and Jeffrey's return. Lyndsey tried to recall the name of Gilbert's boat…Karen or had it been Kreen.

CHAPTER 39

LYNDSEY PAUSED AT THE BOTTOM OF THE HILL THEN WALKED A short distance to the foot of the dock. A short stroll took her out to the dock's end. To her left, Karyn-Anita bobbed at the ends of her docking lines. She was a white boat about twenty to twenty-four feet long, with an outboard motor mounted on her stern and a small cabin towards the bow. The cabin sheltered the engine controls and the helm's steering wheel. A branch of light pink roses had been painted beneath her name, which had been painted in gold letters. The gold letters glittered in the bright, mid-day sunlight. Out towards the middle of East River, a blue and white power boat on its mooring pointed leisurely to East River Bay.

Lyndsey shielded her eyes and looked out onto the waters beyond East River Bay. The water of Mahone Bay had a slight chop to it. A breeze blowing in from the sea dressed most of the wave tops with picturesque whitecaps. Further out on Mahone Bay, she spotted a large whitecap. A closer look revealed her error. The whitecap turned out to be a small boat, which appeared to be heading in towards East River Bay. Lyndsey hoped it was Richard and Jeffrey. Her watch hit high noon, and they were due in if Gilbert had been right.

Out on board Rose Bud, Richard stood at the helm. He directed Rose Bud under Jeffrey's watchful eye and directions. About a hundred metres from the dock, he guided her through the gap into

East River, where ahead stood their destination, the McClaken's dock. He spotted what had to be Lyndsey and waved out to her. Jeffrey ordered him to ease up on the throttle and joined Richard in hailing Lyndsey. Richard guided the Rose Bud smoothly up to the side of the dock that stood vacant. There, Jeffrey jumped over, line in hand, to the docking ladder and tied off Rose Bud's bow. Richard manoeuvred closer to the dock and Jeffrey jumped back on board. He took up the stern docking line, and together, Richard and Jeffrey secured the Rose Bud to the dock and her outbound mooring lines. Richard then climbed up onto the dock where Lyndsey greeted him with a kiss that lingered. Jeffrey joined them on the dock. Lyndsey ended the kiss. She turned to Jeffrey, smiled and, pleaded, "Please Uncle Jeffrey…you've just got to take me out on a tour of the bay."

Jeffrey looked into Lyndsey's eyes and his heart melted. He tried to look stern but failed badly. Something in Lyndsey's eyes destroyed any resistance he might have possessed. He caved in and said, "Give me fifte'n minets ta git me tour'ing duds on and refu'l Rose Bud ens we'll be out'ta here's."

Richard offered up his assistance. He asked, "Where's the fuel Jeffrey? I'll take care of it while you run up to the house."

"Ov'r yander. Sees dat sheed. Spere fuel toks be in der. Beest takes two, ans put de ones on Rose Bud in'ta de sheed."

Lyndsey watched Richard and Jeffrey walk off towards their destinations. Jeffrey broke into a run at the dock's end and soon disappeared over the hill. Richard went to the shed and retrieved the two gas tanks requested by Jeffrey. He returned to the dock, placed both gas tanks on board Rose Bud and removed the tanks they'd used on the morning run. He placed them in the shed as instructed by Jeffrey.

Fifteen minutes went by and Jeffrey had not returned. Richard entertained Lyndsey by relating to her the details of his morning run with Jeffrey. He ended by explaining away their delayed return: they'd encountered a longer than normal delay at the processing dock. But he concluded by hinting that Jeffrey had fared well with the morning's catch.

Twenty minutes passed and still no sign of Jeffrey. Lyndsey paced up and down the dock. She grew anxious. On nearing Richard, she walked up to him and wrapped her arms about him. Next, she lifted herself up onto her tiptoes and her lips sought out his. Her hands moved down his back paused at his waist then pulled him closer. A squeeze pulled their hips closer together. Lyndsey raised the passion of her kiss and worked her tongue into Richard's mouth. Richard suddenly pulled away from Lyndsey. She pouted at him then smiled on hearing Jeffrey call out from atop the hill.

"I's a com'in. I's a com'in."

Jeffrey raced down the hill and soon stood before the separated lovers. He smiled broadly and said, "Shall wes all bes abourd'n de Loves Boot?"

Lyndsey blushed and stood back, while Jeffrey climbed down the dock and jumped onto Rose Bud. Once there, he released her outbound mooring lines and pulled her up close to the dock. Richard guided Lyndsey to the dock ladder and helped her step down to boat level. Jeffrey wrapped his arms about her waist and lifted her onboard. Richard then climbed down the ladder and joined them aboard Rose Bud. Jeffrey commented to Lyndsey, "You twos beest bees ready to take in an eyesful and then soome. It's a might preeety out dar."

Richard stooped down and connected one of the gas tanks up to the engine fuel line. He primed the line then proceeded to release Rose Bud from the dock.

Jeffrey fired up the engine and shifted it into reverse. Rose Bud pulled away from the dock. A shift into forward and Rose Bud quickly carried its crew out onto East River Bay and headed towards Mahone Bay. Jeffrey's promise quickly became a reality in Lyndsey's eyes. Her mind became enthralled by the beauty surrounding them. Jeffrey took them out past Deep Cove and seaward beyond Blandford. There, he steered Rose Bud northeast and headed towards St. Margaret's Bay. East Ironbound Island appeared on their starboard, with Pearl island beyond it on the horizon. Jeffrey soon had them looking upon the lighthouse and rocks of Peggy's Cove. All three waved at the tourists walking or sitting upon the rocks.

From there, Jeffrey took them directly into Peggy's Cove, turned about and took them back out onto St. Margaret's Bay. They explored many coves and inlets, then finally ended up in a long inlet Jeffrey referred to as Ha'ck'ts Coove. Richard looked it up on the chart of St. Margaret's bay and pointed out Hackett's Cove to Lyndsey. At the extreme end of the cove, Jeffrey eased off on the throttle. He took his cell phone out and pressed a speed-dial number. After a brief conversation in which he repeated himself often, he hung up and returned the cell phone to his jacket pocket. He switched the engine off and dropped Rose Bud's anchor. Ten or fifteen minutes later, a small motorized skiff pulled up to their side. Jeffrey pulled out his wallet and paid the skiff's captain for the goods he'd delivered. The captain handed Jeffrey three large bags, then pulled away and headed off towards a dock across the cove.

Jeffrey set the bags down, retrieved a small folding table from under Rose Bud's bow and set it up. He placed the three bags on the table and said proudly, "Beest dang fishh-n-cheeps in de worlt. Deegs in an enjoys."

Richard looked into the cabin and spotted what looked like a cluster of folding chairs up under the bow. He retrieved three of the folding chairs and set them up around the table.

Lyndsey sat down first then Jeffrey sat down across from her. Richard took up a spot between the two. The three large orders of fish and chips disappeared in short order. All three settled back in their chairs and relaxed. Lyndsey wiped her face and cleaned off a dab of tartar sauce. She looked over to Jeffrey, started to smile, and then paused. Her dimples popped outward and forced Lyndsey's baby face to the forefront. Her mouth opened and words of thanks started to flow out.

Jeffrey's jaw dropped, He uttered, "Yer weecome Hope. Gad I loves dem dimples."

Lyndsey and then Richard's jaws dropped together. Lyndsey asked, "Who did you just call me?"

"Ooops. I's done did et."

"Done did what?" a baffled Richard asked.

"Leet de cat out'ta de bag."

"Say what!" demanded Lyndsey.

"Oh. Oooh. Gilbe't's a gon'na kills me. He iis."

"Slow down Jeffrey. Nobody is going to kill you. We wouldn't allow it."

"Ya doesn't member me does ye…Lynd…sie?"

"You're our dearly beloved Uncle Jeffrey, right?" questioned Lyndsey.

Richard moved to Lyndsey's side. Over the next hour, Jeffrey explained with great effort the reasoning behind his strange conversation. A shocked Richard and dumbfounded Lyndsey listened and clung to each of Jeffrey's words. Lyndsey bit pensively on her lower lip. She quickly cast aside momentary spells of anger towards her parents, Liam and Letitia. A heart attack at 52 had denied her of Dad's love. Why had he never revealed her past? Memories of Mom—Letitia, Lyndsey's special Lettie suffering through her prolonged battle with cancer drew tears to her eyes. Their love and devotion she'd never doubted. Recollections of treasured childhood moments with her parents touched her heartstrings. Their love had embraced and supported her throughout life. Lyndsey's doubts vanished. Richard spotted Lyndsey's tears and touched his napkin gently to her cheeks and eyes. Images of Hope filled her thoughts. Hope's words, 'I was chosen' echoed in her heart. She sighed, "Yes little sister, we were chosen."

In the end, after Jeffrey had managed to partially explain away his cat-out-of-the-bag declaration, he raised the anchor, started the engine and headed Rose Bud out of Hackett's Cove back towards East River. Richard and Lyndsey's sworn vows to protect Jeffrey from any harm Gilbert might see fit to inflict upon him soon had Jeffrey's happy carefree smile back on his face.

Lyndsey remained seated in her chair with Richard at her side. Snuggled close together her head rested on his chest. He smiled at her and placed an occasional kiss on her windblown hair. She recalled the morning's bathroom exchange with Hope giggles broke her cycle of gentle tears. Lyndsey and Richard shifted positions and embraced. Their lips shared a tender kiss.

Rose Bud bumped up against her dock and it shocked Lyndsey out of her trance-like state. They kissed then Richard joined Jeffrey and secured the docking lines. Lyndsey stood up and stepped back. She watched Richard help Jeffrey stow away the table and chairs. After Richard had climbed up the dock ladder, Lyndsey stepped towards the ladder. Jeffrey went to her side. Lyndsey turned to him and embraced him firmly. She burst into tears. Jeffrey offered her a hanky. Lyndsey dried her eyes then tried to get her sobbing under control. Finally, she raised her head from Jeffrey's shoulder and kissed him long and hard on the cheek.

She blurted out, "I love you. We love you." She smiled then finished with, "Thank you, Uncle Jeffrey. You're a true sweetheart, a keeper."

Lyndsey reached out to the dock ladder and stepped over to it. She climbed up the ladder and joined Richard up top on the dock. Jeffrey joined them five minutes later. During that five minutes, Lyndsey fought hard to refrain herself from taking off and running up the hill to Gilbert's house.

Richard placed his arm around Lyndsey's waist and the three of them stepped forward. Jeffrey took on a quiet resolve as the distance to Gilbert's grew shorter. When they walked out of the path onto Gilbert's lawn, Jeffrey held himself back. Lyndsey placed her free arm around his shoulder and pulled him close to her side. They stopped, and Lyndsey kissed him on his cheek. Jeffrey blushed then smiled. Lyndsey 's arm slipped down to Jeffrey's waist and all three walked across the lawn together.

When they were twenty feet from the front door, Gilbert and Hope stepped out of the house. Lyndsey broke free from Richard and Jeffrey. She raced over the last twenty feet and leaped past Gilbert to Hope. Gilbert looked to Richard and Jeffrey. He turned ashen. Lyndsey wrapped her arms around Hope and kissed her hard on the lips. She burst into tears and called out, "I love you, sis!"

CHAPTER 40

HOPE FELL BACKWARDS. SHE LANDED ON THE DOORSTEP. LYNDSEY tumbled with Hope and landed stretched out on top of her, pinning her to the doorstep. A shocked Hope cried out, "What's gotten in to you, girl? Have your cookies crumbled?"

Lyndsey hugged Hope and stared lovingly into her eyes. She whispered, "No sis. I love you.

"Sister? Whose sister?" Hope asked.

Lyndsey released Hope. She gazed longingly at Hope and softly declared "You, sister! Yes. You're the playmate that filled my imaginary childhood cravings. The sister I never had and the sister fate has blessed and reunited me with."

Hope stared questioningly back at Lyndsey. Richard ran over to Gilbert's side. He looked at Gilbert and asked, "Are you OK, Gilbert? It happened by accident, an honest, but good one."

Jeffrey stood back and lowered his head in shame. He hadn't intended to let the cat out of the bag; it had just happened. Jeffrey really liked Richard and Lyndsey. They treated him good and didn't mock his shortcomings in speech, among other things. He looked up with a tear in his eye when summoned by Gilbert.

"Come on over Jeffrey. It's OK. It had to happen. You did what I never could bring myself to do, now git over here!"

Jeffrey hesitated then finally walked towards Gilbert.

Gilbert held his arms outward and beckoned Jeffrey to join him.

Slowly—very slowly—Jeffrey walked the last ten feet to his older brother's open arms.

Gilbert stepped towards Jeffrey and embraced him. The two brothers then released themselves and looked towards the girls. First Gilbert, then Jeffrey smiled, at Hope and Lyndsey.

Hope looked up at her two uncles and pleaded, "Would one of you two please explain what's gotten into Lyndsey?"

Gilbert spoke first. He said, "OK." He sat down on the doorstep next to Hope and signaled Jeffrey and Richard to join him. Richard chose to sit at Lyndsey's side. He wrapped his arm about her shoulder. Jeffrey sat down in front of Hope and Gilbert.

Gilbert spoke first. He frowned and said, "Please do not think the worst of me, Hope. My fear of losing you—"

"You'll never lose me, Uncle Gilbert," Hope injected. She reached out and hugged Gilbert.

"But, please hear me out first."

"It will never ever happen, you will never lose me! Never, ever", Hope avowed. She declared Gilbert's fear to be naught but a needless worry.

Gilbert cautioned her. He said, "Let me explain. Then, God willing, you'll continue to feel that to be true of my dreaded secret."

Nobody spoke. Gilbert released Hope from his grasp. He heaved a sigh then revealed the truth to Hope, Lyndsey, and Richard.

"It all took place at the time of your parents' fatal accident. Yes. I've spoken to you of it over the years. However, I could not bring myself to reveal the whole truth."

Gilbert paused. He looked deep into Hope's then Lyndsey's eyes and confessed, "It's true. The two of you are sisters. Please don't ask how. Just listen and I'll explain."

Hope turned, looked to Lyndsey, and then reached out and pulled Lyndsey toward herself out of Richard's grasp. This time, she kissed Lyndsey square on the lips and sobbed.

Gilbert then spoke. He unburdened his heart. He told the truth.

"The accident denied you both of parents that loved you dearly. Twenty-one years have passed since the fatal accident robbed you of your parents and me of true, life-long friends. Their names were, Allan and Sandy McDonald. I did not witness the accident. A couple that had been on the scene did and later related the details to our family. Allan, your Father, did not survive the crash. Sandy, your Mother, passed on before the ambulance arrived. The man, a doctor on the scene, acted of his own accord and removed the child Sandy bore from her womb. That child, Hope…was and is you. There was an investigation. The man had been a well-respected doctor. Therefore, the investigation had not resulted in charges being laid. On the contrary, he had been hailed a hero."

Gilbert sobbed. He recalled how happy he and Karyn had been upon being granted custody of that child. He pulled himself together and continued to relate the truth.

"Karyn and I were not blessed. We could not have children of our own. Allan and Sandy had both grown up in foster care. They had no family outside of Lyndsey and you Hope. Yes Hope, you were truly a gift from God. Lyndsey, you were but three years old at the time. Richard's Grandfather, William Ramsay was a guest in our home at the time. He took a shine to you…and you to him. Over the week following the accident, the two of you and his wife Maureen were never far apart. Actually on the day of the accident they had taken you and Jeffery on an outing.

"Ta de Lunsinborgs Museeum it was," Jeffrey announced. After a pause he added, "Wes gots ttreeat'd ta iceee creams and sodeee poops! Real biiiig Bluuuebeeerrries coonesss de weres!"

Everyone laughed on hearing Jeffrey share his memories of the day's outing.

Gilbert waited until the laughter subsided then continued, "Mother and Pappy could not take you in at the time. William knew a family close to him that suffered as did Karyn and I. God bless him. He arranged things such that Karyn and I received custody of the baby, and we were blessed with our Hope. Lyndsey went on to bless the lives of William's friends. William returned every year or two. He always kept us up to date on Lyndsey's progress. I have a photo album that will attest to that fact. Pappy and I attended Lyndsey's graduations and later her wedding, but not the reception.

Pappy cried that day. He taught me a lesson, a lesson I'll never forget. Real men do cry."

Gilbert fell silent. His head dropped, and tears streamed down his cheeks. Hope and Lyndsey shuffled over and embraced him. The threesome displayed the power of love that day, a lesson that made Pappy proud once he'd learned the cat was finally out'ta de bag and no longer a deeply buried family secret.

Gilbert continued, "We raised and loved you as our daughter, Hope. In gratitude to the gift from Heaven that Allen and Sandy had entrusted to us, Karyn and I insisted that you have your Dad's surname, McDonald. We were up front with you most of the way. We explained why we were your Aunt and Uncle and not your Mom and Dad."

Hope hugged Gilbert, I'll always love you like a Dad. A special Dad, you chose me." Together, Gilbert, Hope and Lyndsey hugged. They started to sob, cried lightly, then burst into tears.

Jeffrey looked on, then said, "I tought Lynd…sie loook'd a tad famil'r Den I remembeeered it alls."

Gilbert looked up to Jeffrey. Through tear-blurred eyes, he said, "I know. It scared me. It shouldn't have. I've always known this would one day come to be."

"Den…I din't do bad?" Jeffrey asked.

"No. Jeffrey. It had to be. You did what I couldn't"

Jeffrey stood up. Richard followed his lead. After a moment, Gilbert, Hope, and Lyndsey joined them. Richard opened the front door. The two newly reunited sisters stepped into the house side by side. Next, Gilbert ushered Jeffrey and Richard inside, then he stepped inside and closed the door.

Hope asked, "Uncle Gilbert…Father. Could we see that album you spoke of?"

Gilbert did not answer. He walked out of the room and returned five minutes later with the album in hand. He went to Hope and Lyndsey who sat together on the sofa and handed it to them. Jeffrey and Richard sat down, one on each arm of the sofa. Gilbert sat down next to Hope.

Hope opened the album to its first page. A tiny blond girl in a polka-dot dress looked out at them.

Jeffrey blurted out, "I's member dat un."

Everyone looked at Jeffrey.

Jeffrey revealed his memory, "Dat wer de day Mama pit de beat'in onta ya Gilly."

Gilbert frowned then smiled.

Jeffrey continued his story, "Lynd...sie mudd'r an fadd'r lef't her at yer old plac ta sit fer. Pappy en Mama an yer ladyyy Karyyyns steeped out. Ya wer leeft ta kere fer Lynd...sie an I's. We play't hid en seeeks. Member Gilly?"

Gilbert nodded.

Jeffrey spoke on, "Lynd...sies don hid regh't goood. climp't up inta de dry'r an hid h'rsef into it." Jeffrey started to laugh and then abruptly stopped. He continued, "Den yar kit'ty kat strip's jump'd daw'n stated de dry'r. Member. tumpity...tump...tumpity...tump. Den Mama com'd hoom real orly an sa'd, 'Whot dat naise?' Bouys den't ya git et!"

Lyndsey shouted out, "What! You guys stuck me into the dryer and started it?"

Gilbert burst out in laughter. Through tears of joy he answered, "No. You climbed in all by yourself. Stripes, our old cat, jumped down, hit the start button, and fluff-dried you."

Everyone joined Gilbert and laughed heartily. Gilbert's deepest fears were not to be realized. The revelation had started a long overdue healing process, and once again weaved the reunited family closer together.

CHAPTER 41

RING...RING. GILBERT JUMPED UP FROM THE SOFA. FOUR QUICK steps carried him across the room to answer the telephone. He picked it up after the third ring, but before the fourth.

"Hello, Gilbert here."

The room fell silent and waited for Gilbert to speak again.

"Yes. He's here. I'll put him on the line. No. It's no problem at all. Good talking to you, Roger."

Gilbert placed his hand over the mouthpiece. He called Richard to the phone then directed him to pick up the phone in the kitchen. Once Richard had picked up the kitchen phone, Gilbert hung up his extension. He returned to the sofa and the memories of the photo album.

"Hi Roger, what's up?"

"It's John...Richard."

"What's wrong?"

"Not to worry. He's OK."

"No lies."

"No lies. Things have taken a turn about for the best. John's back to work and much happier."

"Then why did you call?"

"John's made a decision. He feels good about it. I felt it best to call and warn you."

"Warn me about what, Roger. I thought everything was OK?"

"It is. Trust me. An attorney will be calling on Lyndsey with papers to be signed. John's sticking by his guns and wants to marry Tessa. She's agreed. John wants a quick, uncontested divorce."

Richard fell silent and recalled the conversation he'd had with John prior to leaving on the trip. Doubts about Tessa bubbled to the surface of his mind. What trick did the lady hold up her sleeve this time? Richard knew he'd have a difficult time accepting her into the family circle.

"Roger. I don't trust her. What's your read on it?"

"Richard, he is taking full responsibility. He's your bother. Tessa she's a good legal assistant. I dislike what she did, trust is a major employee—employer element in the legal profession. She crossed the line and has been terminated. Richard, there is an added twist she claims that she's is carrying John's child your niece or nephew. It's best right now to show a little compassion."

"Please—I should show compassion? She's destroyed and tearing apart the remnants of my family. She's after Lyndsey's share, right?"

"Wrong. John has been very generous in the divorce settlement. All he wants is their house. Lyndsey at the probate of your Dad's will as John's spouse received a 10% share of the business. Through the uncontested divorce settlement her 10% share is retained by her."

"And Tessa wants?"

"She claims to simply want to marry her child's father, John. Actually with the probated share designated to Lyndsey on the disbursement of the estates, any future wife of John would not be entitled to any share of the business, through your Dad's will." Roger paused then continued, "There's no strings attached. Let's face it, Richard. John and Lyndsey—it never stood right by me. However, I have attached strings to John and especially Tessa. I met with John, he agreed not to move on the I Dos with Tessa until the paternity test comes back and confirms first that Tessa is pregnant and second, that John is the father. John agreed to the terms and signed a prenuptial agreement that must pass the paternity stage before it comes into effect. Tessa, she signed. Simply stated, she signed with hesitation from my point of view. It will take a little time. Its uncontested status along with the papers and the supporting documents being filed will help cut the time needed for a final decree. It could be under three months, but don't hold me to it. John is protected and Lyndsey will be free."

"Speaking of which, were you aware of the connections between..."

"Then it has come out?"

"Yes."

"William did what he thought proper at the time."

"Then why has there been so much secrecy, Roger?"

"Liam and Lettie were childless. William and Maureen were visiting at the time of Allan and Sandy's fatal accident. It was one of only two or three trips down east that saw Maureen accompany William. Lyndsey had bonded with him and Maureen. Actions had to unfold quickly. Gilbert and Karyn were best friends with Allan and Sandy. They were also naturals for Hope. Noreen and I had our boys, Liam and Lettie well, they were ready. They had love to share with little Lyndsey. Face it, Richard. Right or wrong, many lives were blessed and touched by this love. John and Lyndsey's marriage shocked everyone. Noreen, your Mom and Grandmother chatted with Lyndsey, damn near till the cows came home, then continued until they sensed resentment in Lyndsey. We expected you and Lyndsey to reconnect on your return following your graduation. Bill, your Dad, felt John sought out Lyndsey to 'One-Up-You'. However, we respected and accepted Lyndsey and your assurances that the marriage was meant to be. You stood as John's Best Man at their wedding."

Richard sighed. He said, "Yes I did." After a pause he whispered, "But I never stopped the loving." After a short pause he asked, "Lyndsey and Hope, are they blood relatives to our Ramsays?"

"No! There is definitely no direct connections."

The line fell silent as neither man spoke. Images of his parents and grandparents graves saddened Richard's thoughts. He pondered the idea of returning home and working with John at their family's marine business. Had John actually sought out Lyndsey in his absence to 'One-Up-Him?' In anger and frustration he tightened his grasp on the phone.

Roger broke the silence, "Nobody anticipated the tragic accident and loss of your parents and grandparents. We never saw John and Tessa connecting, never sensed the presence of their affair. Add in John's outburst in my office and his abusive treatment of Lyndsey was another shocker. Personally, I always liked the two of you as a couple. It just seemed natural."

Richard remained silent. The accident had reduced them to a family of three. Roger's revelations of his Dad's concerns over John's intentions towards Lyndsey angered him. Laughter from the living room cast aside his anger.

Roger broke their silence, "Richard, give it time. Each of us needs it now, more than ever. I need to speak on behalf of your Grandfather. William swore me to secrecy. You know what he stood for! God, he was more a Father to me than my own. God rest their souls."

"So, Lyndsey retains her shares. Walks away free. What's the catch? Are the common properties shared between John and me safe? I'm sorry, Roger. It'll take a while—quite a while before I'll come to trust Tessa."

"Understood, I understand where you're coming from. But trust me on this, Richard. It'll all work out for the best. I'll take care of your interest."

"Then please assure me you'll also be there for Lynd..."

"It's not a question; it's a personal guarantee Richard. I will be there, along with Noreen. We'll be there like family for you, John and Lyndsey." Roger paused, then with hesitation added, "Tessa, given a passage of time and circumstance, yes, Tessa too."

Richard sighed. An image of Lyndsey silhouetted against the beach flashed through his mind. Subconsciously, he prayed that this time it wouldn't happen too fast—that maybe, just maybe, he'd get it right and Lyndsey would once again become his princess...his soul mate. "Roger who can we expect to call on Lyndsey? With the documents, I mean legal papers initiating the uncontested divorce?"

"You'll recognize him, Walter Lizards. He jumped at the opportunity to head down east, something about looking up a friend."

An image of Mr. Lizards eased Richard's concerns. A familiar face would help Lyndsey face what had to be.

"OK Roger. I'll break the news to Lyndsey."

"Thanks Richard. I appreciate it. Take care and enjoy your trip."

"Thanks Roger."

"Not a problem. Just—"

"I know. Just trust me. And Roger, take care of John. I just can't trust Tessa. It'll take a stretch of time and then some."

Richard hung up the phone. He stood there in the kitchen and reflected over his conversation with Roger. He remained in the kitchen lost in personal thoughts. Images of Grandfather and Grandma, Dad and Mom captivated his thoughts.

"Meow—meow," a familiar voice called out to Richard through the kitchen door. He walked over to the door and opened it. A flash of yellow fur brushed his legs and raced into the house. Bailey quickly jumped up onto the kitchen counter. Richard rubbed and massaged Bailey's head and chest. The feisty feline purred loudly in response to Richard's attention.

"Is everything OK Richard?" Gilbert called out.

"It's perfect Gilbert," Richard replied. Richard smiled inwardly, then walked back out into the living room and rejoined the others Bailey followed closely on his heels.

Jeffrey laughed on spotting Bailey and declared, "De kit'ty kat dun com'd hoom." The room roared with laughter. Richard walked up to the sofa and took up his place on the sofa arm nearest to Lyndsey.

Lyndsey looked up from the photo album at Richard. She asked, "Everything OK? How's Roger?" After a pause and no answer she asked, "How's John?"

Richard grinned, leaned over, kissed Lyndsey by the ear, and whispered, "Fine. All's fine. He had some updates to pass along. Roger is Roger, and John is good. They've allowed him to return to work."

Lyndsey sighed. She said, "Good. The work will be good for him."

Richard straightened back up and looked down at the album. He spotted the cause of all the laughter, a picture of Lyndsey at five in a swimming pool. Her hands were on the back of a shy-looking, little blonde boy and had pulled his swimsuit down over the cheeks of his butt. Lyndsey had a mischievous look on her face. It was one Richard knew well. He burst into laughter. The others joined him.

Richard demanded, "Where'd you get these pictures from…really?"

Gilbert stopped laughing long enough to answer. He said, "Your Grandfather. No, really. He was quite a character, and we all loved his visits." Gilbert then returned to his fit of laughter.

The remainder of the evening played out through the pages of the photo album. It passed from Lyndsey's childhood to her teens, with a picture of Richard and her at their prom. It ended with a scattering of photos taken at her wedding to John. The gathering broke up shortly after the album's last page had been turned over. The clock on the mantel struck the midnight hour.

Jeffrey stood up and excused himself. He said, "Sorr'y, da morn com soon. I's beest be tuck'n me head'n."

Hope, then Lyndsey stood up and in turn embraced and kissed Jeffrey warmly. Gilbert walked Jeffrey to the front door. He handed him a flashlight to aid him on his walk home. Before Jeffrey stepped out through the door, Gilbert embraced him, sobbed once, and then said, "Thanks Jeff. It had to happen. I couldn't do it. Thank you."

Jeffrey stepped out of the door and turned the flashlight on. He turned, waved back to Gilbert and walked off across the lawn towards his house.

Gilbert closed the door. He walked to the kitchen. There, he set out a plate of canned tuna for Bailey. He paused a second in thought, then went to the dining room hutch and retrieved a bottle of Bailey's favourite. Back in the kitchen, he poured out a saucer of rum. Satisfied, Gilbert returned the bottle to its place in the hutch and walked upstairs. On walking down the hallway to his bedroom, he called out, "Good night…Hope, Lyndsey, Richard."

A chorus echoed out to him.

First Hope sang out, "Goodnight Dad—Uncle Gilbert, Lyndsey and Richard."

Lyndsey was next, "Goodnight Uncle Gilbert, Hope and Richard."

Finally Richard called out, "Goodnight Uncle Gilbert, Lyndsey and Hope."

Gilbert reached his bedroom. He stepped inside and closed the door. Once in bed, he drifted off into a sound sleep. A great burden had been lifted off his shoulders and heart that night.

CHAPTER 42

MORNING CAME EARLY TO THE MCCLAKEN HOUSEHOLD. JEFFREY put in his appearance before the sun had risen up in the east. He started up a pot of coffee, then sat down at the table and waited for the others to stir. The smell of coffee drew Richard, then Gilbert to the kitchen like a giant magnet. An alert Jeffrey, coffee mug in hand, greeted them.

"Toops o de marnin'g ta ya's"

Richard sat down opposite Jeffrey. He returned the greeting first, "Morning Jeffrey. Do I have time for a coffee and toast?"

"Honly iff'in ders a slice'r too in it fer I."

Gilbert joined them. At the counter he put the toaster to work then he carried two fresh mugs of coffee to the table. After he'd taken his place at the table, he passed Richard one of the mugs. Gilbert raised his mug, toasted the morning, and returned Jeffrey's greeting, "Top of the morning to you also, Jeffrey. Toast is underway."

A brief silence befell the table. Gilbert ended it with a quick quote from his passion Shakespeare, "'*What from the cape can you discern at sea?*'"

Richard followed with, "'*Nothing at all: it is a highwrought flood; I cannot, 'twixt the heaven and the main, Descry a sail.*'" Richard smiled and said, "*Othello, Act II Scene I.*"

"Lard spars me. Now ders twoo o dem," Jeffrey becried.

Before Gilbert could continue the Shakespearean verse, Hope and Lyndsey walked into the kitchen.

Jeffrey looked up. He rejoiced, "I's bin sav'd by twoo fare damsils. Tank ye Lard."

Hope took over command of the kitchen. She served up the first four slices of toast, started the second round, and poured out coffee for herself and Lyndsey. Next, Hope set out the peanut butter and a jar of homemade jam. After an ample supply of toast had been produced, Hope joined the others at the table.

Gilbert jovially boasted, "Hope and Lyndsey have offered up their assistance on my lobster run. Are there any objections?"

Richard chuckled. He spoke out, "Lyndsey hauling lobster? Good God. Gilbert, she's scared to death of spiders."

Lyndsey gave Richard the look. Before he could rebut it, she stuck out her tongue at him. Gilbert intervened. He ordered a time out with a wave of his hands. He then called out, "Children. We'll have none of that at the table."

Lyndsey pouted in protest and declared, "I'm not a child!"

When Gilbert turned to address Lyndsey, Jeffrey closed the issue. He raised his hands to his ears, stuck his tongue out then popped out both eyes. His hands fluttered. He almost attained a full 'Bugshit McClaken' salute before Gilbert caught on to his antics. The girls and Richard burst into laughter. Gilbert whipped around, but failed to catch Jeffrey in the act. Jeffrey, a master of the maneuver, sat erect in his chair with both arms crossed against his chest.

Gilbert tried to bluff him into a confession. He declared, "I saw that!"

"Doodn't."

"Did."

Yer doodn't!"

"Did."

"No wers…doodn't"

"Didn't"

"Sees ya doodn't"

Hope stepped in. She called out, "Uncle Gilbert, Uncle Jeffrey, enough already."

Jeffrey's hand whizzed across the table and snatched the last piece of toast. He winked at Gilbert and said, "Dar I's gots yer."

At that point, Gilbert joined the others in their laughter.

Jeffrey chewed, then swallowed the last of the toast. He stood up looked to Richard and summoned him to duty, "Wees beest be oon ar wers. De hurly boid gits de lobbies."

Richard moved to Jeffrey's side, and by doing, so declared his allegiance for the morning's lobster run.

Gilbert stood up. He moved over behind the girls then placed a hand on each of their shoulders.

Hope looked to Lyndsey and whispered, "We've been ordered to battle stations, Sis. Not to worry, I'm a good teacher."

Jeffrey and Richard stepped off towards the front door. Gilbert followed. Hope stopped at the refrigerator and withdrew two jugs of water and two large, plastic bags filled with an assortment of energy snacks. The two sisters left the kitchen and joined the men outside. The walk down to the dock seemed much shorter than yesterday's to Richard and Lyndsey.

The morning tide stood almost halfway up the pilings of the dock. Jeffrey and Richard made a good team. In short order, they had boarded Rose Bud and cast off her docking lines. Jeffrey fired up the motor, left it in idle, and allowed Rose Bud to drift quietly away from the dock.

Gilbert and the girls took a little longer to board. With all three safely on board, Gilbert started the motor. It took a little persuasion, but finally relented. It sputtered first, then roared and finally settled back to a smooth idle. Hope cast off the docking lines.

Lyndsey watched her crew mates carry out their duties. The Karyn-Anita drifted out towards Rose Bud. Lyndsey looked towards the shore then glanced up the hill. She froze for a second or two. Standing atop the hill Lyndsey spotted the spirit of Grace Ramsay. Its hands waved and pointed towards Jeffrey and Rose Bud. Lyndsey turned towards Jeffrey's boat. She waved out to Richard and Jeffrey. They returned her hail. Lyndsey turned back towards the hill. Grace Ramsay's spirit stood there gazing down at the lobster crews on the water.

Hope caught Lyndsey's unease and focused line of sight. She asked, "What's up, girl? You look a tad nervous."

Lyndsey gazed up towards the spirit. She hesitated then asked, "Is the old homestead haunted?"

Hope laughed lightly and repeated her earlier assurances to Lyndsey, "Sis! Trust me, Uncle Jeffrey's home, the homestead is not haunted." She shook her head moved to Lyndsey's side and whispered, "Unless one gives credence to the tales of Grammy Ramsay. She often claimed she'd heard a convincing tale or two from the lips of her Great-grandfather." She paused then said, "Relax. Uncle Jeffrey's house is not haunted."

The two boats bumped sides. Richard pushed Rose Bud free, and Jeffrey shifted into forward gear. Rose Bud pulled away from Karyn-Anita and moved out towards East River Bay. Lyndsey caught Jeffrey glancing upwards towards the spirit and wave. Jeffery's wave convinced, Lyndsey, that Grace Ramsay's spirit was definitely, Uncle Jeffrey's *Good Neighbour Fairy?* Gilbert shifted into forward gear and set Karyn-Anita off in Jeffrey's wake. Lyndsey took another look up onto the hill. The spirit had vanished. Its message had not. Lyndsey fully understood that the journey out to the Floating Islands would take place on board Rose Bud. Thoughts of Jeffrey filled her mind. Their unique, charming and loveable Uncle Jeffrey would soon be subjected to a young niece with a determined mind and a fixed agenda.

The trip out took thirty minutes. Then the real action started out beyond East River Bay on Mahone Bay. Gilbert manoeuvred up to the trap marker. Hope hauled the trap and retrieved its contents. Lyndsey jumped back away from Hope on their first exercise. She'd expected to see large red crab-like creatures that did not object to being manhandled and removed from the traps. She had been wrong. At the second float, Hope handed Lyndsey a pair of heavy gloves and a chest high apron. Lyndsey slid her hands into the gloves and slipped into the apron, but once again at that trap she refrained from offering Hope a helping hand.

At the third trap, Hope hauled Lyndsey to her side and employed her as an aide. Together, they hauled the trap up to the surface. It proved to be the tenth haul out before Lyndsey summoned up the courage to remove a lobster from its trap. On the fifteenth, Hope took a break. She stood back and watched Lyndsey step smoothly through the process. Through the remainder of the run, the sisters worked well together. The lobster run ended with the last trap lowered back down into the water by Lyndsey. Karyn-Anita with Gilbert at her helm set off to rendezvous with Rose Bud, Jeffrey and Richard.

Seven minutes out from the processors dock, he could not restrain himself any longer. Shakespeare of Mahone Bay burst forth in an artful rendition of 'The Merchant of Venice.'

"'*In sooth, I know not why I am so sad: It wearies me; you say it worries you; But how I caught it, found it, or came by it, What stuff tis made of, whereof it is born, I am to learn; And such a want-wit sadness makes of me, That I have much ado to know myself.*'"

Hope joined in, "'*Your mind is tossing on the ocean; There, where your argosies with portly sail, Like signiors and rich burghers on the flood, Or, as it were, the pageants of the sea, Do overpeer the petty traffickers, That curtsy to them, do them reverence, As they fly by them with their woven wings.*'"

Richard called out from Rose Bud, "*Tis alas... Shakespeare's 'The Merchant of Venice' Act I Scene I.*"

Rose Bud bumped up against the dock. Jeffrey uttered a quiet, "Tank YE Lard." He jumped onto the dock and tied off the fore and aft docking lines. From up on the dock, he assisted Gilbert in securing Karyn-Anita to the dock ahead of Rose Bud.

Forty-five minutes passed before their catches had been unloaded and sold to the processors. Richard released first Karyn-Anita's, then Rose Bud's, docking lines and jumped back onboard Rose Bud.

Jeffrey pulled away from the dock first. Gilbert followed. They moved slowly out of the inner harbour until they'd passed the restricted no wake zone. Once there, Jeffrey hit the throttle and Rose Bud responded. She leapt up out of the water then crashed back down. With Jeffrey at the helm, she raced like a free spirit across the waters of Mahone Bay. Karyn-Anita followed in her wake. Gilbert held back on the throttle, preferring not to push his motor to the limit.

Jeffrey pointed out towards two islands off on the horizon. He shouted out, "Dars a ways pas dat Big Tancooookie Islend bes a plece Gilly wan't ner goes neer ta."

"What's his problem? Bad shoals about them?"

"Na. Lik'in mose folks…her's bout. Dy's scart."

Rose Bud, with Jeffrey at the helm, altered course and headed northward she left Big Tancook Island in her wake and eastward out towards the vast Atlantic. Richard looked towards her aft out to the island and wondered, *Could the diary speak of a sad truth that once happened? Did a demonic soul stand guard over the remains of riches once uncovered by my ancestors?* Little doubt remained in his mind. He would have to step upon the islands before their visit ended. He walked back up into the cabin. There, he leaned over and begged Jeffrey to perform the honours. He said, "I've got to go there the islands, will you take me?"

Jeffrey turned, looked directly at Richard, and asked, "Doon't yoous bees a teell'n Gilly. Hee'd nay heer oof it."

"Never, never," Richard called back. He then avowed, "You can trust me on that one."

"OK. Den…I'll's takes ya. Butt nat noow."

"Great. Thanks Jeffrey. You'll not regret it."

Rose Bud slowed on entering East River Bay then slipped through the entrance to East River. She slid across the river to her dock. There, she bumped up against the dock's pilings. Jeffrey and Richard worked the docking lines. They had them secured and had climbed up onto the dock well before Karyn-Anita entered East River.

Aboard Karyn-Anita, Lyndsey and Hope stood together and chatted. Hope revealed a conversation she'd had with her best friend-forever Eugette. She pointed a finger at Lyndsey and declared, "You been had, girl! Your past has returned to haunt you."

Lyndsey frowned. The reference to haunt reminded her of occurrences she felt drawn to yet leery of pursuing.

Hope grinned, lowered her finger and revealed Eugette's revelation, "Lunenburg, the Fisheries Museum of the Atlantic. Do you recall anything special about that day?" She grinned and added, "Besides the Beach?"

Lyndsey blushed and stated, "No."

"You don't recall by chance hiring two eager kittie-sitters?"

Lyndsey smiled warmly and revealed a recollection of the museum visit.

"Dang! Megan and Taylor are two genuine sweethearts. Their Gramma, Maria is Eugette's Mom, and she bakes the best chocolate chip peanut butter cookies ever baked. Well while driving the wee ones home, Maria had some serious flashbacks to days past. Anyway, to make it short and sweet—Maria recalled a sweet little blonde kid that once lived next door to her parents home that Maria grew up in. She recalled that the girl's parents were both killed in the horrific accident that turned into a blessing with my birth. Well Maria sensed...no Maria saw something in you that made her wonder whatever became of that sweetheart? She actually thinks she saw something in your face that made her think..."

Thump. Karyn-Anita bumped up against the dock. Gilbert had guided Karyn-Anita through the gap into East River and up to the dock. Hope jumped up and shouted, "Later Sis. We got'ta secure the docking lines."

Gilbert killed the engine. Jeffrey and Richard assisted Hope and Lyndsey in securing Karyn-Anita and helped its crew back up onto the dock.

Lyndsey took a light ribbing over her trap hauling, but received both Gilbert and Hope's endorsement. To Richard's kidding, they responded by declaring Lyndsey a fit and capable lobster mate. Together, the five departed the dock and walked up the hill towards home. Jeffrey left them at his house. It had been a successful lobster run, and everyone looked forward to a hot shower. In silence, the remaining four walked together, tired, but satisfied with the efforts they'd put forth.

CHAPTER 43

ON ENTERING THE HOUSE, GILBERT OFFERED THE GIRLS FIRST GO at the showers. Naturally, neither chided or declined the offer. After the girls had departed, Gilbert suggested a celebration of their successful lobster run. Richard nodded his approval. Gilbert retrieved a bottle of white rum from the dining room hutch. He rejoined Richard in the kitchen, with Bailey in hot pursuit at his heels. Gilbert poured out two healthy tumblers of rum. He filled Bailey's saucer, endearing himself anew and forever to the old feline's heart.

Talk centred on the beauty of Mahone Bay. Richard had been impressed with the Village of Chester. Gilbert referred to the bay and its beautiful islands as the original Thousand Islands. He boldly stated to Richard, "The ones you grew up with were merely a sprinkling from Heaven, whereas Mahone Bay and its islands…is the true gateway to Heaven!"

Richard having just experienced the second of two enchanted days upon the bay, did not attempt to debate Gilbert on the matter. The appearance of Hope put a stopper on their conversation. Gilbert greeted Hope and told Richard to take up residence in the vacated shower. Richard accepted his offer. He left the kitchen.

Hope called out after him, "It's the one off Uncle Gilbert's bedroom."

Richard called back his thanks. Upstairs, he encountered Lyndsey in the hallway. She smiled at him. Richard liked the view. A towel suited Lyndsey well. He stopped in front of her.

Lyndsey stood up on her toes and kissed him. She jumped back and uttered a, "Yuk!", then stood back and pointed him towards the shower.

Richard hesitated. They'd not had a moment alone since their arrival. He took five minutes and updated Lyndsey on the news related to him by Roger. He tried to omit the part about John and Tessa's pending marriage, but Lyndsey probed all the details out of him. Richard looked deep into Lyndsey's face and eyes for a sign of her true reaction. He did not find it there.

Lyndsey finally spoke. She said, "It is best this way. I could never return to him. I'll never feel for him the way I once did. I hope they'll be happy."

"That's it?"

"Fraid so."

Richard laughed. He chided her, "Yer talk'n like dem."

Lyndsey smirked then smiled. Her dimples popped out and she released her towel. It fell to the floor. She pouted and chirped, "Dooes dey loooks leke dis beloons ta a tru Blu-nooser?"

Richard's jaw dropped. Before he could reply, Lyndsey stooped, picked up the towel, and fled into her bedroom. He watched the bedroom door swing shut behind a naked Lyndsey. The temptation to follow her into the bedroom subsided when Richard heard the heavy footsteps of Gilbert climbing up the stairs.

He turned and fled to Gilbert's bedroom. There, he found the door to Gilbert's en suite bath and entered it. In a flash, Richard stripped and stepped into the shower enclosure. Five minutes into his shower, Richard discovered the meaning behind the term '*Go take a cold shower.*' Within a minute of Gilbert stepping into the main bathroom shower, Richard, then Gilbert, screamed out in shock. Ice-cold water hit their bodies and sent them scurrying for relief at the far ends of their showers. The image of Lyndsey's naked body had vaporized from Richard's mind in a flash. Richard bit his tongue and timidly reached through the stream of ice water.

He turned off the water, then whipped the shower door open and grabbed a towel. It took a moment to recover Richard toweled himself dry. He wrapped the towel about his waist, picked up his soiled clothes and went to his bedroom.

Inside the bedroom, Richard quickly dressed himself in a set of clean clothes then went back downstairs. On the way, he shuddered on hearing the water running and Gilbert singing loudly in the shower. Down in the kitchen, Richard found Hope and Lyndsey seated at the table with Mr. Lizards. Richard stopped. He tried to excuse himself, but Mr. Lizards urged him to join them. He explained that all the details had been attended to. Richard sat down at the far end of the table.

Lyndsey held up two photos and passed them over to Richard.

Mr. Lizards explained, "I dropped in on a mutual friend. One, I met at the Blue Buzzard Tavern in Newmarket. He passed along these photos he took of you two onboard the Digby Ferry, the '*Princess of Acadia*'."

Richard laughed. He held the photos up and eyed them longingly. The photos showed a happy couple enthralled by their partner's presence accompanied by one relaxed cat lost in dreamland. He passed them back to Lyndsey then gazed longingly at the real thing.

Hope piped up, "Bring on de preacher." She looked to Mr. Lizards and asked, "Per chance do you perform the doing in addition to the undoing."

Mr. Lizards lowered his head. He apologized, "Sorry. I see the need. I'm willing, but unable to oblige." He paused then updated them on the latest news from Roger. "No need to worry about your work piling up on you back home, Lyndsey. Roger tells me Mike has everything caught up and under control."

"It's totally caught up?" Lyndsey asked.

"Totally," Walter replied then added, "Totally, if one excludes a Nora Bobinski."

"Little, harmless lovable Nora?" Lyndsey frowned and asked.

"Yes ma'am. Little Nora has taken a shine to Mike. She is persistently trying to fix Mike up with her daughter, Lori. Claims if he weren't so young she give him a go however she insists he'd be a perfect man for her dear sweet Lori."

Lyndsey closed her eyes and said, "Poor Mike. Nora's a sweetheart. But ..."

The kitchen burst into laughter then fell silent on Gilbert's arrival. He stepped into the kitchen and hailed a greeting to Mr. Lizards, "Welcome. Welcome to our home, Mr. Lizards, right?" Gilbert walked over and shook hands with Mr. Lizards.

Mr. Lizards pleaded, "Please. Walter is just fine. I'd prefer it, really."

Gilbert looked at the kitchen clock, he asked, "Would you have time to visit and enjoy some Maritime hospitality?" He pointed to the bottle of white rum that sat on the counter.

Walter smiled broadly and avowed his love of Maritime hospitality.

Gilbert picked up the bottle of white rum from the counter and signaled everyone to follow him. Hope and Lyndsey remained in the kitchen. Gilbert led Walter and Richard off into the living room. There, he politely asked Walter for his car keys. "Tis but a wee measure of safety, we ask the same of all our guests."

Walter extracted a set of car keys from his front pocket. He handed them over to Gilbert.

"I thanks ye me son," Gilbert said to Walter. He added, "You'll be spending the night I will assume. Hope and Lyndsey will share a bedroom. Walter, we'll bunk you out overnight."

No objections were raised. Richard stepped over to Walter and asked him for news from the home front. Walter explained all matters had now been fully addressed. He stated that to his knowledge, all was going well. He'd conducted a very good meeting with John and Roger in the presence of Tessa. Walter explained, "Both John and Tessa appeared to be happy but definitely not to the degree I see with you love birds at this end. Everything is on hold pending the results of the paternity tests. References to that fact were an issue with her. As least, that's my read. He sends his best to you."

Hope and Lyndsey cut him off. They entered the living room carrying a tray apiece. Hope's bore an ice bucket and two large bottles of cola. Lyndsey's bore five large tumblers and a saucer. They set the trays down on the coffee table. A flash of yellow raced into the room and sat down by the coffee table.

Gilbert topped off a tumbler to Walter's specifications. He next placed Bailey's saucer on the floor. To Walter, he explained, "Bailey here…well he's a cat after my heart. If you're not careful he'll drink you under the table."

Walter raised his eyebrows.

Richard added, "Bailey is—no—was Grandpa Ramsay's drinking partner."

Walter set his glass down. He burst into laughter then said, "Say no more. I knew William well. He spoke often of a Bailey, but I assumed he spoke of a drinking buddy. I never realized that buddy was a cat until now. However I can attest to, William's boasting of a Bailey and their solid friendship."

Bailey cast a disdainful eye at Walter on hearing him question his kinship with his master. The disdain vanished throughout the balance of the evening, Gilbert and Walter swapped tales of grandeur, each trying and at times outdoing the other. Gilbert's stories centred on his time spent teaching at the university and out upon the bay hauling in he estimated a million and then some lobsters. Walter naturally ran his tales out of his legal past, and to Richard's pleasure, threw in more than one or two tales that included the antics of his Grandpa Ramsay.

Bailey worked his way through two saucers of rum. A fit of friskiness hit him around 11:30 pm. Bailey leapt into the bay window. He pawed the glass madly. This drew the attention of all present. Gilbert explained Bailey's action by alluding to the large moth population. Everyone laughed and bought into his explanation, except Lyndsey. She looked out the window past Bailey and spotted his quarry. It had been none other than the spirit of Grace Ramsay. Lyndsey, after a pause, laughed along with the others. The spirit no longer frightened her. She knew its quest, and had resolved herself to assisting the young spirit in attaining her goal.

The clock struck midnight. Lyndsey and Hope excused themselves and retired upstairs together. Richard suspected a session of girl-talk would ensue before the two crawled under the covers for the night. He reasoned the two reunited sisters had a lifetime of experiences to share. He remained downstairs until Gilbert and Walter entered into a hearty debate over Shakespeare. Richard wisely and politely excused himself. He claimed possession of mere amateur status in the realm of Shakespeare. The boastful Shakespearean quotations of Gilbert and Walter, assured Richard that he was not a Bardolater.

The clock struck 4:00 am when Walter declared Gilbert the winner and master of his trade. They shared one last round then staggered upstairs. Gilbert set Walter up in the fourth bedroom, then staggered down to his and collapsed on the bed. The house fell silent. Robust snoring from three of the bedrooms disturbed the silence throughout the night. Otherwise not a sound could be heard.

CHAPTER 44

ONE WEEK LATER, JOHN SURRENDERED TO TESSA'S DEMANDS. THE time back at work had eased his tension and stress levels. He agreed to follow Richard and Lyndsey's lead and head down to Nova Scotia. The meeting he had with Roger and Mr. Lizards had convinced him to put off any plans to visit a justice of the peace since he had agreed to granting Lyndsey an uncontested divorce. The clincher came with Roger's advice and plea for him to hold off until Tessa's paternity test results were in and his divorce decree finalized. Roger advised him repeatedly that it could be under three months, but he'd best not hold him to it. At times the passage of time and justice failed to meet the needs of those it served.

Tessa savored the taste of victory. She sat behind the wheel and drove as they departed Newmarket that afternoon. Tessa's sharp comments and actions quickly irked John, but he suppressed his reactions. Their destination carried them down the trail recently traveled by Richard, Lyndsey and Bailey. Twenty-four hours later, John drove Tessa's Oldsmobile off the Digby Ferry. Tessa entered Nova Scotia determined to find financial security. She could never have anticipated the events that would unfold.

From Digby, the route John and Tessa took followed Hwy 101 straight through to Windsor where, they stopped for the night. Tessa prearranged their overnight stay at a quaint out of the way

Victorian home operating as a Bed and Breakfast. It provided them with a pleasant introduction to Maritime hospitality which John enjoyed but Tessa refused to share her impressions.

Tessa arose bright and refreshed the next morning and left John sleeping soundly after a night of torrid sex. Downstairs, she ate a light breakfast. At 9:00 am, John had not yet made an appearance. Tessa went out to her vehicle. There, she pulled out the photocopied pages of the old diary. Richard had dropped off a copy at John's house before he headed out to Nova Scotia. Tessa then returned to the room. She sat down at the table and flipped through the pages until she reached the section that had captured her interest.

John stirred. Tessa jumped up and pulled the shades. The darkened room settled John down. He drifted back into a deep sleep. Tessa started to reread the pages. The prospect of getting her hands on the buried treasure hinted at in the diary's yellowed pages appealed to her greedy nature. Denied of the ten percent share awarded Lyndsey, Tessa resolved herself to settling on nothing less than the alluded-to treasure. She recalled with anger the words of Walter Lizards. Lyndsey, John's spouse of record is entitled to her 10% share of the Ramsay business interest. Henceforth, there being no provisions for secondary spouses, the future spouse of Richard will receive a 10% share of the Ramsay business interest. Tessa pounded her left fist into the palm of her right hand in frustration. She reasoned John's soon to be ex–Lyndsey had no right to a 10% share of the Ramsay business interest. Once her wedding vows were exchanged with John, she'd fight the bitch for her soon to be rightful share! The diary alluded to a treasure on an island. Greed had driven her through two husbands. The third, once secured, she reasoned could be replaced…if the treasure's rewards justified it. Tessa would sooner be damned than share the treasure with any of her soon to be new family, including John.

John awoke at 11:00 am. Tessa stripped and slid back under the sheets after he started to stir. She massaged him until he had risen to a state of readiness then crawled up onto his hips. John's eyes popped open and he smiled as Tessa slid him into her sexual nerve centre. Their late morning romp ended quickly. It satisfied John, but only tempered Tessa's needs. She faked it by collapsing onto his chest and moaning. John bought her sales job. Tessa rolled off after a brief moment. A quick, shared shower did not arouse John. Tessa stepped out of the shower and left John to himself. Half an hour later, they were back on the road again.

John chose to take Route 14, which ran from Windsor almost directly to Chester. An hour later, they arrived in Chester. Hungry, John pulled into the parking lot of the Lobster Pot Pub & Eatery. Inside, they seated themselves at a table along a long window that looked out onto the harbour. Their waitress, Eugette, welcomed them then departed after they'd placed an order: two lobster platters and a jug of draft beer.

She returned shortly with their jug of beer and two mugs to find the couple in a heated argument. The lady loudly expressed her view that beer was a non-alcoholic beverage. Eugette wisely delivered their jug of beer and mugs and left the couple to resolve their difference of opinion. Fifteen minutes later, she returned with their meals. Tessa ordered a second jug of beer. John, an experienced lobster diner, made short work of his broiled crustacean. He then assisted Tessa in the art of lobster dining. After she'd eaten half her lobster and John the other, Tessa excused herself. She stepped off to the lady's washroom. John ordered a third jug of beer in her absence.

Tessa walked out of the washroom. She stopped at the bar and made an inquiry. "How does a person go about securing passage out to the Floating Islands?" The bartender turned ashen on hearing Tessa's question.

Tessa raised her eyebrows. She chided, "What? You mean this little town has no real men living in it?"

The bartender recovered. He answered, "Yes M'am. We do. Liv'n ones. Alive cause de don't tempts fate."

"Oh, really, well I need one with balls! Care to point one out to me? It shouldn't be difficult. How many real men can there be in this shit-assed little town? One...Two tops."

The bartender turned red in the face. The little brunette had pissed him off. If not for the knowledge gained growing up in this so-called *'shit-assed little town'*, he'd take the bitch out there himself.

Barnie unknowingly spoke his thoughts, "I'd give you the thrill of yer lifetime…before I tossed you off onto the island." Then, he mumbled, "Then, I'd flee, leaving you on the island to die a satisfied woman."

Tessa heard his spoken thoughts and mumbled boast. She roared, "In your dreams, fish-boy. I ain't met the man capable of delivering what Little Tessa needs."

She prodded, "What, at a loss for words? Or just don't know any real men?"

Barnie's eyes flashed red. He slammed both hands down hard on the bar then cast his eyes out over the floor. The pub had its normal patrons for the hour: mostly lobstermen—laid-back and relaxed now that the lobster season had come to an end. He spotted Martin and Slick at one table. One table over sat a stranger. Barnie figured this to be the unfortunate mate of the fiery bitch. Next to the stranger, he spotted Pappy McClaken and Lenny. Where was Pappy's son? *Why?* He fretted, *wasn't BugShit McClaken about when needed?* He sighed on spotting Meat *Ned Stone*, and the *Sliver* wee Mikie Slivers seated at the far end of the pub.

Barnie boldly called out, "Attention. May I have your attention please?"

All eyes, including John's, turned towards the bar and Barnie.

Barnie took a deep breath. He stated the facts as he'd come to know them, "Gentlemen. Please take note of the LADY IN RED, this fine young lady!" He paused, then continued, "This fine young lady. Why she's a look'n fer passage out to the Floating Islands! Do I have any takers?"

Barnie and the room fell silent.

Enraged, John slammed his stein of beer on the table stood and ran over to Tessa's side. He shouted into her face, "What in hell are you up to?" Beer and spit flew out of his mouth with each word.

The pub remained silent. Tessa sneered. She chirped, "Shut up, and trust me."

Barnie looked at the bitch's mate. He envied him but pitied him in matters beyond the sack. John grabbed Tessa and attempted to pull her towards the door.

Meat broke the silence, he called back to Barnie, "Is de lady crazy?"

John released Tessa and screamed back at Meat, he demanded an apology, "Asshole—Apologize to my lady!" His face and neck reddened with his soaring blood pressure.

Barnie sneered. He knew Meat would never retract his words. His hand dropped off the bar and picked up a fish bonker that he kept under the bar in case of emergencies. Barnie felt one coming on. John moved towards Meat. The fish bonker in Barnie's hand flew through the air. With a solid *Whack!* It struck John on the head. He staggered then twisted around and grabbed the bar's countertop. His head throbbed. In rage, he stared at Barnie and his blood stained fish bonker. Barnie grinned and warned a stunned John, "Shut yer pie hole or I'll be treating ya to another sampling of me friend here."

Mikie took the floor and all present by surprise. He stood up and walked up to the bar. Meat tried to restrain his lobster-mate but failed. Mikie could not resist a damsel in distress, at least not one with a chassis like Tessa's. Once Mikie had set his eyes upon Tessa's chest and ample cleavage, his decision had been made. Hell! He'd take the lady to the Devil's doorstep and back for a good up-front look-see. Mikie stopped directly in front of Tessa. He eyed her head to toe with a short pause at the low-cut top of her dress.

John moved towards Mikie. Barnie stopped him. Mikie's eyes finished their inspection. Tessa had passed. He looked up and deep into Tessa's eyes. Mikie stood a mere five foot zero in height. Short compared to Tessa's five foot two.

Tessa laughed. She sneered then snarled, "What! This is the best you can do? A midget?"

Mikie shrugged his shoulders. He smiled and said, "Don't be chiding me short-comings. I's been over-compensated fer where it counts de most."

Tessa's eyes shot down to Mikie's crotch. Her sneer changed to a smile.

"I'll pay you a thousand dollars to take me and my man out to the Floating Islands and back."

Mikie teetered. He jacked the price up. Had the lady been going solo ten bucks and a sampling of the goods would have made him a happy man.

Mikie shot back, "If he's coming da price is five grand. But I's don't step a foot on the islands."

Tessa grabbed his hand, stuffed it inside her top, and pressed it hard against her left breast.

Mikie faltered. First, he stood there blank faced. Slowly, realization of his situation set in. Mikie smiled broadly and squeezed his fingers against Tessa's breast, then fondled the prize presented to him.

Tessa smiled warmly. She pulled Mikie's hand off her breast and retorted, "Two grand. Not a penny more."

Mikie gulped. He said, "Sold."

John glared at Mikie. Barnie waved his fish bonker at John. The threat worked. John remained at the bar and stared on in anger.

"When, where, what time?" Tessa demanded.

Mikie held his hand out. Tessa took it to be a demand for cash payment. She ripped open her purse and flipped through it. To Mikie's astonishment and all present, she withdrew and slapped two one-thousand-dollar bills into his open hand.

"Two days time...Saturday morning, down by the docks and launch ramp, 5:00 am. Be there! I'll be aboard 'Total Satisfaction', and I wait for no woman with a man." He paused, then stated, "Total Satisfaction would be me boat. Like me...she delivers."

Tessa withdrew two fifty-dollar bills, snapped the purse shut and wheeled around to face Barnie. She laid the bills on the bar.

"Keep the change, Fish-Boy! And don't go a blabbing our travel plans to those damned East River McClakens."

She turned back to face Mikie and said, "We'll be there."

Tessa moved towards the door. John followed. Tessa looked back at Mikie and said, "Nice fingers!"

John followed Tessa out of the Lobster Pot Pub & Eatery. He unlocked the passenger door, but did not open it. Tessa grabbed the keys from him. She then opened the driver's door and slide in behind the wheel. She started the engine. Then reached across the seats and opened the passenger door. "Get in!" she yelled.

John obeyed. Tessa chided him, "Knock off the silent treatment. He squeezed my boob; got the thrill of his lifetime…and I saved us three grand."

She backed out of the parking lot then drove off in search of their accommodation. John's head throbbed. Tessa's actions had angered him. Tessa turned left at Route 3. They ended up registered at a weather beaten inn that claimed they served up the best breakfast east of the Pacific. John paid in advance for their anticipated three night stay. He accepted the room key from the desk clerk. The clerk's directions led them to their room. A minor spat broke out once they entered their room. It centred on Tessa's earlier claim that beer was not an alcoholic beverage. The clock in their room struck 7:00 pm. John fell silent. He stepped outside and retrieved their luggage. A bottle of rye whiskey retrieved from his overnight bag started to settle his nerves.

Tessa restrained herself. She had sworn off alcohol at John's insistence after he agreed to her settlement terms and marriage pending the results of her tests. She saw no reason to cause another flare up before Junior passed out for the night. The child possibly growing inside her was Tessa's insurance policy. Tessa knew the value of that policy.

John's anger eased up after several healthy servings of whisky. He joined Tessa at the table. Together, they read over the photocopied pages from Grace Ramsay's diary. Their main focus fell on the pages that alluded to buried treasure. The clock struck midnight. John felt the effects of a hangover take hold. He reached toward the bottle of rye whiskey in search of a long overdue third drink.

Tessa restrained him. Instead, she offered up a meal John could not refuse. Tessa served up the works to John: no-holds-barred raw sex. It carried them through the next half hour. John begged off on Tessa's offer of a rerun. Mikie's finger squeeze had faded from John's mind. He drifted off to sleep sated.

CHAPTER 45

OPEN SEASON ON LOBSTER CLOSED TWO DAYS AFTER MR. LIZARDS departed the company of Gilbert's household. He headed to the airport a happy man, and a wiser man, with a dozen fresh lobsters packed to accompany him on his flight home and a Mahone Bay lobster run under his belt. He was wiser because he'd met a true master and practitioner of Shakespeare, one who had drawn and quartered a hitherto, self-proclaimed Bardolater—Walter Lizards, in an open debate of Shakespeare's works. Yes, Gilbert had definitely earned the respect of Walter Lizards. Still, Walter departed a satisfied man. He had worked on the team that set in motion the actions needed to free young Lyndsey from the bonds of what he considered to be a bad marriage.

With lobster season closed, Gilbert focused all his energies on his duties at the university. That left Richard and Lyndsey free to do some day-tripping around the area. On day one they took in part of the Evangeline Trail. Their travels carried them to Annapolis Royal, Port Royal, and the Habitation, a reconstruction of a fur-trading post, one of the earliest European settlements in North America. It had first been built under the direction and efforts of settlers that included Samuel de Champlain in 1605. From there, they traveled to Delaps Cove and hiked along a wilderness trail to an amazing waterfall. Their return trip took them through Bridgetown, Berwick, and Kentville. At Kentville they returned to East River via Route 12 and Chester.

On their second free day, Jeffrey suggested they take Rose Bud out and explore the bay. He recommended a run out to Big Tancook Island. He'd actually winked and alluded to a secluded cove on its seaboard side that just might provide the pair an excellent spot for a private picnic. Richard accepted Jeffrey's offer. Hope packed them a picnic lunch before she left with Gilbert for a day of volunteer work in Halifax. Through Gilbert's urging, she'd become involved in an adult literacy tutoring program.

Richard and Lyndsey set off at 10:00 am. Richard carried their lunch down to the dock. There, he helped Lyndsey climb aboard Rose Bud. He checked the two fuel tanks. They were full. Satisfied, Richard cast off the docking lines and fired up the motor. Rose Bud glided out onto East River Bay with Richard at its helm. A blue sky and calm sea out on Mahone Bay showed promise for a great day.

They took the scenic route and worked their way towards Big Tancook Island. Richard consulted the onboard charts and pointed out the many islands by name to Lyndsey as they motored past them. He did not seek out the Floating Islands. Jeffrey had made it a condition of their trip and Richard had accepted. He looked forward to his trip to those islands with Jeffrey on Saturday morning.

At noon, they passed between Big and Little Tanacook Islands. Richard slowed on reaching the seaboard side of Big Tanacook. On reaching the midpoint of the island, he spotted the cove alluded to by Jeffrey. Richard pulled the throttle back and slowly slid into the cove. Safely inside a sheltered nook, Richard killed the motor. Next, he put out both sets of bumpers on the sides of Rose Bud. She drifted closer to shore then bumped up against a low rock wall. Richard climbed up on the bow. From there he jumped ashore, with bowline in hand. After securing the line and Rose Bud to a large tree, he then caught the stern line tossed to him by Lyndsey and tied it off on a weathered pine tree. Next, he accepted the picnic lunch from Lyndsey then helped her ashore.

Jeffrey had not lied. The cove placed Richard and Lyndsey in a secluded spot. They sat down and glanced out over the sea. Their minds sucked in the solitude of their situation. The gentle surf eased all worries from their minds: minds that titillated over what might lay in store for them before another sunset ended their day.

Lyndsey broke the silence. She whispered, "Not to be a spoiler, but my tummy is rumbling."

Richard laughed and replied, "Let's check out Hope's lunch."

Lyndsey stood up, went to the picnic lunch, and opened it up. She set out a small tablecloth on the ground. From the picnic hamper, she pulled out a selection of sandwiches, egg salad, chicken salad, and roast beef. Next, she set out a portion of Hope's liquid refreshments.

Two bottles of iced beer drew Richard's eye. He joined Lyndsey at the picnic spot.

Lyndsey said, "Mmm. I'll take the chicken salad."

Richard picked up a can of cola and pulled its tap off. He passed it to Lyndsey. Lyndsey passed him the roast beef sandwich. Richard took the sandwich and a bottle of beer. They ate in silence. The third sandwich, egg salad, they shared. Once they'd eaten, Lyndsey returned the tablecloth and leftovers to the hamper. She joined Richard where he sat under a large tree. Richard placed his arm over her shoulder, and Lyndsey snuggled up against him. Again, they stared out to sea. Each waited for the right moment to touch the other in a giving way.

"I want you," Lyndsey murmured.

"Then take me."

"No it's your turn."

"You're a temptress."

Richard stood up. He reached down and took Lyndsey's hand.

"Rise up My Lady."

Lyndsey closed her hand on Richard's and allowed him to pull her up. Hand in hand they walked out onto the cove's point. A gentle sea breeze touched their faces. The hot afternoon sun warmed their bodies.

Richard turned and faced Lyndsey. He said, "I love you, Lyndsey."

"How do you love me?"

"More than I know how."

"I'll teach you."

Richard did not reply. He stepped up to Lyndsey and took her into his arms. Their lips touched and lingered. The kiss raised their body temperatures and passions. Richard stepped away from Lyndsey. He walked around behind her then stepped up to her back. His hands moved to her front and started to slowly massage Lyndsey's lower belly. Her head dropped back onto his shoulder.

Richard worked his way to the bottom of Lyndsey's top. His fingers worked the top up over her midsection, then he slid it up and free of her body. A gentle lift pulled it over her head and to her finger tips. Released it fell to the ground. Then he reached for her bra straps. These he pulled down over her shoulders. The sun hit Lyndsey's breasts and warmed them. Richard released the bra hooks. It fell to the ground. Lyndsey now stood naked from the waist up.

Richard's hands moved to her breasts. Slowly, he massaged them. Lyndsey's head fell back onto his chest. He kissed her neck lovingly. His hands released her breasts and dropped to her waist. There they fumbled, then finally worked her belt free. The button of her shorts offered no resistance. Next, Richard slid her zipper down. The shorts dropped to the ground. Richard's fingers glided under the elastic of Lyndsey's briefs. He pulled them down over her hips. The two lovers swayed. The briefs fell to the ground atop Lyndsey's shorts.

Lyndsey pushed her butt against Richard's hips. He sighed.

Richard's hands slid down her belly and paused in response to each sigh. Eager fingers softly touched and excited Lyndsey's passions. She stepped free of her shorts/briefs and parted her thighs. Richard's fingers extended their search one slid down and entered her. It slowly massaged Lyndsey. Its motion heightened her passions. She sighed. Her thighs trembled. She eased herself down onto a bed of lush green grass.

Lyndsey looked up at Richard and smiled provocatively. Before Richard could react, she reached up and tackled Richard. He willingly tumbled to the ground. She pulled his T-shirt up over his head, blinding him and arresting his arms.

Helpless, Richard lay back and relaxed on the grass.

Lyndsey attacked his shorts. In a flash, she had his briefs down around his knees. She left them there and gazed longingly at Richard's exposed body. A smile broke on her face. Satisfied that she was not alone in her heated desire, Lyndsey took hold of Richard's exposed sexual desire and massaged it slowly taking ownership of it. Richard thrust his hips and moaned. Lyndsey loved the power she now held over him.

Her actions increased to match his passions. Richard groaned, collapsed and sighed uncontrollably with his orgasm. His thighs trembled. Lyndsey reached up and pulled Richard's T-shirt up over his head and completely off.

Richard sighed, "Sorry, I couldn't hold back."

"I know."

"What about your need?"

"Trust me. I'll get mine on the second round."

"Second?"

"Trust me. It's now my turn."

Lyndsey's lips touched Richard's. Slowly she reignited his passions. Time stood still and vanished while each willingly ignited the other's need. Sensing Richard's readiness, Lyndsey straddled him and guided him to her passion. She placed her hands on his chest and started to rotate her hips. The motion increased in intensity with their rising passions. Richard started to ebb. Lyndsey slowed her movements Richard responded and rose up anew.

Richard groaned. Lyndsey moaned. She drove her hips to his one last time. Together they climaxed. Lyndsey collapsed onto Richard's chest. She sobbed. Her chest heaved. Inside, she felt Richard twitching and quickly retreat. She lay atop Richard. Their bodies trembled. Lyndsey released her arms from around Richard's neck she slid off him and rolled to his side. They lay there naked for a time. The sun caressed them. The gentle sea breezes slid refreshingly over their exposed bodies.

Finally, Lyndsey rose up and collected her clothes.

Richard followed her lead, once dressed he watched Lyndsey while she dressed. After he'd observed Lyndsey completely clothe herself, Richard stood up. He returned the hamper to Rose Bud. Lyndsey stood and watched.

Richard returned. He walked up to her and whispered, "I love you, teacher."

Lyndsey placed her arms around his neck. Her lips moved to his. Their kiss lingered. Lyndsey pulled away when she heard a branch snap.

Together they walked down to the boat. Richard helped Lyndsey climb up onto the bow. He waited until she'd safely returned to the stern. Then he untied stern line and tossed it to Lyndsey. On releasing the bowline he jumped up onto Rose Bud's bow.

Lyndsey stood at the stern and glanced up into the forest along the shore. Just before Richard started the motor, a soft song in the wind touched her ears and heart, *'Two lovers—two lovers lost in love's joys. Sharing—embracing the true joys of love's giving nature.'* She trembled, and the motor roared to life.

Richard stood at the helm, and guided Rose Bud back out of the little nook, and into the cove. There, he shifted into forward gear and set off towards East River. Rose Bud left the cove in her wake. Lyndsey at the stern stared longingly back at the cove's point. It disappeared when Rose Bud rounded a jut of land along the island. The run back to East River carried the couple over a gentle sea. The island faded on the horizon. A chilly sea breeze chased Lyndsey into the shelter of Rose Bud's cabin. Where she embraced Richard and rested her head on his chest. On gliding past Deep Cove on East River Bay Richard pulled the throttle back and Rose Bud's bow settled back into the sea. Startled by the vessels action Lyndsey awoke from a sleepy daze. They kissed as Rose Bud slipped into East River at 5:00 pm. Hope stood on the dock and hailed their return. She helped Richard in securing the docking lines and helped Lyndsey up onto the dock. Richard climbed up onto the dock with the picnic hamper in hand. He looked down the dock and spotted Hope and Lyndsey at the base of the hill. Satisfied that Rose Bud was secure, he set off after them.

Hope walked at Lyndsey's side up the hill. Her arm was about Lyndsey's waist.

With a grin and nod of the head, she asked, "So. Did you see another sunset?"

Lyndsey smiled, but did not reply.

"You did—don't be denying it girlie. I see it in your eyes. And sis yer top be insides out."

Lyndsey chuckled. She put her arm on Hope's waist. They walked back up to the house in silence secure in each other and the future that lay ahead of them.

CHAPTER 46

FRIDAY MORNING, RICHARD ACCEPTED GILBERT'S OFFER. HE accompanied Gilbert on his daily run into Halifax. On arriving in Halifax, they ate breakfast together. Then, Gilbert dropped Richard off down at the waterfront's *Historic Properties.* Richard spent the day exploring the many historic sites and general attractions in the downtown area. His first stop, the *Marine Museum of the Atlantic,* held him captive through the balance of Friday morning and well into the afternoon.

Hope and Lyndsey slept in that Friday morning. Their late night sister-to-sister session had lasted well into the early hours of Friday morning. After a breakfast of fruit salad, they set off together in pursuit of Uncle Jeffrey.

Jeffrey heard the girls' voices once they'd drawn near to the shed. He stepped out of the shed and waved to them. Hope's demure approach set Jeffrey on the alert. He sensed that the visit had a purpose. He loved his niece dearly, but did not relish the idea of being the brunt of Gilbert's disdain. Jeffrey could not recall an instance in which Hope had come calling after she'd received Gilbert's approval on one of her requests. No, Jeffrey reasoned, if Hope tries her Uncle Jeffrie Dearest routine...he'd just plain oout say NOpe.

Hope stepped away from Lyndsey. She strutted over to Jeffrey. Her hands went to his shoulders, and she kissed his forehead.

Jeffrey jumped back. He chirped, "I's ain't a dooing et."

"Doing what Uncle Jeffrey?"

"Doon't knoows. Jist ain't a dooing et.

Lyndsey joined Hope and Jeffrey. Her demure attitude, subtler than Hope's, did not alarm Jeffrey. With a smile, she said, "We had a great time yesterday, Richard and I. Thank you for allowing us the use of Rose Bud."

Jeffrey blushed. He answered, "Me pleesure. Lynd…sie. Doo…ja finds de cove?"

Lyndsey blushed.

Hope declared, "Oh. I'd say they found the cove…and a little more." She stepped back from Lyndsey and Jeffery, resolved to observe Uncle Jeffery's willpower melt like butter on a skillet, under Lyndsey's charm and manipulation.

Jeffrey dropped his guard. Hope, he could resist. Lyndsey and Hope together formed a formidable feminine force. A force determined to melt Uncle Jeffrey's heart and get their way with him.

Lyndsey played her trump card…Richard. She looked at Jeffrey and said, "Richard and I. We found the cove. Your directions were easy to follow."

"I's trii'd ta mak'm simp'le."

Lyndsey smiled. She continued to play her trump card, "Richard tells me you're a legend on the bay. Your charts are so well marked. We had no trouble identifying any of the islands or landmarks. He really respects your mastery of the sea. We're blessed to have a dear such as you to call Uncle…Uncle Jeffrey."

"Oh. Richie whys hees a purty goood seaman heesel'f."

Hope stood back and watched her older sister work Jeffrey over. She recognized the early signs of submission in Jeffrey. Though not near the meltdown point, Jeffrey's resolve showed signs of faltering.

"True. Richard comes from a family with a lifelong involvement in the marine business. It did not surprise us at all…to discover a man of your capabilities heading up the family's Nova Scotia link. Richard refers to you as 'A true natural.'"

"I's triies. I's dooes."

Lyndsey delivered her knockout punch. She said, "Richard and I need your help. Well, your help and the use of Rose Bud with you at her helm. We need to seek out a piece of our family's history."

"Ooh. Gilly. Hees moore goood bout dat histree stooff."

"It's not the book history stuff that Richard and I need help on. We need to go out to the Floating Islands."

"Goosh. Lynd...sie. Whys ye noot jest says so. I's teek'n Richie out dar Siterday. De day aft'r taday. Deedn't hees teells ya.?"

Lyndsey blushed. Her dimples popped out and melted Jeffrey's heart. She apologized by saying, "I'm so terribly sorry...Uncle Jeffrey. Yes Richard mentioned it in passing yesterday. I feel so silly for not remembering. It must have been the magic of being out on the bay and all. It is such a beautiful place to be."

Jeffrey blushed. He said, "Noo yer noot sillly. Yer jest a pritty lil niecee o'mine...whoo happin ta be in loove. Jest rimeend Richie ta be doown bye de doock comes fivvees oo'cloock tamorro morn'n." He embraced Lyndsey, kissed her cheek and boasted quietly in her ear, "Oooh de wee one's a goi'ng ta be soo joyfuuul ta bees a joinn'ng ups wwit de twoo's a ya ans a heed'ng ta de issslind. Tis alls shess everrs ask'd a mees. Tas gooes ta de islands."

Hope moved over to Jeffrey. She pleaded, "Oh...Oh please Uncle Jeffrey. Can I go with you?"

Jeffrey's face grew stern. In a firm voice he rejected Hope's plea, "I's soorry Hope. Bout I's kan't. Bout maybee Lynd...sie weel lets ya."

Hope turned to Lyndsey and pleaded her case anew. She played her part very good. Lyndsey teetered, but did not cave in to Hope's pleas. Jeffrey commended Lyndsey and suggested she talk first to Richard before rejecting Hope outright. Lyndsey agreed to Jeffrey's suggestion. The girls each kissed and thanked Jeffrey for his help. They left their uncle and walked back up to Gilbert's house.

After the girls left, Jeffrey strutted about the shed. He felt great. It wasn't often that Jeffrey got to refuse one of Hope's impulses. The idea of Hope having an older sister, one who could give her wise council like Gilbert so often provided pleased him. Hope and Lyndsey walked back to Gilbert's in silence. Once they'd entered the kitchen, Hope exploded, "Girlie, you are something else. Why, I swear. You worked Jeffrey over like a pro. Good God. I pity Richard. You've trained him right from the sandbox! Here, let me fix a drink. We'll celebrate."

Lyndsey frowned. She declined, "Sorry Hope. I'd best decline."

"So, I'm really going to be an auntie. I like it."

"I just want to err on the side of discretion."

Hope frowned then chided. "It was only a dream, a nightmare Lyndsey. Trust me."

"Hope. I can't. I know what I saw in Jeffrey's bedroom. It talked to me. I saw it up on the hilltop the morning we did the lobster run. Uncle Jeffrey's Good Neighbour Fairy, I believe it is Grace Ramsay's spirit. He also looked up towards the hilltop, waved and smiled at it. The night Mr. Lizards visited. Bailey—the window... Uncle Jeffery saw it, and he waved at it."

"Gads I knew you were a Maritimer, Sis! You really saw something in the window?"

"Yes really. Besides if I wasn't with child before yesterday. Well suffice to say my chances have increased ten-fold, after Richard and I picnicked on Jeffery's island."

Hope chuckled then asked, "You really saw something?"

"Yes, furthermore, ghost or no ghost, I'll not chance or question the feelings that have been racing through me lately."

"It's called love sister!"

Lyndsey shrugged her shoulders. She asked, "Does Uncle Jeffrey have a vehicle?"

"Why?"

"I'm hungry. I'd like to go somewhere and get a bite to eat."

"OK. I'll ring Uncle Jeffrey. Maybe he'll join us."

"Yes. That would be nice."

Within ten minutes of Hope's phone call to Jeffrey, he pulled into the yard in his pickup truck. Unlike Gilbert's, it wasn't vintage sixties. To Lyndsey's surprise, it was an extended cab, four-wheel-drive 1996 Ford Pickup Truck. Hope and Lyndsey climbed up into the truck. Hope sat up front, and Lyndsey sat on the rear bench seat.

Jeffrey drove over to Chester. He pulled into the parking lot at the Lobster Pot Pub & Eatery.

Hope commented, "Good food. Good Company. Come on Lyndsey. You'll love it."

Inside the Pub, Hope led Jeffrey and Lyndsey to a table for four over by the waterfront window where they sat down. To Hope's surprise, Barnie the Bartender served their table.

"Hi. Bugshit. Long—"

"Don't be call'n me dat Bernie!"

"Sorry Jeffrey. I could have used you here abouts day b'fore yesterday."

"I's beeen beessie."

"Ya. Whatever."

Barnie grabbed the fourth seat and sat down beside Jeffrey.

"Had a job you could've handled."

"What kind of job?" Hope asked.

"Didn't Pappy tell you? He was here wit Lenny. De saw the whole thing."

"Hees nat due hoome. Tills tanight. Bunkk'd out et Lennie's," Jeffrey explained.

"Right," Barnie acknowledged Jeffrey's comment.

Barnie turned and faced all three seated at the table. He described his encounter with Tessa two days past.

"I had me a real fireball drop in, not a local fer sure. Told me not ta go a blabbing her travel plans ta de damned East River McClakens. Pardon my fine language, Ladies. But she was one foul-mouthed bitch."

"You're excused, Barnie," Hope said. She introduced Lyndsey as her sister.

Barnie did a double take, but did not comment. Instead he continued his recount of the event.

"She paid Mikie two grand—two real, big ones to take her and her man out to the Floating Islands this Saturday morning."

"What?" Lyndsey blurted out.

"Sorry," Barnie said.

He explained the details, "Well, she opened with an offer of a grand. No takers. Mikie took the floor to get a closer look-see at the lady's rack. Sorry ladies, but she had a 'to kill-for body'. Besides, you know Mikie. Anyway, Mikie countered at five grand. Then with God as my witness, the lady grabs Mikie's hand and done shoved in down inside her top a'ginst her things."

"Breasts. The word is breasts, Barnie!" Hope chided.

"I know. Just being polite. Anyway, she pulled Mikie's hand off'n her rack and counter-offered at two grand. Mikie accepted. She slapped two one-thousand-dollar bills into his hand. Betcha Mikie don't wash that hand anytime soon."

"Where'd they go?" Lyndsey asked.

"Don't know. I was just happy to see the bitch and her man leave. Oops. Sorry, ladies."

"No need," Lyndsey said. She turned to Jeffrey and said, "I'm sorry Uncle Jeffrey. I'm not really as hungry as I thought. Can we go home?"

Jeffrey frowned. He asked, "Ya shore ona dat Lynd…sie?"

"Yes."

Jeffrey, Hope and Lyndsey stood up. Lyndsey led them out to Jeffrey's truck. Both Jeffrey and Hope tried to suggest another restaurant to Lyndsey. She would not hear of it. On reaching Gilbert's, Hope and Lyndsey stepped out of the truck. Lyndsey apologized to both for being such a bother. Both declined her apology. Jeffrey drove off. Hope entered the house with Lyndsey. She tried, but could not get Lyndsey to open up to her. Lyndsey went up to her room and lay down on the bed. She resolved herself to not inform Richard of the change of events. An image of Tessa strutted arrogantly through her mind. Lyndsey cursed silently, who else she pondered would be seeking passage to the Floating Islands and calling down the McClakens? Barnie had hit the nail on the head. Tessa was one fiery bitch. Her appearance and performance in Chester left Lyndsey with no doubts on that one. Lyndsey tossed and turned, then finally drifted off to sleep.

CHAPTER 47

WHEN RICHARD STEPPED THROUGH THE FRONT DOOR, HE CARRIED two large packages in his arms.

Gilbert followed his lead. He called out, "Hello, anyone home?" Nobody answered.

They reached the kitchen where Richard placed the packages on the table. A walk about the ground floor led Richard to Hope in the living room. Hope opened her eyes and stared up at Richard from the sofa. Richard greeted the sleepy-eyed beauty with, "Din-din awaits you in the kitchen. Where's Lyndsey hiding out?"

"She made it to the bedroom. You wore the poor girl out yesterday."

"No way, did I really?"

"Well, maybe. No. It must have been all the work we did out in the garden today."

"Could be, Lyndsey loves to garden."

Hope sat up. After a second or two, she stood and used her fingers to comb her tussled mess of strawberry-blonde hair. She offered, "Serve it up. I'll go awaken your princess."

"Thanks, Hope."

Richard left the living room and returned to the kitchen.

Hope stopped outside Lyndsey's bedroom door. A rat-a-tap-tap failed to bring a response. She opened the door and walked inside. There, she found Lyndsey sprawled across the bed. Her arms were wrapped tightly about the pillow. Hope tip toed over to the side of the bed. Lyndsey did not stir. She stooped over and gently ran her fingers up and down Lyndsey's inner thighs. Lyndsey swayed her hips and murmured.

"Oh Richie. Don't stop."

Hope jumped onto the bed, reached out, and tickled a startled Lyndsey's exposed belly.

Lyndsey wriggled and tried to escape. She called out, "Stop it Richard…now." Her eyes popped open. She frowned on seeing Hope staring down at her.

"Oh Richie. Don't stop," Hope mimicked Lyndsey's earlier plea. She pulled her hands free of Lyndsey, curtsied, and said, "Your Highness. The Prince awaits you in the kitchen."

Lyndsey sat up on the bed. A glance at her watch revealed the hour to be 5:00 pm. She climbed off the bed and went to the mirrored dresser. There, she picked up a hair brush and worked it through her hair.

Hope smirked and said, "Should Uncle Gilbert and I excuse ourselves? The prince will undoubtedly be amiss if he doth not seek to ravage his princess."

"My hair is a mess." Lyndsey pulled the brush harder through the golden strands of her hair. She turned, looked at Hope, and said, "Not a word about Jeffrey or our visit to Chester."

"Do I get to go?"

"Richard doesn't know that I know."

"Neither does Uncle Gilbert. Do I get to go?"

"OK. We'll go down to the dock together at 4:30 tomorrow morning."

"Good. We can hide out under the bow of Rose Bud, where Uncle Jeffrey stows away his onboard table and chairs. Once we're well out on Mahone Bay we can reveal ourselves. They'd never turn back then."

"Is that really necessary? After all, Jeffrey will be expecting me to accompany Richard."

"OK. Then I'll hide. You can wait for Richard on the dock."

Lyndsey stuck her hand out. She said, "Deal?" The sisters shook hands.

Hope uttered her acceptance, "Deal, but not a word to Uncle Gilbert. He'd have a kitten."

Hope and Lyndsey left the bedroom and joined Richard and Gilbert in the kitchen. They walked into a buffet of Chinese food set out neatly on the kitchen table.

"Self serve. Grab a plate and load up, girls",Gilbert announced.

Hope and Lyndsey were famished. They surprised Gilbert and Richard with the amount of food they placed on their plates. The surprise grew to shock when both girls reloaded their plates with seconds.

After everyone had eaten their fill and more, Richard cleared the table. He disposed of the waste and cleaned the dishes. When finished, he joined the others in the living room. Within minutes, Richard took over the conversation. He set about describing his trip to the city. To no surprise, he started out with a detailed description of every article on display in the *Marine Museum of the Atlantic.* A good hour dwelt on his tour of the *H.M.C.S. Sackville*, a World War II Navy Flower-class corvette.

"One of only a hundred and twenty-three and the only one of its kind still afloat," Richard boasted. He continued to exalt the Sackville's uniqueness, "She actually engaged German U-boats in battle—protected key Allied convoys and hastened the end of the war."

Lyndsey wondered which WWII Naval Veteran Richard had cornered and pestered with his inquisitive questioning nature. However, it had always been a trait she'd admired in Richard, and Lyndsey quickly lost herself in the details of Richard's adventure. It closed with him declaring the Sackville to be Canada's oldest fighting warship and our official Naval Memorial.

From the *Marine Museum of the Atlantic*, Richard took them on a walk along Halifax's historic waterfront then up to the fortress *The Citadel* that overlooked the city and its harbour, and held within its walls a treasury of military history. Richard finished by producing two paperback books he'd bought. Both were excellent historically accurate accounts of the early settlement of Nova Scotia in the late 1700s. One focused on Halifax, the other on Liverpool. To Lyndsey he boasted, "Look Lynds, Halifax down to the South Shore and through to Liverpool was a beehive of privateers sailing the seas seeking to legally and otherwise line their pockets with silver and gold. I suspect an odd nugget of gold, silver trinket or misplaced gem may have slipped past the eye of an inattentive or bribed official back in the days of yore."

Gilbert nodded his approval and exalted the talents of both authors. He said, "Both wrote with a master historian's pen. When you've finished those books, I have dozens of others awaiting that will set you off on amazing adventures."

Lyndsey smirked then burst into fits of laughter. She looked a Gilbert and pleaded, "Please! Please don't take Richie down a trail to the sea and buried pirate treasures. He's a wanderlust raised on tales of wonder and possibilities by a wanderlust of fame Grandfather—William Ramsay."

Gilbert joined Lyndsey in her laughter. He boasted back, "Say no more. Grampa Isaac and Mom I'm sure added tons of tales to William's repertoire of tales and facts out of the past. I've little doubt a sprinkling of privateers and pirates led an adventure and then some following many a bedtime tale."

Hope piped in, "Surely you do not speak of Grammie? A kinder and gentler soul there could not be."

"Lessen she be sharing the words and rumoured adventures of Grampa Ramsay—Isaac. Adventures that took shape in many a secluded seaside cove." Gilbert retorted.

Hope smiled at Gilbert's boast then declared, "If'in it were down Liverpool way t'was naught but a secluded—"

Lyndsey interrupted Hope, "Beach. Naught but a secluded beach if'ins it's down past Liverpool. They're everywhere! Remember, Richard?"

Richard glanced down at the two paperback books. The sandy sea shores on their covers ignited a sparkle in his eye. Gilbert missed it. Hope and Lyndsey did not. Richard looked up from the books at Lyndsey. He spotted the sparkle in her eyes. Hope's face took on an all-knowing expression, one that Gilbert again missed, but not Richard and Lyndsey. Richard knew at that moment what he must do. It was a moment not unlike the one Jeffrey had experienced out on Hackett's Cove where he'd let the cat out of the bag and revealed the truth about Lyndsey and Hope.

Richard scratched his chest. A sense of relief hit him. He recalled the purchase he made earlier that afternoon. Richard reached up under his sweater. He retrieved the small package from his shirt pocket. A glance around the room confirmed what he'd known. All eyes were on him. He rose up walked over to Lyndsey, then dropped down onto his knees.

Hope beamed. Lyndsey blushed.

Richard spoke directly to Lyndsey, "I once pledged my love to you. We were but toddlers and sandbox bound."

Lyndsey now beamed. She whispered, "I recall."

"I loved you then more than my little heart knew."

"Yes."

"We've been through a lot since then."

"Yes."

"I lost you once."

Lyndsey did not reply.

"I found you."

"And I found you."

Richard opened the package and withdrew a small jewelry box. He fumbled and tried to open it. Finally, it snapped open. The overhead light bounced off of a large diamond and sparkled in Lyndsey's eyes.

Richard's hands shook. He looked into Lyndsey's eyes and asked, "Wi…Will yo… Will You M…"

Hope jumped up and screamed, "Enough all ready. Just say 'YES', Girl!"

Lyndsey slipped out of her chair. She landed on her knees. Her arms embraced Richard. Their lips met. After a long kiss, their lips parted. She whispered, "Yes. Yes. Yes, I'll marry you Richie."

Hope ecstatically demanded, "What's that girl? I can't hear you."

Lyndsey looked up at Hope then returned her eyes to Richard. She repeated herself but this time spoke loud enough for Gilbert and Hope to hear. She said, "Yes. Yes. Yes, I'll marry you, Richie."

Gilbert bounced out of his chair. He raced into the dining room, he returned in a flash with a bottle of champagne in his hands. Lyndsey and Richard had not moved. Gilbert danced about the room. He removed the foil from the bottle's cork then twisted away the cork's wire restraint. It took three twists and tugs along with Hope's help to uncork the bottle. The cork flew through the air. Champagne sprayed out of the bottle and showered down on Richard and Lyndsey. Gilbert called out, "Quick, Hope. Get us some glasses. We've got a celebration on our hands.

Hope dashed into the dining room. She then returned with four tall, crystal wine glasses and a towel. The glasses she passed to Gilbert, the towel to Richard and Lyndsey. Gilbert set the glasses down on the coffee table. He filled them with what remained of the champagne. Richard stood up. He offered Lyndsey his hand. She accepted, and he pulled her up. Richard then took the diamond ring out of its case. He slid it onto the ring finger of a beaming Lyndsey. Hope took the towel and wiped off the faces of Richard and Lyndsey.

Gilbert then presented Lyndsey, Richard, and Hope with glasses of champagne. He lifted his glass and toasted the newly betrothed couple. "May the love Lyndsey and Richard now share continue to grow and shower love upon their tightly entwined souls. Good God, Son, step aside and allow me to hug'n kiss the bride to be." Gilbert stepped up to Lyndsey, embraced her with a trademark *'Gilbert Hug'* then kissed her cheek. She responded by kissing his lips.

Hope stepped up and embraced her sister. After a pause, she released Lyndsey and locked her arms around Richard. She hugged him hard and long then released him. To Lyndsey she said, "He's a keeper, Sis!"

Lyndsey laughed, and then took Richard into her arms and embraced him. The remainder of the evening Lyndsey sat on Richard's lap, or by his side. The two became inseparable. Following the celebrations and toast Lyndsey returned her glass to the coffee table. It remained there less a sip taken at the toast until Bailey joined the celebrations. He eyed the glass and claimed it and its contents with a swipe of his paw, on sensing no eyes were on him.

At midnight, Gilbert excused himself and retired. Hope, then Richard and Lyndsey followed in his footsteps. At Lyndsey's bedroom door, the betrothed shared a long goodnight kiss. They parted and entered their separate bedrooms. Once Hope heard Richard's door shut, she raced into Lyndsey's bedroom, with her alarm clock in hand. There, the sisters chatted until they both fell asleep on Lyndsey's bed but not before they'd set the alarm clock for 4:00 am.

CHAPTER 48

"RING...RING." TESSA ROLLED OVER; SHE ANSWERED THE PHONE, "Hello."

"Four o'clock wake up call. Good morning, Mrs. Ramsay."

"Oh. OK. Thank you, a good morning to you, too."

"Thank you, Mrs. Ramsay. Enjoy a great day."

Tessa hung up the receiver. She sat up, yawned then climbed out of the bed. Next, Tessa went straight to the bathroom. There, she stepped into the shower, pulled the shower curtain, then adjusted the showerhead and finally turned on the water. "Damn!" Tessa swore. She'd forgotten the soap and shampoo. After retrieving both, she stepped back into the shower. Ten minutes later, Tessa stepped out of the shower and dried herself off. Standing in front of the mirror, Tessa inspected her abdomen for signs of swelling. Her desired pregnancy that she assumed was now in its second or third month refused to display itself to the world. Again stress and blindness to reality hid the telltale signs of her body's state. Next, Tessa took the hair-dryer and blow-dried her hair.

John stepped into the bathroom. He walked behind Tessa. There, he stopped long enough to slap her on the butt. Tessa shot him a nasty glare. John stepped past her and entered the shower.

Tessa left the bathroom. She dressed and prepared herself for the day's activities. Before John returned, Tessa removed a small calibre pistol from her overnight bag. After loading it with a fresh magazine, Tessa slipped it into the pocket of her scarlet red jacket. Nothing, absolutely nothing, was going to stand between Tessa and her treasure.

John walked out of the bathroom a second too late to catch Tessa depositing the pistol in her jacket. He dressed then carried their luggage out to the car. He returned to the room. Tessa had brewed a pot of coffee. They sat at the table and administered their early morning java fixes. At 4:35 am, John and Tessa left the room. John locked the door and left the key sitting on the night table. Tessa had clearly stated her dislike of the accommodations. The treasure seeker and her meal ticket left the inn and headed over to Chester for their scheduled meeting with Mikie. John had his doubts in regards to Mikie's reliability. Before the sun set on Mahone Bay, that would become the least of his worries.

They arrived in Chester at 4:50 am. John parked down near the docks. He stepped out of the car and paced the dock. Tessa remained inside the car. At 4:59 am, John heard the sound of an approaching powerboat. He walked to the edge of the dock and looked out over the water.

Mikie guided Total Satisfaction up to the dock. He hailed John and tossed docking lines to him. John secured the lines. He told Mikie to remain onboard then returned to the car. There, under Tessa's directions, he removed their gear from the car's trunk. With a shovel and a pickaxe, in hand, John waited until Tessa slammed the trunk down. He followed her back over to Mikie and Total Satisfaction. John passed their tools down to Mikie. Next, Tessa stepped down the dock ladder and jumped aboard the boat.

The tide was out. It provided Mikie with an opportunity to view Tessa's attributes while she stepped down the ladder.

John joined them on board. He gave Mikie a disapproving look.

Mikie shrugged it off. He said, "Can't be blam'in a man fer admiring a chassis lik'in yer lady's. Trust me red is definitely yer lady's colour. Would her drawers be red and a match ta her out'ta dressings?"

John sneered at Mikie but did not reply. He joined Tessa at the stern and put his arm around her waist. His hand slid down until it settled on Tessa's hip. John had staked his claim of ownership.

Mikie turned to John and said, "How's about lift'n yer hand of the lady's ass and releasing the docking lines."

John followed Mikie's request, but not without giving Mikie a disdainful look. With John back on board Mikie shifted the motor into gear. Total Satisfaction pulled away from the dock and headed out on Mahone Bay. Mikie tried to strike up a conversation. He asked, "Either of you a botanist?"

"No," John answered.

"Then what's with the shovel and pickaxe?"

No answer.

"Well ye'll not find Mikie stepping foot on that God-forsaken place. No Sir…eee. I ain't stupid. An I ain't gots no death wish."

"Stop with the local-yokel chit-chat," Tessa warned Mikie.

"Yes Ma'am."

Tessa stepped away from John. She made Mikie another offer, "I'll toss you another five grand if you'll work my shovel or pickaxe."

Mikie eyed Tessa up and down. He declined, "Sorry Mam. Like I said…Mikie don't set foot on them islands. Not five grand, not even a rumble under yer bed sheets could tempt Mikie. Horny? Hell, yes. Stupid? No!"

Tessa moved back to John's side. Off to the east, a brilliant sunrise cast an array of seaside glitter over the water and morning embraced another new day. Unwilling to risk their return trip, Tessa did not push the subject. Instead, she stared out over the bay and wondered how long their journey would take. It took them out past the Tancook Islands then out beyond both East Ironbound, Flat and Pearl Islands. An hour later, sea smoke appeared. It raced across the surface of the water. Ahead, the sea smoke thickened. Tessa grew anxious. She sensed the end of their outbound journey. Images of glittering jewels flashed through her mind's eye. *Yes,* Tessa reasoned, *my mother ship is about to come in.*

....

Hope stirred. Her eyes opened. A glance at the clock told her it was 3:55 am. She rolled off the bed, went over to the clock, and disarmed the alarm. Lyndsey looked so peaceful, she hated to disturb her but did. Lyndsey responded to Hope's gentle wakeup call. Her eyes blinked open. She sat upright.

Hope chided, "It's time to get things underway, girl."

"OK."

"Don't be so enthusiastic."

Lyndsey climbed off the bed. She glanced down at the clothes she'd slept in.

"They'll do. Trust me," Hope whispered. "Grab a jacket. We best move it before your prince awakens."

Lyndsey picked up her jacket from the corner chair. She followed Hope quietly out of the room. Hope stopped at her bedroom and picked up a jacket for herself. The two girls stepped softly down the staircase. Halfway down, Hope held up. She skipped the eighth step. Lyndsey followed suit. Downstairs, Hope picked up a flashlight in the kitchen then they moved through to the front door without incident.

Outside, they walked quickly side by side. Lyndsey stayed close to Hope's side. She stopped at Richard's SUV, opened the passenger door and retrieved the jeweled rosary from the glove compartment, an eerie sensation drew an image of the rosary's proclaimed rightful owner, Grace Ramsay's spirit in Lyndsey's mind. Resolve washed the ghostly image aside. Lyndsey placed the rosary in her jacket pocket; Hope did not question her actions. There were no streetlights to light their path. At Jeffrey's shed, they turned down towards the dock. Once safely past Jeffrey's house, Hope turned the flashlight on. It lit the path for them on their walk down the hill. Twenty feet from the dock, Hope pointed the light onto the dock.

They both froze. A family of skunks were walking out onto the dock. Hope flashed the light onto her watch. It displayed 4:20 am. Richard and Jeffrey would be making their appearance within twenty minutes. Hope considered tossing a rock at the dock but thought better of it. She turned the flashlight off and sat down on a rock at the side of the pathway. Lyndsey joined her. Time stood still and raced forward all at once. After what seemed an eternity, the skunks lost interest in the dock. Hope allowed a twenty count then stood up. Lyndsey followed her move. The flashlight flicked back on.

At 4:35 am Hope climbed down the dock and jumped onto Rose Bud. She pulled the boat towards the dock and helped Lyndsey aboard. Hope crawled up under the bow then turned the flashlight off. They whispered to each other over the next ten minutes. Everything from bride's maid's dresses to honeymoon locale was discussed. At 4:45 am, the whispers died. A lantern appeared at the top of the hill. Hope tucked herself further into the bow. Lyndsey prepared herself to fend off Richard's arguments. The lantern reached the bottom of the hill. Lyndsey sat down on a chair inside the small cabin. No sense revealing herself to Richard before she had to. Footsteps signaled Richard and Jeffrey's arrival on the dock. Lyndsey took a deep breath and held it. The first argument between the newly betrothed would erupt shortly. The winner in waiting dug her heels in.

....

Jeffrey climbed down the dock ladder. He pulled the docking line, and Rose Bud moved towards the dock. Jeffrey jumped onboard. Richard passed two shovels, a pickaxe and an axe down to Jeffrey. He then followed Jeffrey's example but slipped and fell onto the boat's deck. Lyndsey ran out to his aide. Before Richard could protest Lyndsey's presence, Jeffrey greeted her.

"Goood. Ye mede it. Tought ya mebe sleept'd in."

Richard said, "Not funny, Jeffrey." He looked up at Lyndsey and frowned.

Lyndsey beat him to the punch. She said, "Face it, Richard. From the moment you read aloud Grace's words…my mind was set. Set hard."

"But!"

Richard sat up on Rose Bud's railing. He brushed off his hands.

"No! No ifs ands or buts. I'm going. So don't even think it." She paused then asked, "Are you, Ok?"

"Yes."

"Then we'd best get underway."

"No."

"No? I don't think so. I'm going."

"I don't want to ever lose you again."

"You won't. Besides it's just another island, right?"

Unnoticed by all aboard, Grace Ramsay's spirit slipped onboard. She took up a position at the stern of the boat. The spirit's face glowed in anticipation of the pending journey.

Jeffrey stood motionless and stared at the stern. He smiled warmly towards his *Good Neighbour Fairy*. His fairy—Grace Ramsay's spirit returned a warm grateful glowing smile. In his heart he accepted that the time to grant his *Good Neighbour Fairy* dees onlees ting shees everrs ask't fer had finllees com ta bees. He nodded then busied himself with releasing the docking lines. Rose Bud drifted out towards the centre of East River.

Richard looked longingly at Lyndsey. He searched for the right words to convince her to back down from her stance. If he found the words, they never made it past his lips.

Lyndsey leaned towards Richard. She kissed him then said, "Good. It's settled then. Jeffrey, start the motor. We're going."

Jeffrey obeyed. He primed the gas line then started the motor. It coughed briefly then sputtered and roared. Jeffrey kept the throttle at a low setting. He did not want to disturb the silence any more than necessary. After the motor had warmed up, Jeffrey slipped it into forward gear. Rose Bud glided over the glass-like water out onto East River Bay and headed towards Mahone Bay.

Lyndsey stood up. She sighed and looked back at the dock. Her eyes caught Grace Ramsay's spirit sitting on the transom. Lyndsey smiled. If spirits were capable of love, Lyndsey understood the glow on this spirit's face and the glitter in its eyes. Lyndsey felt relieved the spirit's eyes were not locked onto Richard. That left one of two objects, the open sea ahead and the Floating Islands or Uncle Jeffrey. Lyndsey smirked, offered her hand to Richard then together they stood up. They joined Jeffrey up forward in the cabin. Jeffrey hit the throttle and Rose Bud raced across the glasslike surface of Mahone Bay. Time stood still and flew past Rose Bud's crew in one easy motion. Suddenly Sinner's Island stood in front of them. Jeffrey veered off to starboard and they motored past its leeward side. On clearing Sinner's Island, Jeffrey headed Rose Bud out to sea. He hit the throttle again, and Rose Buds' bow leaped out of the water. Jeffrey veered back towards the east. The bow crashed back down into the sea. A voice screamed out in agony.

"Oouch! Damn it! That hurt!"

Richard looked at Jeffrey. Jeffrey looked back at him. A second, then two passed. They both turned and looked accusingly at Lyndsey.

"What? What is it?" Lyndsey asked innocently.

Hope crawled out from under the bow. A startled Richard and Jeffrey stared down at her in shock. Jeffrey eased back the throttle. He uttered a mild, "Oooh. Oooh. I'm in beeg troub'ls."

Hope stood up. She greeted Richard and Jeffrey, "Hi Guys. Guess who?"

"Oooh. Dees bees a baad sceene. Gilly's gon'na skins mee."

Hope smiled. She reached past Jeffrey and threw the throttle ahead. Rose Bud leapt back out of the water.

"What Uncle Gilbert doesn't know won't hurt him. Let's get going. I can't wait to get there!"

....

Pappy's ears twitched. His eyes popped open. He'd heard the front door close. In a flash, he sat up then climbed out of bed. He went to the sunroom and looked out into a dusky early morning sky that eagerly await'd an approaching sunrise. Off to his left, he spotted a lantern moving through the woods. He concluded it was being carried by someone along the path to the dock. Pappy left the sunroom. In the hall, he switched on the light. At Jeffrey's room, he looked inside. Unable to see Jeffrey, he switched on Jeffrey's bedroom light.

The room was empty. No Jeffrey; Pappy, puzzled; couldn't figure out what Jeffrey would be doing down at the dock at that early hour. Concerned, he went to the kitchen, and picked up the phone. He dialed Gilbert's number.

After four rings Gilbert answered, "Hello?"

"Hi. Gil. Pappy here."

"What? What's wrong, Pappy?"

"Jeffrey has up and taken himself down to the dock. It's 4:45 am. Did he mention plans to you? Hauling is over and done with. It jest don't make sense!"

Gilbert sat up and set his feet on the floor. He said, "Hold on, Pappy. I'll go check with Richard." He set the receiver down on the bed and walked off to Richard's bedroom. On discovering Richard missing, he ran to the girls' rooms, where he also found them missing. Gilbert ran back to his bedroom. He picked up the receiver.

"They're all gone Pappy. This is bad."

"What do you mean…son. What's bad?"

Pappy waited to hear Gilbert's response.

It didn't come for several minutes. Finally Gilbert spoke. His voice trembled.

"I think they've…they've headed out to the islands. The Flo… Floating Islands."

"Don't be stupid."

"No. I'm not stupid. I know."

The phone went silent. Finally, Pappy spoke.

"Git dressed now Gil. Meet me down at the dock."

"I…I can't."

"Yep you can son, do it now! God damn it! Get your ass in gear boy."

"No. I…I can't."

"Jeffrey, Hope, Lyndsey…Richard! Don't tell me they mean nothing to you. I know."

"But…but, you said."

"Forget what an old fool said or didn't say. Just do it. Meet me there!"

"But!"

"Do it!" Pappy slammed the receiver down. He ran to his bedroom and dressed. Fifteen minutes later, Pappy arrived at the dock. He surprised himself with the haste he'd managed. Fifteen minutes from the house to dock for a seventy-plus senior was good time. Real good!

Pappy paced up and down the dock. He glanced impatiently up at the hill and cursed Gilbert for being so slow. Ten minutes passed before Gilbert appeared at the top of the hill. Pappy both cursed and urged his son to move it a little faster.

Gilbert arrived at the dock. He looked flushed.

Pappy climbed down the dock ladder. He pulled the docking line and Karyn-Anita to the dock then stepped on board. To Gilbert, he called out, "Move it, time's-a-wasting."

Gilbert relented. He obeyed Pappy and climbed down the dock's ladder. Onboard Karyn-Anita, he stood and stared, glassy eyed, out onto the bay. Pappy released the docking lines. The boat drifted out onto the river. Pappy fired up the motor. He did not wait for Gilbert to act. Immediately, he shifted the motor into gear and pointed the bow out towards East River Bay. Out on the Bay, Gilbert stood by Pappy's side. He did not speak. Pappy hit the throttle. Karyn-Anita, with Pappy at the helm and Gilbert at his side, headed out towards Mahone Bay—seaward towards the Floating Islands.

CHAPTER 49

ROSE BUD AND HER CREW WERE THE FIRST TO CATCH SIGHT OF the islands. Jeffrey steered towards the larger of the two islands. Sea smoke swirled about the surface of the sea. It thickened up closer to the islands. Jeffrey chose a spot along the leeward side and headed towards it. Twenty feet away, the others discovered that Jeffrey had chosen a landing spot wisely.

Jeffrey guided Rose Bud into the sheltered cove. The water up next to the shore was deep. Low tide would not present them with a problem. Richard automatically flipped out both sets of bumpers climbed up on the bow then took the bowline and jumped to shore. There, he secured the line to a large, windblown pine tree. It stood two feet thick at its base. Jeffrey tossed him a line from the stern Richard caught the line and pulled Rose Bud up alongside the shoreline. Jeffrey threw the shovels and pickaxe onto the island. Next, Lyndsey and Hope stepped ashore. Finally, Jeffrey ended his long absence from the island. He stepped ashore with the axe in hand. Richard released a length of the stern line and allowed Rose Buds' stern to drift away from the rocky shore. He looped its end around a small tree.

Richard grabbed the pickaxe and shovels while Jeffrey kept the axe. Jeffrey surveyed the island. He shouted, "Dems treees bees a tad t'icker dan I's members." He chose to head towards an area where the alders thinned out and led towards a natural pathway. Richard and the girls followed his lead. Beyond the alders, their progress picked up speed. A new obstacle embraced them. The foursome swatted away at a cloud of mosquitoes that eagerly buzzed around their newly discovered meals. Jeffrey stopped swatting and pulled a spray can of insect repellent out of his jacket pocket. He shouted, "Cooveers yer eyes aands I wills spays des bugggers."

Everyone obeyed. Jeffrey sprayed and a heavy mist quickly deterred the hungry mosquitoes from the island's visitors.

"Do we have much further to go, Uncle Jeffrey?" Hope asked.

"Goes wher? Wes ona islind…gorl."

"Well. We're headed towards something, right?" Hope wondered aloud.

Lyndsey reached into her jeans pocket. She withdrew a folded, yellowed paper then unfolded it. The old yellowed map attracted the others to it.

Jeffrey kneeled at Lyndsey's side. He eyed the map then pointed out the island they'd landed on. "Wees her," Jeffrey said. He pointed the island out.

It was the largest one on the map. Next, he pointed to their landing point, then to the area they occupied. Off to the east, the map showed a large clearing. Would it still exist, all parties wondered. The opening on the map stood closer to the seaward side of the island. What looked like a large tree had been drawn at the clearing's northwest end. An arrow pointed away from the tree. It had a 15 marked on it. At the arrow's end, another had been drawn. It pointed off to the east. That arrow had a 10 marked on it.

Jeffrey stood up. He said, "Wees beest bees gitting on ta dar."

The girls groaned but stood up. Lyndsey returned the map to her pocket. Jeffrey picked up both the shovels and pickaxe, Richard the axe. Jeffrey held back and allowed Richard to take the lead. Their troubles lessened ten minutes later. The forest thinned and they entered a wide clearing then stepped cautiously into the opening they'd seen on the yellowed map of the island.

It covered an area about a hundred feet across and sixty feet long. Tall grass and alders covered the eastern side of the clearing and beyond the grass one could catch glimpses of water. Towards the clearing's centre stood two windswept pine trees. Off to the north of them stood an ancient maple tree most of its upper branches void of leaves and dead. On the map it had been indicated by a large M. Beneath the maple stood the spirit of Grace Ramsay. Two did not see it Lyndsey glanced towards the spirit and acknowledged its presence. She reached into her jacket pocket and unnoticed by the others removed the rosary. She walked towards the maple tree. On approaching the tree's base, she dropped the rosary at the spirit's feet. A mist started to move in over the ground around them. She reached into the pocket of her jeans and pulled out the map. A glance at the ground revealed the rosary had disappeared. Lyndsey walked to the maple tree's base. She looked up at the sun, took her directions from it, and paced off fifteen large steps. She stopped. With Richard at her side, she turned eastward and started to pace off another ten steps. At seven, she stopped dead in her tracks. Hope bumped into her back.

"Sorry."

Lyndsey did not hear Hope's apology. Three steps, about eight feet ahead of her, stood an overgrown cavity in the ground. It was covered in small alders and grass. Lyndsey tried to race forward.

Jeffrey grabbed her shoulder and said, "Keerful...Lynd...sie. I's bees her afore. Tis a badd pleece."

Richard ignored Jeffrey's warning. He ran over to the overgrown cavity and stood by its edge. The girls stayed back with Jeffrey. After he'd spent five minutes clearing away the alders, Richard dropped the axe. He waved to Jeffrey and asked for a shovel. Jeffrey tossed it to him. With shovel in hand, Richard moved to drive it into the ground.

"No. Wait!" Lyndsey shouted.

Richard turned and looked at her; he sought an explanation for her outburst. He did not get one. Instead, he stepped aside. Lyndsey took his shovel and stepped into the spot he'd abandoned. She turned slowly to her left then stopped after completing a quarter turn and stared off to the east. Puzzled, Richard eyed Lyndsey and waited. After she'd stepped forward to the cavity's southern edge

Lyndsey looked at Richard and nodded her approval to him. She did not explain her odd action. Nor did she tell him or the others what—or who she'd seen. The sight of Grace Ramsay's spirit twenty feet off to the east had eased Lyndsey's concerns. She smiled on seeing Jeffrey glancing calmly at Grace's spirit. Only after she'd received the spirit's nod of approval did she step aside and allow Richard to proceed. Hope and Jeffrey joined them.

Richard thrust the shovel in the ground immediately upon receiving Lyndsey's approval. The ground below the grassy surface yielded to the shovel with ease. When five minutes went by without incident, Jeffrey took the pickaxe and worked at loosening the soil for Richard. After thirty minutes they'd dug a hole four feet across and one foot deep. Hot from their labour, Jeffrey and Richard took a break. They looked back at the girls. Strangely, the mist had grown dense but not in the area of the hole. A hot sun shone down and warmed those in or up close to the hole. Richard sat down on the ground at the edge of their diggings. Jeffrey sat down beside him.

Hope joined them. She sat down at Jeffrey's side.

Lyndsey did not join the others. She wandered off into the strange mist. Twenty feet from the hole, Lyndsey stopped. With her back to the hole, Lyndsey listened to Grace Ramsay's spirit.

"Thank you. You've done good, girl. We're close I can almost feel it in my bones," the spirit chuckled. "It's a figure of speech. I feel so much closer to Father now. He will come. I can feel—"

"Feel it in your bones?" Lyndsey injected.

"Yes," the spirit said with a smile.

Lyndsey looked away from the spirit back towards the hole and Richard.

"You'll be safe for now. The beast lays at rest but do not dilly-dally too long. I feel a danger greater than the sleeping beast approaching."

Lyndsey frowned then asked, "What kind of danger?"

"I feel it. If I knew its nature I'd tell you. But I don't."

"Should we leave?" Lyndsey asked then turned and looked again back towards the hole and Richard.

"No. I want to plea and bargain for the release of the curse that burdens Father's soul. Go. Get them back to work. Work with them.

Time grows short I fear. The beast mustn't be uncovered and aroused before I approach it!"

On turning back towards the spirit, Lyndsey found herself standing alone. She turned towards the hole. This time, she walked back and joined the others.

Richard stood up. He looked to Lyndsey. His mouth opened. The words never came out. Lyndsey's strange expression worried him. Afraid to ask the question on his lips, Richard turned away from her. He started to dig deeper into the ground. Jeffrey joined him with the pickaxe.

Hope stepped back out of the hole. She joined Lyndsey and asked, "Everything, OK?"

"Just peachy, Sis!"

"Care to explain your walk in the mist? Nothing personal, but you scared the hell out of me."

"Yes, really there's so much rolling around in my head. The diary and too many late nights best explains the odd quirk I've let myself get tied up in."

"No way, I'm sorry for intruding on you, but your odd little quirk had me concerned."

"Trust me. I'm fine." Lyndsey called out to Jeffrey, "How's the digging? Take a break. Hope and I will dig for a bit."

"Noo ways!," Jeffrey replied. He added, Diis bees meens workkks!" Then added, "The sol is toops. Ya knows no racks and eesy diigs."

Lyndsey replied, "Good. Do you think we'll find something? I mean…it's all so strange. Like something you'd read in a book or see in a movie."

Jeffery grinned at Lyndsey. He answered, Iff'n wee fiines de croownd jewels, den wes'll croowns aree twoo princceessess.

Hope chuckled and added, "Well, truth be told, I've got my doubts. But, Uncle Gilbert's fear of this place makes me wonder. Could the deeply imbedded fears of the locals and Uncle Gilbert be justified? God…I hope he never finds out we came here. Now that's a scary thought."

"We'll use the picnic line."

"He'll never buy it."

"Oh. Then I guess we'll just have to give him a little…girl talk."

Hope laughed. They walked back over to the hole. There, they looked down at Richard and Jeffrey. The hole appeared roughly two feet deep. They could not see signs of any rock. Hope and Lyndsey sat down. They watched the men dig and wondered—wondered what, if anything lay beneath the feet of Richard and Jeffrey.

CHAPTER 50

MIKIE PULLED THE THROTTLE BACK. TOTAL SATISFACTION SLOWED in response to his action. Mikie announced their pending arrival, "All hands on deck. Welcome to the Gateway to Hell. Prepare to disembark in ten minutes."

Tessa frowned. Just who did the midget think he had impressed. For a ten-spot, she'd gladly pull out Jewels and fire a slug through his little opinionated head. Tessa gripped the handle of her pistol then relaxed. She pulled her hand out of the jacket. Best to save Jewels, a silver-plated, small-calibre pistol, for its intended use: Tessa's protection and a little persuasion, should the need arise. Tessa left John's side. She walked up into the cabin. There, she stood in silence by Mikie's side. She looked out through the glass window of the cabin.

Ahead of them stood a large forested island shrouded in an eerie mist. Overhead rays from the morning sun appeared to shine directly on and into the island's core. Tessa hoped the sun would quickly burn off the mist.

"We'll approach from the seaward side there are a number of sheltered coves we can pull into."

"Do what you must, captain. Just get me to my destination."

"That, I will do! That I'll do! Though I can't figure why ye'd ever choose ta go dar."

"It's not too late. Name your price. We could use your help."

Mikie looked Tessa over. *Best get one last look at the goods,* he thought. *One last look before the bitch disappears through Hell's Gate screaming and shouting.* Mikie held little hope of ever seeing the pair make the return passage to Chester. Hell, the minute they stepped ashore, Total Satisfaction would be head'n out to sea. Out to sea where Mikie planned to wait just long enough to hear the screaming laments of their demise.

He replied to Tessa's final offer, "Nope. As I said earlier M'am, not even a rumble under yer bed sheets could tempt Mikie. Horny, yes. Stupid, no."

Tessa walked back to where John stood. She said, "We'll be there shortly."

"Yes," John answered then said, "Your idea of adding an Atlantic Cruise aboard Mikie's version of the *Titanic* to our vacation best damned well be worth the trouble and time I've wasted getting here!"

"Trust me. That island holds wealth beyond the wildest dreams of little Grace Ramsay."

"Right, and Grace Ramsay's diary claims another fool."

"Trust me! A legacy awaits us."

"No! But, I'll guarantee you're naught but another hell bent fool in search of nonexistent wealth and fame!"

"A Fool never! Hell-bent! Damn right," Tessa shot back.

Mikie had Total Satisfaction headed into a small but deep cove. His knuckles whitened and his grip on the steering console tightened. The place gave him a bad feeling, a very bad feeling. He made his final announcement, "Ye fools best git ready, I have no intentions of making your landing a long one."

Inside the cove and sheltered from the pounding surf, Total Satisfaction glided closer to the island's shore. Mikie shifted into neutral. Total Satisfaction touched the shore. Mikie screamed, "Jump now. Git your sorry arsses of'fa me boat."

Tessa looked hard at Mikie.

John obeyed Mikie. He stepped onto the running board then jumped onto the island. Mikie threw their tools over to him: a shovel, and a pickaxe. Tessa looked once more to Mikie.

"Git yer ass of'fa me boat!"

Tessa placed one foot up onto the running board. She started to jump.

Mikie shifted into reverse gear. He hit the throttle. Total Satisfaction churned up the salty water. Her stern pulled away from the shore.

On hitting the ground, Tessa stumbled forward. She tumbled head first onto the rocky shore. She yelled out in pain, "Bastard!"

Mikie called out, "I's dat I bees, and a live-bastard at dat. Enjoy Hell. Iff'n de Devil won't take ye I pick up as agreed to. Best make yourselves seen. I'll not return iff'n I don't see yer sorry arsses from a safe distance."

Their arrival on the island occurred at the moment Lyndsey's conversation with Grace Ramsay's spirit ended. Had the spirit sensed their arrival?

John helped Tessa to her feet. He took out a ball of used paper towel and offered it to Tessa.

"What?" Tessa demanded.

"Your chin, you're cut up good and bleeding."

Tessa took the paper towel. She pressed it to her chin then pulled it away. The paper towel blotted up a healthy spattering of her blood. Tessa reapplied the towel to her chin and held it there. She pointed to the shovel and pickaxe on the ground. "Pick them up. Let's get moving."

John obeyed. Tessa looked pissed; he did not risk pushing her buttons. He reasoned it best to humour the lady. John picked up the shovel in one hand, the pickaxe in the other. Silently twinges of doubt added depth to the thoughts that had started to build in John's mind. John's thoughts centred on the odds of a false pregnancy or DNA mismatch releasing him from their prenuptial.

Tessa moved away from the shore. John followed. Neither spoke. The forest lacked the density experienced by Jeffrey, Richard, Hope, and Lyndsey on the leeward side. It had been battered and thinned by countless sea gales over the centuries.

Out from the cove's mouth, Mikie watched the pair disappear into the forest. He sighed in relief then wondered if he'd see them again.

Mist hovered above the forest bed. Tessa stumbled over several large hidden tree roots, but did not fall. John stayed close on her heels. Their progress slowed when the mist thickened. Determined to go on, Tessa did not allow it to stop their progress. Twenty minutes later, Tessa, then John emerged out of the forest. They stood on the southeast corner of the clearing. The tall grass and alders covering the eastern side of the clearing concealed both parties from each other.

John stopped. He struggled to regain his breath. The trek had extracted its toll on John's body. His aversion to physical exertion or anything that resembled exercise had not prepared him for their adventure.

Tessa stared up across the clearing. She spotted the large pine trees close at hand. A glance to the north exposed the large maple tree to her eyes. Intense sunrays hit an area thirty feet in front of the maple tree. Tessa spotted what she took to be two men in that area. She sneered on realizing that they were working the ground—stealing her treasure. Tessa signaled John her intent to move forward.

On closing the gap between themselves and the thieves, Tessa recognized Richard but not Jeffrey. Pissed, she almost raced forward. The opportunity to secure their labours on her behalf held Tessa back. She stopped and stooped down. John followed her lead. Tessa explained her plans and intentions to John. She patted her jacket and Jewels. If the situation needed Jewels' assistance, Tessa resolved herself to making use of it. Under her breath, she uttered an oath to herself, "Nothing, absolutely nothing, will stand between me and my treasure. If it breathes a breath of life I will snuff that breath out before relinquishing the rewards that await me on this island."

Tessa stood up. John joined her. She placed her hand firmly on the pistol grip of Jewels and moved off to claim her reward. John moved along by Tessa's side unaware of Tessa's undeclared companion.

....

Pappy took Karyn-Anita along the route Jeffrey had taken before them. Out past Sinner's Island, Pappy threw the throttle three-quarters forward. Gilbert did not offer his usual protest. Instead, he stood at Pappy's side inside the cabin.

Gilbert tried to fathom the forces that had placed him in his current position. Love leaped to the forefront of his mind. Love of Pappy, Jeffrey, Hope, Lyndsey, and Richard. On that count, Pappy had been right on the money. The diary of Grace Ramsay had intrigued Gilbert, but only for its historical value, content, and connection to his ancestors. True, it had alluded to buried treasure. Riches waiting for the right person to claim them. Riches nobody in the McClaken/Ramsay clan needed. The tragedy that had reunited their two families had also bestowed upon them wealth beyond their worldly needs.

Pappy broke the silence. He related to Gilbert the events both he and Lenny had witnessed at the Lobster Pot Pub & Eatery two days past.

"She were one sassy lady. Had poor Bernie shaking in his boots. The man, come to think about it, he looked at tad familiar, though I couldn't figure why till jest now. It'd wager him to be the other family member you spoke of Lyndsey's ex…right?"

Gilbert's heart sank. He uttered an emotionless, "Yes, could be."

"Regardless, Meat tried to restrain Mikie. It proved a fruitless effort. The lady had taken Mikie's eye. Ya should'a seen it. Mikie strutted up to her, called her out and countered her offer at five big uns, then the lady done shoved his hand inside her top an pressed it against the apple of Mikie's eyes."

"Her breasts, Pappy?"

"Right."

"Then…just say it—breasts."

"Takes away the allure boy. Takes it away."

"Whatever."

Pappy explained how Mikie finally settled on a fee of two thousand dollars to take the pair out to the islands.

Gilbert reacted. He reached in front of Pappy and threw the throttle full forward. Karyn-Anita roared and raced faster towards her destination, the Floating Islands. Gilbert once again fell silent. He still did not know if he could bring himself to step upon the island.

Pappy approached the larger island from the same angle Jeffrey had earlier. He spotted a glimpse of white inside a cove backed the throttle off. He followed his instinct and entered the cove. Rose Bud awaited their arrival. She did not wait long. Pappy pulled up alongside of Jeffrey's boat. He cut the engine, tied a line onto Rose Bud's stern then tied a second one between the bows. He stepped from one vessel to the other. Gilbert reluctantly followed him. Pappy pulled on Rose Buds' stern line. He pulled her in tight to the shoreline. Next, he jumped ashore, held the line, and waited for Gilbert.

Gilbert hesitated. In shock he stared at Pappy standing on the island and goading him to jump ashore and join him. Pappy had no cane! Pappy had gadded about Karyn-Anita and jumped ashore like a limber and agile teenager! Determined to beat his fears and match Pappy's stamina and determination, he took a deep breath, closed his eyes, and jumped ashore. His arrival on the island coincided with Tessa and John's arrival in the clearing. Relieved not to have been dragged screaming through the Gates of Hell by a ragging demonic entity, Gilbert followed Pappy towards the forest. He did not know what lay ahead of him. Relief hit him. He'd finally made the journey that should have been his not Jeffrey's, so many years ago. Each step eased his concerns and fears. Resolve finally hit him. Gilbert moved up behind Pappy…determined to do what had to be done to ensure the safety of his loved ones this time. Determined to keep pace with Pappy's high paced energies and youthful agilities.

CHAPTER 51

TESSA LED JOHN NORTH TOWARDS THE LARGE MAPLE TREE. THEY moved slowly. Tessa veered off to the east into the dense mist. She wanted to make a surprise appearance. Parallel to where the treasure seekers worked their dig, Tessa made her move towards them.

Lyndsey and Hope sat at the edge of the hole. Hope focused on each word Lyndsey spoke. Recollections of times spent in the old homestead and occasional eerie feelings that she had experienced were adding substance to Lyndsey's words.

Hope's curiosity drew her thoughts to her lips. She asked, "Lyndsey, do you really feel the homestead is haunted?" Lyndsey did not answer.

Hope pondered Lyndsey's words, could Grammy Ramsay's creative tales and claims of ghostly encounters have been based on facts. Actual encounters with the author of the diary Grace Ramsay's spirit? Could Uncle Jeffrey's Good Neighbour Fairy be Grace Ramsay's spirit?

Lyndsey continued to relate details of her ghostly encounter, "This is where it all started Hope. Her spirit is with us. It—she sat at your side aboard Rose Bud on our run to the island."

Hope shivered in response to Lyndsey's words. She looked about their immediate surroundings. In her heart she wanted to connect with Grace Ramsay. In her mind the idea of connecting to the great beyond terrified her.

Jeffrey and Richard had reached a depth of just under four feet. No treasure had been uncovered, their resolve and focus started to fade. Tessa stepped out of the mist. She held out the pistol. It pointed directly at Richard. She spoke out, "My, my, my, look at what we've got here."

Jeffrey and Richard jumped then looked up at Tessa. Lyndsey and Hope froze.

Jeffrey dropped his pickaxe, looked to Tessa, and said, "Wheys ye not jest puts dat ting aweys. Wees noo horts ya."

"Right, Clem. What hole did you crawl out of?" Tessa paused. She looked at John. With a snarl, she roared, "Don't just stand there, stupid. Get to work."

John stood frozen. Tessa's actions had stunned him. He slowly dropped the pickaxe then the shovel his moves did not impress Tessa.

She waved the pistol in his face then demanded, "Move it. Are you daft and stupid too? I said, 'Get to work.' Use the pickaxe. Secure my—our, child's financial future. Give the shovel to your prissy little soon to be ex, or her freckle faced friend. It doesn't pay to have slackers on the job site. Now move IT— Fiancé Dearest of mine."

John hesitated a second longer than Tessa wanted. She pointed the pistol directly at a spot between John's eyes. "Now, fool. Now or I'll collect on your life insurance."

John dropped down. He picked up the shovel and pickaxe. He shuffled over to the hole then stepped down into it. John struggled to suppress the disgust he felt towards Tessa. He recalled with pleasure how he'd procrastinated and failed to change the beneficiary on his insurance to Tessa. The hatred and greed he saw in Tessa's face caused Roger's words to echo in his mind. 'Take a timeout John, recall and embrace the love of your Mom, Heed the advice she's shared over the years. Her love is special, embrace it. It is a precious gift.'

"What are you waiting for? Give the shovel to one of the ladies. Make them useful, God!"

Tessa watched John complete her instructions. Once all her workers had stepped into the hole, it became an unworkable situation. Tessa compromised. She ordered everyone but John out of the hole. She put him to work with his pickaxe. He worked the soil beneath his feet and loosened it up. Tessa then set up a rotation; she worked Jeffrey and Richard with the shovels then injected John with the pickaxe, followed by a shift worked by Lyndsey and Hope. During the shifts worked by the girls, Tessa taunted them.

"Come on girls. Move it. Move it. A little effort would be nice. We haven't got all day!"

During the girls' shift, she kept Jewels pointed at the men. Sweat poured off Lyndsey's forehead halfway through her second shift. The hole stood almost five feet deep at its centre.

Tessa eyed Lyndsey. Nothing would make her happier than to be given a reason to deep-six prissy-missy. "That's better. This exercise will tighten up your buttocks. Men like that in a woman. We must not deny them their simple pleasures in life, right girls?" Tessa continued to taunt both girls. Her main focus always fell on Lyndsey. Tessa was irritated to no end over being deprived of the legacy inherited by John's ex.

Lyndsey remained silent. She had never liked Tessa. Hate...detest now best described her feelings towards Tessa. Several times, she'd considered tossing a shovel of earth into Tessa's face. Make the bitch eat dirt. Lyndsey felt a pang of pity for John. Though she had once loved him, she couldn't bring herself to hate him. The idea of him being committed to marrying Tessa satisfied her anger towards him. If he'd thought himself hard done being married to her, Lyndsey would pay a million to know how he felt now.

"OK girls. Out. John it's haul ass time, get your ass to it, work the hole."

Hope aided Lyndsey. She boosted her up out of the hole. Then Richard and Jeffrey each took one of her hands and hoisted Hope out of the hole. The four original treasure hunters sat huddled together across the way from Tessa.

John returned to the hole. Tessa eyed him. She questioned his loyalty. Were things to turn bad, would John stand by her? Jeffrey muttered something to Richard. Tessa pointed the pistol at him. "That's enough, out of you. You speak—you speak to me. Got it?"

Jeffrey nodded. Tessa did not trust the bearded one. If anyone was to make a move, Tessa believed Jeffrey would be the one. He had a strange look in his eye, one Tessa did not trust. She decided he'd be the first to go.

John went to work in the hole. The pickaxe sliced into the earth with ease. He worked the edges first. He'd never been thrust into a situation where a life, possibly his own, stood in peril, unless one counted the fatal car crash of his parents and grandparents. That he rued, had been the beginning of his end. Tessa ate away at his mind. The thought of living out a life in her bonds scared him. Were the opportunity to end her reign of terror presented to him, John now felt himself capable of handling it. He shifted his work efforts toward the centre of the hole. The pickaxe struck an object. It did not ring out but made a dull thud. Nobody called out to him. John assumed the others had not heard. He lifted the pickaxe and drove it down off to the right of where the unseen object lay. Again it struck something. He kicked away at the earth in an effort to uncover the object. Nothing appeared. John stood up and attempted to leave the hole.

Tessa stopped him. "Not so quick lover-boy. Your shift ain't over just yet."

John cursed her silently then returned to working the pickaxe.

....

Determination kept Gilbert up with Pappy. Without his cane, the senior McClaken pushed Gilbert to his limits and hurried their advance towards the island's clearing. Pappy panted lightly and declared, "Gads! This old body sure is slowing down and feeling de ravages of me old age."

"You'd be hard pressed to convince me of that, Pappy. Where'd you come about all the vim and vigor and without your cane to boot?"

"Hurry up son. Time it be a wasting. It hasn't grown over a tad since I was last here. Or someone—something is a hell of a woodsman. It can drag my sorry soul and arse straight to Hell, but not till I saves our loved ones. I'll never stop till they're safe."

Gilbert stepped up his pace and moved up to Pappy's side. Together they raced towards their loved ones Jeffrey, Hope, Lyndsey and Richard.

"It's family. Family needs me. I got'ta be there. No choice. I'm proud of you, son. I know how hard it must be for you. To be here I mean. The place is not without its local lore of years gone by. I'm proud."

A bonding took place. Gilbert felt closer than he'd ever been to Pappy. The two men looked hard into each other's eyes. Without a word, they ran faster side by side in pursuit of their kin. Pappy and Gilbert reached the area where the forest thinned out in half the time it had taken the others.

The area started to look familiar to Pappy, though many years had passed since he'd last visited it, his memories of that visit remained vivid. The one part of the visit he'd never revealed to a living soul remained a dark secret buried deep in his soul. Pappy had vowed long ago to carry that secret with him to his grave. Nothing had happened to change that vow. Not even the current events. He rued over the guilt he bore over what had befallen young Jeffrey that day. The truth be told, Pappy and his Father-In-Law, Old Isaac Ramsay, had been well into the rum that day and dead drunk. They'd no right to be out on the water, let alone drag along the willing and energized young Jeffrey.

Yes, Pappy thought. *Could'a been a bear that day. Could'a been a ghost.* Liquor tended to fog ones memory when taken to the excesses they'd administered themselves that day. *Then again*, he rued, *it'll nary be known by another soul but Old Isaac and me. What the hell*, he thought, had to tell the wife something. *God. Little Jeffrey had come back a mess. Besides, bears roared…and so did ghosts.* Or so he'd once been told. He stepped out of the forest into the clearing. A smile broke out on his face. He cherished the notoriety that the ghost version had bestowed upon him.

Gilbert stepped out of the forest behind Pappy, off to the north above a layer of mist stood a tall, old tree. It looked forbearing standing by itself at that end of the clearing. Ahead of the tree, he spotted what looked like a person standing on a small hill. Unknown to him, it was the pistol-bearing Tessa. She stood above the pile of earth her workers had extracted from the hole.

Pappy slowed down. Gilbert moved up to his side. Together, they walked towards what Gilbert assumed would be Jeffrey, Richard, Hope, and Lyndsey. He'd forgotten Pappy's tale of Bernie's encounter with the bitch of two days past. He'd recall the tale and more before his day ended.

CHAPTER 52

THE SPIRIT OF GRACE RAMSAY HAD NOT ABANDONED LYNDSEY when it vanished. It had stepped forward and sought to free her family of the consequences of her Father's actions.

Actions that had torn her family apart: the words she'd once written in her treasured diary echoed in her soul.

'I no longer fear Hell's Gates. I have stared directly into the eyes of its Master. I pray no other ever comes to stare onto that fearsome and terrifying sight. That island, you must recall our shock at hearing voices drifting out towards us from its mist covered shoreline. There remains no doubt in my mind ... the voices belonged to long dead pirates of the worst kind. We dropped our sail and rowed up to the island's shore and quickly disembarked setting our feet upon welcomed grounds, or so we thought. We uncovered a scattering of gold coins and glittering precious gems. Your greed surfaced and you pocketed the coins and gems, then Hell's Gates opened its guardian that wretched-evil soul we uncovered in gathering those gems reached out and damned our souls! Those eyes reached out from its grave and I swear sought to possess our souls. You spotted the glittering jeweled rosary held so tightly in its hand. All would have been well had we done right! Returned the earth to where it belonged ... firmly packed above that demon from Hell. But no! You'd have nothing to do with that John.'

The words reinforced the once youthful Grace Ramsay's resolve to return the jeweled rosary that her beloved Father John Ramsay had once stolen from the Demon and guardian of Hell's gateway. The Demon had totally destroyed her Uncle Richard's life passions. She approached the beast with caution and resolve, determined to recapture her family's life passions destroyed by her Father's greed.

The sleeping beast sensed the presence of her spirit's essence, but could not identify it as a friend or foe. The approaching spirit's presence concealed the presence of the other intruders. Grace Ramsay's spirit approached the resting beast—the sad tormented soul who'd been left behind by its Captain and crew to stand guard over their booty that fateful day centuries and then some past.

The beast stirred, then awoke from its long slumber, it turned and glared at its intruder. On spotting the jeweled rosary adorning the neck of its intruder, it scowled, then hissed "Mine!"

Grace Ramsay's spirit pulled away from the beast. The youthful female spirit felt doubt start to embrace it and its goal. Images of her Father flashed before her, then quickly faded. She whispered, "And yours it shall be once more."

Torment and anger eased in the beast. It settled down upon not sensing danger from the intruder, the bearer of its treasured gift that had once been ripped from its shattered hand by an intruder not so kind. Young Grace Ramsay's spirit sensed a presence of goodness within the beast. She drew near to it and felt its essence.

"Your name sir, that I may address you." Grace Ramsay's spirit whispered.

"Wil...Wilb...Wilbert, Wilbert Enid be my earthly name," The beast with fading anger replied.

He paused then whispered, "Allow me but a moment to recall the words of my long lost sweet sister Selby." Silence befell the pair. A moment, then two slipped past. Footsteps above disturbed their connection. Wilber tensed.

Grace Ramsay's spirit softly sang, "Wee Willie Wilbert, Wee Willie Wilbert. It will please me to hear the words of sweet Selby."

The softly sung words relaxed Wilbert. He shared Selby's words, "Wilber…Wilbert Enid. Wilbert ... one with promise to be bright and famous, Enid ... Soul Life a woodlark, perhaps one in possession of a soul and life's joys?"

"To be—to be so truly blessed—Oh but to have shared one's life with a sister so sweet and gentle as your Selby."

"Not I," Wilbert moaned. "I failed in life, failed my parents' aspirations for my future. Fell in amongst a truly unsavory lot. Worst of all I failed my sister, dear sweet Selby. Oh, how she loved me, her only sibling, and hated my leaving." Wilbert sighed then revealed, "It was Selby's gift that jeweled rosary. T'was to bring me safely home to her."

Grace Ramsay's spirit sobbed. She then removed the jeweled rosary and passed it to the one she now knew to be Wilbert Enid.

Memories gathered centuries past by Wilbert Enid caressed and eased the tensions his spirit had been burdened with since death. In his long past youth peer pressure, misdirection, greed along with a wealth of bad choices had cruelly embraced his once youthful human form. He turned and gazed upon the jeweled rosary. He whispered, "Mine. I pray blessings be upon you for returning this treasure. True blessings are yours to embrace. You have returned to me a gift I have truly missed. The gift Selby once gave me with the promise it would one day carry me home to her warm loving sisterly embrace."

Grace Ramsay's spirit gained something, something she'd never lived long enough to experience. It felt and embraced the love and kindness of another, a love that eclipsed the love of one's family. The lingering sadness they'd endured faded. Together their heartbeats sang a gentle song of joy. Together, they shared the precious moment and each shed tears of joy. Wilbert gazed at the treasured rosary he held, tears of joy tricked down his cheeks. Sated in love's tender caresses, Wilbert asked of Grace Ramsay's spirit, "Please call upon me to repay you for the treasure you returned to me this day."

Wilbert's offer lifted a burden from her soul. Grace shared the agonies that had burdened her, "I am the spirit of Grace Ramsay. Years past, my Father wronged you. He attacked you and stole your treasured rosary Selby's precious gift. Uncle Richard was unwillingly at his side. Those actions and the resultant curses destroyed Uncle

Richard's soul and life essences. I sought you out to seek forgiveness for Father's actions, his greed. In connecting to your essence and life joys, Father's greed truly saddens me. It cannot and should not be forgiven. I truly erred. I can no longer seek Father's forgiveness. I now merely plead on Uncle Richard's behalf. Please, I beg, forgive him. He is truly worthy of forgiveness and restoration of his spirit's joyful essence. Grace Ramsay's spirit glowed on connecting to Wilbert Enid's essence. A touch of joyfulness embraced her. Images of her Uncle Richard flashed vibrantly in her mind. The joy revealed in his expressions and the return of his robust head of flowing black curls she once had grown to love, showered her with elation. The image of her Father, she could not call forth. It had faded from her trove of treasured memories. The image of Lyndsey's Richard surfaced she caught a likeness of her Uncle Richard in the image.

Thud! Cruuun...ch! Wilbert tensed. He sensed another presence. A threat against the treasure he'd faithfully guarded over the centuries. Thud! Wilbert grew more concerned. Above, John drove the pickaxe hard into the ground. Tessa had really pissed him off. The pickaxe struck something and uttered an eerie crussss...ink then passed through it. A sick feeling shot through John's heart.

The others had heard the distinct sound made by the pickaxe, but none faster than Tessa. Excited, she yelled to John, "What is it. Give it to me, damn you!"

Jeffrey slipped into the hole and stared down at John's feet. John ignored Tessa's ranting. He stooped and extracted the pickaxe's tip from the earth. In a flash, John recoiled away from his discovery. He stared down at his feet and the skull impaled on the pickaxe.

"Give it to me. You son of a bitch! It's MINE, Mine you bastard! Give it to me!"

John recovered. He thought, *Okay bitch. One well-earned reward coming at you!* In a smooth motion, he swung the pickaxe in an around the clock motion. The impaled skull slid off the pickaxe and flew towards an eager Tessa. Jeffrey reeled back away from the pickaxe's flow. He fell down on John's feet.

Gilbert and Pappy together broke into a trot. They raced towards Tessa and the others. Twenty feet away, Gilbert recognized Tessa. He slowed his pace.

Tessa heard their approaching footsteps. She wheeled her pistol-toting hand until it held Gilbert in its sights. She screamed, "Freeze, big-foot, you too, Gramps. It's all mine! Mine, do you hear?"

Gilbert stopped dead in his tracks. Pappy stopped at his side a second or two later. The skull left the shadow of the hole and raced towards Tessa. She spotted it and recoiled. Her trigger finger twitched; a shot fired off. It hit the ground ahead of Gilbert and ricocheted harmlessly off to Gilbert's left. Gilbert and Pappy fell forward. They landed ten feet away from the hole and to the left of those they'd set out to rescue. The skull hit Tessa's midsection. Her left hand swung up and deflected it off to her right. Tessa started to tumble backwards away from the hole. Her right hand and the pistol trained itself on the hole and John.

Wilbert roared out a series of ear piercing howls and screeches that cast a shadow of terror over everyone above. He pulled away from Grace Ramsay's spirit, whose whispered plea had caught his ear.

"Get the lady in red! Send her straight through Hell's Gate!"

His territory had been violated by flesh bearers from the other-side. He roared and rose up out of the ground. "Get out'ta here. Leave us be…or I'll rip your hearts from yer flesh and drag your sorry souls straight to the Gates of Hell." He floated up and passed through Jeffrey and John's bodies then reached towards Tessa. Everyone watched its dirt-caked arms extend out to Tessa.

John tried desperately to climb out of the hole. Terrified and still falling backwards, Tessa repeatedly squeezed her trigger finger. Four shots rang out. They all passed through the apparition reaching out to her. The first bullet hit John in the shoulder. The second grazed his cheek. The third and forth flew harmlessly off into the advancing eerie mist. Richard jumped into the hole and embraced John. He checked for a pulse, finding one, he lifted John up out of the hole with Jeffrey's help. Pappy and Gilbert stood up and ran towards the action unfolding. On nearing the hole, Pappy stared sadly into the eyes of Tessa then turned away from the fear he'd seen. He grabbed Lyndsey's hand and urged her to flee at his side. Lyndsey sobbed and clung desperately to him.

Gilbert, Hope and Jeffrey responded to Pappy's urgings and ran off together back towards the boats. Hope stopped, turned back and attempted to run to Lyndsey's side. Gilbert grabbed her and pulled her back. He screamed, "Now, Hope. Now while we're still alive!"

"Bu...but my sister. She needs me." Hope cried.

Jeffrey joined Gilbert and pulled Hope towards the advancing mist. Together the three ran fleeing back towards the boats.

Lyndsey fought Pappy's grasp desperate to stay at Richard's side. Pappy held on firmly to Lyndsey.

"Rich...Richie," Lyndsey cried out then sobbed, "We're all going to die!!!"

Through watery, tear-stained eyes, Lyndsey stared, horrified, at Richard in the hole. Terrified she waited for death to reach out and seize her. Richard clawed his way out of the hole, ran to and embraced Lyndsey. Their shared embrace eased Lyndsey's fears. Richard's lips touched Lyndsey's then parted, he urged her to flee with Pappy to the boats. Lyndsey obeyed and hesitantly fled away at Pappy's side. They quickly vanished into the mist. Richard picked up John, shifted him onto his shoulders then set off in pursuit of the others. Tessa's soul stared out through her eyes. Mikie's words echoed in her ears, 'I's dat I bees, and a live-bastard at dat. Enjoy Hell. Iff'n de Devil won't take ye…I pick up as agreed to. I'll not return…Iff'n I don't see yer sorry asrses from a safe distance.' Terrified she stared at the apparition. Tessa's face contorted and her hair embraced the whiteness of a raging winter blizzard. Out aboard Total Satisfaction, Mikie heard the shots ring out. Mikie snickered. He hit the throttle. Total Satisfaction leapt out of the water and headed away from the island. Under his breath he wished the Devil well. He knew in his heart that Lucifer would have all he could handle in that bitch. Mikie's knuckles whitened and his grip on the steering column tightened. On sensing the island's presence fade, a man of his word, Mikie relaxed and pulled back on the throttle. He resolved to wait 10 minutes, then keep his word and approach the island from a safe distance.

....

The apparition roared out, "Come hither bitch…I want you!"

Gilbert raced through the woods back towards the boats, Jeffrey and Hope at his side. He shouted, "MOVE IT! Move It! I don't know what we just witnessed. I don't want to." He took Hope's hand and said, "Let's git the fuck out'ta here!"

Jeffrey's jaw dropped, he stared over at Gilbert, shocked on having heard his brother's profanity. Hope uttered a silent series of tsk, tsks at her uncle's rare profanity. Jeffrey struggled to keep up to Gilbert and Hope, while fighting to suppress a series of snickers brought on by Gilbert's profanity. Richard gained ground on Pappy and Lyndsey as they fled. He quickly caught up with them. Each step Richard took lightened the load of John on his shoulders. Urged on by Richard, Pappy and Lyndsey ran at his side towards the boats. They all looked back into the mist on hearing a series of renewed eerie shrieks and howls, rise out of the mist. Determined, they raced on towards the safety of the boats.

Back at the hole, Tessa stared at the howling apparition. Terrified, she turned scrambled off the pile of dirt she lay on and headed off, terrified and screaming profanities towards Mike's agreed upon pick up point.

CHAPTER 53

GILBERT'S PARTY ARRIVED BACK AT THE COVE AND THE BOATS first. At the shore, he picked up the stern line and pulled Rose Bud and her tethered mate Karyn-Anita towards himself. He held the line while Jeffrey helped Hope aboard Rose Bud, then joined her. After Hope and Jeffrey were aboard, Gilbert removed the line's end from the tree that had held it and tossed the line to Jeffrey. Next, he untied Rose Buds' bowline, coiled the line up then jumped over onto Rose Buds' bow.

"Shouldn't we wait until everyone returns before casting off?" Hope shouted.

"No damn it!. Definitely…no," Gilbert shouted.

"But!"

"No. I saw that thing. You saw it. If Pappy, John, Richard and Lyndsey arrive back without it on their heels, I'll go back ashore and pick them up."

Hope turned ashen, she screamed, "No! Give me 10 minutes. I'll go back and meet them!"

"God Damn it...No!" Gilbert screamed back at her.

Afraid Hope would leap back onto the island he raced to Hope embraced and attempted to stop any plans she might have nurtured about going back onto the island. Hope's body trembled.

With her head pressed against Gilbert's chest, Hope muttered, "No. I'm going back. I'll not abandon them in this hell hole!" She sobbed hard then declared, "I'll not lose the sister the past denied me!"

Gilbert tightened his embrace, "There's no way you're setting foot on that island again. I'll never allow it!" Gilbert stroked her hair in an attempt to calm her fears.

Unnoticed, Jeffrey stepped onto Rose Bud's bow and jumped back onto the island. He set off in search of Pappy, Lyndsey, Richard and John. To Gilbert and Hope he shouted back, "Take the boats out of the cove and wait for me! I'll get Pappy, Lyndsey and Richard. Get out of the cove. I'll be OK." Jeffrey disappeared into the mist before Gilbert and Hope could react. Gilbert stared out at Jeffrey. The clarity of his brother's words rocked him. They echoed in his mind, *'Take the boats out of the cove and wait for me! I'll get Pappy, Lyndsey and Richard. Get out of the cove. I'll be OK.'* He hadn't heard Jeffrey speak so clearly since that day in their youth long past. The day he'd shirked his duties and exposed Jeffrey to the hell hole of an island, he now stared at in disbelief. Had his ears deceived him?

Hope twisted and turned in the grasp of Gilbert's arms. Her anger and dismay turned into uncontrolled sobs and heartfelt tears. The boats drifted away from the island. Gilbert relaxed his protective hold and embrace that had held Hope a captive. He patted her back and whispered, "Hold tight, Hope." He treated Hope to an emotional hug, kissed her forehead, then released her. He boarded Karyn-Anita and released her lines from Rose Bud. To Hope he shouted, "We'll drift out of the cove then will head back in once Jeffrey, Pappy, Richard and Lyndsey return. We'll pick them up then get away from this God forsaken hell hole!"

Gilbert settled back and waited for Pappy, Jeffrey, Richard and Lyndsey to make their appearance. He knew ghosts, spirits, or anything dead could not travel across water. Pappy had etched that lesson into his mind when he'd been naught but a young lad. Pappy's confession at Mama's funeral had only reinforced the lifelong lessons. Yes. Gilbert would keep himself and Hope a safe distance from shore until he knew for certain that no danger from the other side—the spirit world—existed.

....

Ten minutes later Jeffrey caught sight of Richard and his burdened shoulders. He ran faster and quickly came to Richard's side. Pappy and Lyndsey raced up and embraced Jeffrey, then Pappy attempted to hoist John off Richard's shoulders onto his.

Jeffrey shoved him away from Richard and shouted, "No, Dad. Let me do that!"

He stopped Pappy's attempt to hoist John onto his shoulders from Richard's.

Jeffrey repeated himself, "No, Dad. Let me do that!"

Pappy looked up in shock. He'd not heard Jeffrey speak so clearly in decades. Not since their last terrifying trip to the island. He helped Jeffrey shift John off Richard onto his shoulders. Lyndsey embraced Richard. They all took one last look back in the direction of the clearing and its hole. Nobody spoke. Pappy swore under his breath that he'd never set foot upon the island again. Not, even if he lived to be a centurion. They all stepped off running towards the cove. A tear trickled down his cheek. He'd once again recalled Jeffrey's words, "No, Dad. Let me do that!"

Richard helped Jeffrey carry John over the last 100 feet to the cove. Nearing the water the mist grew lighter. Out on the water hints of sunshine brightened the horizon. On arriving at the cove they set John down and checked out his vital signs and wounds. Pappy and Lyndsey waved frantically to Gilbert aboard Karyn-Anita and Hope on Rose Bud both adrift off the island. Both boat engines roared to life after they had spotted Pappy and Lyndsey. Hope raced Rose Bud frantically back into the cove. She arrived back in the cove ahead of Gilbert. Rose Bud bumped up against the cove's shore.

Hope shifted her into neutral then abandoned the controls she helped Lyndsey aboard Rose Bud then embraced her. Jeffrey helped Richard place John on board then took control of the helm. Once Richard had stepped aboard, he shifted the motor into gear. Rose

Bud pulled away from the island. Gilbert eased Karyn-Anita into the cove. He waved to Jeffrey in passing Rose Bud. He shifted the motor into neutral and glided up towards the shore. Pappy jumped too soon. The cove's icy water greeted him with a great splash. Gilbert tossed a line out to Pappy and pulled him to the boat. Back on board Pappy tore off his jacket and ripped off his shirt. He grabbed a sweater from a cabin hook, toweled himself off then donned the sweater. Gilbert removed his jacket he passed it to Pappy then wasted little time in heading out of the cove away from the island. At the helm, Gilbert crossed the line. He drove the throttle full forward. Karyn-Anita flew across the water towards an anxious Rose Bud and crew awaiting her outside the cove.

....

Tessa scrambled through the forest trail, Wilbert Enid's apparition in hot pursuit. A renewed series of ear piercing howls and curses reached out to Total Satisfaction and startled Mikie. He stared at the island's shore and spotted Tessa's red clothing racing towards the shoreline. Tessa stumbled on a bed of rocks fifteen feet away from the water.

Her pursuer screamed out to her, "Hiss…sss. Stop you Bitch. You're mine!"

Mikie's jaw dropped. He stared out at Tessa and her pursuer. Tessa spotted him she crawled over the rocks, regained her footing and ran to the water. Terrified she leapt into the water with abandon and swam towards Total Satisfaction. Frozen Mikie stared at the scene unfolding before his eyes. On seeing Tessa hit the water Mikie watched in shock as her howling pursuer stopped at the water's edge and did not pursue her. A misty vapour surrounded the apparition. Mikie watched its eyes follow the woman's frantic swim towards Total Satisfaction. Mikie's heart raced and pounded inside his chest, his jaw dropped on spotting a smaller apparition suddenly appear and ease up to the demonic beast's side. The blood red in the beast's eyes faded. Its eyes turned towards the one at its side. Frozen, Mikie stared in fear at the pair on the shoreline. His racing heart eased on seeing the beast's once blood red eyes turn a gentle, pleasing green.

Mikie started to utter a series of long forgotten prayers, "Our Father, Who art in heaven, Hallowed be 'thy name"

The pair on the shoreline turned away from him and the water. They quickly vanished back into the island's mist shrouded forest.

"Thy Kingdom come—" Mikie's prayers continued.

Fifty feet off Total Satisfaction's bow Tessa came fully into Mikie's line of vision. Each stroke drew her closer to her goal, Total Satisfaction and Mikie.

Like Mikie, she too had started to shout out long forgotten prayers, "Hail Mary full of grace blessed be thy name—"

Mikie heard the splashes of Tessa's frantic swimming. He stared at her. The fear he saw captured on her face shocked him. A seasoned man of the sea, Mikie reacted to Tessa's peril. He took hold of Total Satisfaction's controls and steered her towards Tessa. Ten feet away, he shifted into neutral and tossed a line out to Tessa, she grabbed hold of it. Working together, the rescue quickly unfolded. Once Tessa had been brought safely aboard, Mikie grabbed several blankets from the cabin and wrapped Tessa securely inside them. The two embraced, stared towards the island, and continued to utter their long forgotten prayers. A lifetime of blessings passed between them. Mikie's years of seamanship guided him through his hesitant state of mind. He took control of the helm shifted into gear and headed Total Satisfaction, her captain and new found blessing back home. Reality reclaimed Mikie later as Total Satisfaction bumped up against the docks in Chester. He secured her to the dock then returned to Tessa's embrace. Secure in each other's arms they continued to pray.

....

Gilbert's heart pounded against his chest. He looked back towards the island and shuddered on hearing a fading voice shout out.

"Hiss…sss. Stop you Bitch. You're mine!"

He watched the Floating Islands and the howling voice both grow faint then vanish from sight, ears and mind. In his mind he pondered, "Are they gone?" In his heart, Gilbert resolved, prayed and hoped that the island and its inhabitants' destination would be Hell and points beyond. He quickly turned and joined Pappy waving to Jeffrey and Richard. Their boats moved closer together, towards a reunion filled with rejoicing out on the Atlantic. In the distance a faint image above the sea hinted that the Tancook Islands and the safety of Mahone Bay awaited them.

CHAPTER 54

GILBERT VEERED TO PORT AND RACED TOWARDS ROSE BUD. THE distance closed quickly. The wind had picked up. Whitecaps dotted the surface of the Atlantic. Gilbert pulled the throttle back ten feet away from Rose Bud. He hailed Jeffrey and Richard.

Jeffrey answered, "Everyone's A OK. Just a little wet, but OK."

"And the girls are?"

Jeffrey pointed to Rose Bud's cabin and shouted "They're tending to John. He's started to come around slowly." He paused then added, "We radio'd in and asked Lenny to meet us at the dock with some assistance. I suggested Doc Rose Jr. but Lenny flatly stated he'd get Doc Rose Sr. or his retired nurse, Isabelle."

"Anything we can do to help?" Pappy called back.

Jeffrey waved. He pointed towards the northwest. Then shouted, "We'd best get ourselves back home, the wind has picked up—could get rough. Head back to East River, but stay close at hand. We'll talk, back at the dock, OK?" He paused then called back out to Gilbert, "Move it, Gillie! We'll see you at the dock."

Gilbert waved back, and pushed the throttle ahead. Karyn-Anita picked up speed and set off with Gilbert at the helm towards East River Bay. He eyed Rose Bud until Jeffrey had her under way. The run back to East River Bay took two hours.

During that time, Hope and Lyndsey remained huddled in the cabin with John. Together they tended to his wounds. Using Jeffrey's onboard first aid kit, the girls had cleaned and bandaged John's grazed cheek. Hope used her first aid training and treated his wounded shoulder. The bullet appeared to have passed cleanly through with no signs of bone or blood vessel damage. Lyndsey cradled John's head on her lap. Wiping his forehead with a towel she struggled to deal with her feelings. Each bout of shivering that John passed through rekindled memories of the love they had shared. Flashbacks to Lyndsey's night of horrors in Newmarket cast her rekindled memories into an icy cold shower. John's eyelids flickered he attempted to rub them clear, but the pain in his shoulder caused him to flinch. Hope quickly removed the flask of white rum from the first aid kit. She opened it and eased its spout between John's lips. The rum hit John's pleasure sensors.

He smiled and said, "Thanks Lyns... I really needed that!"

John focused on the Lyndsey in his mind. The Lyndsey his eyes gazed at appeared to have taken on a new look. Her hair, although not red was definitely not blonde. He settled on strawberry-blonde as his ex's new hair colour. Her freckled cheeks puzzled him. Hope gave him a second serving of white rum. John smiled then slipped back into a hazy refuge. He found himself standing in a hole with a pickaxe in hand. He looked up at Tessa. The anger imbedded in her face fed his ire and really pissed him off! A shudder ran through him on spotting a pistol in Tessa's hand. Bam! Bam! John's body twisted and reacted to the scene playing out in his mind. Hope tossed the flask aside. The pain expressed on John's face drew a frown to hers.

Jeffrey passed the helm to Richard then reached under the bow and pulled out two blankets. He tossed one to Lyndsey. The other one he placed over John. He smiled at Lyndsey and said, "Best cover up girl. The wind will chill you to the bone before we get home."

Lyndsey acted on Jeffrey's suggestion she wrapped the blanket around herself. The woolen blanket quickly dampened the chill and occasional shiver she'd been feeling. Hope tucked the blanket securely around John. Lyndsey slid away from John. She stood up and joined Jeffrey and Richard. Lyndsey's emotions continued to confuse her heartstrings. Hope sat at John's side. His head rolled with Rose Bud's motion and his face found Hope's chest. The feel of John's face against her eased some of Hope's tension. A flashback of his anger displayed in Roger's office raised doubts in her mind. The angry drunken exchange Lyndsey had described raised her doubts anew. The warmth of his face and breath concerned her, was a fever setting in? Would his condition worsen? The sensation of touching the man triggered her caring nature. Hope snuggled up to John and the vibration of the motor quickly lulled her to sleep.

....

Gilbert pulled the throttle back on approaching the gap into East River. He guided Karyn-Anita through the gap, then safely up to her dock. Lenny, Old Doc Rose and his nurse Isabelle stood on the dock awaiting their arrival. At the dock, Pappy tossed the docking lines to Lenny who secured the lines to the dock. Once up on the dock Gilbert thanked Old Doc Rose and Isabelle profusely for responding to their need. He then pointed out to Rose Bud about to shoot through the gap.

Jeffrey stood at the stern, Richard eased back on the throttle Lyndsey followed Jeffrey's lead and stood by with a docking line to assist in the docking of Rose Bud. Hope slept soundly snuggled up next to John in the cabin. Rose Bud bumped up against the dock, Lyndsey and Jeffrey tossed their docking lines to the welcoming party on the dock. The bump awoke Hope and John from their sound sleep. Hope offered John her hand then helped him up into a standing position. Assured that John had recovered from the shock of his ordeal, Richard and Jeffrey helped him up onto the dock. Hope and Lyndsey stepped up to Jeffrey and each kissed him on a cheek then hugged him. John stared at the girls with a bewildered look on his face. A quick round of introductions took place during the walk up to Gilbert's house.

....

Old Doc Rose set up his first aid centre in the kitchen. Isabelle eased John into a chair. She then ran about the kitchen and bathroom gathering together a supply of towels and set a kettle of water to boil on the stove.

Richard approached John, his face contorted. The words he wanted to scream at his brother never surfaced. He chuckled and said, "I'm at a loss to explain our latest adventure, brother. I suspect Mom and Dad, along with Grandma and Grandpa, played a major role and convinced *'The angels above and our creator'* to save our sorry arses today!"

John smirked. Before he could respond Old Doc Rose and Isabelle chased everyone but John out of the kitchen. Isabelle removed the bandages, gauze and wrappings Hope had applied to John's wounds. Both openly commented on how lucky John was to have received up front treatment that they believed had stabilized him and averted any chance of early infection. Doc, assisted by Isabelle, worked his medical magic on John. In wrapping up he handed John a sample supply of pain killers and antibiotics to combat infection and relieve any pain that arose. Satisfied with his work, Doc suggested they head to the living-room and join John's partners in crime.

Everyone in the living-room cheerfully greeted the return of Doc, Isabelle and John. Hope, seeing John shirtless and bandaged, raced off to find clothing for him. She returned with an extra, extra large red flannel shirt from Gilbert's closet. With Hope's help, John slipped into the shirt.

Gilbert embraced Doc and Isabelle. "You're amazing, Doc. You and Isabelle just get better with time. You're the best."

Doc laughed then replied, "Trust me Gil, I'm trying to embrace this retirement concept." He pointed at Pappy and Lenny and said, "Some of our local Old Farts have mastered the concept. I suspect Isabelle and I never will."

Mild laughter broke out throughout the room. Doc walked up to Lyndsey. He smiled then embraced her and added, "Welcome, home, sweetheart. What a charming, beautiful young lady you've become." He paused then shouted, "Look Gil, she's got her sister's dimples!"

Lyndsey stuttered, "Are, are you the dd—doctor that saved my sister's life?

Before Doc could answer, Lyndsey wrapped him in her arms and burst into fits of uncontrolled sobbing. Hope ran to them and embraced both in her arms. Slowly Lyndsey's sobbing abated. Doc, Hope and Lyndsey moved off into the hallway, where Doc retold the details of the day he'd come upon their parents' accident. Each word warmed Lyndsey's heartstrings. Time stood still. She fought back tears on failing to recall any childhood memories of her birth parents Sandy and Allan. Brushing aside her tears she recalled the love of her adoptive parents Liam and Letitia—her Mom and Dad.

Richard and John reconnected by sharing cares, concerns and magical memories they'd shared and lived as brothers. No mention was made of the day's shared adventure, or the recent loss they'd suffered with the tragic accident and death of their grandparents and parents. John apologized profusely over his ill conceived affair with Tessa. He glanced across the room to the hallway where Doc, Lyndsey, Hope stood chatting up a storm and radiating an aura of positivity.

He confessed his past motives to Richard, "Rich, I never deserved her. Yes! My anger, jealousy of you led me to seeking Lyndsey's attentions in your absence. Dad and Grandfather's stern criticism of all I did fueled my anger. I clung to our family's planned gathering that never came to be. I needed a window of opportunity to rekindle family connections. Lyndsey assured me she'd work with me to nurture a new and refreshed relationship with them."

John sobbed lightly then added, "I was wrong! Definitely shocked and elated when our occasional outings grew more frequent and took on personal shared passions.

Richard cut John off. He took John's hands in his and said, "Brother, our lives have taken a twist of late beyond my wildest imaginations. We cannot change the past. We are, and always will be, family!"

"But.", John interrupted.

"No buts, brother, no buts! We are family, you, me and now this amazing Maritime reconnection to the McClaken/Ramsay Clans and Lyndsey, definitely Lyndsey." He paused then added, "I sense Hope has taken a hesitant shine to you."

John smirked and said, "I doubt it. After the episode in Roger's office and my drunken follow up with Lyndsey—topped off with today's adventure? It's highly unlikely any woman would. Who is she, Rich? How are we really connected? On regaining my senses back on the boat, I could have sworn her to be a Strawberry-Blonde freckled distant cousin of Lyndsey! There's a look I can't explain."

Richard laughed and said, "It's the dimples John, the dimples, she's Lyndsey's sister."

John's jaw dropped in disbelief.

Gilbert, Jeffrey and Pappy sat together on the sofa.

"He called me Dad!" Pappy boasted. He repeated himself, "Called me Dad!" tears trickled down Pappy's cheeks.

Gilbert smiled, on recalling the exchanges he had with Jeffrey out on the water. The wind had stolen a touch of the clarity from their voices out there. However, he couldn't recall having heard Jeffrey speak so clearly since their childhoods. He asked, "What's up Jeff? It's amazing that your stutter has vanished. We're truly blessed!"

Jeffrey shrugged then asked, "I stuttered?"

Gilbert pondered Jeffrey's question. Could it be his brother never sensed or realized he had a speech impediment that had fed the schoolyard bullies with ammunition over the years? He cast aside an image of Barnie, bartender at the Lobster Pot Pub & Eatery. The image had interrupted his positive thoughts and celebration of the Jeffrey standing before him. "Yes, you stuttered and I blamed myself. I should have been the one out with Pappy and Grandpa Ramsay that day! Barnie would never have tried to cross my path. He'd never have taunted and called me Bugshit McClaken!"

Jeffrey flinched on hearing Barnie's name mentioned and topped off with the nickname he'd detested throughout life. Today's adventure out on the Floating Islands had somehow rekindled the tight connection the brothers had shared in their youth. It had definitely cast aside Gilbert's guilt over its outcome. Jeffrey smiled back at his brother. The grin on Gilbert's face cast aside a short lived frown. It elated him. He shared anew his recollection of the encounter on the island. "It's weird, eerie really! Back on the island, at the hole, when all that screeching and howling erupted, something icy yet warm touched me. I just can't explain it, Gil. Something touched me. It may sound crazy but I believe it passed straight through me."

"Really Jeff? I will not doubt your word. After what I saw on the island, we'd best take it to be a blessing in disguise."

"Yes Gil. I swear it actually passed straight through me. The truth be told—I swear it touched my soul. It was icy but I sensed a warm embracing presence."

Jeffrey's words caught Pappy's ear and ire. He jumped up stared over at Jeffrey and declared, "We'll be having none a'dat der swear'in stuff me son!"

Both Gilbert and Jeffrey chuckled at Pappy's outburst. It reminded them of the Pappy of their youth. Gilbert stepped towards Jeffrey and embraced him in one of his trademark hugs. The brothers quickly cast aside the day's island adventure. They recalled and shared a treasure trove of their childhood adventures, each adding a touch of exaggeration to their version. Pappy willingly injected tidbits of his recollections and versions of the long past adventures.

Dusk started to make its presence known. Gilbert stood and headed off to the kitchen. He switched on a series of light switches. On his return 10 minutes later he announced, "Those needing a change of clothes and a quick shower, best git to it before I lay claim to all the hot water."

Lyndsey and Hope hugged Doc then turned and bolted to the stairs and the two available showers. Everyone chuckled on their departure. Jeffrey shook his head and declared "Now that's definitely a matched set of dynamite sisters!"

The laughter broke out anew. Gilbert suggested they eat in. He offered to order pizzas at Happy Charlie's Pizza Shack. Pappy countered with an offer to treat everyone to an outing on his tab. He suggested they step out in style and dine at Michaela's Dockside Pub and Seafood Emporium over in Hubbards. Pappy boasted, "Trust me. They serve up the absolute best Fish and Chips this side of de Atlantic! Ask Lenny or takes a gander at the jiggling belly on the old lad."

Lenny heard his name spoken in jest. He defended his honour, “Tis but the last stages of me body toning program at the Fitness Centre in Chester.”

Everyone laughed in response to Lenny’s declaration. Once the laughter passed Pappy retorted, “Ah—Fer those so inclined they also serves up a wide selection ov’en dem healthy veggie and fat free offerings.”

Lenny replied, “Then I’ll be dining on one of dem healthy tings fer sure.”

Laughter broke out anew. Before it settled down Pappy and Jeffrey excused themselves and headed off to their house to freshen up. Gilbert offered up rounds of white rum, to Richard, John, Lenny and Doc. To Isabelle he served up a chilled glass of white wine. Doc took to laughing on spotting Bailey strutting into the living-room.

“Meow, meow...meo...!”

Doc suppressed his chucking. He inquired, “Am I seeing things? Could that possibly be William Ramsay’s rum loving drinking partner Bailey?”

Gilbert answered Doc’s question. He quickly visited the kitchen and returned with a large sized saucer. Richard endeared Bailey’s lifelong loyalties anew by filling the saucer with a healthy serving of rum. Conversations broke out anew between the remaining parties, Gilbert, Richard, John, Lenny, Doc and Isabelle, along with an occasional comment from Bailey.

CHAPTER 55

THE FOLLOWING TWO WEEKS DISAPPEARED IN A MELTING POT OF reunion joys and discoveries. The McClaken and Ramsay Clans embraced their newly rekindled family connections. The years of separation melted away. At the one week mark, Roger and his wife, Noreen, joined a growing list of special guests at the McClaken homes in East River. Richard and Lyndsey missed their arrival since they had disappeared two days earlier. Only Hope knew their whereabouts. She refused to drop a hint to anyone. After the second day of their absence, nobody bothered to ask again. Everyone focused on welcoming the new arrivals.

Hope's shadow never fell far from John's side. Their island adventure had shaken and rocked them both. John's arrogance and short fuse had vanished. In shared confidences with Hope he confessed to having crossed the line and destroying his marriage. Over time he shared recollections of his time on the island. Like how he had sensed an eerie sensation on having tossed the skull at Tessa. He recalled for her the icy warmth that rocked him on being shot.

John declared, "I believed myself to be a dead-man. My God the icy feeling that touched and passed through me, the ear piercing howls. I swear something touched my soul. Hell...I prayed as I crumbed to the ground!"

Hope's jaw dropped. She uttered an extended uuhmm then said, "Uncle Jeffrey! He felt the same icy-chill. Said it lasted mere seconds then passed. To everyone's amazement he lost his severe stutter and speech impediments." She paused then added, "Off the record everyone I talk to recalls having heard the ear piercing howls."

The two bonded over that first week. Roger's arrival and updates set both their minds and hearts at ease. Roger updated them on Tessa's situation. She had never been pregnant. John clasped Roger's hands and thanked him before Roger relayed the latest details. Under Tessa's instructions her attorney had withdrawn her lawsuit demanding personal compensation and financial support. In lieu of that compensation she requested a $10,000 donation to Michael Slivers, referred to as her salvation and the *'Truly Blessed'*, in her attorney's documents."

Hope's jaw dropped and she burst into laughter. Both Roger and John stared at her in wonderment. Hope recovered and with a broad grin on her face asked, "Surely you don't mean the *Sliver* Mikie Slivers of East River Bay?"

Both Roger and John stared at Hope with question marks on their faces. Roger replied, "Legally he is listed as Michael S. Slivers of East River Bay, Nova Scotia."

Following a second outburst of laughter Hope simply replied, "OK."

The conversation shifted to lunch options once Noreen joined the group. Roger revealed a desire to sample some real down east seafood and hinted at lobster being his first choice. Noreen suggested she'd prefer an offering that did not come cloaked in a shell. Hope suggested they head out to the Lobster Pot Pub & Eatery in Chester. Roger agreed and treated them to the outing.

At the Lobster Pot, Barnie personally tended to their table on spotting Hope. Eager to pump Hope and her friends for some loose tidbits of local gossip, Barnie looked at John and asked, "Gid-day friend. Have you seen your lady about town of late?" Barnie handed out the menus and snickered.

"What lady?" John asked then added, "I'm with Hope."

Barnie snickered then replied, "Your lady in red! You know, the same hot little lady in red that turned de *Sliver* hornie Mikie into a raging forest fire!"

John did not answer.

"Ok! I can take a hint." Barnie chuckled then added, "Sorry to hear she dropped you for Mikie. She must have liked Mikie's magic fingers."

John frowned and grew tense. Hope sensed his tension she stood up looked at Barnie and said, "Enough Barnie! We dropped in for a bite to eat and some relaxation. Not to be interrogated!" Hope sat back down.

"OK!" Barnie replied. He added, "I'll be back for your orders."

"Let's leave," Hope suggested.

"No," John said then added, "We came to enjoy a good meal and a little relaxation. Let's do it. Relax and enjoy a good meal."

Roger nodded his agreement, everyone focused on their menus until Barnie returned. Once they'd placed their orders, Noreen and Hope stood up and excused themselves. They headed off to the lady's room. On their return to the table Barnie was delivering their meals.

"Bon Appétite," Barnie said after the ladies had returned.

Before he left the table Barnie smiled and said to John, "I don't know if Mikie took you and your ex out to the islands. I don't want to know what happened out there if he did."

Hope sneered. She snapped, "Enough, Barnie."

Barnie smiled, he started to slowly walk away and said, "They must 'a seen a ghost or Satan himself. Her hair is whiter than snow. And both your man's ex and Mikie have rediscovered Jesus!" He chuckled aloud then added, "Tried to save me but I'm not ready to visit the Promised Land." Satisfied, Barnie strutted back to the bar.

Everyone enjoyed their meals. Conversation avoided Barnie's comments and it centred instead on the planning and excitement surrounding the wedding plans that were afoot. Edging on the side of discretion, Barnie remained at the bar. He sent Eugette to clear away the post meal plates, serving utensils and deliver the bill. In parting, Hope slipped Eugette a twenty dollar tip. She asked Eugette, "What's with Barnie? Did he OD on a batch of nasty pills?"

Eugette chucked and replied, No! But he is uptight over the transformation of Mikie. It scares him."

Hope and John exchanged concerned glances with Eugette then walked out to the parking lot where Roger and Noreen awaited them. Roger had covered the meal on his credit card.

....

It was early on Saturday morning a week later when Richard and Lyndsey returned. They walked into Gilbert's kitchen to a rowdy chorus of oooh's and aaah's, followed by an endless series of hugs from all present. Lyndsey picked up on Hope's silent cue. The sisters slipped out of the kitchen and headed up to Hope's bedroom. On stepping into the room, Hope shut the door and embraced Lyndsey. Once they had reconnected conversations shifted to details of the wedding plans Hope had arranged over the past week. Lyndsey asked, "Are you still good to stand for me, be my Matron of Honour? John has agreed to stand and be Rich's Best Man?"

"I'm there, girl!" Hope shouted with glee.

They hugged anew. Lyndsey chided, "Should we be planning a double? I saw you hanging off John back there in the kitchen."

Hope blushed paused in thought then replied, "A hesitant and qualified uh um no."

Lyndsey laughed and chided anew, "Doth I detect a maybe? Hope I can assure you that I did loved him and believed he loved me." She frowned then said, "If not for that bitch Tessa, I believe I'd still love him! Trust me I'll never love him again as I once did."

Unable to contain her curiosity Hope asked, "Has a date been set for the big day Richard—You wedding bells and I dos?" She anxiously awaited the answer.

Lyndsey remained silent for several moments. With each moment Hope's anxiety levels soared skyward. Finally Lyndsey spoke, "I signed the divorce papers that Mr. Lizards brought to the house. The papers and the supporting documents have been filed; the uncontested status could help cut the time needed for a final decree. However we've been told to give it three months. Roger, Mr.

Lizards and their associates tell us it could finalize in under three months, but we cannot bank on it."

Hope rolled her eyes. She asked, "The date and exchange of I dos? When Sis? When do I get to stand for you?"

"On the September Labour Day weekend's Saturday."

"That's close to four months away girl. What if the decree comes in early? August is a fantastic time of the year in East River. You are going to do it here, right?"

"Yes. But not until September."

"Rats! I wanted a summer wedding. Grammy's rose hedge would be in full bloom. It would be an amazing setting for you and Richard to exchange your—I dos."

"It will be in September."

"Rats, again!"

"I repeat, it will be in September. However if you'll have me, I'll stay—"

Hope wrapped Lyndsey in her arms and shouted in glee, "Have you girl! You're the sister I've just discovered, the imaginary sibling of my childhood and invisible playmate that entertained me and shared my dreams."

Sobs were exchanged then Lyndsey repeated, "It will be in September. However if you'll have me, I'll stay—here, while Richard and John head home and tend to business. They should put in an appearance."

A short silence ensued. Then Lyndsey grinned and confessed, "I've walked down the aisle to Richie's side 10,000 times over since we bumped into each other in that sand box."

Hope sighed, "Say no more girl. I spotted those amazing sparkles and twinkles in your eyes and Richard's the day I met you!" She paused then added "Now they've turned into a never ending display of fireworks!"

Talk shifted to Hope updating Lyndsey on the status of the wedding plans she'd set in place. Everything was set to go as planned. Roger had agreed to walk Lyndsey down the aisle. The only items in need of immediate action called on Hope to alter the date to September. She grabbed her cell phone and speed dialed the company booked to supply and set up the tents, tables and chairs. Ring—ring on the second ring her call was answered.

"Steve's Event Tents, the best event organizers east of the Pacific. Charming Steve here at your service. How may I assist you?"

"Hi Steve It's Hope McDonald. I'm call..."

"About the Big Gala I Dos Event set to go in East River. Has a date been set?"

"Yes. It has."

"Name it and we'll be there."

"It will be the Saturday of the September Labour Day weekend."

"Oh. Not this weekend?"

"No."

"Not a problem. Cheer up lassie, September the weather is great in de Maritimes."

"Is that a Promise?"

"Guaranteed lassie, I've reserved a perfect weather forecast for the big day, clear blue skies, at worse a cloud or two, and but a hint of fall in de air."

"Guaranteed?"

Steve replied, "Absolutely me lassie. Relax and have yerself a great day. Stevie and the boys will be there, guaranteed." Then he closed the call with, "Cheers, Hope. Have yourself a great weekend."

Hope returned her cell phone to her hip pocket. She jumped off the bed and declared, "Best git your ass a mov'in girl! There be tings that needs doing! We'd best be heading off to Chester and get you fitted for your gown. They have Mom and Dad's wedding photos and have agreed to create a replica of the gown Mom wore on her wedding day."

They returned to the kitchen and received a thunderous round of applause. Hope cut their visit short. She ushered Lyndsey towards the door and commandeered Noreen. Together they headed off to Chester for Lyndsey's fitting session. Outside the seamstress's shop they bumped into the town's newest attraction, Mikie decked out in a 50's era dark grey suit topped off with a matching vintage fedora hat. Mikie's companion, the once vibrant temptress Tessa, wore a simple white on white flowered dress. Both carried opened bibles and on making eye contact encouraged the threesome to embrace the Lord's word. Tessa proclaimed, "Salvation and its eternal everlasting blessings can be yours, ladies."

Lyndsey almost replied. Shocked on recognizing Tessa and disgusted by her self-righteousness, she turned from the pair and walked towards the seamstress's shop door.

"Repent, unrepentant ones," The newly reborn Tessa chided. "Forgiveness is not reserved solely for the chosen ones. Given signs of repentance, the door is open to whores and sluts of your ilk!"

Disgusted, the three entered the seamstress's shop. Following the fitting they stopped in at the Lobster Pot Pub & Eatery for a quick lunch then headed back to East River.

The week flew by faster than everyone had anticipated. Roger and Noreen were treated to Gilbert's culinary masterpiece the McClaken Lobster Lasagna. Then reluctantly all shared several rounds of parting hugs. Roger and Noreen drove off to the Halifax Airport and their flight home.

Richard and John followed Roger's lead three days later. Their departure lingered a hug and more beyond Roger and Noreen's departure. Lyndsey reluctantly released Richard with assurances from Hope that September would reunite the love sick couple. Hope hugged Richard then embraced John and shared a short kiss. The couple were close but had not committed to a relationship. Both were reluctant and needed time. Lyndsey gazed longingly at Richard as he entered the SUV. A twist of the ignition key started the engine. Desperate for one more taste of her man, Lyndsey popped her head through the open driver's window and shared an extended and passionate parting kiss with Richard. The couple parted. Richard and John waved heartily out of their windows and the SUV drove out of the driveway. Lyndsey wrapped herself in a consoling hug. Tears streamed down her cheeks. Hope, Gilbert and Jeffrey embraced her. Once the SUV had driven out of sight they parted. Hope strolled with Lyndsey over to Grammy Ramsay's rose hedge. Its blooms cast an alluring rose fragrance over the sisters. Unnoticed, Bailey watched the SUVs departure secure under the cover of Grammy's rose hedge. Not a single kittie tear was shed.

Hope hugged Lyndsey and whispered, "Before you know it Sis, he'll be standing here watching you walking towards him to exchange your wedding vows."

The sisters fell silent. They gazed longingly out over the rose hedge and the glittering waters of East River Bay.

....

Back in Newmarket the brothers quickly lost themselves in a busy summer of work. John sold the house he and Lyndsey had lived in as a married couple. It carried too many memories and recent heartaches. Richard moved out of his townhouse and the brothers moved in together and shared their grandparents' home. They arranged to rent out their parents' condo apartment. Both were reluctant to sever that connection to their parents.

In East River, Professor Gilbert McClaken focused on preparing his materials for the new school year. Come September it would once again place a heavy demand on his personal—professional time and resources. However both would, at times over the summer, play second fiddle to a priority commitment Gilbert M. McClaken: part-time lobster-fisherman, part-time Professor of English, had taken on in the spring. Gilbert had committed to preparing and delivering a culinary feast of seafood delights at Lyndsey and Richard's wedding set for the Saturday of September's Labour Day weekend. On occasion, Hope chided her uncle for neglecting his commitment to the approaching new school year.

In early July, Hope convinced Lyndsey to volunteer and become an Adult Literacy Tutor. On learning that a dedicated Tutor had suffered a massive heart attack and passed away, Lyndsey opted to work with his student over the summer. Her student Jack a semi-retired tradesman, excelled in sharpening his reading and mathematics skills. He had pleaded with his former tutor to continue their sessions over the summer months. Devastated over the death of his tutor and friend Jack jumped at the opportunity to work with Lyndsey. Quickly student and tutor bonded working two evenings each week. Family financial pressures had forced Jack Evans to abandon the classroom at the age of 12. He had become a seasoned tradesman but struggled with reading comprehension and the ability to balance his chequing account. Jack's enthusiasm ignited thoughts of a new career direction in his Tutor, Lyndsey. At Jack's request, Lyndsey had researched Toastmasters International. Jack's brother had recommended it as a great avenue to develop one's self confidence and communication skills. Together they had met up with a local Toastmaster over coffee. Both Jack and Lyndsey had walked away enthused and eager to explore Toastmasters International and other educational options. A university graduate with a degree in Business Administration, Lyndsey pined over the option of returning to university and earning a Bachelor of Education Degree. In observing Gilbert eagerly putting together his new curriculum for the new school year, Lyndsey's excitement grew. She reasoned, if one student two evenings a week could be so rewarding to a tutor and their student, what would it be like to stand before a classroom full of eager students?

Jeffrey passed the summer overhauling the engines on Rose Bud and Karyn-Anita. Pappy assisted him, but focused mainly on assisting only with the required repairs the vessels and their engine controls needed. The warm summer days quickly slipped forward into the Dog Days of late July and a hot humid August.

Hope had taken on the task of coordinating the planning for September's big event. Once all the arrangements had been secured her focus shifted to Lyndsey. The sisters bonded closer together with each passing day. At times Hope envied her sister's long late evening phone connections with Richard. John called but not anywhere as frequently as Richard. Suddenly the odd chill of an approaching September sent an air of excitement through East River and the McClaken households. Back in Newmarket travel plans had been finalized by the Ramsay boys, Roger and Noreen. Richard and John flew out midweek on the Wednesday. Roger and Noreen on the Thursday.

Jeffrey insisted on escorting Hope and Lyndsey to the airport to meet Richard and John. He borrowed Lenny's shiny new jet black SUV. The trip took them just over an hour. Jeffrey remained silent through most of the ride. Hope and Lyndsey chatted up a storm until Lyndsey fell silent at the Hwy 102 exit to the airport. Once they had parked in the airport parking garage they followed the crowd of garage arrivals through to the passengers' arrivals area in the airport. There they discovered that the flight had arrived early. A glance up at the arrivals escalator spotted Richard and John. Lyndsey froze. Hope bounced up and down waving frantic greetings to John and Richard. Jeffrey smiled proudly at the girls who were quickly embraced in the arms of Richard and John. The embraces lingered. Arriving passengers altered their directions and walked past the embracing couples. All smiled warmly on the reunited lovers. Jeffrey waited a bit then a tad longer until the arrivals area cleared. He tapped Richard on the shoulder. After a pause the couples released their embraced partners. John and Richard greeted Jeffrey who in turn welcomed both home with hearty handshakes and an enthusiastic hug. Together they retrieved their luggage and returned to Lenny's SUV. Richard engaged his seat belt. A smile burst out on his face, as he watched Lyndsey open the driver's door and settle into the driver's seat. The return trip to East River passed in the blink of an eye. Conversations shared the busy summers each had experienced. On arriving in East River Chef Gilbert greeted them with a barbecued feast of whisky-maple marinated Atlantic salmon. Bailey joined the revelers and returned several times to compliment the chef and received a complimentary second and third serving. Everyone turned in early that evening. Exhausted but elated with the excitement of their day.

Roger called before heading to the airport in Toronto. He advised them that he had booked a car rental and would drive directly out to East River on their flight's arrival. Following a short delay in departing Toronto, Roger and Noreen arrived in Halifax. On arriving at East River warm and hearty greetings were exchanged. Great laughter ensued on Roger announcing that their flight had been delayed in Toronto due to heavy fog. Gilbert was relieved of his culinary duties that evening. Lenny joined them. They headed out to Michaela's Dockside Pub and Seafood Emporium in Hubbards, where Lenny refused to dine on Pappy's offer to order him a Veggie Dietarian's Delight. Summer activities were chatted up by everyone.

Lenny and Pappy entertained all by swapping and exaggerating tales of epic proportion out of their youth. Lyndsey shared her adult literacy tutoring experience and her thoughts on looking into pursuing a Bachelor of Education Degree and a teaching career. Richard totally supported her expressed ambitions. Gilbert beamed with pride. Inwardly he pondered the possibility of the family gaining a third teacher if Hope followed Lyndsey's lead. The evening of celebration and reunion wrapped up. Everyone headed home tired and eager to set in motion the plans for Saturday's wedding.

Gilbert arose first. He prepared a hearty breakfast buffet that quickly drew everyone to the kitchen and dining room. Once again Gilbert's breakfast offerings amazed everyone. Lyndsey and Hope assisted in delivering Gilbert's creations to the buffet table. The buffet wrapped up. Everyone shifted to coffee, tea and idle chit-chatting. Hope and Lyndsey headed upstairs to check Lyndsey's bridal dress and the bridesmaids dresses.

Noreen followed. Eugette stopped in with her twins Taylor the ring bearer and Megan the flower girl. She was directed towards the stairs. However, Taylor and Megan diverted her plans. On spotting Bailey both youngsters chased him around the kitchen in glee shouting, "Bailey—Bailey our ice cream kittie kat! Our ice cream kittie kat! Comes here and we'll cat-sits you kittie."

All the men folk laughed heartily. Once settled down, the children were lassoed by Eugette and they were ushered upstairs, so Mom could try on her bridesmaid's dress and Megan her flower girl dress. Halfway upstairs Taylor escaped and ran down to the kitchen in pursuit of Bailey. Upstairs on seeing Lyndsey, Megan leaped in a series of joyful bounces shouting, "Taylor...Taylor, come see Bailey's Mommie, the ice cream kittie-kat lady! She's up here."

Lyndsey on seeing and hearing Megan's joyful outburst stooped down in front of her. Megan leaped to Lyndsey and hugged her. She pleaded, "Can we Taylor and me babysit Bailey? Please... please... please!" Megan squirmed herself free of Lyndsey. She pleaded anew, "Can Taylor and me babysit Bailey? Please... please...please!"

All the ladies laughed along with Lyndsey, who replied, "Yes. Bailey would love to be entertained by his favourite kittie-kat sitters. But first we need you to try on your flower girl's dress. We want you to be the prettiest wee lassie at my wedding tomorrow. Megan agreed. Once she stepped back out of her dress Megan ran off to rejoin Taylor and Bailey downstairs. Lyndsey's wedding gown, Hope's matron of honour dress, Eugette's and Noreen's bridesmaids' dresses all received full approval. Following the fittings, the ladies all remained upstairs sharing memories of weddings past and the wedding soon to be. Megan shared a secret that her Mom, the widow Maria Lamont had revealed to her that morning. A secret she'd promised to never repeat in the company of others. Boldly she stated, "We're friends—right ladies?"

Everyone nodded and whispered together, "Bestest friends forever—for sure, absolutely a guaranteed given."

"Well, seeing as I'm not in the company of others," Eugette declared, "I won't really be revealing Mom's secret!"

The bedroom fell silent. Eugette spoke. "Back in the days before Momma knew my dearly departed Poppy and Momma was but the age of my Taylor and Megan...there was a young charmer, a devoted companion, and defender in her life!"

Eugette paused to garner added impact to her words. She smiled and boasted, "That blue eyed sweetheart. That gentle hearted—young boy who could have become my Pappy...saved my Momma on many occasions from schoolyard bullies like Barnie. And ladies that charmer is right here in this house." She paused once more. With every lady's ears glued to her words Eugette continued, "Yes! She boasted Momma's childhood sweetheart is right here in this house. She dreamt often of one day walking down the aisle to eagerly leap into his arms in wedded bliss! Who you ask? None other than the charming, dashing and handsome love of my Momma's eye and heart. The one and only Jeffy—Jeffrey McClaken!"

The room burst into ahs, ums and idle chitter chatter among the ladies. Eugette smiled boldly. Then stated, "Momma is attending tomorrow's gala celebration. Sure would be nice to see our two young lovers torn apart by life and life's circumstance reunited!"

Hope and Lyndsey smiled boldly at each other and their eyes connected. Silently the reconnected sisters plotted their dearly loved uncle's fate.

Downstairs Gilbert lost himself in preparing food for the wedding reception. Jeffrey busied himself grooming the grounds. The actions of both were completed under Hope's watchful eye and guidance. The huge tents, tables, chairs and settings arrived and were set up early Friday afternoon. That evening everyone gathered and celebrated in Gilbert's kitchen. The gala kitchen party broke up in the early morning hours of Saturday, shortly before Bailey passed out from his participation in the revelry.

Jeffrey awoke late Saturday morning. A quick bath recharged him. The hot water felt good, especially after the celebrations of the previous night. Dried and invigorated, Jeffrey stood before the vanity's mirror. He ran a brush through his hair. Satisfied with the results, he fluffed his beard. He frowned. Something about the beard did not sit well with him. Jeffrey took the scissors out and started to trim his beard. Half an hour later he stepped out of the bathroom. He startled Pappy. Along with a newly trimmed beard Jeffrey had worked the scissors through his once shoulder length hair. Jeffrey's new look set Pappy into a fit of snickering and rapidly fired compliments.

"Whoa! Look'n good," Pappy commented. He jested, "Something stuck in yer eye? Like a lady?" Pappy walked up to Jeffrey and embraced him. He inhaled the scent of Jeffrey's hair gel then teased, "Perhaps I's should be a booking accommodations over at Lenny's tonight. Tings could be gitt'n hot an deen somes here abouts ta'night!"

"No. No. Nothing like that! Thought my beard and hair needed a little trim. Did I cut too much off?"

"No, it looks right smart." Pappy winked then said, "Trust me son. She'll like it."

"Who Pappy? Who will like it? Jeffrey asked.

Together, Pappy and Jeffrey stepped outside then made their way up to Gilbert's house. Along the pathway Pappy nudged Jeffrey and said, "Son—The Widow Lamont, Eugette's Mom, Maria. I caught her eyeing you up and down at Gilbert's gala kitchen party."

"No Pappy, you're mistaken." Jeffrey answered.

"Right, Pappy chided back, "Your Pappy still has vibrant and sharp 20-20 eyesight. Blame it on me age, son." He chuckled and added, "But the girls saw it too!"

Jeffrey looked curiously into Pappy's eye on their walk through the tent set up on Gilbert's lawn. On reaching Gilbert's he asked, "Really?"

Pappy entered Gilbert's first. He walked through to the living room where the others had gathered. When Jeffrey made his appearance behind his Father it took everyone by surprise. The sisters jumped up. They strutted off to Jeffrey and did a comical look-see walk about their neatly groomed and trimmed uncle. Hope stepped up at Jeffrey's left—Lyndsey to his right. They treated him to a double kiss one on each cheek. Jeffrey blushed then scolded his nieces, "Get out of here. You're both too young for me. Besides, I fear I'm too much man. The both of you together couldn't handle me."

The sisters strutted around their uncle anew, each echoing the other in a series of catcalls. They each whispered to Jeffrey, "Mmm... mm that'll make the Widow Lamont a happy lady!"

Pappy, Gilbert, and Roger joined in on the friendly jesting.

Gilbert rescued his brother. He offered up coffee to Jeffrey and Pappy. Pappy hinted at a preference for a little touch of white rum. Jeffrey accepted the original offer of coffee. Pappy helped himself to a glass then half filled it with his stated preference and added two ice cubes.

Hope moved to Lyndsey's side. She whispered, "Time's a wasting girl. Those blue jeans won't cut it at your big event. We'd best get you ready for your man."

Lyndsey nodded agreement they headed upstairs to prepare for the wedding

Noreen joined them.

. . . . . .

All the clocks and watches in East River struck the magic hour together. Richard stood nervously in front of Grammy McClaken's prized rose bushes. The rose bush had strangely burst forth in a second prolific bloom that Labour Day Weekend. On a cue from the minister, he turned to see the bridal party enter the tent. Hope, maid of honour led, followed by bridesmaids, Eugette and Noreen, with Megan the flower girl and Taylor the ring bearer following. Maria smiled on seeing her grandchildren. Megan was tossing flower petals and Taylor was totally focused on carrying the rings to where Richard stood with John, the best man, at his side. Roger walked proudly at Lyndsey's side. The childhood fantasies of Lyndsey and Richard became a reality before their supportive and loving family and friends gathered at the outdoor ceremony. Pappy, Gilbert and Jeffrey stood off to the side up by the rose hedge. They made a great team. Each claimed to be the 'Best Available Man' at the show. Gilbert's culinary delights pleased everyone at the reception under the big tent. Later the men worked to prove themselves worthy of the title up on the dance floor.

The band announced a short break. A chorus of boos echoed out from the dance floor. The loudest boos came from the McClakens—Gilbert, Jeffrey and Pappy. Everyone quieted down on seeing Lyndsey standing alone in front of Grammy Ramsay's rose hedge. She held her bridal bouquet and its companion a miniaturized copy—the new traditional 'tossing bouquet'. Quickly, all the single ladies anxiously gathered together in front of Lyndsey. A special one slipped in unnoticed, flower girl Megan Savoy. Lyndsey held the tossing bouquet out and displayed it for all to admire. Then she turned her back to the anxious ladies and tossed the bouquet back over her head. Gleeful shouts of anticipation greeted the tossed bouquet throughout its flight. It landed in the extended hands of a thrilled recipient five year old flower girl Megan. Ecstatic she walked proudly over to where Hope stood and proudly said, "These are for you Auntie Hope."

Hope crouched down accepted Megan's offering and hugged her. Into Megan's ear she whispered, "Thank you sweetheart. It is beautiful." Hope stood and took Megan's hand in hers. They walked over and joined a beaming Eugette and Maria. Loud applause followed them.

Again everyone quieted down on seeing Richard carry a chair over to Lyndsey. She followed his cue and sat on the chair. Richard knelt down at her feet. He lifted Lyndsey's gown and exposed her leg and thigh. Ooos and aaahs broke the silence. Richard reached out and toyed with Lyndsey's garter. Slowly he moved it down to her ankle and slipped off her shoe. The garter slid over her foot into Richard's waiting hand. He stood up. Hope and the bridesmaids gathered around the groom. Playfully they twisted him about to induce dizziness into his mind. The twisting stopped. Richard stood with his back to the bachelors, widowers and single men who all awaited Richard's traditional tossing of the garter. Good luck awaited the man who caught it. Tradition held that he would be the next one to marry.

Lenny shouted out, "Where's de McClaken lads? If I got'ta be up here then they best bees up here's wit me!"

Spontaneous laughter broke out. Hope, the bridesmaids and the ladies in attendance glanced about in search of their quarry. Once spotted all the McClaken men were surrounded and nudged over to where all the garter contestants stood.

The ladies laughingly called out to Richard, "Toss it, toss it, toss it, toss it, toss it, toss it!"

Richard hooked the garter on his left thumb. He pulled the loose end of it away from his thumb then released it. The garter flew off his thumb upwards to the tent top and towards the awaiting contestants. Suddenly it started to tumble downward.

The ladies shouted out to their men, "Git it, git it, we're next—we're next!"

To everyone's glee and one's shock the garter touched Jeffrey's forehead then fell into his hands. Suddenly he stood all alone. All the other bachelors, widowers and single men had fled. They left Jeffrey to fend for himself. Maria walked over to Jeffrey. The band played a slow love song. Jeffrey and Maria waltzed around the dance floor. Richard and Lyndsey joined them in dance. They were quickly joined by Roger and Noreen, along with couples eager to dance away the night. Eugette danced with John, Hope nudged Gilbert up onto the dance floor. Lenny and Pappy eagerly headed to the cash bar until they were intercepted by the Wright sisters Janella and Aimée.

Just before sunset Jeffrey made an encouraged departure. A kiss on Jeffrey's cheek by Maria sealed his fate. They slipped away under a watchful eye or two. The sunroom at his home proved to be their destination.

....

Lyndsey quietly returned from the house dressed in her going away outfit. She stood at Richard's side. The tent fell silent. Gazing out through teary eyes of joyfulness the newlyweds thanked everyone for having attended and added special joys and enthusiasm to their special day of love and commitment. Responding to the traditional tinkling of spoons on tea cups they embraced and kissed. The joys they had felt in exchanging their vows echoed in their hearts and minds.

'A gentle sea breeze blew in over a glittering sea. We exchanged 'I dos' and our two hearts were joined. Standing before Grammy Ramsay's rose hedge, as newlyweds, we were quickly covered in a shower of pink rose petals. Overhead, a group of soaring sea gulls sang their lonesome song of love and the sea. Below them in wedded bliss, our hearts rejoiced in the knowledge that all that glitters is not gold, but when that glitter comes from the sea, it carries a treasure known only to the heart.'

The End

EPILOGUE

SHARING MY PASSION AND LOVE OF THE WRITTEN WORD WITH THE readers of my novel 'Seaside Glitter' has been a pleasure and treasured blessing. In publishing it and sharing its adventure with the world I've come to realize a personal dream—a goal that I once believed was unachievable. I am now a published author. Throughout the creative writing process I challenged and forced myself to step beyond many personal fears and inhibitions. How could I possibly do a public book signing session? I was a confirmed introvert. Like many introverts I reached out to an organization and its members, that I now call my *Fellow Toastmasters.* I learned to share ideas and present them in public arenas. I received valued feedback through their evaluations of my speeches and storylines. I applied the feedback when editing the novel. I dared to step beyond my comfort zones in many ways. I freely encourage any fellow introverts to follow in my footsteps. I have even succeeded in overcoming a dislike or misunderstanding of written words shared in the form of poetry. On a visit to our daughter the teacher's home I dared myself to pen my thoughts of the moment in poetic form. Did I succeed? I'll leave that decision in your hands as you read my thoughts and I run off to another creative adventure in the world of the written word.

....

PS fellow introverts and extroverts feel free to explore the world of a potential new you. Visit *toastmasters.org* I did. And today I'm a published author, poet *(I believe)* and a DTM Distinguished Toastmaster.

'Life's Gift Treasured in the Kiss of Dewdrops'

Sunshine and dewdrops morning kisses treasured
Roses and lilies bring joy to one's morning
Apple blossoms and bumble bees embrace summer's joys
Gentle breezes caressed with evening's mist

Life's journey is blessed with each step taken on its path
Shouts of joy from youthful playful lips
Children rejoicing in life's treasures and pleasures
Parents busy tied up in the pleasures of parenthood

Sunflowers brighten our day morning through to dusk
Skitters and other hungry critters seek us out
Weeds and other unloved flowers embrace our gardens with delight
Life a never-ending blessing filled with
joys begging to be discovered

Fresh cut grass, bark mulch and a dash of fer-
tilizer bring joy to gardeners
Butterflies, humming birds, finches and crows
Flittering wings, flapping wings call out to each new day's morn
Oh where oh where have I awakened to
Could I be on hill, dale or a heavenly secluded glen?
But isn't life such a pleasant to be treasured gift

Misty dews and raindrops too make a morning joyful
Cricket chirps and grasshopper flips catch and hold attentive ears
Kitty cats oh and puppies too greet each morning joyfully

For all so oft each morn quickly turns into an evening

Boastful cries of deeds once tried
Seldom allude to failures
Success it's said awaits each one bold enough to embrace adventure
And success we know awaits each of our daily actions

Morning kisses and door-side hugs enrich
each embraced and hugged one's day
Throughout the day each hug recalled enriches one anew
To be alone for too long a time can sadden one's emotions
So on each new day and throughout its way
Cast a happy joyful smile on those you meet

Written by Wayne Turner November 2015

ABOUT THE AUTHOR

Seaside Glitter IS THE FIRST PUBLISHED NOVEL OF AUTHOR, WAYNE Turner. Wayne recalls a love of the written word that he can trace back to his childhood in Ottawa, Ontario. As the years passed, he found himself stretching fact into fiction and adding fiction to facts while writing letters and postcards to friends and family. A course in Creative Writing was the advice offered by those close to the author and an old love was rekindled as Wayne wrote short story after short story. The first seeds of Seaside Glitter were planted in the writer's mind while he sat on the rocks of Peggy's Cove, with his wife on one side and a daughter on the other, and stared out at two islands shrouded in an eerie mist. Wayne's love of the sea and all of its mysteries drew him back to the pristine shores of Nova Scotia where he now resides.

REFERENCES

REFERENCE IS MADE TO THE WORKS OF SHAKESPEARE QUOTED, '*Othello, Act II Scene I*', '*The Merchant of Venice Act I Scene I*'

Reference is made to **Toastmasters International**, referring to the organization's educational programs focused on supporting individuals worldwide looking to develop their personal and professional communications and leadership skills. *toastmasters.org*

Reference is made to Nova Scotia Tourism's provincial tourism '***Doers & Dreamers' Travel* Guide**'. The guide's content is not directly quoted. However it is the provincial guide tourists are encouraged to tote along on their visits to Nova Scotia.

Recollection of a pleasant stay we once enjoyed at ***Ocean Hillside Bed & Breakfast*** in Digby, Nova Scotia. Did I exaggerate their welcoming of our dignified and at times refined cat Bailey? I highly recommend you call ahead, to book and confirm both your reservation and their pet policy.

CPSIA information can be obtained
at www.ICGtesting.com
Printed in the USA
LVOW03s1409130617
537895LV00003B/3/P